RANDOM
HOUSE

LARGE
PRINT

Also by Henning Mankell
Available from Random House Large Print

The Man from Beijing

The Troubled Man

The Troubled Man

HENNING MANKELL

Translated from the Swedish by Laurie Thompson

RANDOM HOUSE
LARGE PRINT

Translation copyright © 2011 by Laurie Thompson

Published in the United States of America by Random House Large Print in association with Alfred A. Knopf, New York.
Distributed by Random House, Inc., New York.

Cover photograph by Mark Dye
Cover design by Barbara de Wilde

Originally published in Sweden as **Den orolige mannen** by Leopard Förlag, Stockholm, in 2009. Copyright © 2009 by Henning Mankell.

The Library of Congress has established a cataloging-in-publication record for this title.

ISBN: 978-0-7393-7811-3

www.randomhouse.com/largeprint

Printed in the United States of America

10 9 8 7 6 5 4 3 2

This Large Print Edition published in accord with the standards of the N.A.V.H.

People always leave traces.
No person is without a shadow.

You forget what you want to remember
and remember what you would prefer to forget.

—Graffiti on buildings in New York City

Contents

The Troubled Man

Prologue

The story begins with a sudden fit of rage.

The cause of it was a report that had been submitted the previous evening, which the prime minister was now reading at his poorly lit desk. But shortly before that, the stillness of morning held sway in the Swedish government offices.

It was 1983, an early spring day in Stockholm, with a damp fog hovering over the city and trees that had not yet come into leaf.

When Prime Minister Olof Palme finished reading the last page, he stood up and walked over to a window. Seagulls were wheeling around outside.

The report was about the submarines. The accursed submarines that in the fall of 1982 were presumed to have violated Swedish territorial waters. In the middle of it all there was a general election in Sweden, and Olof Palme had been asked by the Speaker to form a new government since the non-socialist parties had lost several seats and no longer had a parliamentary majority. The first thing the new government did was to set up a commission to investigate the incident with the submarines, which had never been forced to surface. Former defense minister Sven Andersson was chairman of the commission. Olof Palme had now read his report and was none the wiser. The conclusions were incomprehensible. He was furious.

But it should be noted that this was not the first time Palme had gotten worked up about Sven Andersson. His aversion really dated back to the day in June 1963, just before Midsummer, when an elegantly dressed gray-haired fifty-seven-year-old man was arrested on Riksbron in the center of Stockholm. It was done so discreetly that nobody in the vicinity noticed anything unusual. The man arrested was Stig Wennerström, a colonel in the Swedish air force who had been exposed as a spy for the Soviet Union.

When he was arrested, the prime minister at the time, Tage Erlander, was on his way home from a trip abroad, one of his few vacations, to one of Reso's resorts in Riva del Sole. When Erlander stepped off the airplane and was mobbed by a large crowd of journalists, not only was he totally unprepared, he also knew next to nothing about the incident. Nobody had told him about the arrest, and he had heard nothing about a suspicious Colonel Wennerström. It is possible that the name and the suspicions had been mentioned in passing when the minister of defense held one of his infrequent information sessions with the prime minister, but not in connection with anything serious, anything specific. There were always rumors circulating about suspected Russian spies in the murky waters that constituted the so-called Cold War. And so Erlander's response was less than illuminating. The man who had been prime minister without a break for what seemed like an eternity—twenty-three years, to be exact—stood there openmouthed and had no idea what to say since neither Defense Minister Andersson nor anybody else involved had informed him of what was going on. During the last part of his journey home, from Copenhagen to Stockholm, which barely took an hour, he could have been filled in and thus been prepared to say something to the excited journalists; but nobody had met him at Kastrup Airport and accompanied him on the last leg of the flight.

During the days that followed, Erlander came very close to resigning as prime minister and leader of the Social Democrats. Never before had he been so disappointed in his colleagues in government. And Olof Palme, who had already emerged as Erlander's chosen successor, naturally shared his mentor's anger at the nonchalance that had resulted in Erlander's humiliation. Palme watched over his master like a savage bloodhound, as they used to say in circles close to the government.

He could never forgive Sven Andersson for what he had done to Tage Erlander.

Subsequently, a lot of people wondered why Palme included Andersson in his governments. However, it was not particularly difficult to understand why. Of course Palme could have refused; but in practice it simply wasn't possible. Andersson had a lot of power and a lot of influence among the grass roots of the party. He was the son of a laborer, unlike Palme, who had direct links to Baltic nobility, had officers in his family—indeed, he was a reserve officer himself—and had come from the well-to-do Swedish upper class. He had no grassroots support in the party. Olof Palme was a defector who was no doubt serious about his political allegiance to the Social Democrats, but nevertheless, he was an outsider, a political pilgrim who had wandered into the party.

Now Palme could no longer contain his fury. He turned to face Sven Andersson, who was sitting hunched up on the gray sofa in the prime minister's office. Palme was bright red in the face, and his arms were twitching in the strange way they did when he lost his temper.

"There is no proof," he roared. "Only claims, insinuations, nods and winks from disloyal navy officers. This investigation has shed light on nothing at all. On the contrary, it has left us wallowing in political swamps."

A couple of years before, in the early hours of October 28, 1981, a Soviet submarine had run aground in Gåsefjärden Bay off Karlskrona. The bay was not only Swedish territorial water, but also a military restricted area. The submarine was labeled U-137, and the captain on board, Anatoli Michailovitch Gushchin, maintained that his craft had gone off course because of an unknown defect in its gyrocompass. Swedish naval officers and local fishermen were convinced that only an

extremely drunk captain could have managed to pene-
trate that far into the archipelago without running
aground earlier.

On November 6, U-137 was towed out into international waters and disappeared. But on that occasion
there had been no doubt at all that it was a Russian
submarine in Swedish territorial waters. However, it
was never established if it had been an intentional vio-
lation of Swedish sovereignty or a case of drunkenness
at sea. No respectable navy would admit, of course,
that their commanding officer had been drunk while
on duty.

So their denial was regarded as proof that he had
been. But where was the proof now?

No one knows what former minister of defense Andersson had to say in his own defense and that of his
investigation. He made no notes, and Olof Palme was
assassinated a year or so afterward; he left no witness
accounts either.

So it all began with a fit of rage. This story about the
realities of politics, this journey into the swamps where
truth and lies are indistinguishable and nothing is
clear.

PART 1

Invasion of the Swamps

1

The year Kurt Wallander celebrated his fifty-fifth birthday, he fulfilled a long-held dream. Ever since his divorce from Mona fifteen years earlier, he had intended to leave his apartment in Mariagatan, where so many unpleasant memories were etched into the walls, and move out to the country. Every time he came home in the evening after a stressful and depressing workday, he was reminded that once upon a time he had lived there with a family. Now the furniture stared at him as if accusing him of desertion.

He could never reconcile himself to living there until he became so old that he might not be able to look after himself anymore. Although he had not yet reached the age of sixty, he reminded himself over and over again of his father's lonely old age, and he knew he had no desire to follow in his footsteps. He needed only to look into the bathroom mirror in the morning when he was shaving to see that he was growing more and more like his father. When he was young, his face had resembled his mother's. But now it seemed as if his father was taking him over—like a runner who has been lagging a long way behind but is slowly catching up the closer he gets to the invisible finish line.

Wallander's worldview was fairly simple. He did not want to become a bitter hermit growing old in isolation, being visited only by his daughter and perhaps now and then by a former colleague who had suddenly remembered that Wallander was still alive. He had no religious hopes of there being something in store for him on the other side of the black River Styx. There would be nothing but the same darkness that he had once emerged from. Until his fiftieth birthday, he had harbored a vague fear of death, something that had become his own personal mantra—that he **would be dead for such a long time.** He had seen far too many dead bodies in his life. There was nothing in their expressionless faces to suggest that their souls had been absorbed into some kind of heaven. Like so many other police officers, he had experienced every possible variation of death. Just after his fiftieth birthday had been celebrated with a party and cake at the police station, marked by a speech full of empty phrases by the former chief of police, Liza Holgersson, he had bought a new notebook and tried to record his memories of all the dead people he had come across. It had been a macabre exercise and he had no idea why he had been tempted to pursue it. When he got as far as the tenth suicide, a man in his forties, a drug addict with more or less every problem it was possible to imagine, he gave up. The man had hanged himself in the attic of the condemned apartment building where he lived, hanging in such a way that he was guaranteed to break his neck and hence avoid being slowly choked to death. His name was Welin. The pathologist had told Wallander that the man had been successful—he had proved to be a skillful executioner. At that point Wallander had abandoned his suicide cases and instead stupidly devoted several hours in an attempt to recall the young people or children he had found dead. But he soon gave that up as well. It was too repugnant. Then he felt ashamed of what he had been trying to do and burned the notebook, as if his efforts were both perverted and illegal. In fact, he was basically a cheerful person—it was just that he had allowed another side of his personality to take over.

Death had been his constant companion. He had killed people in the line of duty—but after the obligatory investigation he had never been accused of unnecessary violence.

Having killed two people was the cross he had to bear. If he rarely laughed, it was because of what he had been forced to endure.

But one day he made a critical decision. He had been out near Löderup, not far from the house where his father used to live, to talk to a farmer who had been the target of a very nasty robbery. On the way back to Ystad he noticed a real estate agent's sign picturing a little dirt road where there was a house for sale. He reacted automatically, stopped the car, turned around, and found his way to the address. Even before he got out of the car it was obvious to him that the property was in need of repair. It had originally been a U-shaped building, the bottom half clad in wood. But now one of the wings was missing—perhaps it had burned down. He walked around the house. It was a day in early fall. He could still remember seeing a skein of geese migrating south, flying directly above his head. He peered in through the windows and soon established that only the roof badly needed to be fixed. The view was enchanting; he could just make out the sea in the far distance, and possibly even one of the ferries on the way to Ystad from Poland. That afternoon in September 2003 marked the beginning of a love story with this remote house.

He drove straight to the real estate agent's office in the center of Ystad. The asking price was low enough that he would be able to manage the mortgage payments. The very next day he returned to negotiate with the agent, a young man who spoke at breakneck speed and gave the impression of living in a parallel universe. The previous owners were a young couple who had moved to Skåne from Stockholm but almost immediately, before they even had time to buy furniture, decided to split up. Yet there was nothing hidden in the walls of the empty house that scared him. And the most important thing was crystal clear: he would be able to move in without delay. The roof would last for another year or two; all he needed to do was to redecorate some of the rooms, perhaps install a new bath and maybe acquire a new stove. But the boiler was less than fifteen years old, and all the plumbing and electrical fittings no older.

Before leaving, Wallander asked if there were any other potential buyers. There was one, said the agent, looking distinctly worried, as if he really wanted Wallander to get the house but at the same time implying that he had better make his mind up fast. But Wallander had no intention of rushing in blindly. He spoke to one of his colleagues whose brother was a home inspector and managed to arrange for the expert to inspect the house the very next day. He found nothing wrong apart from what Wallander had already noticed. That same day Wallander spoke to his bank manager and was informed that he could rely on a mortgage big enough to buy the house. During all his years in Ystad, Wallander had saved up a lot of money without ever thinking much about it. Enough for the down payment.

That evening he sat at his kitchen table and made detailed financial calculations. He found the occasion solemn and significant. By midnight he had made up his mind: he would buy the house, which had the dramatic-sounding name of Black Heights. Despite the late hour, he called his daughter, Linda, who lived in a new development just off the main road to Malmö. She was still awake.

"You must come over," said Wallander excitedly. "I've got news for you."

"What? In the middle of the night?"

"I know it's your day off tomorrow."

It had been a complete surprise to him a few years earlier when, during a walk along the beach at Mossby

Strand, Linda told him she had decided to follow in his footsteps and join the police force. It cheered him up instantly. In a way it was as if she was giving new meaning to all the years he had been a police officer. When she finished her training, she was assigned to the Ystad force. The first few months, she lived with him in the apartment in Mariagatan. It was not an ideal arrangement; he was set in his ways, and he also found it hard to accept that she was grown up now. But their relationship was saved when she managed to find an apartment of her own.

When she arrived in the early hours, he told her what he was planning to do. The next day she accompanied him to the house and said immediately that it was perfect. No other house would do, only this one at the end of a dirt road at the top of a gentle slope down to the sea.

"Granddad will haunt you," she said. "But you don't need to be afraid. He'll be a sort of guardian angel."

It was a significant and happy moment in Wallander's life when he signed the contract of sale and suddenly found himself standing there with a bunch of keys in his hand. He moved in on November first, having redecorated two rooms but having refrained from buying a new stove. He left Mariagatan without the slightest doubt that he was doing the right thing. A southeasterly gale was blowing the day he moved in.

That first evening, with the storm raging, he lost electricity. Wallander sat in his new home in pitch darkness. There was groaning and creaking coming from the rafters, and he discovered a leak in the ceiling. But he had no regrets. This was where he was going to live.

There was a dog kennel outside the house. Ever since he was a little boy Wallander had dreamed of having a dog. By the time he was thirteen he had given up hope, but out of the blue he got one as a present from his parents. He loved that dog more than anything else in the world. Looking back, it felt like the dog, Saga, had taught him what love could be. When she was three years old, she was run over by a truck. The shock and sorrow were worse than anything he had experienced in his young life. More than forty years later, Wallander had no difficulty recalling all those chaotic emotions. **Death strikes,** he sometimes thought. It has a powerful and unforgiving fist.

Two weeks later he acquired a dog, a black Labrador puppy. He wasn't quite a purebred, but he was nevertheless described by the owner as top class. Wallander had decided in advance that the dog would be called Jussi, after the world-famous Swedish tenor who was one of Wallander's greatest heroes.

Nearly four years after he bought the house, on January 12, 2007, Wallander's whole life changed in an instant.

As he stepped out into the hall a few paces behind Kristina Magnusson, whom he liked viewing from behind when nobody was looking, the phone rang in his office. He considered ignoring it, but instead he turned and went back in. It was Linda. She had a few days off, having worked on New Year's Eve, during which Ystad had been unusually lively, with lots of cases of domestic violence and assaults.

"Do you have a minute?"

"Not really. We're on the verge of identifying some crooks in a big case."

"I need to see you."

Wallander thought she sounded tense. He started to worry, as he always did, that something might have happened to her.

"Is it anything serious?"

"Not at all."

"I can meet you at one o'clock."

"Mossby Strand beach?"

Wallander thought she was joking.

"Should I bring my bathing suit?"

"I'm serious. Mossby Strand. But no bathing suit."

"Why do we have to go out there in the cold with this icy wind blowing?"

"I'll be there at one o'clock. So will you."

She hung up before he could ask anything else. What did she want? He stood there, trying in vain to think of an answer. Then he went to the conference room with the best television set and sat for two hours going through CCTV camera footage for the case he was working on, the brutal attack and robbery of an elderly arms dealer and his wife. As twelve-thirty approached, they were still only halfway through. Wallander stood up and announced that they could review the rest of the tapes after two o'clock. Martinsson, one of the officers Wallander had worked with longest in Ystad, looked at him in surprise.

"You mean we should stop now? With so much still to do? You don't usually break for lunch."

"I'm not going to eat. I have an appointment."

He left the room, thinking that his tone of voice had been unnecessarily sharp. He and Martinsson were not only colleagues, they were also friends. When Wallander threw his housewarming party out at Löderup it was of course Martinsson who gave a speech in praise of him, the dog, and the house. We are like an old hardworking couple, he thought as he left the police station. An old couple who are always bickering, mainly to keep each other on our toes.

He went to his car, a Peugeot he'd had for the last four years, and drove off. How many times have I driven along this road? How many more times will I drive along it? As he waited for a red light to change, he remembered something his father had told him about a cousin Wallander had never met. His cousin used to be captain of a ferry plying between several islands in the Stockholm archipelago—short trips, no more than five minutes at a time, but year in, year out, the same crossings. One afternoon in October something snapped inside him. The ferry had a full load, but he suddenly changed course and headed straight out to sea. He said later that he knew there was enough diesel in the tank to take him as far as one of the Baltic states. But that was all he said, after he was overpowered by angry passengers and the coast guard raced out to put the ferry back on course. He never explained why he did what he did.

But in a vague sort of way, Wallander thought he understood him.

As he drove west along the coast road he could see dark thunderclouds building up on the horizon. The radio had warned that there was a risk of more snow in the evening. Shortly before he passed the side road to Marsvinsholm he was overtaken by a motorcycle. The rider waved at him and made Wallander think of something that frightened him more than anything else: that one of these days Linda would have a motorcycle accident. He had been totally unprepared when, several years earlier, she turned up outside his apartment on her newly bought bike, a Harley-Davidson covered in glittering chrome. His first question when she took off her crash helmet was whether she had lost her mind.

"You don't know about all my dreams," she had said with a broad, happy grin. "Just as I'm sure I don't know all yours."

"I don't dream about a motorbike, that's for sure."

"Too bad. We could have gone for rides together."

He had gone so far as to promise to buy her a car and pay for all her gas if she got rid of the motorcycle. But she refused, and he knew that the battle was lost. She had inherited his stubbornness, and he would never be able to take the motorcycle away from her, no matter what temptations he could offer.

When he turned into the parking lot at Mossby

Strand, which was deserted and windswept, she had taken off her helmet and was standing on top of a sand dune, her hair fluttering in the wind. Wallander switched off the engine and sat looking at her, his daughter in the dark leather outfit and the expensive boots from a factory in California that she had paid nearly a month's wages for. Once upon a time she was a little girl sitting on my knee, Wallander thought, and I was the biggest hero in her life. Now she is thirty-six, a police officer just like me, with a brain of her own and a big smile. What more could I ask for?

He stepped out into the wind and plowed his way through the soft sand until he was standing by her side. She smiled at him.

"Something happened here," she said. "Do you remember what?"

"You told me that you were going to become a police officer. On this very spot."

"I'm thinking of something else."

Wallander realized what she was getting at.

"A rubber dinghy drifted ashore here, with two dead men inside it," he said. "So many years ago that I can't remember exactly when. An incident from a different world, you might say."

"Tell me about that world."

"That couldn't possibly be why you made me come here."

"Tell me anyway!"

Wallander stretched out his hand toward the water.

"We didn't know much about the countries on the other side of the sea. We sometimes pretended the

Baltic states didn't exist. We were cut off from our nearest neighbors. And they were cut off from us. But then that rubber dinghy came ashore, and the investigation took me to Latvia, to Riga. I went behind the iron curtain that no longer exists. The world was different then. Not worse, not better, just different."

"I'm going to have a baby," said Linda. "I'm pregnant."

Wallander held his breath, as if he didn't understand what she'd said. Then he stared at her stomach, hidden behind her leather suit. She burst out laughing.

"There's nothing to see. I'm only in the second month."

Looking back, Wallander remembered every detail of that meeting with Linda, when she told him her staggering news. They walked down to the beach, leaning into the howling wind. She answered his questions. When he arrived back at the police station an hour late, he had almost forgotten all about the investigation he was in charge of.

Shortly before the end of that day, just as it was beginning to snow again, they finally found pictures of the two men who had probably been involved in the arms theft and brutal murder. Wallander summed up what they all knew: that they had taken a big step toward solving this case.

When the meeting ended and everybody was gathering together their papers, Wallander felt an almost irresistible urge to tell them about the great joy he had just been gifted with.

But he said nothing, of course.

He wouldn't allow his colleagues to come that close to his private life, not ever.

2

On August 30, 2007, shortly after two in the afternoon, Linda gave birth to a daughter, Kurt Wallander's first grandchild, at Ystad Hospital. The delivery was normal, and also punctual—on the exact day predicted by her midwife. Wallander had taken the precaution of being on vacation at the time, and he spent the day trying to mix a bucket of cement in order to repair cracks under the porch roof next to the front door. It wasn't all that successful, but at least it kept him occupied. When the phone rang and he was informed that from now on he was entitled to call himself Granddad, he started crying. The feeling took him by surprise, and for a while he was utterly defenseless.

It wasn't Linda who called, but the baby's father, financier Hans von Enke. Wallander didn't want to reveal how emotional he was, so he merely thanked von Enke for the news, sent his greetings to Linda, and hung up.

Then he went for a long walk with Jussi. Skåne was still luxuriating in the heat of late summer. There had been thunderstorms during the night, and now, after the rain, the air was fresh and easy to breathe. At last Wallander was able to admit to himself that he had often wondered why Linda had never before expressed a desire to have children. Now she was thirty-seven years old, in Wallander's opinion far too late in life for a woman to be a mother. Mona had been much younger when Linda was born. He had kept an eye on Linda's relationships from a discreet distance; he had preferred some boyfriends to others. Occasionally he had been convinced that she had finally found the right man—but then it was suddenly all over, and she never told him why. Even though Wallander and Linda were very close, there were certain things they never discussed. One of the taboo subjects was having children.

That day on the windswept beach at Mossby Strand was the first he had heard about the man she was going to have a child with. It was a complete surprise to Wallander, who had thought his daughter wasn't even in a steady relationship at the time.

Linda had met Hans von Enke through mutual friends in Copenhagen, at a dinner to celebrate an engagement. Hans was from Stockholm, but had been living in Copenhagen for the last couple of years, working for a finance company that specialized in setting up hedge funds. Linda had found him somewhat self-important, and had been annoyed by him. She informed him, rather fiercely, that she was a simple police officer, badly paid, and had no idea what a hedge fund was. It ended up with them going for a long evening stroll through the streets of Copenhagen, and deciding to meet again. Hans von Enke was two years younger than Linda, and didn't have any children either. Both of them had decided from the very start, without saying as much but nevertheless being quite clear about it, that they were going to try and have children together.

Two days after the revelation, Linda came in the evening to Wallander's house with the man she had decided to live with. Hans von Enke was tall and thin, balding, with piercing bright blue eyes. Wallander immediately felt uncomfortable in his presence, found his way of expressing himself off-putting, and wondered what on earth had inspired Linda to take a shine to him. When she had told him that Hans's salary was three times as big as her father's, and that in addition he received a bonus every year that could be as much as a million kronor, Wallander had concluded depressingly that it must be the money that attracted her. That thought annoyed him so much that the next time he saw Linda he asked her outright. They were sitting in a café in the middle of Ystad. Linda had been so angry that she had thrown a roll at him and stormed out. He had hurried after her and apologized. No, it had nothing to do with the money, she explained. It was genuine and all-consuming love, something she had never experienced before.

Wallander made up his mind to try hard to view his future son-in-law more sympathetically. Via the Internet and with the aid of the bank manager who handled his modest affairs in Ystad, Wallander found out as much as he could about the finance company Hans worked for. He discovered what hedge funds were, and many more details alleged to be the basis of a modern finance company's activities. Hans von Enke invited him to Copenhagen and took him on a tour of his opulent offices at Rundetårn. Afterward, Hans invited him to lunch, and when Wallander returned to Ystad he no longer had the feeling of inferiority that had affected him at their first meeting. He called Linda from the car and told her that he had begun to appreciate the man she had chosen.

"He has one fault," said Linda. "He doesn't have enough hair. Otherwise he's okay."

"I'm looking forward to the day when I can show him my office."

"I've already shown him. Last week when he was here visiting. Didn't anybody tell you?"

Needless to say, nobody had said a word about it to Wallander. That evening he sat at his kitchen table, pencil in hand, and worked out Hans von Enke's annual salary. He was astonished when he saw the final figure. Once again he had a vague feeling of unease. After all his years in the police force, his own salary was barely 40,000 kronor per month. He regarded that as a high wage. But he wasn't the one getting married. The money might or might not be what would make Linda happy. It was none of his business.

In March Linda and Hans moved in together in a big house outside Rydsgård that the young financier had bought. He started commuting to Copenhagen, and Linda carried on working in Ystad. Once they had settled in, Linda invited Kurt to dinner at their place the following Saturday. Hans's parents would be there, and obviously they would like to meet Linda's father.

"I've spoken to Mom," she said.

"Is she coming too?"

"No."

"Why not?"

Linda shrugged.

"I think she's unwell."

"What's the matter with her?"

Linda looked long and hard at him before answering.

"Too much booze. I think she's drinking more than ever now."

"I didn't know that."

"There's a lot you don't know."

Wallander accepted the invitation to dinner to meet Hans von Enke's parents. The father, Håkan von Enke, was a former commander in the Swedish navy and had been in command of both submarines and surface vessels that specialized in hunting down submarines. Linda wasn't sure, but she thought that at one time he had been a member of a team that decided when military units were allowed to open fire on an enemy. Hans von Enke's mother was named Louise and had been a language teacher. Hans was an only child.

"I'm not used to mixing with the nobility," Wallander said somberly when Linda finished speaking.

"They're just like everybody else. I think you'll find you have a lot to talk about."

"Such as?"

"You'll find out. Don't be so negative."

"I'm not being negative! I just wonder . . ."

"We'll be eating at six o'clock. Don't be late. And don't bring Jussi. He'll just make a nuisance of himself."

"Jussi's a very obedient dog. How old are they, Hans's parents?"

"Håkan will be seventy-five shortly; Louise is a year or two younger. And Jussi never takes any notice of what you tell him to do—you should know that, since you've failed to train him properly. Thank God you did better with me."

She left the room before Wallander had time to reply. For a moment or two he tried to get annoyed by the fact that she always had to have the last word, but he couldn't manage it and returned to his papers.

It was drizzling unseasonably over Skåne on Saturday when he set off from Ystad to meet Hans von Enke's parents. He had been sitting in his office since early morning, yet again, for who knows how many times, going through the most important parts of the investigation material concerning the death of the arms dealer and the stolen revolvers. They thought they had identified the thieves, but they still had no proof. I'm not looking for a key, he thought. I'm hunting for the slightest sound of a distant tinkling from a bunch of keys. He had worked his way through about half of the voluminous documentation by three o'clock. He decided to go home, sleep for an hour or two, then get dressed for dinner. Linda had said Hans's parents were sometimes a bit formal for her taste, but given that, she suggested her father wear his best suit.

"I only have the one I wear at funerals," said Wallander. "But perhaps I shouldn't put on a white tie?"

"You don't need to come at all if you think it's going to be so awful."

"I was only trying to make a joke."

"You failed. You have at least three blue ties. Pick one of those."

As Wallander sat in a taxi on the way back to Löderup at about midnight, he decided that the evening had turned out to be much more pleasant than he had expected. He had found it easy to talk to both the retired commander and his wife. He was always on his guard when he met people he didn't know, thinking they would regard the fact that he was a police officer with barely concealed contempt. But he hadn't detected any such tendency in either of them. On the contrary, they had displayed what he considered to be genuine interest in his work. Moreover, Håkan von Enke had views about how the Swedish police were organized and about various shortcomings in several well-known criminal investigations that Wallander tended to agree with. And he in turn had an opportunity to ask questions about submarines, the Swedish navy, and the current downsizing of the Swedish defense facilities, to which he received knowledgeable and entertaining answers. Louise von Enke hardly spoke but sat there for most of the time with a friendly smile on her face, listening to the others talking.

After he had called a cab, Linda accompanied him as far as the gate. She held on to his arm and leaned her head on his shoulder. She did that only when she was pleased with him.

"So I did okay?" asked Wallander.

"You were better than ever. You can if you make an effort."

"I can what?"

"Behave yourself. You can even ask intelligent questions about things that have nothing to do with police work."

"I liked them. But I didn't get to know her very well."

"Louise? That's the way she is. She doesn't say much. But she listens better than all the rest of us put together."

"She seemed a bit mysterious."

They had come out onto the road and stood under a tree to avoid the drizzle, which had continued to fall all evening.

"I don't know anyone as secretive as you," said Linda. "For years I thought you had something to hide. But I've learned that only a few mysterious people are in fact hiding something."

"And I'm not one of them?"

"I don't think so. Am I right?"

"I suppose. But maybe people sometimes hide secrets they don't even know they have."

The taxi headlights cut though the darkness. It was one of those bus-like vehicles becoming more and more common with cab companies.

"I hate those buses," said Wallander.

"Don't start getting worked up now! I'll bring your car tomorrow."

"I'll be at the police station from ten o'clock on. Go in now and find out what they thought of me. I'll expect a report tomorrow."

She delivered his car the following day, shortly before eleven.

"Good," she said as she entered his office, as usual without knocking.

"What do you mean, 'Good'?"

"They liked you. Håkan had a funny way of putting it. He said: 'Your dad is an excellent acquisition for the family.'"

"I don't even know what that means."

She put the car keys on his desk. She was in a hurry since she and Hans had planned an outing with his parents. Wallander glanced out the window. The clouds were beginning to open up.

"Are you going to get married?" he asked before she disappeared through the door.

"They very much want us to," she said. "I'd be grateful if you didn't start nagging us too. We want to see if we're compatible."

"But you're going to have a baby?"

"That will be fine. But being able to put up with each other for the rest of our lives is a different matter."

She disappeared. Wallander listened to her rapid footsteps, the heels of her boots clicking against the floor. I don't know my daughter, he thought. There was a time when I thought I did, but now I can see that she's more and more of a stranger to me.

He stood by the window and gazed out at the old water tower, the pigeons, the trees, the blue sky emerging through the dispersing clouds. He felt deeply uneasy, an aura of desolation all around him. Or maybe it was actually inside him? As if he were turning into an hourglass with the sand silently running out. He continued watching the pigeons and the trees until the feeling drifted away. Then he went back to his desk and continued doggedly reading through the reports piled high in front of him.

Wallander spent Christmas with Linda's family. He observed his granddaughter, who still hadn't been given a name, with admiration and restrained joy. Linda insisted that the girl looked like him, especially her eyes, but Wallander couldn't see any similarities, no matter how hard he tried.

"The girl should have a name," he said as they sat drinking wine on Christmas Eve.

"All in good time," said Linda.

"We think the name will announce itself one of these days," said Hans.

"Why am I named Linda?" she asked out of the blue. "Where does that come from?"

"You can blame me," said Wallander. "Mona wanted to name you something different; I can't remember what. But as far as I was concerned, you were Linda from the very beginning. Your granddad thought you should be called Venus."

"Venus?"

"As you know, he wasn't always all there. Don't you like your name?"

"I've got a good name," she said. "And you don't need to worry. If we get married, I'm not going to change my surname. I'll never be Linda von Enke."

"Perhaps I should become a Wallander," said Hans. "But I don't think my parents would like that."

Over the next few days, Wallander spent his time organizing all the paperwork that had accumulated during the past year. It was a routine he had instigated years ago—before ringing out the old year, make room for all the junk that would build up during the one to come.

The evening the verdicts in the arms theft trial were made public, Wallander decided to stay at home and watch a movie. He had invested in a satellite dish and now had access to lots of film channels. He took his service pistol home with him, intending to clean it. He was behind in his shooting practice and knew he would need to submit to a test by the beginning of February at the latest. His desk wasn't cleared, but he had no pressing business. I'd better make the most of the opportunity, he thought. I can watch a movie tonight; tomorrow might be too late.

But after he got home and took Jussi out for a walk, he started to feel restless. He sometimes felt abandoned in his house out in the wilds, surrounded by empty fields. Like a wrecked ship, he sometimes thought. I've run aground in the middle of all these brown muddy fields. This restlessness usually passed quickly, but tonight it persisted. He sat in the kitchen, spread out an old newspaper, and cleaned his gun. By the time he'd finished it was still only eight o'clock. He had no idea what inspired him, but he made up his mind, changed his clothes, and drove back into Ystad. The town was always more or less deserted, especially on weekday evenings. No more than two or three restaurants or bars would be open. Wallander parked his car and went to a restaurant in the square. It was almost empty. He sat at a corner table, then ordered an appetizer and a bottle of wine. While he was waiting for the food, he gulped down a few glasses. He told himself he was swilling the alcohol in order to put his mind at rest. By the time the food arrived, he was already drunk.

"The place is dead," said Wallander. "Where is everybody?"

The waiter shrugged.

"Not here, that's for sure," he said. "Enjoy your meal."

Wallander only picked at the food. He dug out his cell phone and scrolled through the numbers in his address book. He wanted to talk to someone. But who? He put the phone down since he didn't want anyone to know that he was drunk. The wine bottle was empty, and he had already had more than enough. But even so, he ordered a cup of coffee and a glass of cognac when the waiter came to tell him the place was about to close. He stumbled when he got to his feet. The waiter gave him a tired look.

"Taxi," said Wallander.

The waiter called from the telephone attached to the wall next to the bar. Wallander could feel himself swaying from side to side. The waiter replaced the receiver, and nodded.

The wind was icy cold when Wallander came out into the street. He sat in the backseat of the taxi and was almost asleep by the time it turned into his drive-way. He left his clothes in a pile on the floor, and passed out the moment he lay down.

Half an hour after Wallander fell asleep, a man hurried into the police station. He was agitated, and asked to speak to the night duty officer. It happened to be Mar-tinsson.

The man explained that he was a waiter. Then he put a plastic bag on the table in front of Martinsson. In it was a gun, similar to the one Martinsson had.

The waiter even knew the name of the customer, since Wallander was well known in town.

Martinsson filled out a criminal offense form, then sat there for a long time staring at the revolver.

How on earth could Wallander have forgotten his service weapon? And why had he taken it to the restau-rant?

Martinsson checked the clock: just after midnight. He really should have called Wallander, but he didn't.

That conversation could wait until tomorrow. He wasn't looking forward to it.

3

When Wallander arrived at the police station the following day, there was a message waiting for him at the front desk, from Martinsson. Wallander swore under his breath. He was hungover and felt awful. If Martinsson wanted to speak to him the moment he arrived, it could mean only that something had happened that required Wallander's immediate presence. If only it could have waited for a couple of days, he thought. Or at least a few hours. Right now all he wanted to do was to close the door to his office, unplug his phone, and try to get some sleep with his feet on his desk. He took off his jacket, emptied an open bottle of mineral water, then went to see Martinsson, who now had the office that used to be Wallander's.

He knocked on the door and went in. The moment he saw Martinsson's face he realized it was serious. Wallander could always read his mood, which was important since Martinsson swung constantly between energetic exhilaration and glum dejection.

Wallander sat down in the guest chair.

"What happened? You only write me notes like that if something important has come up."

Martinsson stared at him in surprise.

"You mean you have no idea what I want to talk to you about?"

"No. Should I?"

Martinsson didn't reply. He merely continued looking at Wallander, who began to feel even worse than he had before.

"I'm not going to sit here guessing," he said in the end. "What is it you want?"

"You still have no idea why I want to talk to you?"

"No."

"That makes things harder."

Martinsson opened a drawer, took out Wallander's service pistol, and put it on the desk in front of him.

"I take it you know what I'm talking about now?"

Wallander stared at the revolver. A shudder ran down his spine, and almost succeeded in banishing his hangover. He recalled having cleaned his gun the previous evening—but then what happened? He groped around in his memory. The gun had migrated from his kitchen table to Martinsson's desk. But how it had gotten there, what had happened in between, he had no idea. He had no explanations, no excuses.

"You went to a restaurant last night," said Martinsson. "Why did you take your gun with you?"

Wallander shook his head incredulously. He still couldn't remember. Had he put it in his jacket pocket when he drove into Ystad? No matter how unlikely that seemed, apparently he must have.

"I don't know," Wallander admitted. "My mind's a blank. Tell me."

"A waiter came here around midnight," said Martinsson. "He was agitated because he had found the gun on the bench you had been sitting on."

Vague fragments of memory were racing around in

Wallander's mind. Maybe he had taken the gun out of his jacket when he'd used his cell phone? But how could he possibly have forgotten it?

"I have no idea what happened," he said. "But I suppose I must have put the gun in my pocket when I went out."

Martinsson stood up and opened the door.

"Would you like a coffee?"

Wallander shook his head. Martinsson disappeared into the hall. Wallander reached for the gun and saw that it was loaded. He broke into a sweat. The thought of shooting himself flashed through his mind. He moved the gun so that the barrel was pointing at the window. Martinsson came back.

"Can you help me?" Wallander asked.

"I'm afraid not this time. The waiter recognized you. You'll have to go from here straight to the boss."

"Have you already spoken to him?"

"It would have been dereliction of duty if I hadn't."

Wallander had nothing more to say. They sat there in silence. Wallander tried to find an escape route that he knew didn't exist.

"What will happen now?" he asked eventually.

"I've been trying to read up on it in the rule book. There will be an internal investigation, of course. There's also a risk that the waiter—Ture Saage is his name, incidentally, if you didn't know that already—might leak information to the press. Nowadays you can earn a few kronor if you have the right kind of information to sell. Careless, drunken policemen could well sell a few extra copies."

"I hope you told him to keep his mouth shut?"

"Of course I did! I even told him he could be arrested if he leaked any details of a police investigation. But I think he saw through me."

"Should I talk to him?"

Martinsson leaned over his desk. Wallander could see that he was both tired and depressed. That made him feel sad.

"How many years have we been working together? Twenty? More? At first you were the one who told me what to do. You told me off, but you also gave credit when it was due. Now it's my turn to tell you what to do. Nothing. You could only make things worse. Don't speak to the waiter; don't speak to anyone. Except for Lennart. And you need to see him now. He's expecting you."

Wallander nodded and stood up.

"We'll try to make the best of this," said Martinsson.

Wallander could tell from his tone of voice that he was not particularly hopeful.

Wallander reached out for his gun, but Martinsson shook his head.

"That had better stay here," he said.

Wallander went out into the hallway. Kristina Magnusson was passing, a mug of coffee between her hands. She nodded to him. Wallander could tell that she knew. He didn't turn around to check her out as he usually did. Instead he went into a bathroom and locked the door. The mirror over the sink was cracked. Just like me, Wallander thought. He rinsed his face, dried it, and contemplated his bloodshot eyes. The crack divided his face in two.

Wallander sat down on the toilet seat. There was another feeling nagging at him, not just the shame and the fear following what he had done. Nothing like this had ever happened before. He couldn't recall ever having handled his service issue pistol in a way that broke the rules. Whenever he took it home he always locked it away in the cabinet where he kept a licensed shotgun that he used on the very infrequent occasions he hunted hares with his neighbors. But there was something affecting him much more deeply than having been drunk. Another sort of forgetfulness that he didn't recognize. A darkness in which he could find no lamps to light.

When he finally stood up and went to see the chief of police, he had been sitting in the bathroom for over twenty minutes. If Martinsson called to say I was on my way, they probably think I've run off, he thought. But it's not quite as bad as that.

Following two female police chiefs, Lennart Mattson had taken up his post in Ystad the previous year. He was young, barely forty, and had risen surprisingly quickly through the police bureaucracy, which is where most senior officers came from nowadays. Like most active police officers, Wallander regarded this type of recruitment as ominous for the ability of the police force to carry out its duties properly. The worst part was that Mattson came from Stockholm and complained often that he had difficulty understanding the Skåne dialect. Wallander was aware that some of his colleagues made an effort to speak as broadly as possible whenever they had to talk to Mattson, but Wallander refrained from such malevolent demonstrations. He had decided to keep to himself and not get involved in anything Mattson was doing, as long as he didn't interfere too much in real police work. Since Mattson also seemed to respect him, Wallander had not had any problems with his new boss so far.

But he realized that things had now changed once and for all.

The door to Mattson's office was ajar. Wallander knocked and went in when he heard Mattson's high-pitched, almost squeaky voice.

A patterned sofa and matching armchairs had been squeezed into the office with considerable difficulty. Wallander sat down. Mattson had developed a technique of never opening a conversation if it could possibly be avoided, even if he was the one who had called the meeting. There was a rumor that a consultant from the National Police Board had sat in silence with Mattson for half an hour before standing up, leaving the room without a word having been spoken, and flying back to Stockholm.

Wallander toyed with the idea of challenging Mattson by not saying anything. But that would only have made him feel worse—he needed to clear the air as quickly as possible.

"I have no excuse for what happened," he began. "I accept that it is indefensible, and that you have to take whatever disciplinary steps the regulations specify."

Mattson seemed to have prepared his questions in advance, since they came out like machine-gun fire.

"Has it happened before?"

"That I've left my gun in a restaurant? Of course not!"

"Do you have an alcohol problem?"

The question made Wallander frown. What had given Mattson that idea?

"I'm a moderate drinker," Wallander said. "When I was younger I suppose I drank a fair amount on the weekend. But I don't do that anymore."

"But nevertheless you went out boozing on a week-day evening?"

"I didn't go out **boozing**. I went out for dinner."

"A bottle of wine and a cognac with your coffee?"

"If you already know what I drank, why are you asking? But I don't call that boozing. I don't think any sane person in this country would call it that. Boozing is when you swill down schnapps or vodka, probably straight from the bottle, and drink in order to get drunk, not for any other reason."

Mattson thought for a moment before his next question. Wallander was annoyed by his squeaky voice and wondered if the man sitting opposite him had the slightest idea of what police work in the field entailed, what horrific experiences it could involve.

"About twenty years ago you were apprehended by some of your colleagues for driving under the influence. They hushed it up, and nothing came of it. But you must understand that I wonder if you do in fact have an alcohol problem that you have been keeping under wraps, and which has now led to a most unfortunate consequence."

Wallander remembered that occasion all too well.

He had been in Malmö and had dinner with Mona. It was after their divorce, at a time when he still imagined he would be able to persuade her to come back to him. They had ended up arguing, and he had seen her being picked up outside the restaurant by a man he didn't recognize. He was so jealous and upset that he took leave of his senses and drove home, instead of getting a hotel room or sleeping in the car. His colleagues brought him back to his apartment and parked his car there, and he heard nothing more about it. One of the officers who had arrested him that night was now dead; the other had retired. But evidently rumors were still buzzing around the station. That surprised him.

"I'm not denying that. But as you said yourself, it was twenty years ago. And I assure you, I don't have an alcohol problem. If I choose to eat out one night in the middle of the week, I can't see why that should be anybody's business but my own."

"I will have to take the necessary steps. Since you are due some vacation time and are not involved in a serious investigation at the moment, I suggest you take a week off. There will have to be an internal investigation, of course. That's all I can say at the moment."

Wallander stood up. Mattson remained seated.

"Is there anything you'd like to add?" he asked.

"No," said Wallander. "I'll do what you suggest. I'll take time off and go home."

"It would be best if you left your gun here."

"I'm not an idiot," said Wallander. "Irrespective of what you think."

Wallander went back to his office and fetched his

jacket. Then he left the police station via the garage and drove home. It occurred to him that he might still have alcohol in his blood after yesterday's gallivanting, but since things couldn't get any worse than they were, he kept on going. A strong northeasterly wind had blown up. Wallander shuddered as he walked from the car to his front door. Jussi was leaping around inside his kennel, but Wallander didn't have the strength even to think about taking him for a walk. He undressed, lay down, and went to sleep. By the time he woke up it was twelve o'clock. He lay there motionless, his eyes open, and listened to the wind battering the house walls.

The feeling that something wasn't as it should be had started nagging at him again. A shadow had descended over his existence. How had he not even missed the gun when he woke up? It was as if somebody else had been acting in his stead, and then had switched off his memory so that he wouldn't know what had happened.

He got up, dressed, and tried to eat, although he still felt sick. He was very tempted to pour himself a glass of wine, but he resisted. He was doing the dishes when Linda called.

"I'm on my way," she said. "I'm just checking that you're at home."

She hung up before he had chance to say a single word. She arrived twenty minutes later, carrying her sleeping baby. Linda sat down opposite her father on the brown leather sofa he had bought the year they moved to Ystad. The baby was asleep on a chair next to her. Kurt wanted to talk about her but Linda shook her head. Later, but not now; first things first.

"I heard what happened," she said. "But even so, I feel as if I don't know anything about it."

"Did Martinsson call?"

"Yes, right after he spoke to you. He was very unhappy about it all."

"Not as unhappy as I am," said Wallander.

"Tell me what I don't know."

"If you've come here to interrogate me you might as well leave."

"I just want to know. You're the last person I'd ever have expected to do something like this."

"Nobody died," said Wallander. "Nobody even got hurt. Besides, anyone can do anything. I've lived long enough to know that."

Then he told her the whole story, from the restlessness that had driven him out of the house in the first place, to not knowing why he had taken his gun with him. When he had finished she said nothing for a long time.

"I believe you," she said eventually. "Everything you're telling me comes down to one single fact, one single circumstance in your life. That you are far too lonely. You suddenly lose control, and there's nobody around to calm you down, to stop you from rushing off. But there's still something I wonder about."

"What?"

"Have you told me everything? Or is there something you're not saying?"

Wallander wondered for a moment if he should tell

her about the strange feeling of a shadow closing in on him. But he shook his head; there was nothing more to tell her.

"What do you think's going to happen?" she asked. "I can't remember what the rule book says."

"There'll be an internal investigation. After that, I have no idea."

"Is there a chance they'll fire you?"

"I figure I'm too old to be fired. Besides, the offense isn't all that serious. But they might force me into early retirement."

"Wouldn't that appeal to you?"

Wallander was chewing away at an apple when she asked him that question. He hurled the core at the wall with all his strength.

"You've just said that my problem is loneliness!" he roared. "What would it be like if I was forced to retire? I'd have nothing at all left."

Wallander's bellowing woke the baby up.

"I'm sorry," he said.

"You're scared," she said. "I can understand that. I would be too. I don't think anybody should apologize for being scared."

Linda stayed until the evening, made him dinner, and they spoke no more about what had happened. Kurt escorted her to the car through the cold, gusting wind.

"Will you manage?" she asked.

"I'll always get by. But thank you for asking."

· · ·

The following day Wallander had a call from Lennart Mattson, who wanted to see him without delay. When they met, he was introduced to an internal affairs officer from Malmö who had come to interrogate him.

"Whenever it suits you," said the investigator, whose name was Holmgren and who was about the same age as Wallander.

"Now," said Wallander. "Why put it off?"

They shut themselves away in one of the police station's smallest conference rooms. Wallander made an effort to be precise, not to make excuses, not to trivialize what had happened. Holmgren took notes, occasionally asked Wallander to take a step backward, repeat an answer, and then continue. It seemed to Wallander that if the roles had been reversed, the interrogation would doubtless have proceeded in exactly the same way. It took slightly more than an hour. Holmgren put down his pen and looked at Wallander—not in the way one would look at a criminal who had just confessed, but as somebody who had messed things up. He seemed to be feeling sorry for the trouble Wallander found himself in.

"You didn't fire a shot," said Holmgren. "You forgot your gun when you drank too much at a restaurant. That's serious—there's no getting away from that— but you haven't actually committed a crime. You haven't assaulted anyone; you haven't taken bribes; you haven't harassed anyone."

"So I'm not going to be fired, you don't think?"

"Hardly. But it's not up to me."

"But your guess would be . . . ?"

"I'm not going to guess. You'll have to wait and see."

Holmgren began collecting his papers and placing them carefully in his briefcase. He suddenly paused.

"It's obviously an advantage if this business doesn't get into the hands of the media," he said. "Things always take a turn for the worse when we can't hush up this sort of thing and keep it inside the police force."

"I think we'll be okay," Wallander said. "There's been no mention of it so far, so that's an indication that nothing has been leaked."

But Wallander was wrong. That same day there was a knock on his door. He had been lying down, but he got up because he thought it was one of his neighbors. When he opened the door, a photographer took a flash picture of Wallander's face. Standing next to the cameraman was a reporter who introduced herself as Lisa Halbing, with a smile Wallander immediately classified as fake.

"Can we talk?" she asked aggressively.

"What about?" wondered Wallander, who already had a pain in his stomach.

"What do you think?"

"I don't think anything."

The cameraman took a whole series of pictures. Wallander's first instinct was to punch him, but he did no such thing, of course. Instead he demanded that the cameraman promise not to take any photographs inside the house; that was his private domain. When both the cameraman and Lisa Halbing promised to respect his privacy, he let them in and invited them to sit down at his kitchen table. He served them coffee and the remains of a sponge cake he'd been presented with a few days earlier by one of his neighbors who was an avid baker.

"Which newspaper?" he asked when he had finished serving coffee. "I forgot to ask."

"I should have said." Lisa Halbing was heavily made up and was trying to conceal her excess weight beneath a loose-fitting tunic shirt. She was in her thirties, and looked a bit like Linda—although his daughter would never have worn so much makeup.

"I work for various papers," Halbing said. "If I have a good story, I sell it to the one that pays best."

"And right now you think I'm a good story, is that it?"

"On a scale of one to ten you might just about scrape into four. No more than that."

"What would I have been if I'd shot the waiter in the restaurant?"

"Then you'd have been a perfect ten. That would obviously have been worth a front-page headline."

"How did you find out about this?"

The cameraman was itching to pick up his camera, but he kept his promise. Lisa Halbing was still wearing her forced smile.

"You realize of course that I'm not going to answer that question."

"I assume it was the waiter who tipped you off."

"It wasn't, in fact. But I'm not going to say anything more about that."

Looking back, it was clear to Wallander that one of his colleagues must have leaked the details. It could have been anyone, even Lennart Mattson himself. Or the investigating officer from Malmö. How much would they have earned? All the years he had been a police officer, leaks had been a continuing problem, but he had never been affected himself until now. He had never contacted a journalist, nor had he ever heard the slightest suggestion that any of his close colleagues had done so either. But then, what did he know? Precisely nothing.

Later that evening he called Linda and warned her about what she could expect to read in the following day's paper.

"Did you tell them the honest truth?"

"At least nobody can accuse me of lying."

"Then you'll be okay. Lies are what they're after. They'll make a meal of it, but I don't think there'll be any repercussions."

Wallander slept badly that night. The following day he was waiting for the phone to ring, but he had only two calls. One was from Kristina Magnusson, who was angry about the way the incident had been blown out of proportion. Shortly afterward, Lennart Mattson called.

"It's a pity you made a statement to the press," he said disapprovingly.

Wallander was furious.

"What would you have done if you'd been confronted by a journalist and a cameraman on your front doorstep? People who knew every detail of what had happened? Would you have shut the door in their face, or lied to them?"

"I thought it was you who had contacted them," said Mattson lamely.

"Then you are even more stupid than I thought you were."

Wallander slammed down the phone and unplugged it. Then he called Linda on his cell phone and said she should use that number if she wanted to talk to him.

"Come with us," she said.

"Come with you where?"

She seemed surprised.

"Didn't I tell you? We're off to Stockholm. It's Håkan's seventy-fifth birthday. Come with us!"

"No," he said. "I'm staying here. I'm not in a party mood. I've had enough of that after my evening at the restaurant."

"We're leaving the day after tomorrow. Think about it."

When Wallander went to bed that night he was convinced that he wasn't going anywhere. But by the next morning he had changed his mind. The neighbors could take care of Jussi. It might be a good idea to make himself scarce for a few days.

The following day he flew to Stockholm. Linda and her family drove. He checked into a hotel across from the Central Station. When he leafed through the evening newspapers, he noted that the gun story had already been relegated to an inside page. The big news story of the day was an unusually audacious bank robbery in Gothenburg, carried out by four robbers wearing ABBA masks. Reluctantly, he sent the robbers his grateful thanks.

That night he slept unusually soundly in his hotel bed.

4

Håkan von Enke's birthday party was held in a rented party facility in Djursholm, the upmarket suburb of Stockholm. Wallander had never been there before. Linda assured him that a business suit would be appropriate—von Enke hated dinner jackets and tails, although he was very fond of the various uniforms he had worn during his long naval career. Wallander could have worn his police uniform if he'd wanted to, but he had taken his best suit with him. Under the circumstances, it didn't feel right for him to use his uniform.

Why on earth had he agreed to go to Stockholm? Wallander asked himself as the express train from Arlanda Airport came to a halt in the Central Station. Perhaps it would have been better to go somewhere else. He occasionally used to take short trips to Skagen in Denmark, where he liked to stroll along the beaches, visit the art gallery, and lounge around in one of the guesthouses he had been using for the past thirty years. It was to Skagen that he had retreated many years ago when he had toyed with the idea of resigning from the police forcce. But here he was in Stockholm to attend a birthday party.

When Wallander arrived in Djursholm, Håkan von Enke went out of his way to make him welcome. He seemed genuinely pleased to see Wallander, who was placed at the head table, between Linda and the widow of a rear admiral. The widow, whose name was Hök, was in her eighties, used a hearing aid, and eagerly re-filled her wineglass at every opportunity. Even before they had finished the soup course she had started telling slightly smutty jokes. Wallander found her interesting, especially when he discovered that one of her six children was an expert in forensic medicine in Lund—Wallander had met him on several occasions and had a good impression of him. Many speeches were delivered, but they were all blessedly short. Good military discipline, Wallander thought. The toastmaster was a Commander Tobiasson, who made a series of witty remarks that Wallander found highly amusing. When the admiral's wife fell silent for a little while due to the malfunctioning of her hearing aid, Wallander wondered what he could expect when he celebrated his own seventy-fifth birthday. Who would come to the party, assuming he had one? Linda had told him that it had been Håkan von Enke's own idea to rent the party rooms. If Wallander understood the situation correctly, his wife, Louise, had been surprised. Usually her husband was dismissive of his birthdays, but he had suddenly changed his mind and set up this lavish spread.

Coffee was served in an adjacent room with comfortable easy chairs. When everyone had finished eating, Wallander went out into a conservatory to stretch his legs. The restaurant was surrounded by spacious grounds—the estate had previously been the home of one of Sweden's first and richest industrialists.

He gave a start when Håkan von Enke appeared by his side out of nowhere, clutching something as un-PC as an old-fashioned pipe and a pack of tobacco. Wallander recognized the brand: Hamilton's Blend. For a short period in his late teens he had been a pipe smoker himself, and used the same tobacco.

"Winter," said von Enke. "And we're in for a snowstorm, according to the forecast."

Von Enke paused for a moment and gazed out at the dark sky.

"When you're on board a submarine at a sufficient depth, the climate and weather conditions are totally irrelevant. Everything is calm; you're in a sort of ocean basement. In the Baltic Sea, twenty-five meters is deep enough if there isn't too much wind. It's more difficult in the North Sea. I remember once leaving Scotland in stormy conditions. We were listing fifteen degrees at a depth of thirty meters. It wasn't exactly pleasant."

He lit his pipe and eyed Wallander keenly.

"Is that too poetic a thought for a police officer?"

"No, but a submarine is a different world as far as I'm concerned. A scary one, I should add."

The commander sucked eagerly at his pipe.

"Let's be honest," he said. "This party is boring both of us stiff. Everybody knows that I arranged it. I did it because a lot of my friends wanted me to. But now we can hide ourselves away in one of the little side rooms. Sooner or later my wife will come looking for me, but we can talk in peace until then."

"But you're the star of this show," said Wallander.

"It's like in a good play," said von Enke. "In order to increase the excitement, the main character doesn't need to be onstage all the time. It can be advantageous if some of the most important parts of the plot take place in the wings."

He fell silent. Too abruptly, far too abruptly, Wallander thought. Von Enke was staring at something behind Wallander's back. Wallander turned around. He could see the garden, and beyond it one of the minor roads that eventually joined the main Djursholm–Stockholm highway. Wallander caught a glimpse of a man on the other side of the fence, standing under a lamppost. Next to him was a parked car, with the engine running. The exhaust fumes rose and slowly dispersed in the yellow light. Wallander could tell that von Enke was worried.

"Let's get our coffee and then shut ourselves away," he said.

Before leaving the conservatory, Wallander turned around again; the car had vanished, and so had the man by the lamppost. Perhaps it was someone von Enke had forgotten to invite to the party, Wallander thought. It couldn't have been anyone looking for me, surely—some journalist wanting to talk to me about the gun I left in the restaurant.

After they picked up their coffee, von Enke led Wallander into a little room with brown wooden paneling and leather easy chairs. Wallander noticed that the room had no windows. Von Enke had been watching him.

"There's a reason for this room being a sort of bunker," he said. "In the 1930s the house was owned for a few years by a man who owned a lot of Stockholm nightclubs, most of them illegal. Every night his armed couriers would drive around and collect all the takings, which were brought back here. In those days this room contained a big safe. His accountants would sit here, adding up the cash, doing the books, and then stash the money away in the safe. When the owner was arrested for his shady dealings, the safe was cut up. The man was called Göransson, if I remember correctly. He was given a long sentence that he couldn't handle. He hanged himself in his cell at Långholmen Prison."

He fell silent, took a sip of coffee, and sucked at his pipe, which had gone out. And that was the moment, in that insulated little room where the only sound was a faint hum from the party guests outside, that Wallander realized Håkan von Enke was scared. He had seen this many times before in his life: a person frightened of something, real or imagined. He was certain he wasn't mistaken.

The conversation started awkwardly, with von Enke reminiscing about the years when he was still on active duty as a naval officer.

"The fall of 1980," he said. "That's a long time ago

now, a generation back, twenty-eight long years. What were you doing then?"

"I was working as a police officer in Ystad. Linda was very young. I'd decided to move there in order to be closer to my elderly father. I also thought it would be a better environment for Linda to grow up in. Or at least, that was one of the reasons why we left Malmö. What happened next is a different story altogether."

Von Enke didn't seem to be listening to what Wallander said. He continued along his own line.

"I was working at the east coast naval base that fall. Two years before I had stepped down as officer in charge of one of our best submarines, one of the Water Snake class. We submariners always called it simply the Snake. My posting at the marine base was only temporary. I wanted to go back to sea, but the powers that be wanted me to become part of the operations command of the whole Swedish naval defense forces. In September the Warsaw Pact countries were conducting an exercise along the East German coast. MILOBALT, they called it. I can still remember that. It was nothing remarkable; they generally had their fall exercises at about the same time as we had ours. But an unusually large number of vessels were involved, since they were practicing landings and submarine recovery. We had succeeded in finding out the details without too much effort. We heard from the National Defense Radio Center that there was an awful lot of radio communication traffic between Russian vessels and their home base near Leningrad, but everything seemed to be routine; we kept an eye on what they were doing and made a note of anything we thought important in our logbooks. But then came that Thursday—it was September 18, a date that will be the very last thing I forget. We had a call from the duty officer on one of the fleet's tugs, HMS **Ajax**, saying that they had just discovered a foreign submarine in Swedish territorial waters. I was in one of the map rooms at the naval base, looking for a more detailed chart of the East German coast, when an agitated national serviceman burst into the room. He never managed to explain exactly what had happened, but I went back to the command center and spoke to the duty officer on the **Ajax**. He said he'd been scanning the sea with his telescope and suddenly noticed the submarine's aerials some three hundred yards away. Fifteen seconds later the submarine surfaced. The officer was on the ball, and figured out that the submarine had probably been at periscope depth but had then started to dive when they saw the tug. The **Ajax** was just south of Huvudskär when the incident happened, and the submarine was heading southwest, which meant that she was parallel with the border of Swedish waters but definitely on the Swedish side of the line. It didn't take long for me to find out if there were any Swedish submarines in the area: there were not. I requested radio contact with the **Ajax** again, and asked the duty officer if he could describe the conning tower or the periscope he had seen. From what he said I realized immediately that it was one of the submarines of the class NATO called Whiskey. And at the time they were used only by the Russians and the Poles. I'm sure you'll understand that my heart started beating faster when I established that. But I had two other questions."

Von Enke paused, as if he expected Wallander to ask what the two questions were. Some peals of laughter could be heard on the other side of the door, but they soon faded away.

"I suppose you wanted to know if the submarine was in Swedish territorial waters by mistake," said Wallander. "As was claimed when that other Russian submarine ran aground off Karlskrona?"

"I had already answered that question. There is no naval vessel as meticulous with its navigation as a submarine. That goes without saying. The submarine the **Ajax** had come across intended to be where it was. The question was what exactly it was up to. Why was it reconnoitering and surfacing, apparently not expecting to be discovered? It could have been a sign that the crew was being careless. But of course, there was also another possibility."

"That the submarine wanted to be discovered?"

Von Enke nodded, and made another attempt to light his reluctant pipe.

"In that case," he said, "to encounter a tugboat would be ideal. A vessel like that probably wouldn't even have a catapult to attack you with. Nor would the crew be trained for confrontation. Since I was in charge at the base, I contacted the supreme commander, and he agreed with me that we should immediately send in a helicopter equipped for tracking down submarines. It made sonar contact with a moving object we decided was a submarine. For the first time in my life I gave an order to open fire in circumstances other than training exercises. The helicopter fired a depth charge to warn the submarine. Then it vanished, and we lost contact."

"How could it simply disappear?"

"Submarines have many ways of making themselves invisible. They can descend into deep troughs, hugging the cliff walls, and thus confuse anybody trying to trace them with echo sounders. We sent out several helicopters, but we never found any further trace of it."

"But couldn't it have been damaged?"

"That's not the way it goes. According to international law, the first depth charge must be a warning. It's only later that you can force a submarine up to the surface for identification."

"What happened next?"

"Nothing, really. There was an inquiry, and they decided that I'd done the right thing. Maybe this was the overture for what was to follow a couple of years later, when Swedish territorial waters were crawling with foreign submarines, mainly in the Stockholm archipelago. I suppose the most important result was that we had confirmation of the fact that Russian interest in our navigational channels was as great as ever. This happened at a time when nobody thought the Berlin Wall would fall or the Soviet Union collapse. It's easy to forget that. The Cold War wasn't over. After that incident, the Swedish navy was granted a big increase in funding. But that was all."

Von Enke drained the rest of his coffee. Wallander

was about to stand up when his host started speaking again.

"I'm not done yet. Two years later, off we went again. By then I'd been promoted to the very top of the Swedish naval defense staff. Our HQ was in Berga, and there was a combat command on duty around the clock. On October 1 we had an alarm call that we could never have imagined, even in our wildest dreams. There were indications that a submarine, or even several, were in the Hårsfjärden channel, very close to our base on Muskö. So it was no longer just a case of trespassing in Swedish territorial waters; there were foreign submarines in a restricted area. No doubt you remember all the fuss?"

"The newspapers were full of it, and television reporters were clambering around on slippery rocks."

"I don't know what you could compare it to. Perhaps a foreign helicopter landing in a courtyard at the heart of the royal palace. That's what it felt like, having submarines close to our top secret military installations."

"That was when I'd just received confirmation that I could start working in Ystad."

Suddenly the door opened. Von Enke gave a start. Wallander noted that his right hand was on its way to the breast pocket of his jacket. Then he let it fall back onto his knee again. The door had been opened by a semi-inebriated woman who was looking for a bathroom. She withdrew, and they were alone again.

"It was in October," von Enke resumed once the door had closed. "It sometimes felt as if the whole

Swedish coast was under siege by unidentified foreign submarines. I was glad I wasn't the one responsible for talking to all the journalists who had gathered out at Berga. We had to convert a few barrack rooms into press rooms. I was extremely busy all the time, trying to find one of those submarines. We'd lose all our credibility if we couldn't manage to force a single one to the surface. And then, at last, came the evening when we had trapped a submarine in the Hårsfjärden channel. There was no doubt about it; the command team was convinced this was it. I was the one responsible for giving the order to open fire. During those hectic hours I spoke several times to the supreme commander and the new minister of defense. His name was Andersson, if you recall—a man from Borlänge."

"I have a vague memory of him being called 'Red Börje.'"

"That's right. But he wasn't up to the job. He no doubt thought the submarines were pure hell. He went back home to Dalarna and we got Anders Thunborg as minister of defense. One of Palme's blue-eyed boys. A lot of my colleagues didn't trust him, but the contact I had with him was good. He didn't interfere; he asked questions. If he got an answer, he was satisfied. But once when he called me I had the distinct impression that Palme was in the room with him, standing by his side. I don't know if that was true. But the feeling was very strong."

"Anyway, what happened?"

Von Enke's face twitched, as if he was annoyed by

Wallander interrupting him. But when he continued there was no sign of that.

"We had cornered the submarine in such a way that it couldn't move without our permission. I spoke to the supreme commander and told him that we were about to fire depth charges and force the sub up to the surface. We needed another hour to prepare for the operation, and then we would be able to reveal to the world the identity of this submarine that had invaded Swedish territorial waters. Half an hour passed. The hands on the wall clock seemed to be moving unbearably slowly. The whole time, I was in touch with the helicopters and the surface vessels surrounding the submarine. Forty-five minutes passed. And then it happened."

Von Enke broke off abruptly, then stood up and left the room. Wallander wondered if he had been taken ill. But after a few moments the commander returned, carrying two glasses of cognac.

"It's a chilly winter evening," he said. "We need something to warm us up. Nobody seems to have missed us, so we can carry on chatting in this bunker."

Wallander waited for the rest of the story. Even if it wasn't perhaps totally engrossing, listening to old stories about submarines, he preferred von Enke's company to having to talk to people he didn't know.

"That's when it happened," repeated von Enke. "Four minutes before the attack was due to take place, the phone rang—the direct line to Defense Command Sweden. As far as I know it was one of the few lines guaranteed to be safe from bugging, and it was also fitted with an automatic scrambler. I was given an order that I would never have expected in a thousand years. Can you guess what it was?"

Wallander shook his head, and wrapped his hand around his glass to warm up the brandy.

"We were ordered to abort the depth charge attack. Naturally, I was dumbstruck and demanded an explanation. But I didn't receive one—not then, at least. Just the specific order that on no account should any depth charges be fired. Obviously, I had no choice but to obey. There were only two minutes left when the helicopters were informed of the decision. None of us at Berga could understand what was going on. It was exactly ten minutes before we received our next order. If possible, it was even more incomprehensible. Our superiors seemed to have taken leave of their senses. We were ordered to back off."

Wallander was becoming more interested.

"So you were told to let the submarine get away?"

"Nobody actually said that, of course. Not in so many words, at least. We were ordered to concentrate our attention on a different part of the Hårsfjärden channel, at its very edge, south of the Danzig straits. A helicopter had made contact with another submarine. Why was that one more important than the one we had encircled and were just about to force up to the surface? My colleagues and I were at a loss. I asked to speak to the supreme commander in person, but he was busy and couldn't be interrupted. Which was very odd, because he was the one who had authorized the operation not long before. I even tried to speak to the minister of defense or his private secretary, but everyone seemed to have vanished, unplugged their phones, or been instructed to say nothing. The supreme commander and the minister of defense instructed to say nothing? By whom? The government could have done it, of course, or the prime minister. I had agonizing stomach pains for several hours. I didn't understand the orders I'd been given. Aborting the operation went against my experience and instincts. I came very close to refusing to obey. That would have been the end of my military career. But I still had a grain of common sense left. And so we moved all our helicopters and two surface vessels to the Danzig straits. I asked for permission to keep at least one helicopter hovering over the place where we knew the submarine was hiding, but that was not granted. We should leave the area, and do so immediately. Which we did. With the expected result."

"Which was?"

"Needless to say, we didn't find a submarine near the Danzig straits. We continued searching for the rest of the night. I still wonder how many thousand liters of fuel the helicopters used up."

"What happened to the submarine you had encircled?"

"It disappeared. Without a trace."

Wallander thought over what he had heard. Once, in the far distant past, he had completed his national military service with a tank regiment in Skövde. He had unpleasant memories of that period of his life. On being called up he had tried to join the navy, but he had been sent to Västergötland. He had never had any trouble accepting discipline, but he did find it difficult to understand a lot of the orders they were given. It often seemed that chaos ruled, despite the fact that they were supposed to imagine themselves in a potentially lethal confrontation with an enemy.

Von Enke emptied his cognac glass.

"I started asking questions about what had happened. I shouldn't have. I soon noticed that it was not a particularly popular thing to do. Even some of my colleagues whom I had regarded as my best friends objected to my curiosity. But all I wanted to know was why these counter-orders had been issued. I'm convinced that we were closer than we'd ever been before, or have been since, to finally making a submarine surface and identify itself. Two minutes away, no more than that. At first I wasn't the only one to be upset about the situation. Another commander, Arosenius, and an analyst from Defense Command Sweden were part of the top-level team that day. But after a few weeks they both started keeping me at arm's length. They didn't want to be associated with the way I was stirring things up and asking questions. And eventually I gave up as well."

Von Enke put his glass down on the table and leaned forward toward Wallander.

"But I haven't forgotten it, of course. I still keep trying to understand what happened—not just on that day when we allowed a submarine to give us the slip. I keep rehashing everything that happened during those years. And I think that now, at long last, I'm beginning to get some idea of what was really going on."

"You mean, why you weren't allowed to force that submarine to surface?"

He nodded slowly, lit his pipe again, but said nothing. Wallander wondered if the story he had heard was destined to remain unfinished.

"I'm curious, of course. What was the explanation?"

Von Enke made a dismissive gesture.

"It's too early for me to say anything about it. I still haven't come to the end of the road. So right now I have nothing more to say. Perhaps we'd better go and join the other guests."

They stood up and left the room. Wallander went back to the conservatory, and bumped into the woman who had disturbed them. Only now did he reflect on the way von Enke had moved his right hand when she had burst into the room—at first very decisively, but then slowing down and eventually dropping it back onto his knee.

Even if it seemed almost inconceivable, Wallander could think of only one explanation. Von Enke was carrying a gun. Was that really possible? he thought as he stared out through the window at the deserted garden. A retired naval commander carrying a gun at his seventy-fifth birthday party?

Wallander simply couldn't believe it. He dismissed the thought. He must have been imagining things. One bewildering experience must have led to another. First the idea that von Enke was scared, and then that he was carrying a gun. Wallander wondered if his intuition was fading, just as he was beginning to grow more forgetful.

Linda came into the conservatory.

"I thought you must have left."

"Not yet. But soon."

"I'm sure both Håkan and Louise are glad you came."

"He's been telling me about the submarines."

Linda raised an eyebrow.

"Really? That surprises me."

"Why?"

"I've tried to get him to tell me about that lots of times. But he always refuses, says he doesn't want to. He seems to get annoyed."

Hans shouted for her, and Linda left. Wallander thought about what she had said. Why had Håkan von Enke chosen to tell him his story?

Later, when Wallander had returned to Skåne and thought about the evening, there was another thing that intrigued him. Obviously there was a lot in what von Enke had said that was unclear, vague, difficult for Wallander to understand. But with regard to the way in which it had been served up, as Wallander put it, there was something he couldn't figure out. Had von Enke planned to tell him all that during the short time he knew that the father of his son's girlfriend was going to attend the party? Or had it happened at much shorter notice, sparked by the man under the lamppost on the other side of the fence? And who was that man?

5

Three months later—on April 11, to be more precise—something happened that forced Wallander to
think back yet again to that evening in January.

It happened without warning and was totally unexpected by everyone involved. Håkan von Enke disappeared without a trace from his home in the
Östermalm district of Stockholm. Every morning, von
Enke went for a long walk, regardless of the weather.
On that particular day, it was drizzling all over Stockholm. He got up early, as usual, and shortly after six
was enjoying his breakfast. At seven o'clock he
knocked on the bedroom door in order to wake up his
wife, and announced that he was going out for his
usual walk. It generally lasted about two hours, except
when it was very cold; then he would shorten it to one
hour, since he used to be a heavy smoker, and his lungs
had never recovered. He always took the same route.
From his home in Grevgatan he would walk to Valhallavägen and from there turn off into the Lill-
Jansskogen woods, following an intricate sequence of
paths that eventually took him back to Valhallavägen,
then southward along Sturegatan before turning left
into Karlavägen and back home again. He would walk
fast, using various walking sticks he had inherited from
his father, and was always sweaty by the time he arrived
back home and tumbled into a hot bath.

This particular morning had been like all the others, apart from one thing: Håkan von Enke never came home. Louise was very familiar with his route—she used to accompany him sometimes, but she stopped when she could no longer keep up with his pace. When he didn't turn up, she started to worry. He was in good shape, no doubt about that; but nevertheless he was an old man and something might have happened to him. A heart attack, or a burst blood vessel perhaps? She went out to look for him, having first established that he hadn't taken his cell phone, in spite of their agreement that he always would. It was lying on his desk. She came back at one o'clock, having retraced his footsteps. The whole time, she was half expecting to find him lying dead by the side of the road. But there was no sign of him. He had vanished. She called two, maybe three friends he might conceivably have visited, but nobody had seen him. Now she was sure that something had happened. It was about two when she called Hans at his office in Copenhagen. Although she was very worried and wanted to report Håkan's absence to the police, Hans tried to calm her down. Louise reluctantly agreed to wait a few more hours.

But Hans called Linda immediately, and from her Wallander heard what had happened. He was trying to teach Jussi to sit still while he cleaned his paws—he had been taught what to do by a dog trainer he knew in Sturup. He was just about to give up on the grounds that Jussi had no ability whatsoever to learn new habits when the phone rang. Linda told him about Louise's worries and asked for his advice.

"You're a police officer yourself," Wallander said. "You know the routine. Wait and see. Most of them come back."

"But this is the first time he's deviated from his routine in many years. I understand why Louise is worried. She's not the hysterical type."

"Wait until tonight," said Wallander. "He'll come back; you'll see."

Wallander was convinced that Håkan von Enke would turn up and that there would be a perfectly logical explanation for his absence. He was more curious than worried, and wondered what the explanation would be. But von Enke never did return, not that evening or the next one. Late in the evening of April 11 Louise reported her husband missing. She was then driven around the narrow labyrinthine roads in the Lill-Jansskogen woods in a police car, but they failed to find him. The following day her son traveled up from Copenhagen. It was then that Wallander began to realize something serious must have happened.

At that point he had still not returned to work. The internal investigation had dragged on and on. And to make matters worse, in the beginning of February he had fallen badly on the icy road outside his house and broken his left wrist. He had tripped over Jussi's leash because the dog still hadn't learned to stop pulling and dragging, or to walk on the correct side. His wrist was put in a cast and Wallander was given sick leave. It had been a period of short temper and frequent outbursts of anger, aimed at himself and Jussi and also at Linda. As a result, Linda had avoided seeing him any more than was necessary. She thought he had become like his father—surly, irritable, impatient. Reluctantly, he accepted that she was right. He didn't want to turn into his father; he could cope with anything else, but not that. He didn't want to be a bitter old man who kept repeating himself, both in his paintings and in his opinions about a world that grew increasingly incomprehensible to him. It was a time when Wallander strode around and around his house like a bear in a cage, no longer able to ignore the fact that he was now sixty years old and hence inexorably on his way into old age. He might live for another ten or twenty years, but he would never be able to experience anything but growing older and older. Youth was a distant memory, and now middle age was behind him. He was standing in the wings, waiting for his cue to go onstage to begin the third and final act, in which everything would be explained, the heroes placed in the spotlight while the villains died. He was fighting as hard as he could to avoid being forced to play the tragic role. He would prefer to leave the stage with a laugh.

What worried him most was his forgetfulness. He would write a list when he drove to Simrishamn or Ystad to do some shopping, but when he entered the shops he would realize he had forgotten it. Had he in fact ever written one? He couldn't remember. One day, when he was more worried than usual about his memory, he made an appointment with a doctor in Malmö who advertised herself as a specialist in "the problems of old age." The doctor, whose name was Margareta Bengtsson, received him in an old house in the center of Malmö. In Wallander's prejudiced view she was too young to be capable of understanding the miseries of old age. He was tempted to turn around and leave, but he controlled himself, sat down in a leather armchair and began talking about his bad memory that was getting worse all the time.

"Do I have Alzheimer's?" Wallander asked as the interview drew to a close.

Margareta Bengtsson smiled, not condescendingly but in a straightforward and friendly way.

"No," she said. "I don't think so. But obviously, nobody knows what's lurking around the next corner."

Around the next corner, Wallander thought as he walked back to his car through the bitterly cold wind. When he got there he found a parking ticket tucked under a windshield wiper. He flung it into the car without even looking to see how much he had been fined and drove home.

A car he didn't recognize was waiting outside his front door. When Wallander got out of his own car, he saw Martinsson standing by the dog kennel, stroking Jussi through the bars.

"I was just going to leave," said Martinsson. "I left a note on the door."

"Have they sent you to deliver a message?"

"Not at all—I came entirely of my own accord to see how you were."

They went into the house. Martinsson took a look at Wallander's library, which had become extensive over the years. Then they sat at the kitchen table, drinking coffee. Wallander said nothing about his trip to Malmö and the appointment with the doctor. Martinsson nodded at his plastered hand.

"The cast will come off next week," said Wallander. "What does the gossip have to say?"

"About your hand?"

"About me. The gun at the restaurant."

"Lennart Mattson is an unusually taciturn man. I know nothing about what's going on. But you can count on our support."

"That's not true. You no doubt support me. But the leak must have come from somewhere. There are a lot of people at the police station who don't like me."

Martinsson shrugged.

"That's life. There's nothing you can do about it. Who likes me?"

They talked about everything under the sun. It struck Wallander that Martinsson was now the only one left of the colleagues who were at the police station when he first moved to Ystad.

Martinsson seemed depressed as he sat there at the table. Wallander wondered if he was ill.

"No, I'm not ill," said Martinsson. "But I'm resigned to the fact that it's all over now. My career as a police officer, that is."

"Did you also leave your gun in a restaurant?"

"I just can't take it anymore."

To Wallander's astonishment, Martinsson started crying. He sat there like a helpless child, his hands wrapped around his coffee cup as the tears ran down his cheeks. Wallander had no idea what to do. He had occasionally noticed that Martinsson was depressed over the years, but he had never broken down like this before. He decided simply to wait it out. When the phone rang he unplugged it.

Martinsson pulled himself together and dried his face.

"What a thing to do!" he said. "I apologize."

"Apologize for what? In my opinion anyone who can cry in front of another man displays great courage. Courage I don't have, I'm afraid."

Martinsson explained that he felt he had lost his way. He found himself questioning more and more the value of his work as a police officer. He wasn't dissatisfied with the work he did, but he worried about the role of the police in the Sweden of today. The gap between what the general public expected and what the police could actually do seemed to be growing wider all the time. Now he had reached a point where every night was a virtually sleepless wait for a day he knew would bring more torture.

"I'm packing it in this summer," he said. "There's a firm in Malmö I've been in contact with. They provide security consultants for small businesses and private properties. They have a job for me. At a salary significantly higher than what I'm getting now, incidentally."

Wallander recalled another time many years ago when Martinsson had made up his mind to resign. On that occasion Wallander had managed to persuade him to soldier on. That must have been at least fifteen years ago. He could see that this time, it was impossible to talk his colleague out of it. It wasn't as if his own situation made his future in the police force particularly attractive.

"I think I understand what you mean," he said. "And I think you're doing the right thing. Change course while you're still young enough to do it."

"I'll be fifty in a few years' time," he said. "You call that young?"

"I'm sixty," said Wallander. "By then you're definitely on a one-way street to old age."

Martinsson stayed a bit longer, talking about the work he would be doing in Malmö. Wallander realized the man was trying to show him that despite everything, he still had something to look forward to, that he hadn't lost all his enthusiasm.

Wallander walked him to his car.

"Have you heard anything from Mattson?" Martinsson asked tentatively.

"There are four possible options," Wallander told him. "A 'constructive reprimand,' for instance. They can't do that to me. That would make a laughingstock of the whole police force. A sixty-year-old officer sitting before some police commissioner like a naughty schoolboy, told to mend his ways."

"Surely they aren't seriously considering that? They must be out of their minds!"

"They could give me an official warning," Wallander went on. "Or they could give me a fine. As a last resort, they could give me the boot. My guess is I'll get a fine."

They shook hands when they came to the car. Martinsson vanished into a cloud of snow. Wallander went back into the house, leafed through his calendar, and established that three months had now passed since that unfortunate evening when he forgot his service pistol.

He remained on sick leave even after the cast had been removed. On April 10 an orthopedic specialist at Ystad Hospital discovered that a bone in Wallander's hand had not healed as it should have. For a brief, horrific moment Wallander thought they were going to break his wrist again, but the doctor assured him that there were other measures they could take. But it was important that Wallander not use his hand, so he couldn't go back to work.

After leaving the hospital, Wallander stayed in town. There was a play by a modern American dramatist on at the Ystad theater, and Wallander had been given a ticket by Linda, who had a bad cold and couldn't go herself. As a teenager she had thought briefly about becoming an actress, but that ambition passed quickly. Now she was relieved she had realized early on that she didn't have enough talent to go on the stage.

After only ten minutes, Wallander started checking his watch. The play was boring him. Moderately talented actors were wandering around in a room and reciting their lines from various places—a stool, a table, a window seat. The play was about a family in the process of breaking up as a result of internal pressures, unresolved conflicts, lies, thwarted dreams; it completely failed to engage his interest. When the first intermission came at last, Wallander grabbed his jacket and left the theater. He had been looking forward to the production, and he felt frustrated. Was it his fault, or was the play really as boring as he found it?

He had parked his car at the train station. He crossed over the tracks and followed a well-trodden path toward the rear of the station building. He suddenly felt a blow in the small of his back and fell over. Two young men, eighteen or nineteen, were standing over him. One of them was wearing a hooded sweater, the other a leather jacket. The one with the hood was carrying a knife. A kitchen knife, Wallander noted before being punched in the face by the one in the leather jacket. His upper lip split and started bleeding. Another punch, this time on the forehead. The boy was strong and was hitting hard, as if he was in a rage. Then he started tugging at Wallander's clothes, hissing that he wanted his wallet and cell phone. Wallander raised an arm to protect himself. The whole time, he was keeping an eye on the knife. It then dawned on him that the kids were more scared than he was, and that he didn't need to worry about that trembling hand holding the weapon. Wallander braced himself, then aimed a kick at the kid with the knife. He missed, but grabbed ahold of his hand and gave it a violent twist. The knife flew away. At the same time, he felt a heavy blow to the back of his neck, and he fell down again. This time the blow had been so hard that he couldn't stand up. He managed to raise himself onto his knees, and he felt the chill from the wet ground through his pant legs. He expected to be stabbed at any moment. But nothing happened. When he looked up, the kids had disappeared. He rubbed the back of his head, which felt sticky. He slowly got to his feet, realized that he was in danger of fainting, and grabbed hold of the fence surrounding the tracks. He took a few deep breaths, then made his way gingerly to the car. The back of his neck was bleeding, but he could take care of that when he got home. He didn't seem to have any signs of a concussion.

He sat behind the wheel for a while without turning the ignition key. From one world to another, he thought. First I'm sitting in a theater but don't feel a part of what's happening. So I leave and then find my-self in a world I often come across from the outside; but this time I am the one lying there, injured, under threat.

He thought about the knife. Once, at the very be-ginning of his career, as a young police officer in Malmö, he had been stabbed in Pildamm Park by a madman run amok. If the knife had entered his body only an inch to one side it would have hit his heart. In that case he would never have spent all those years in Ystad, or seen Linda grow up. His life would have come to an end before it had started in earnest.

He remembered thinking at the time: **There's a time to live, and a time to die.**

It was cold in the car. He started the engine and switched on the heat. He relived the attack over and over again in his mind. He was still in shock, but he could feel the anger boiling up inside him.

He gave a start when somebody knocked on the window, afraid that the young men had come back.

But the face peering in through the glass was that of a white-haired elderly lady in a beret. He opened the door a little.

"Don't you know it's forbidden to leave your engine running for as long as you have?" she said. "I'm out walking my dog, but I've been checking my watch and know how long you've been standing here with the engine on."

Wallander made no reply, simply nodded and drove off. That night he lay in bed without being able to sleep. The last time he looked at the clock it was 5:00 A.M. The following day Håkan von Enke disappeared. And Wallander never reported the attack he had suffered. He told no one, not even Linda.

When von Enke failed to turn up after two days, Wallander's future son-in-law called and asked him to go to Stockholm. Since he was still out sick, he agreed. Wallander realized that it was in fact Louise who had asked for help. He made it clear that he didn't want to meddle in police business; his colleagues in Stockholm were dealing with the case. Police officers who interfered in other forces' work and poked their noses where they shouldn't were never popular.

The evening before Wallander left for Stockholm, one of those pleasant evenings in early spring when it was growing noticeably lighter, he paid a visit to Linda. As usual, Hans was not at home; he always worked late on what Wallander referred to wryly as "financial speculations." That had led to the first and so far only argument between him and his prospective son-in-law. Hans had protested that he and his colleagues were not involved in anything as simple as that. But when Wallander asked what they did do, he had the impression that the answer referred in fact to speculations in foreign exchange and shares, derivatives and hedge funds (things that Wallander freely admitted he didn't understand). Linda had intervened and explained that her father had no idea about mysterious and hence frightening modern financial goings-on. There had been a time when Wallander would have been upset by what she said, but now he noticed the warmth in her voice and simply flung his arms out wide as a sign that he submitted to her judgment.

But now he was sitting in the house shared by his daughter and her partner. The baby, who still hadn't been given a name, was lying on a mat by Linda's feet. Wallander observed her, and it occurred to him, perhaps for the first time, that his own daughter would never sit on his knee again. When one's own child has a child, some things are gone forever.

"What do you think happened to Håkan?" Wallander asked. "What's your view, both as a police officer and as Hans's partner?"

Linda replied immediately—she had clearly been prepared for the question.

"I'm sure something serious has happened. I'm even afraid he might be dead. Håkan isn't the type of person who just vanishes. He would never commit suicide without leaving a note. Mind you, he would never commit suicide, period; but that's another matter. If he had done something wrong, he would never slink off without taking his punishment. I simply don't believe that he disappeared of his own free will."

"Can you explain?"

"Do I need to? Surely you understand what I mean."

"Yes, but I want to hear it in your own words."

Wallander noted yet again that she had prepared herself meticulously. Linda was not merely somebody talking about a relative; she was also a shrewd young police officer setting out her view of the case.

"When you talk about something not happening of the victim's own free will, there are two possibilities. One is an accident—he fell through thin ice or was run over by a car, for instance. The other is that he was subjected to premeditated violence, abducted or killed. The accident explanation no longer seems feasible. There are no reports of him in the hospital. So that possibility can be ruled out. That leaves only the other possibility."

Wallander raised his hand and interrupted her.

"Let's make an assumption," he said. "You and I know this happens much more often than you might think. Especially where older men are concerned."

"You mean that he might have run off with some woman?"

"Something along those lines, yes."

She shook her head firmly.

"I've spoken to Hans about that. He says there are definitely no skeletons in the closet. Håkan has been faithful to Louise throughout their marriage."

Wallander interrupted again.

"What about Louise? Has she been faithful?"

That was a question Linda hadn't asked herself, he could see. She hadn't yet learned all the possible twists that can take place in an interrogation.

"I can't believe she hasn't. She's not the type."

"Not a good response. You should never say a person is 'not the type.' That exposes you to an underestimation."

"Let me put it this way: I don't think she's had any affairs. But obviously, I can't be certain. Ask her!"

"I have no intention of doing any such thing! It would be a disgraceful move in the current circumstances."

Wallander hesitated before asking the next question that came into his head.

"You and Hans must have discussed this over the last few days. He can't have been glued to his computer all the time. What does he have to say? Was he surprised when Håkan vanished?"

"Why wouldn't he have been surprised?"

"I don't know. But when I was in Stockholm, I had the impression that Håkan was worried about something."

"Why didn't you say so?"

"Because I tried to banish the thought. I told myself I was imagining things."

"Your intuition doesn't usually let you down."

"Thank you. But I'm becoming less and less sure about that—as I am about so many other things."

Linda didn't respond. Wallander studied her face. She'd put on a bit of weight after her pregnancy; her cheeks had become fuller. He could see from her eyes that she was tired. His thoughts turned to Mona, and how she was always angry because he never made any move to help her when Linda woke up crying during the night. I wonder how Linda is really feeling, he thought. When you have a child, it's as if every heart-string is stretched to the limit. One or two are likely to snap.

"Something tells me you're right," she said eventually. "Now that I think about it, I can remember situations, barely noticeable at the time, when he seemed worried. He kept looking over his shoulder."

"Literally or figuratively?"

"Literally. He kept turning around. I didn't think about it before."

"Can you remember anything else?"

"He was very careful about making sure the doors were locked. And he insisted that some lights be left on around the clock."

"Why?"

"I don't know. But the desk lamp in his study always had to be on, and the light in the hall next to the front door."

An old naval officer, Wallander thought, making sure navigational channels were properly illuminated during the night by specific lighthouses.

At that point the baby woke up, and Wallander held her until she stopped crying.

On the train to Stockholm, he continued to think about those lights that had to be kept on. It was something he needed to investigate. Perhaps there was an innocent explanation. The same thing might apply to the disappearance of Håkan von Enke. So far he had no idea how to find that out. But he hoped that no matter what, there would be a plausible and undramatic explanation.

6

At the end of the 1970s he and Mona had gone on a trip to Stockholm. Wallander seemed to recall that they stayed at the Maritime Hotel in the Söder district, so he called and reserved a room for two nights. When he got off the train he wondered whether he should go to the hotel by subway or take a taxi. He ended up walking, his heavy bag slung over his shoulder. It was still cold, but it was sunny, and no rain clouds were gathering on the horizon.

As he walked through the Old Town he thought about that trip with Mona. It was her idea. She had suddenly realized that she'd never set foot in the country's capital city and thought it was high time to remedy such a scandalous omission. They spent four days there. Mona had recently gone back to school and so had no income or paid vacation. They arranged for Linda to stay with a classmate for a few days—she was due to begin third grade in the fall. If his memory served him correctly, it was the beginning of August.

Warm days, and the occasional thunderstorm followed by oppressive heat that encouraged them to go for walks through the parks, where they could enjoy the shade of the many trees. That was more than thirty years ago, he thought as he approached Slussen and started walking up the hill to the hotel. Thirty years, a whole generation; and now I'm back. But this time on my own.

When he entered the lobby he didn't recognize it at all. Had it really been this hotel they'd stayed at? He shook off a sudden feeling of unease, dismissed all thought of the past, and took the elevator up to his room on the second floor. He turned down the bed-spread and lay down. It had been a tiring journey— he had been surrounded by screeching children, and to make things worse, a party of drunk young men had joined the train at Alvesta. He closed his eyes and tried to sleep. When he woke up with a start he checked the clock and found that he had dozed off for ten minutes at most. He stood up and walked over to the window. What had happened to Håkan von Enke? If he tried to fit together all the pieces of the jigsaw puzzle, what he had heard from Linda and what he knew from his own experience, what was the result? He didn't have even the beginnings of a solution.

He had arranged to arrive at Louise's place at seven o'clock that evening. Once again he decided to walk. As he passed the royal palace, he paused. He had been here with Mona, he was quite sure of that. They had stopped on the bridge where he was now and agreed that their feet hurt. The memory was so vivid that he could hear their conversation echoing in his ears. There were moments when he was overwhelmed by sadness thinking about how their marriage had collapsed. This was one of them. He looked down into the swirling water and thought about how his life was now centered increasingly on recalling things from the past that he now realized he missed.

Louise von Enke had made a pot of tea. She was visibly suffering from lack of sleep, but she was remarkably composed even so. The living room walls were adorned with paintings of the von Enke family and various battle scenes in muted colors. She saw him looking at the pictures.

"Håkan was the first naval officer in the family. His father, grandfather, and great-grandfather were all army officers. One of his uncles was chamberlain to King Oscar—I don't remember if it was Oscar the First or Second. The sword standing in the corner over there was awarded to another relative by Karl XIV for services rendered. Håkan always says that his job was to supply the king with suitable young ladies."

She fell silent. Wallander listened to the ticking of a clock on the mantelpiece above an open fire and the distant hum of traffic in the street outside.

"What do you think happened?"

"I don't know. I really don't."

"The day he disappeared, was there anything that felt unusual? Did he behave any differently from the way he usually did?"

"No. Everything was the same as it always was. Håkan has his routines, even if he's not a pedant."

"What about the previous days? The week before?"

"He had a cold. One day he skipped his morning walk. That was all."

"Did he have any mail? Did anyone call him? Did he have any visitors?"

"He spoke once or twice to Sten Nordlander, his closest friend."

"Was he at the party in Djursholm?"

"No, he was away then. Håkan and Sten met when they worked in the same submarine—Håkan was in command and Sten was chief engineer. That must have been the end of the sixties."

"What does he have to say about Håkan's disappearance?"

"Sten is just as worried as everyone else. He can't explain it either. He said he'd be pleased to talk to you while you're here."

She was sitting on a sofa opposite Wallander. The evening sun suddenly illuminated her face. She moved into the shade. Wallander thought she was one of those women who try to hide their beauty behind a mask of plainness. As if she had read his mind, she gave him a hesitant smile. Wallander took out his notebook and wrote down Sten Nordlander's telephone number. He noticed that she knew it by heart, and his cell number as well.

They spoke for an hour without Wallander feeling that he'd learned anything he didn't know already. Then she showed him her husband's study. Wallander examined the desk lamp.

"So this is the lamp he used to have on all night."

"Who told you that?"

"Linda mentioned it. This lamp and others."

She closed the thick curtains as she responded. Wallander could detect a faint smell of tobacco.

"He was afraid of the dark," she said, brushing some dust off one of the heavy, dark-colored curtains. "He thought it was embarrassing. It probably started while he was in his submarines, but it was much later that he became really afraid, long after he'd stopped going to sea. I had to promise never to mention it to a soul."

"But your son knows about it? And he in turn told Linda . . ."

"Håkan must have mentioned it to Hans without my knowing."

The phone rang in the distance.

"Make yourself at home," she said as she disappeared through the tall double doors.

Wallander found himself eyeing her in the same way he observed Kristina Magnusson. He sat down on the desk chair made of rust brown wood with a green leather back and seat. He looked slowly around the room. He switched on the desk lamp. There was dust around the switch. Wallander ran his finger over the polished mahogany desktop, then lifted up the blotter. That was a habit he had acquired from his early days as an apprentice of Rydberg's. Whenever they came to a crime scene containing a desk, that was always the first thing Rydberg did. As a rule there was nothing underneath it. But he had explained, in a way that indicated a mysterious subtext, that even blank space could be an important clue.

There were a few pens and pencils on the desk, a magnifying glass, a porcelain vase in the shape of a swan, a small stone, and a box full of thumbtacks. That was all. He swiveled slowly around on the chair and scanned the room. The walls were covered in framed photographs—of submarines and other naval vessels; of Hans wearing the white cap all Swedes get when they pass their graduation exams; of Håkan in his dress uniform, he and Louise walking through a ceremonial arch of swords raised by the honor guard at their wedding; of old people, nearly all the men in uniform. There was also a painting on one of the walls. Wallander went to study it more closely. It was a Romanic depiction of the Battle of Trafalgar, Nelson dying, leaning against a cannon, surrounded by sailors on their knees, all of them crying. The painting surprised him. It was a piece of kitsch in an apartment characterized by good taste. Why had Håkan displayed it? Wallander carefully removed the picture and examined the back. There was nothing written on it. It's too late to start making a thorough search of the whole room, he thought. It's nearly eight-thirty, and it would take several hours. It would make more sense to start tomorrow morning. He went back to one of the two connected living rooms. Louise emerged from the kitchen. Wallander thought he could detect a faint whiff of alcohol, but he wasn't sure. They agreed that he would come back the following day at nine o'clock. Wallander put on his jacket in the hall and prepared to leave, but suddenly he had second thoughts.

"You look tired," he said. "Are you getting enough sleep?"

"I manage the odd hour here and there. How can I sleep soundly when I don't know anything?"

"Would you like me to stay overnight?"

"It's kind of you to offer, but it's not necessary. I'm used to being on my own. Don't forget, I'm a sailor's wife."

He walked back to his hotel, stopping for dinner at an Italian restaurant that looked cheap. The food confirmed that assumption. In the hope of avoiding a sleepless night, he took half of one of his sleeping pills. Sadly, this seemed to be one of the few pleasures left to him: beckoning the onset of sleep by unscrewing the lid of the white bottle.

The next day began like his visit the previous evening: with Louise offering him a cup of tea. He could see that she had hardly slept a wink.

She had a message to pass on, from Chief Inspector Ytterberg, who was in charge of the investigation into von Enke's disappearance. Could Wallander please give him a call. She handed him a cordless phone, then stood up and went into the kitchen. Wallander could see her reflection in a wall mirror; she was standing in the middle of the floor, motionless, with her back to him.

Ytterberg spoke with an unmistakable northern accent.

"It's a full-scale investigation now," he began. "We're pretty sure something must have happened to him. I gathered from his wife you were going to work through his papers."

"Haven't you done that already?"

"His wife has been through them without finding anything. I assume she wants you to double-check."

"Do you have any leads at all? Has anyone seen him?"

"Only one unreliable witness who claims to have seen him in Lill-Jansskogen. That's all."

There was a pause, and Wallander heard Ytterberg telling someone to go away and come back later.

"I'll never get used to this," said Ytterberg when he resumed the conversation. "People seem to have stopped knocking on doors and just barge in."

"One of these days the national police commissioner will tell us all to sit in open-plan offices in order to increase our efficiency," said Wallander. "We'll be able to hear one another's witnesses and help out in other people's investigations."

Ytterberg chuckled. Wallander decided that he had found an excellent contact in the Stockholm police force.

"One more thing," said Ytterberg. "In his active days, Håkan von Enke was a high-ranking naval officer. So it's routine that the Säpo crowd will shove an oar in. Our security service colleagues are always on the lookout for a possible spy."

Wallander was surprised.

"Are you saying he's under suspicion?"

"Of course not. But they have to have something to show when next year's budget comes under discussion."

Wallander moved farther away from the kitchen.

"Just between you and me," he said in a low voice, "what do you think happened? Forget all the facts—what does your experience tell you?"

"It looks pretty serious. He might have been ambushed in the woods and abducted. That's what I think is most likely at the moment."

Ytterberg asked for Wallander's cell phone number before hanging up. Wallander returned to his cup of tea, thinking he would have much preferred coffee. Louise returned from the kitchen and looked inquiringly at him. Wallander shook his head.

"Nothing new. But they are taking his disappearance extremely seriously."

She remained standing by the sofa.

"I know he's dead," she said out of the blue. "I've refused to think the worst so far, but now I can't put it off any longer."

"There must be some basis for that conviction," said Wallander cautiously. "Is there anything in particular that makes you think that way right now?"

"I've lived with him for forty years," she said. "He would never do this to me. Not to me and not to the rest of the family either."

She hurried out of the room. Wallander heard the bedroom door close. He waited for a moment, then stood up and tiptoed into the hall and listened outside. He could hear her crying. Although he wasn't an emotional type, he could feel a lump in his throat. He drank the rest of his tea, then went to von Enke's study, where he had been the previous evening. The curtains were still drawn. He opened them and let in the light. Then he started searching through the desk, one drawer at a time. It was all very neat, with a place for everything. One of the drawers contained several old pipes, pipe cleaners, and something that looked like a duster. He turned his attention to the other pedestal. Everything was just as neatly filed—old school reports, certificates, a pilot's license. In March 1958 Håkan von Enke had passed a test enabling him to pilot a single-engine plane, conducted at Bromma Airport. So he didn't spend all his life down in the depths, Wallander thought. He imitated not only the fish, but the birds as well.

Wallander took out von Enke's reports from the Norra Latin grammar school. He had top grades in history and Swedish, and also in geography. But he only just scraped by in German and religious studies. The next drawer contained a camera and a pair of earphones. When Wallander examined the camera, an old Leica, more closely, he noticed that it still had film. Either twelve pictures had been taken, or there were twelve exposures still available. He put the camera on the desktop. The earphones were also old. He guessed that they might have been state-of-the-art some fifty years ago. Why had von Enke kept them? There was nothing in the bottom drawer apart from a comic book with colored pictures and speech bubbles retelling the story of **The Last of the Mohicans**. The comic had been read so often that it almost disintegrated in Wallander's hands. He recalled what Rydberg had once said to him: **Always look for something that doesn't fit in with the rest.** What was a copy of Classics Illustrated from 1962 doing in the bottom drawer of Håkan von Enke's desk?

He didn't hear Louise approaching. Suddenly she was there, in the doorway. She had removed all trace of her emotional breakdown, and her face was newly powdered. He held up the comic.

"Why did he keep this?"

"I think he got it from his father on a special occasion. He never told me any details."

She left him to his own devices again. Wallander opened the remaining large drawer, at waist height between the two pedestals. Here the contents were anything but neatly ordered—letters, photographs, old airline tickets, a doctor's certificate, a few bills. Why was everything jumbled up here, but not anywhere else? He decided to leave the contents of this drawer untouched for the time being, and left it open. The only thing he removed was the doctor's certificate.

The man he was trying to track down had been vaccinated many times. As recently as three weeks ago he had been vaccinated against yellow fever, and also tetanus and jaundice. Stapled to the certificate was a prescription for antimalarial drugs. Wallander frowned. Yellow fever? Where might you be traveling to if you needed to be vaccinated against that? He returned the document to the drawer without having answered the question.

Wallander stood up and turned his attention to the bookcases. If the books told the truth, Håkan von Enke was very interested in English history and twentieth-century naval developments. There were also books on general history and a lot of political memoirs. Wallander noted that Tage Erlander's memoirs were standing next to Stig Wennerström's autobiography. To his surprise Wallander also discovered that von Enke had been interested in modern Swedish poetry. There were names Wallander didn't recognize, others of poets he knew a little about—such as Sonnevi and Tranströmer. He took out some of the books and noted that they showed signs of having been read. In one of Tranströmer's books somebody had made notes in the margin, and at one point had written: "Brilliant poem." Wallander read it, and he agreed. It was about the sighing of coniferous forests. There were what appeared to be the complete works of Ivar Lo-Johansson, and also of Vilhelm Moberg. Wallander's image of the missing man was changing all the time, deepening. Nothing gave him the impression that the commander was vain and merely wanted to demonstrate to the world that he was interested in the arts. Wallander hated those types.

Wallander left the bookcases and turned his attention to the tall filing cabinet, opening drawer after drawer. Files, letters, reports, several private diaries, drawings of submarines labeled "Types commanded by me." Everything was neat and tidy, apart from that desk drawer. Nevertheless, something was nagging at Wallander without his being able to put his finger on it. He sat down at the desk again, and contemplated the open filing cabinet. There was a brown leather armchair in one corner of the room, a table, and a reading lamp with a red shade. Wallander moved from the desk chair to the reading chair. There were two books on the table, both of them open. One was old, Rachel Carson's **Silent Spring.** He knew it was one of the first books warning that the advance of Western civilization constituted a threat to the future of the planet. The other book was about Swedish butterflies—short blocks of text interspersed with color photographs. Butterflies and a planet under threat, Wallander thought. And a chaotic desk drawer. He couldn't see how the various parts fit together.

Then he noticed a corner of a magazine sticking out from under the armchair. He bent down and picked up an English, or possibly American, journal on naval vessels. Wallander thumbed through it. There was everything from articles on the aircraft carrier **Ronald Reagan** to sketches of submarines still at the drawing-board stage. Wallander put the magazine down and looked again at the filing cabinet. **Seeing without seeing.** That was something Rydberg had warned him about: not noticing what you were really looking for. He went through the filing cabinet once again and found a duster in one of the drawers. So he keeps everything in here spotless, Wallander thought. Not a speck of dust on any of his papers, everything ship-shape. He sat down on the desk chair and looked again at the open drawer that was such a mess, unlike everything else. He started to work his way carefully through the contents, but he found nothing to raise an eyebrow. All that worried him was the mess. It stuck out like a sore thumb; it didn't seem to be how Håkan von Enke would have arranged things. Or did chaos come naturally to him, and it was the orderliness that broke the pattern?

He stood up and ran his hand over the top of the unusually tall filing cabinet; there was a folder lying out of sight, and he took it down. It contained a report about the political situation in Cambodia, written by Robert Jackson and Evelyn Harrison, whoever they might be. Wallander was surprised to discover that it came from the U.S. Department of Defense. It was dated March 2008, only just out. Whoever had read it had evidently felt strongly about it, underlining several sentences and making margin notes with big, forceful exclamation marks. It was titled **On the Challenges of Cambodia, Based on the Legacies of the Pol Pot Regime.**

He went back into the living room. The teacups had been cleared away. Louise was standing at one of the windows, gazing down into the street. When he cleared his throat, she turned so quickly that she gave the impression of being frightened, and Wallander was reminded of the way her husband had behaved at the party in Djursholm—the same kind of reaction, he thought. They are both worried, scared, and seem to be under some kind of threat.

He hadn't intended to ask the question, but it simply came out of its own accord when he remembered Djursholm.

"Did he have a gun?"

"No. Not anymore. Håkan probably had one when he was still on duty. But here at home? No, he's never had one here."

"Do you have a summer cottage?"

"We've talked about buying a place, but we never got around to it. When Hans was little we used to spend every summer on the island of Utö. In recent years we've gone to the Riviera and rented an apartment."

"Is there anywhere else he might keep a gun?"

"No. Why are you asking?"

"Perhaps he has some kind of store somewhere. Do you have an attic? Or a basement?"

"We keep some old furniture and souvenirs from his childhood in a room in the basement. But I can't believe there could be a gun there."

She left the room and came back with a key to a padlock. Wallander put it in his pocket. Louise asked him if he'd like more tea, but Wallander said no. He couldn't bring himself to say that he would love a cup of coffee.

He went back to the study and continued leafing through the report on Cambodia. **Why had it been lying on top of the filing cabinet?** There was a footstool beside the easy chair. Wallander placed it in front of the filing cabinet and stood on tiptoe so that he could see the top of the cabinet. It was covered in dust, except for where the folder had been lying. Wallander replaced the stool and remained standing. It suddenly dawned on him what had attracted his attention.

There seemed to be papers missing, especially in the
filing cabinet. To make sure, Wallander worked his
way through everything one more time, both the
things in the desk drawers and those in the filing cabinet. Everywhere, he found traces of documents having
been removed. Could Håkan have done it himself?
That was a possibility; or it could have been Louise.

Wallander went back to the living room. Louise was
sitting on a chair that Wallander suspected was very
old. She was staring at her hands. She stood up when
he came into the room and asked again if he would like
a cup of tea. He accepted this time. He waited until
she had poured his tea, and noticed that she didn't take
a cup herself.

"I can't find anything," Wallander said. "Could
someone have been through his papers?"

She looked quizzically at him. Her tiredness made
her face look gray, almost twisted.

"I've been searching through them, of course. But
who else could have?"

"I don't know, but it looks as if some papers are
missing, as if disorder has been introduced into all
those neat and tidy files. I could be wrong."

"No one has been in his study since the day he disappeared. Except for me, naturally."

"I know we've talked about this already, but let me
ask you again. Was he neat by nature?"

"He hated untidiness."

"But he wasn't a pedant, I seem to remember you
saying."

"When we have visitors for dinner, he always helps

me set the table. He checks to make sure the cutlery and glasses are where they should be. But he doesn't use a ruler to get the lines exactly right. Does that answer your question?"

"It certainly does," said Wallander gracefully.

Wallander drank his tea, then went down to the basement to take a look at the family's storeroom. It contained a few old suitcases, a rocking horse, plastic boxes full of toys used by earlier generations, not just Hans. Leaning against the wall were some skis and a dismantled device for developing photographic negatives.

Wallander sat down cautiously on the rocking horse. The thought struck him as suddenly and relentlessly as the thugs had attacked him only a few days ago: Håkan von Enke was dead. There was no other possible explanation. He was dead.

That realization not only made him feel sad, it also troubled him.

Håkan von Enke was trying to tell me something, he thought. But unfortunately, in that bunker in Djursholm, I didn't understand what.

7

Wallander was woken up as dawn was breaking by a young couple arguing in the room next door. The walls were so thin that he could hear clearly the harsh words they were exchanging. He got out of bed and rummaged through his toiletry bag for a pair of earplugs, but he had evidently left them at home. He banged on the wall, two heavy blows followed by one more, as if he were sending one final swearword via his fist. The argument ceased abruptly—or maybe they continued arguing in voices so low that he couldn't hear what they were saying. Before going back to sleep he tried to recall if he and Mona had also had an argument in the hotel when they visited the capital. It happened occasionally that they dredged up pointless trivialities— always trivialities, never anything really serious—that made them angry. Our confrontations were never colorful, he thought, always gray. We were miserable or disappointed, or both at the same time, and we knew it would soon pass. But we would argue nonetheless, and we were both equally stupid and said things we immediately regretted. We used to send whole flocks of birds shooting out of our mouths and never managed to grab them by their wings.

He fell asleep and dreamed about somebody— Rydberg, perhaps, or possibly his father?—standing in the rain, waiting for him. But he had been delayed, perhaps by his car breaking down, and he knew he would be told off for arriving late.

After breakfast he sat in the lobby and dialed Sten Nordlander. Wallander began with his home number. No reply. No reply on the cell either, although he was able to leave a message. He said his name and his business. But what was his business, in fact? Searching for the missing Håkan von Enke was a job for the Stockholm police, not for him. Perhaps he could be regarded as a sort of improvising private detective—a title that had acquired a bad reputation after the murder of Olof Palme.

His train of thought was interrupted by his cell phone ringing. It was Sten Nordlander. His voice was rough and deep.

"I know who you are," he said. "Both Håkan and Louise have talked about you. Where can I pick you up?"

Wallander was waiting on the sidewalk when Sten Nordlander pulled up. His car was a Dodge from the mid-fifties, covered in shiny chrome and with whitewall tires. No doubt Nordlander had been a sort of Teddy Boy in his youth. Even now he was wearing a leather jacket, American-style boots, jeans, and a thin undershirt despite the cold weather. Wallander couldn't help wondering how on earth von Enke and Nordlander had become such good friends. At first glance he found it impossible to think of two people who seemed more different. But judging by outward appearances was always dangerous. That reminded him of one of Rydberg's favorite sayings: **Outward appearances are something you should nearly always ignore.**

"Jump in," said Sten Nordlander.

Wallander didn't ask where they were going; he merely sank back into the red leather seat that was no doubt authentic. He asked a few polite questions about the car, and received similarly polite answers. Then they sat in silence. Two large dice in woolly material were swinging back and forth in the rear window. Wallander had seen lots of similar cars in his early youth. Behind the wheel were always middle-aged men wearing suits that glistened just as much as the chrome fittings on the cars. They came to buy up his father's paintings by the dozen, and paid in notes peeled off thick bundles. He used to call them "the Silk Knights." He discovered later they had humiliated his father by paying far too little for his paintings.

The memory made him feel sad. But it was in the past, impossible to resurrect.

There were no seat belts in the car. Nordlander saw that Wallander was looking for one.

"This is a classic car," he said. "It's excused from the obligatory seat belts."

They eventually came to somewhere or other on Värmdö—Wallander had lost his sense of distance and direction long ago. Nordlander pulled up outside a brown-painted building containing a café.

"The woman who owns the café used to be married to one of Håkan's and my mutual friends," said Nordlander. "She's a widow now. Her name's Matilda. Her husband, Claes Hornvig, was first officer on a Snake that both Håkan and I worked on."

Wallander nodded. He recalled that Håkan von Enke had referred to that class of submarine.

"We try to give her business whenever we can. She needs the money. And besides, she serves pretty good coffee."

The first thing Wallander noticed when he entered the café was a periscope standing in the middle of the floor. Nordlander explained which decommissioned submarine it had come from, and it dawned on Wallander that he was in a private museum for submarines.

"It's become a habit," explained Nordlander. "Anyone who ever served on a Swedish submarine makes at least one pilgrimage to Matilda's café. And they always bring something with them—it's unthinkable not to. Some stolen china, perhaps, or a blanket, or even items from the controls. Bonanza time of course was when submarines were being decommissioned and sent to the scrap yard. Lots of ex-servicemen turned up to collect souvenirs, and there was always somebody determined to find something to grace Matilda's collection. The money didn't matter; it was a question of salvaging something from the dead submarine."

A woman in her twenties emerged from the swinging doors leading into the kitchen.

"Matilda and Claes's granddaughter Marie," said Nordlander. "Matilda still puts in an appearance now and again, but she's over ninety now. She claims that her mother lived to be a hundred and one and her grandmother a hundred and three."

"That's right," said the girl. "My mom's fifty. She says she's only lived half her life."

They were served a tray of coffee and pastries. Nordlander also helped himself to a slice of cheesecake. There were a few other customers at other tables, most of them elderly.

"Former submarine crew?" Wallander wondered as they made their way to the room farthest away from the street, which was empty.

"Not necessarily," said Nordlander. "But I do recognize some of them."

This room in the heart of the café had old uniforms and signal flags hanging from the walls. Wallander had the feeling that he was in a props store for military films. They sat down at a table in the corner. On the wall beside them was a framed black-and-white photograph. Sten Nordlander pointed it out.

"There you have one of our Sea Snakes. Number two in the second row is me. Number four is Håkan. Claes Hornvig wasn't with us on that occasion."

Wallander leaned forward in order to get a better view. It wasn't easy to distinguish the various faces. Nordlander informed him that the picture had been taken in Karlskrona, just before they had set off on a long trip.

"I suppose it wasn't exactly our ideal voyage," he said. "We were due to go from Karlskrona up to the Kvarken straits, then on to Kalix and back home again. It was November, freezing cold. If I remember correctly there was a storm blowing the whole time. The ship was tossing and turning something awful—the Baltic Sea is so shallow, we could never get down deep enough. The Baltic Sea is nothing more than a pool."

Nordlander attacked the pastries with eager intent. It didn't seem to matter what they tasted like. But suddenly he laid down his fork.

"What happened?" he said.

"I know no more than you or Louise."

Nordlander pushed his coffee cup violently to one side. Wallander could see that he was just as tired as

Louise. Someone else who can't get to sleep, he thought.

"You know him," Wallander said, "better than most. Louise said you and Håkan were very close. If that's the case, then your view of events is more important than most others."

"You sound just like the police officer I spoke to in Bergsgatan."

"But I **am** a police officer!"

Sten Nordlander nodded. He was very tense. You could tell how worried he was from his fixed expression and his tight lips.

"How come you weren't at his seventy-fifth birthday party?" Wallander asked.

"I have a sister who lives in Bergen, in Norway. Her husband died unexpectedly. She needed my help. Besides, I'm not exactly a fan of big dos like that. Håkan and I had our own celebration. A week earlier."

"Where?"

"Here. With coffee and cookies."

Nordlander pointed to a naval cap hanging on the wall.

"That's Håkan's. He made a present of it when we had our little celebration."

"What did you talk about?"

"What we always talk about. What happened in October 1982. I was serving on the destroyer **Halland**. It was about to be decommissioned. It's now a museum piece in Gothenburg."

"So you weren't only a chief engineer on submarines?"

"I started out on a torpedo boat, then it was a corvette, then a destroyer, then a submarine, and in the end back to a destroyer. We were deployed to the west coast when the submarines started appearing in the Baltic Sea. At about noon on October 2, Commander Nyman announced that we should head for the Stockholm archipelago at full speed because we were needed as backup."

"Were you in contact with Håkan during those hectic days?"

"He called me."

"At home or on board?"

"On the destroyer. I was never at home then. All leave was canceled. We were on red alert, you could say. Bear in mind that this was the blissful time before cell phones had become common currency. The sailors manning the destroyer's telephone exchange would come down and inform us that we had a call. Håkan usually called at night. He wanted me to receive his call in my cabin."

"Why?"

"I suppose he didn't want anybody else to hear what we were talking about."

There was something surly and reluctant in the way Sten Nordlander answered questions. He sat there mashing the remains of the pastry with his fork.

"We spoke to each other practically every night between the first and the fifteenth of October. I don't think he was supposed to talk to me the way he did, but we trusted each other. His responsibility weighed heavily on his shoulders. A depth charge can go off course and sink a submarine instead of forcing it up to the surface."

By now Nordlander had turned the remains of his pastry into an unappetizing mess. He put down his fork and dropped a paper napkin over his plate.

"He called me three times that last night. Very late—or rather, early: it was dawn when he called the last time."

"And you were still on board the destroyer?"

"We were less than a nautical mile southeast of Hårsfjärden. It was windy, but not too bad. We were on full alert. The officers were informed about what was happening, of course, but the rest of the crew knew only that we were ready for action, not why."

"Were you really going to be ordered to start hunting down the submarine?"

"We couldn't know what the Russians would do if we forced one of their submarines to surface. Perhaps they might try to rescue it? There were Russian vessels north of Gotland, and they were moving slowly in our direction. One of our radio officers said he'd never experienced so much Russian radio traffic before, not even during their major maneuvers along the Baltic coast. They were agitated, that was obvious."

He paused when Marie came in and asked if they wanted any more coffee. Both said no.

"Let's consider the most important thing," said Wallander. "How did you react to the order to let the trapped submarine go?"

"I couldn't believe my ears."

"How did you hear about it?"

"Nyman suddenly received an order to back off, proceed to Landsort, and wait there. No explanation was given, and Nyman wasn't the type to ask unnecessary questions. I was in the engine room when I was told there was a phone call for me. I ran up to my cabin. It was Håkan. He asked if I was alone."

"Did he usually do that?"

"Not usually, no. I said I was. He insisted it was important that I speak the truth. I remember feeling angry about that. Then I realized he had left the operations room and was calling from a phone booth."

"How could you know that? Did he say so?"

"I heard him inserting coins. There was a phone booth in the officer's mess. Since he couldn't be away from the command center for more than a couple of minutes, only as long as it would take to go to the bathroom, he must have run there."

"Did he say so?"

Nordlander looked searchingly at him.

"Is it you or me who's the policeman here? I could hear that he was out of breath!"

Wallander didn't allow himself to be provoked. He merely nodded, indicating that Nordlander should continue.

"He was agitated, both furious and scared, I think you could say. He insisted that it was treason, and that he was going to disobey orders and bomb that damned submarine up to the surface no matter what they said. Then his money ran out. It was as if somebody had cut through a tape."

Wallander stared at him, waiting for a continuation that never came.

"That's a strong word to use. Treason?"

"But that's exactly what it was! They released a submarine that had invaded our territorial waters."

"Who was responsible?"

"Somebody in the high command, possibly more than one person, who got extremely cold feet. They didn't want to force a Russian submarine up to the surface."

A man carrying a cup of coffee came into the room, but Nordlander glared so aggressively at him that he turned immediately and went to look for a table in another room.

"I don't know who was responsible. It might be easier to answer the question Why? but even so it would only be speculation. What you don't know, you don't know."

"Sometimes it's necessary to think aloud. Even for police officers."

"Let's suppose there was something on board that submarine that the Swedish authorities couldn't be allowed to get their hands on."

"What might that be?"

Sten Nordlander lowered his voice—not much, but sufficiently for Wallander to notice.

"Maybe you could extend that assumption and suggest that it wasn't 'something' but 'someone.' How would it have looked if it turned out there was a Swedish officer on board? For example."

"What makes you think that?"

"It wasn't my idea. It was one of Håkan's theories. He had lots of them."

Wallander thought for a moment before continuing. He realized that he should have noted down everything Nordlander said.

"What happened after that?"

"After what?"

Nordlander was starting to get cross. But whether it was because of all the questions or due to worry in connection with his friend's disappearance, Wallander couldn't decide.

"Håkan told me that he started to ask questions," Wallander said.

"He tried to find out what had happened. But nearly everything was top secret, of course. Some documents were even classified as ultra-secret so that they would remain under lock and key for seventy years. That's the longest time anything can be kept secret in Sweden. The normal limit is forty years. But in this case some of the papers were embargoed for seventy years. In all probability not even that nice little Marie who served us coffee and pastries will live long enough to be able to read them."

"But then again, she belongs to a family with good genes," said Wallander.

Sten Nordlander didn't react.

"Håkan could be difficult if he'd set his mind on something," Nordlander continued. "He felt just as violated as the Swedish territorial waters had been. Someone had failed in their duty, and failed in spades.

A lot of journalists started digging into the submarines incident, but that wasn't good enough for Håkan. He really wanted to know the truth. He staked his career on it."

"Who did he speak to?"

Nordlander's reply came quickly, like a crack of the whip in order to buck up an invisible horse.

"Everybody. He asked everybody you can think of. Perhaps not the king, but you never know. He asked for an interview with the prime minister, that's definite. He called Thage G. Peterson, that fine old Social Democrat in the cabinet office, and asked for a meeting with Palme. Peterson said the PM's diary was full, but Håkan wouldn't be put off. 'Get out the reserve diary then,' he insisted. 'The one in which urgent meetings can always be fitted in.' And he actually did get an interview. A few days before Christmas 1983."

"Did he tell you about it?"

"I was with him."

"When he met Palme?"

"I was his chauffeur that day, you could say. I sat in the car outside, waiting for him, after watching him, in his dress uniform and a dark overcoat, vanish through the entrance door to the most exalted dwelling in the land after the royal palace. The visit lasted about half an hour. After ten minutes a traffic cop knocked on the window and said that drop-offs were allowed but parking was forbidden. I rolled down the window and informed him that I was waiting for somebody currently discussing very important business with the prime minister and had no intention of moving. After that I was left in peace. When Håkan eventually came back, there were beads of sweat on his forehead."

They had driven off in silence.

"We came here," said Sten Nordlander. "And we sat at this very table. As we got out of the car it started snowing. We had a white Christmas in Stockholm that year. It stayed white until New Year's Eve. Then it rained."

Marie returned with her coffeepot. This time they both had their cups refilled. When Sten Nordlander complied with Swedish tradition and popped a cube of sugar into his mouth before taking a sip of coffee, Wallander noticed that he had false teeth. The discovery made him feel sick for a few moments. Perhaps because it reminded him that he should visit the dentist far more often than he did.

According to Sten Nordlander, von Enke gave a detailed account of his meeting with Olof Palme. He had been well received. Palme asked a few questions about his military career, and spoke ironically about his own status as a reserve officer. Palme listened attentively to what von Enke had to say. And what he had to say was unambiguous. When it came to his relationship with his employer, the Swedish defense forces, von Enke had violated every convention there was. By approaching the prime minister on his own initiative he had burned all bridges with the supreme commander and his staff. There was no going back now. He felt obliged to say exactly what he thought about the whole business. He spoke for over ten minutes before coming to the main point. And Palme listened, he said. With his mouth half open, and looking him in the eye from start to finish. Afterward, when von Enke had reached the end of his diatribe, Palme thought for a while before asking questions. He wanted to know first of all if the military had been certain about the nationality of the submarine, and if it definitely was from one of the Warsaw Pact countries. Håkan responded by asking a different question, Nordlander said. He wondered where else it could have come from. Palme didn't reply, merely pulled a face and shook his head. When Håkan started to speak about treason and a military and political scandal, Palme interrupted and said this was a discussion that should take place in a different context, not during a private interview with the prime minister. That was as far as they got. A secretary peered discreetly around the door and reminded Palme of another meeting that was scheduled to begin. When Håkan came out he was sweating, but also relieved. Palme had listened to him, he said. He was full of optimism and convinced that things would now start moving. The prime minister doubtless understood what Håkan had said about treason. He would corner his minister of defense and his supreme commander and demand an explanation. Who had opened the cage and let the submarine escape? And above all, why?

Sten Nordlander glanced at his watch.

"What happened next?" Wallander asked after a short pause.

"It was Christmas. Everything stood still for a few days, but just before the New Year, Håkan was summoned to the supreme commander. He was given a stern reprimand for going behind his superior's back and meeting Olof Palme. But Håkan was bright enough to realize that the main criticism was aimed at the prime minister, who should never have agreed to meet a naval officer who had gone astray."

"But Håkan must have continued to ferret away? Surely he didn't give up, despite having been reprimanded."

"He's continued ferreting away ever since. For twenty-five years."

"You are his closest friend. He must have spoken to you about the threats he received."

Nordlander nodded, but said nothing.

"And now he's disappeared."

"He's dead. Somebody killed him."

The response came promptly and firmly. Nordlander talked about Håkan's death as if it were obvious.

"How can you be so sure?"

"What is there to be doubtful about?"

"Who killed him? And why?"

"I don't know. But perhaps he knew something that eventually became too dangerous."

"It's been twenty-five years since those submarines entered Swedish waters. What could be dangerous after all these years? Good lord, the Soviet Union no longer exists. The Berlin Wall has come down. And East Germany? All that belongs to a bygone era. What specters could suddenly emerge now?"

"We think it's all over and done with, that the final curtain has fallen. But it could be that somebody merely stepped into the wings and changed costume.

The repertoire may be different, but everything is being acted out on the same stage."

Sten Nordlander stood up.

"We can continue another day. My wife is expecting me now."

He drove Wallander back to his hotel. Just before they parted, Wallander realized he had another question to ask.

"Was anyone else really close to Håkan?"

"No one was close to Håkan. Except Louise, perhaps. Old sea dogs are usually reserved. They like to keep to themselves. I wasn't really close to him myself. I suppose you could say we were **close-ish,** if that's possible."

Wallander could tell that Nordlander was hesitant about something. Was he going to say it, or wasn't he?

"Steven Atkins," said Nordlander. "An American submarine captain. A year or so younger. I think he'll be seventy-five next year."

Wallander took out his notebook and wrote down the name.

"Do you have an address?"

"He lives in California, not far from San Diego. He used to be stationed at Groton, the big naval base."

Wallander wondered why Louise hadn't mentioned Steven Atkins. But that wasn't something Wallander wanted to trouble Nordlander about—he seemed to be in a hurry and was revving the engine impatiently.

Wallander watched the gleaming car drive off up the hill.

Then he went to his room and thought about what

he had heard. But there was still no sign of Håkan von Enke, and Wallander felt that he wasn't a single step closer to solving the problem.

8

The following morning Linda called to ask how Stockholm was. He didn't beat around the bush but told her Louise seemed to be convinced that Håkan was no longer alive.

"Hans refuses to believe that," she said. "He's certain that his father isn't dead."

"But deep down he probably suspects it's as bad as Louise says."

"What do you think?"

"It doesn't look good."

Wallander asked if she had spoken to anyone in Ystad. He knew she was sometimes in touch with Kristina Magnusson privately.

"The internal affairs team has returned to Malmö," she said. "That probably means they'll be reaching a decision on your case any time now."

"I might get the boot," Wallander said.

She sounded almost indignant when she responded.

"It was incredibly silly of you to take the pistol to the restaurant with you, but if that leads to you getting fired we can assume that several hundred other

Swedish police officers will get their marching orders as well. For much worse breaches of discipline."

"I'm assuming the worst," said Wallander gloomily.

"When you've shrugged off that self-pity we can talk again," she said and hung up.

Wallander thought she was right, of course. He would probably get a warning, possibly a fine. He picked up the phone again to call her back but thought better of it. There was too big a risk that they might start arguing. He got dressed, had breakfast, and then called Ytterberg, who had promised to see him at nine o'clock. Wallander asked if they had any leads, but they didn't.

"We got a tip that von Enke had been seen in Södertälje," said Ytterberg. "God only knows why he should want to go there. But there was nothing in it. It was just a man in a uniform. And our friend wasn't wearing a uniform when he set off on his long walk."

"All the same, it's odd that nobody seems to have seen him," said Wallander. "As I understand it, lots of people go jogging or walk their dogs in Lill-Jansskogen."

"I agree," said Ytterberg. "That's something that worries us as well. But nobody seems to have seen him at all. Come at nine o'clock and we can have a chat. I'll be waiting for you in reception."

Ytterberg was tall and powerfully built, and reminded Wallander of a well-known Swedish wrestler. He glanced at Ytterberg's ears to see if there was any of the cauliflower-like disfigurement so common among wrestlers, but he could see no sign of an earlier wrestling career. Despite his bulk, Ytterberg was light on his feet. They hardly touched the ground as he hurried along the hallways with Wallander in tow. They eventually came to a messy office with a gigantic inflatable dolphin lying in the middle of the floor.

"It's for one of my grandchildren," Ytterberg explained. "Anna Laura Constance is going to get it for her ninth birthday on Friday. Do you have any grandchildren?"

"I've just gotten my first. A granddaughter."

"Named?"

"Nothing yet. They're waiting for a name to emerge of its own accord."

Ytterberg muttered something inaudible and flopped down on his chair. He pointed to a coffeemaker on the windowsill, but Wallander shook his head.

"We are assuming that he's been the victim of a violent crime," said Ytterberg. "He's been missing for too long. The whole business is very odd. Not a single clue. There were lots of people in the woods, but nobody saw anything. It's the nearest you can get to going up in smoke. It doesn't make sense."

"So he deviated from his routine and didn't go there at all, is that it?"

"Or maybe something happened to him before he got as far as the woods. Whatever the facts are, it's very odd that nobody saw anything. You can't just kill a man in Valhallavägen without anyone noticing. Nor can you just drag somebody into a car without a fuss."

"Could he have disappeared willingly, then, despite everything?"

"That seems to be the obvious conclusion to draw. But then again, nothing else suggests that."

Wallander nodded.

"You said Säpo had shown an interest in his disappearance. Have they been able to make a contribution?"

Ytterberg screwed up his eyes, looked at Wallander, and leaned back in his chair.

"Since when has Säpo made a sensible contribution to anything at all in this country? They say it's just routine to take an interest when a high-ranking military officer disappears, even if he did retire ages ago."

Ytterberg poured himself a cup of coffee. Wallander shook his head again.

"Von Enke seemed to be worried at his seventy-fifth birthday party," he said.

Wallander had decided that Ytterberg was reliable, so he told him in detail about the episode in the conservatory when von Enke had seemed frightened.

"I also had the impression," Wallander went on, "that there was something he wanted to tell me. But nothing he said explained his agitation, or seemed a significant confidence."

"But he was afraid?"

"I think so. I remember thinking that a submarine commander is hardly the type to worry about imagined dangers. Spending so much time under the sea should have made him immune to that."

"I know what you mean," said Ytterberg thoughtfully.

An excited female voice suddenly started screeching in the hallway. Wallander gathered that she was objecting vehemently to being "interrogated by a damn buffoon." Then everything was quiet again.

"One thing gave me food for thought," said Wallander. "I searched his study in the apartment in Grevgatan and had the impression that someone had been rummaging around in his files. It's hard to be more precise, but you know what it's like. You discover a kind of system in the way a person puts his belongings in order, especially the many documents we all accumulate—**the flotsam and jetsam of our lives,** as an old chief inspector once put it to me. But then it breaks down. There are strange gaps. In general everything was very neat, but one desk drawer was a real mess."

"What did his wife say?"

"That nobody had been there."

"In that case there are only two possibilities. Either she's been rummaging around, but for some reason doesn't want to admit it. It could be simply that she doesn't want to admit to her curiosity—perhaps she finds it embarrassing, who knows? Or he did it himself."

Wallander thought hard about what Ytterberg had said. There was something he should have picked up on, a link that suddenly occurred to him, only to fade away again just as quickly. He hadn't managed to pin it down.

"What about the secret service boys? Säpo?" Wallander wondered. "Could they have something on him?

An old suspicion lying in a dusty drawer somewhere that recently became interesting again?"

"I asked them that exact question. And got a very vague answer. It could mean almost anything. It could well be that the man they sent to see me didn't know any details. That's not impossible. We've all suspected that Säpo has quite a few secrets they keep to themselves even if they seem bad at staying quiet about what they know."

"But was there anything on von Enke?"

Ytterberg flung out his arms wide and accidentally hit his coffee cup, which tipped over and spilled. He hurled the cup angrily into the garbage can, then wiped down his desktop and all the soaking wet documents with a towel that had been lying on a shelf behind the desk. Wallander suspected that the coffee cup episode was not a one-off.

"There was nothing at all," Ytterberg said when he had finished wiping. "Håkan von Enke is a thoroughly honest and honorable member of the Swedish military. I spoke to somebody whose name I forget who has access to the records of naval officers. Håkan von Enke was promoted rapidly, became a commander very quickly. But then things came to a halt. His career leveled off, you might say."

Wallander thought for a while, his chin resting on his hand, remembering what Sten Nordlander had said about von Enke putting his career on the line. Ytterberg was cleaning his fingernails with a letter opener. Somebody passed by in the hall, whistling. To his surprise Wallander recognized the tune—it was an old hit song from World War II. "We'll meet again, don't know where, don't know when . . ." He hummed it quietly to himself.

"How long are you staying in Stockholm?" Ytterberg asked, breaking the silence.

"I'm going back home this afternoon."

"Give me your phone number and I'll keep you informed."

Ytterberg escorted him as far as the door leading to Bergsgatan. Wallander walked toward Kungsholmstorg, flagged down a taxi, and returned to his hotel. He went to his room, hung the "Do Not Disturb" sign on the door handle, and lay down on the bed. He journeyed back in his mind to the birthday party in Djursholm. He thought of it in terms of taking off his shoes and **approaching on tiptoe** his recollections of how Håkan von Enke had behaved and what he had said. He reviewed his memories for anything that didn't ring true. Perhaps he had been wrong. Maybe what he had diagnosed as fear wasn't that at all. A person's facial expression can be interpreted in many different ways. Nearsighted people who screw up their eyes are sometimes mistaken for rude or contemptuous. The man he was trying to track down had been missing now for six days. Wallander knew they had now passed the point where most missing persons are found. After such a long time, they either return or at least show some sign of life. But there was no trace at all of Håkan von Enke.

He simply vanished, Wallander told himself. He went out for a walk and didn't come back. His passport was at home; he had no money with him; he didn't even take his cell phone. The phone was one of the points that made Wallander stop and think. It was a riddle that demanded a solution, an answer. Håkan could simply have forgotten the phone, of course. But why do so the morning he disappeared? It seemed implausible and strengthened the probability of the theory that his disappearance was not voluntary.

Wallander prepared for the journey back to Ystad. An hour before the train was due to leave, he had lunch at a restaurant near the station. He passed the time on the train by solving a couple of crossword puzzles. As usual there were a few words he couldn't figure out, and he was forced to sit there worrying about them. He was back at his house by nine o'clock. When he collected Jussi he was almost bowled over by the dog's delight at being reunited with him.

Wallander called Martinsson's direct line at the police station. Martinsson's recorded voice informed him that he was away all day at a seminar in Lund on illegal immigration. Wallander wondered if he should call Kristina Magnusson, but he decided not to. He solved a couple more crosswords, defrosted the freezer, then went for a long walk with Jussi. He felt bored and restless as a result of not being able to work. When the phone rang he grabbed the receiver. A young woman with a chirpy voice asked him if he was interested in a massage machine that could be stored in a closet and took up very little space even when it was in use. Wallander slammed the receiver down, but then regretted snapping at the girl, who hadn't done anything to deserve it.

The phone rang again. He wondered if he should answer, but after a pause, he did. There was a crackling noise in the background, as if the call was coming from far away. Eventually he heard a voice.

It was speaking English.

It was a man who asked if he was talking to the right person: he was hoping to reach Kurt, Kurt Wallander.

"That's me," shouted Wallander in an attempt to make himself heard through all the background noise. "Who are you?"

It seemed as if contact had been lost. Wallander was just about to replace the receiver when the voice became audible again, more clearly now, nearer.

"Wallander?" he said. "Is that you, Kurt?"

"Yes, that's me."

"Steven Atkins here. Do you know who I am?"

"Yes, I know," Wallander shouted. "Håkan's friend."

"Has he been found yet?"

"No."

"Did you say 'no'?"

"Yes, I said 'no.'"

"So he's been missing for a week now?"

"Yes, more or less."

The line started crackling again. Wallander assumed Atkins was using a cell phone.

"I'm getting worried," Atkins shouted. "He's not the kind of man who simply vanishes."

"When did you last speak to him?"

"On Sunday last week. In the afternoon. Swedish time."

The day before he disappeared, Wallander thought.

"Was it you who called, or did he call you?"

"He called me. He said he'd reached a conclusion."

"What about?"

"I don't know. He didn't say."

"Is that all? A conclusion? Surely he must have said something else?"

"Not at all. He was always very careful when he spoke on the phone. Sometimes he called from a public phone."

The line crackled and faded again. Wallander held his breath; he didn't want to lose the call.

"I want to know what's going on," said Atkins. "I'm worried."

"Did he say anything about going away?"

"He sounded happier than he had been in a while. Håkan could be very gloomy. He didn't like growing old; he was afraid of running out of time. How old are you, Kurt?"

"I'm sixty."

"That's nothing. Do you have an e-mail address, Kurt?"

Wallander spelled out his address with some difficulty, but he didn't mention that he hardly ever used it.

"I'll send you a message, Kurt," Atkins shouted. "Why don't you come over and visit? But find Håkan first!"

His voice grew fainter again, and then the connection was broken. Wallander stood there with the receiver in his hand. **Why don't you come over?** He replaced the receiver and sat down at the kitchen table, notepad and pencil in hand. Steven Atkins had given

him new information, straight into his ear, from distant California. He thought back through the conversation with Atkins, line by line, point by point. The
day before he disappeared, Håkan von Enke called
California—not Sten Nordlander or his son. Was that
a conscious choice? Had that particular call come from
a public phone? Had von Enke gone out into the
streets of Stockholm in order to make that call? It was
a question with no answer. He continued writing until
he had worked his way meticulously through the
whole conversation. Then he stood up, stood some six
feet away from the table, and stared at his notebook,
like a painter studying what was on his easel from a
distance. It was Sten Nordlander, of course, who had
given Steven Atkins Wallander's phone number. That
wasn't especially surprising. Atkins was just as worried
as everybody else. Or was he? Wallander suddenly had
the feeling that Håkan von Enke had been standing
next to Steven Atkins when he made that call to Sweden. Then he dismissed the thought.

Wallander was growing tired of this case. It wasn't
his job to track down the missing person or to speculate about the various circumstances. He was filling his
inactivity with specters. Perhaps this was a test run for
all the misery he would be bound to endure once he
had also gone into retirement?

He prepared a meal, did some cleaning, then tried to
read a book he had been given by Linda—about the
history of the police force in Sweden. He was dozing
off over the book when the phone woke him.

It was Ytterberg.

"I hope I'm not disturbing you," he began.

"Not at all. I was reading."

"We've made a discovery," said Ytterberg. "I thought you should know."

"A dead body?"

"Burned to a cinder. We found him a few hours ago in a burned-out boardinghouse on Lidingö. Not that far from Lill-Jansskogen. The age is about right, but there's no firm evidence that it's him. We're not saying anything to his wife or to anybody else right now."

"What about the press?"

"We're saying nothing at all to them."

Wallander slept badly again that night. He kept getting out of bed, starting to read his book then putting it down again almost immediately. Jussi was lying in front of the open fire, watching him. Wallander sometimes allowed him to sleep indoors.

Shortly after six the next morning Ytterberg called. The body they found wasn't Håkan von Enke. A ring on a charred finger had led to the identification. Wallander felt relieved, and went back to sleep until nine. He was having his breakfast when Lennart Mattson called.

"It's all over," he said. "The Employee Administration Board has decided to dock you five days' pay for forgetting your pistol."

"Is that all?"

"Aren't you pleased?"

"I'm more than pleased. So I assume I can come back to work. On Monday."

And he did. Early Monday morning Wallander was at his desk once more.

But there was still no trace of Håkan von Enke.

9

The missing person remained missing. Wallander went back to work and was surrounded by smiling faces as his colleagues realized how mild his punishment had been. It was even suggested that they should start a collection to cover his fine, but nothing came of that. Wallander suspected that one or two of those welcoming him back with open arms were in fact concealing considerable schadenfreude, but he made up his mind to ignore that. He was not going to go around looking for potential hypocrites; he didn't have the time. He would only sleep even worse at night if he lay in bed working himself up about colleagues sneering at him behind his back.

His first serious case was an assault that had taken place on a ferry between Ystad and Poland. It was an exceptionally brutal attack, and a classic situation: no reliable witnesses and everybody blaming everybody else. The assault had occurred in a cramped cabin; the victim was a young woman from Skurup who was making the unfortunate trip with her boyfriend, who she knew was prone to jealousy and couldn't hold his liquor. During the crossing they had joined up with a group of young men from Malmö who had only one goal in mind: to drink themselves silly.

Wallander conducted the investigation on his own, with occasional help from Martinsson. He didn't need much in the way of assistance; the perpetrator was no doubt among the men the young woman had met during the crossing—one or more of whom had beaten her up and almost ripped off her left ear.

There were no new developments in the Håkan von Enke case. Wallander spoke almost every day to Ytterberg, who still couldn't believe that the commander had run away of his own accord. This belief was supported by the facts that von Enke had left his passport at home and that his credit card hadn't been used. But the main thing was the man's character, Ytterberg maintained. Håkan von Enke simply wasn't the kind of man who disappeared. He would never abandon his wife. It didn't add up.

Wallander spoke frequently to Louise. She was always the one who called, usually at about seven in the evening, when he was at home, eating a sloppily prepared dinner. Wallander could hear that she had reconciled herself to the thought that her husband was dead. In response to a direct question, she told him she was now getting a decent night's sleep with the aid of sleeping pills. Everybody is waiting, Wallander thought as he replaced the receiver. He seems to be missing without a trace, gone up in the proverbial smoke and disappeared through the chimney of our existence. But is his body really lying hidden somewhere, rotting away? Or is he having dinner at this very moment? On a different planet, under another name, sitting opposite some celebrity we don't know about?

What did Wallander think? His experience told him that the former submarine commander was dead. Wallander was afraid it would one day be revealed that his death was due to some banal cause, such as a mugging gone wrong. But he wasn't sure. Perhaps there was still a small chance that von Enke had chosen to disappear, even if they couldn't see why.

The one who dug in her heels deepest and refused to believe that von Enke had been killed was Linda. He's not the kind of man anyone can kill, she insisted, indignantly, when she and Wallander met in their usual café while the baby slept soundly in her stroller. But not even Linda could guess why he would want to run away. Hans never called, but listening to Linda's theories and questions, Wallander had the impression that the two of them were as one in their convictions. But he didn't ask, didn't want to interfere; it was their life, nobody else's.

Steven Atkins started sending long e-mails to Wallander, page after page. The longer Atkins's messages became, the shorter the replies Wallander managed to produce. He would have liked to write more, but his English was so shaky that he didn't dare venture into complicated sentence structure. Nevertheless, he learned that Steven Atkins now lived close to the major naval base just outside San Diego in California, Point Loma. He owned a little house in an area populated almost exclusively by ex-servicemen. On the next block, Atkins claimed, there were "enough former sailors to man a submarine, more likely several, right down to the last position." Wallander asked himself what it would be like to live in a neighborhood filled exclusively with former police officers. He shuddered at the thought.

Atkins wrote about his life, his family, his children and grandchildren, and he even attached pictures of them. Wallander had to ask Linda for help viewing them. They were sunlit photographs, with naval ships in the background, Atkins himself in uniform, and his large family smiling at Wallander. Atkins was bald and slim, and had his arm wrapped around the shoulders of his equally slim and smiling but not bald wife. Wallander thought the photo looked like an advertisement for dish soap, or some new breakfast cereal. Smiling and waving at him from the computer screen was the ideal, happy American family.

Wallander could see from his calendar that it was now exactly a month since Håkan von Enke had left his apartment in Grevgatan, closed the door behind him, and never returned. Wallander had just had a long phone conversation with Ytterberg. It was May 11, and rain was pouring down over Stockholm. Ytterberg sounded depressed—hard to tell if it was because of the weather or the state of the investigation. Wallander was wondering how he could pin down the right person to charge in connection with that sorry business on board the ferry. In other words, the conversation had been between two tired and distinctly grumpy police officers. Wallander wondered if Säpo was still showing an interest in the disappearance.

"A man by the name of William comes to see me now and again," said Ytterberg. "To tell you the truth, I don't know if that's his first or last name. And I can't say I'm all that interested. The last time he was here I had a sudden urge to throttle him. I asked if they had any information they could give me that might make things a bit easier for us. A helping hand from one professional to another, which you might think is a matter of common courtesy in a democratic country like Sweden. But needless to say, they didn't. Or at least, that's what William said. You can never know if people in his trade are telling the truth. Their whole way of operating is a sort of game based on lies and deception. Obviously, ordinary police officers like you and me occasionally pull the wool over people's eyes, but it's not what you'd call the cornerstone of our professional operations."

After the call Wallander returned to the file of interrogation notes lying open on the desk in front of him. Next to the file was a photograph of a badly injured woman's face. That's why I do what I do, he told himself. Because her face looks like that, because somebody nearly beat her to death.

When Wallander came home that evening, he found that Jussi was ill. He was lying in his kennel, didn't want to eat or drink. Wallander broke into a cold sweat and immediately called a veterinary surgeon he knew who had once helped him nail a man who had been attacking young horses grazing in their paddocks around Ystad. He lived in Kåseberga and promised to come.

His examination suggested that Jussi had eaten something that disagreed with him, and that he would soon be well again. Jussi spent that night on a mat in front of the open fire, and Wallander kept checking to make sure he was all right. The next morning Jussi was back on his feet, albeit unsteadily.

Wallander was relieved. When he arrived at his office and switched on his computer, it occurred to him in passing that he hadn't heard from Steven Atkins in five days. Perhaps there was nothing else to say, no more photographs to send. But shortly before noon, just as Wallander was starting to think about whether to go home for lunch or to eat somewhere in town, he had a call from reception. He had a visitor.

"Who is it?" Wallander asked. "What does he want?"

"He's a foreigner," said the receptionist. "He seems to be a police officer."

Wallander went down to the front desk. He realized immediately who his visitor was. He wasn't wearing a police uniform, but that of the U.S. Navy. It was Steven Atkins standing there with his cap under his arm.

"I didn't mean to turn up without warning," he said. "But I got the arrival time in Copenhagen wrong. I called you at home and on your cell phone and didn't get a reply, so I came here."

"This is a surprise," said Wallander. "But you are most welcome, of course. Am I right in thinking that this is your first visit to Sweden?"

"Yes. My dear friend Håkan was always inviting me to come visit, but I never got around to it."

They had lunch at the restaurant in town that Wallander considered to be the best. Atkins was a friendly man who took an interest in his surroundings. He asked questions that were genuine and not just polite, and he listened carefully to the answers. At first Wallander found it hard to imagine that Atkins had been in command of a submarine, especially one of the biggest nuclear-powered types in the U.S. Navy. He seemed much too jovial. But of course, Wallander had no idea what kind of person made a good submarine commander.

What motivated Atkins to travel to Sweden was purely and simply his concern about what had happened to his friend. Wallander was touched when he saw how worried Atkins was. An old man missing another old man—a friendship that was obviously very close.

Atkins had checked in to the Hilton at Kastrup Airport, then rented a car and driven to Ystad.

"I had to see what it was like, driving over that incredibly long bridge," he said with a laugh.

Wallander was jealous of the man's glistening white teeth. After the meal he called the police station and informed them that he wouldn't be in for the rest of the day. Then they drove out to Wallander's house. Atkins turned out to be very fond of dogs, and got on with Jussi like a house on fire. They went for a long walk with Jussi on his leash, following paths around the fields with occasional stops to admire the sea views and the undulating countryside. Atkins suddenly turned to face Wallander, and bit his lip.

"Is Håkan dead?"

Wallander understood his intention. Atkins had fired off his question so that Wallander wouldn't be able to hide behind an evasive or not fully truthful response. He wanted a clear and definite answer. He was the submarine commander demanding to know whether a ship had been lost.

"We don't know. He vanished without a trace."

Atkins stared at him for quite a while, then nodded slowly. They resumed walking and were back at the house half an hour later. Wallander made coffee. They sat down at the kitchen table.

"You told me about the last phone conversation you and Håkan had," said Wallander. "Why would anyone say he had reached a conclusion if the person he was talking to had no idea what he was talking about?"

"Sometimes people believe that others know what they're thinking," said Atkins. "Perhaps Håkan thought I knew what he meant."

"You must have had a lot of conversations. Was there a theme that kept cropping up? Something more important than the rest?"

Wallander hadn't prepared his questions. They simply tumbled out on their own, as if they were inevitable.

"We were roughly the same age," said Atkins, "both children of the Cold War. I was twenty-three when the Russians launched their **Sputnik.** I remember I was scared to death, frightened they were going to aim it at us. Håkan told me once that he'd had similar thoughts, but more innocent, not so hair-raising. The Russians were there all right, but they weren't quite the monsters for him that they were for me. We were affected by all kinds of things in those days. I remember Håkan was worried because Sweden wasn't a member of NATO. He saw that as a catastrophic error of judgment. In his opinion, neutrality wasn't only wrong and dangerous, but outright hypocrisy. We were on the same side. Sweden wasn't in some sort of neutral no-man's-land, no matter what the politicians maintained. When Wennerström was unmasked, Håkan called me—I can still remember it clearly. It was June 1963. I was second-in-command on a submarine that was about to be deployed in the Pacific Ocean. He wasn't indignant at the fact that Wennerström was guilty of treason and had been spying for the Russians. He was exultant about that! At long last the Swedish people would realize what had been going on. The Russians had infiltrated the whole Swedish defense system. There were defectors wherever you looked, and when the day came for Russia to move in and occupy his country, the only thing that could save Sweden would be NATO membership. You asked if there was a theme that kept cropping up in our conversations. Yes, we always talked about politics. Including about how politicians reduced the possibility of maintaining the balance of power between us and the Russians. I can't recall a single conversation we had that didn't contain some kind of political discussion."

"If your conversations were always dominated by politics," Wallander wondered, "what could have been the conclusion he reached? Were there any previous occasions when he reached a conclusion that made him exultant?"

"Not as far as I can recall. But we've known each other for nearly fifty years. A lot of memories have faded away."

"How did you meet?"

"In the way that all important meetings take place. By pure and peculiar coincidence."

It had started raining when Atkins told the story of his first meeting with Håkan von Enke. He was a much better storyteller than the man Wallander had listened to in the windowless room in Djursholm during the birthday party. But perhaps it has to do with the language, Wallander thought. I'm used to thinking that stories in English are so much richer or more important than stories I hear in my own language.

"It was nearly fifty years ago," said Atkins in his low voice. "August 1961, to be precise. In a place where you might least expect to find two young naval officers. I had flown to Europe with my father, who was a colonel in the U.S. Army. He wanted to show me Berlin, that little isolated fortress in the middle of the Russian Zone. We flew Pan Am from Hamburg, I recall; the plane was full of military servicemen—there were hardly any civilians on board, apart from some priests dressed in black. The situation was tense, but at least there were no lines of tanks from east and west, confronting each other like deer in heat. But one evening, not far from Friedrichstrasse, my father and I suddenly found ourselves in a crowd of people. Across from us a group of East German soldiers was busy setting up a barbed-wire fence that would eventually become a wall built of cinder blocks and cement. Standing next to me was a man of about my own age, dressed in a uniform. I asked where he was from, and he said he was Swedish. Of course it was Håkan. That was our first meeting. We stood there watching Berlin be divided by a wall—a world was amputated, you might say. Ulbricht, the East German leader, claimed that it was a measure 'to protect freedom and lay the foundation of the socialist state that would continue to flourish.' But that day, as the Berlin Wall began to be built, we saw an old woman standing on the other side, weeping. She was shabbily dressed and had a big scar on her face; she might have had some kind of false plastic ear, but neither of us was sure. But what we both saw, and would never forget, was that she stretched out a hand in a sort of helpless gesture toward those soldiers who were building a wall before her very eyes. That poor woman was not nailed to a cross, but she was reaching out **toward us.** I think that was the moment when we both realized what our duty was: to keep the free world free, and to make sure that no other countries ended up within prison-like walls. We became even more convinced a few weeks later when the Russians resumed nuclear weapons testing. By then I had returned to Groton, where I was stationed, and Håkan was on a train back to Sweden. But we had each other's addresses in our pockets, and that was the beginning of a friendship that still continues. Håkan was twenty-eight at the time, and I had just celebrated my twenty-seventh birthday. Forty-seven years is a very long time."

"Did he ever visit you in America?"

"Oh yes, often. He must have come over fifteen times, maybe more."

The reply surprised Wallander. He had been under the impression that Håkan von Enke made only the occasional visit to the U.S.A. Wasn't that what Linda said? Or did he misremember?

"That's about one trip every three years," said Wallander.

"He was a big fan of America."

"Did he usually stay long?"

"Rarely less than three weeks. Louise was always with him. She and my wife got along well. We looked forward to their visits."

"Perhaps you know that their son, Hans, works in Copenhagen?"

"I've arranged to meet him this evening."

"I take it you know that he lives with my daughter?"

"Yes, I know. But I'll have to meet her another time. Hans is very busy. We're going to meet after ten this evening in my hotel. I'm flying to Stockholm tomorrow to see Louise."

It had stopped raining. An airplane on its descent into Sturup flew low over the house, making the windows rattle.

"What do you think happened?" Wallander asked. "You knew him better than I did."

"I don't know," said Atkins. "I don't like saying that. I'm not the kind of person who avoids giving a straight answer. But I can't believe he would leave of his own free will, abandoning his wife and son, and now even a grandchild, leaving them to fret and worry. I have to throw up my hands, even though I don't want to."

Atkins emptied his cup and stood. It was time for him to return to Copenhagen. Wallander explained the best way of getting to the main road into Ystad and then to Malmö. Just as Atkins was about to leave, he took a little stone out of his pocket and handed it to Wallander.

"A present," he said. "An old Indian once told me about a tradition in his tribe; I think it was the Kiowa. If a person has a problem, he carries a stone—preferably a heavy one—in his clothes, and lugs it around until he has solved his difficulties. Then he can get rid of the stone and continue on his way through life more easily. Pop this stone in your pocket. Leave it there until we know what has happened to Håkan."

It's just an ordinary granite pebble, Wallander thought after he had waved good-bye to Atkins as he drove away down the hill. He also remembered the stone that had disappeared from the desk in the apartment in Grevgatan. He thought about what Atkins had said about his first meeting with Håkan von Enke. Wallander couldn't remember anything about those days in August 1961. That was the year he celebrated his thirteenth birthday, and all he could recall was the battering he received from his hormones, which resulted in his life consisting of dreams—dreams about women, real or imagined.

Wallander belonged to the generation that grew up in the 1960s. But he had never been involved in any of the political movements, had never joined any of the protest rallies in Malmö, never really understood what the Vietnam war was all about or had any interest in freedom movements in countries he had barely heard of. Linda often reminded him how poorly informed he was. He usually dismissed politics as a higher authority that restricted the ability of the police to enforce law and order, and that was it. He generally voted in elections but was never sure about whom to vote for. His father had been a dyed-in-the-wool Social Democrat, and that was the party he usually supported. But rarely with any real conviction.

The meeting with Atkins had unsettled him. He searched for a Berlin Wall inside himself, but failed to find one. Was his life really so restricted that major events taking place in the outside world never had much effect on him? What aspects of life had upset him? Pictures of children who had been badly treated, of course—but he had never been sufficiently moved to do anything about it. His excuse was always that he was too busy with work. I sometimes manage to help people by making sure that criminals are removed from the streets, he thought. But aside from that? He gazed out over the fields where nothing was yet growing, but he failed to find what he was looking for.

That evening he straightened his desk, and dumped onto it all the pieces of a jigsaw puzzle Linda had given him as a birthday present the previous year. It was a painting by Degas. He sorted the pieces methodically, and managed to complete the bottom left-hand corner of the puzzle.

The whole time, he continued to wonder what had

happened to Håkan von Enke. But it was mainly his own fate he was thinking about.

He kept searching for the Berlin Wall that didn't exist.

10

One afternoon in the beginning of June, Wallander drove to the marina in Ystad and walked to the bench farthest out on the jetty. It was one of his favorite retreats, a confessional without a priest, a place he often went when he wanted to be left alone to come to terms with something that was troubling him. It had been a cold spring, wet and windy, but now the first ridge of high pressure had drifted in over Skåne. Wallander took off his jacket, looked up at the sun, and closed his eyes. But he opened them again immediately. He was remembering the words of one of his father's neighbors. **You had a father who was very fond of you.** He had often asked himself if that was true. The fact that he had become a police officer was something his father could never get over. But there must have been so much more to his life. Mona thought her father-in-law was awful and refused to accompany Wallander when he went to visit him. He and Linda ended up being the only ones in the car whenever he drove to Löderup.

His father was always friendly toward his granddaughter. He displayed a degree of patience with Linda that neither Wallander nor his sister, Kristina, had experienced when they were young.

He was an elusive man, somebody you could never pin down, Wallander thought. Am I becoming like him?

A man about his own age was sitting on the rail of his little fishing boat, cleaning a net. He was concentrating, and humming to himself as he worked. As Wallander contemplated him, it occurred to him that he would love to change places—from the bench to the net, from the police station to a handsome boat made of varnished wood.

His father was an unsolved riddle as far as he was concerned. Was he himself just as much of a riddle to Linda? What would Wallander's granddaughter say about her grandfather? Would he be no more than a shadowy and silent old police officer who sat alone in his house, visited less and less often by fewer and fewer people? That's what I'm afraid of, Wallander thought. And I have every reason in the world to be afraid. I certainly haven't cherished and taken good care of my friendships.

In many cases it was too late now. Some of the people who had been close to him were dead. Rydberg above all, but also his old friend the racehorse trainer Sven Widén. Wallander had never understood those who claimed you didn't need to lose touch with people simply because they were dead, that you could keep on talking to them in their graves. He had never managed to do that. The dead were faces he barely remembered anymore, and their voices no longer spoke to him.

Reluctantly he stood up from the bench. He would have to go back to the police station. The investigation into the assault on the ferry was closed and a man had been found guilty, although Wallander was convinced that there had been two men involved in the attack. It was half a victory: one person was found guilty, one got justice, if that was possible after having your face smashed in. But another person had slipped through the net.

It was three in the afternoon by the time Wallander returned from his excursion to the bench on the jetty. There was a note on his desk saying Ytterberg had called and wanted to speak to him. Whoever had taken the call had noted that it was urgent. Everything was always urgent in Wallander's life as a policeman. He had never received a non-urgent message. So he didn't return the call right away, but first read a memo from the National Police Board that Lennart Mattson had asked him to comment on. It was about one of the reorganizations that were constantly being imposed on various local police forces. This time it was about setting up a system to ensure a bigger police presence in the streets on holidays and weekends, not only in the big cities but also in towns like Ystad. Wallander read through the document and was annoyed by the pompous and bureaucratic language in which it was couched. When he finished he was aware that he didn't really understand what it had said. He wrote a few meaningless comments and put it all in an envelope that he would deposit in the chief's in-box when he left for the day.

Then he called Ytterberg, who answered immediately.

"You called," said Wallander.

"Now she's disappeared too."

"Who?"

"Louise. Louise von Enke. She's vanished as well."

Wallander held his breath. Were his ears deceiving him? He asked Ytterberg to repeat himself.

"Louise von Enke has disappeared."

"What happened?"

Wallander could hear paper rustling. Ytterberg was searching through his notes. He wanted to give an exact report.

"These last few years the von Enkes have had a cleaning woman from Bulgaria. She has a residence permit. Her name's the same as the capital, Sofia. She works for them on Mondays, Wednesdays, and Fridays, three hours in the morning. She was there on Monday and everything seemed to be as usual. When she left the apartment at about twelve o'clock on Monday, Louise said she was looking forward to seeing her again on Wednesday. When Sofia turned up at nine o'clock Wednesday, the apartment was deserted, but that was nothing out of the ordinary. Louise wasn't always at home, and Sofia thought no more about it. But when she arrived this morning she realized something was wrong. She is certain that Louise has not been home since Wednesday. Everything was exactly as she left it. Louise has never before gone away for this long without giving advance warning. But there was no message, nothing, only the empty apartment. Sofia called the son in Copenhagen, who said he last spoke to his mother on Sunday—in other words, five days ago. So he called me next. Incidentally, do you know what line of business he's in?"

"Money," said Wallander. "He deals exclusively with money."

"That sounds like a fascinating job," said Ytterberg thoughtfully.

Then he returned to his notes.

"Hans gave me Sofia's number and we worked our way through the apartment together. The Bulgarian lady knew exactly what was in all the cabinets and drawers. And she said what I least wanted to hear. I assume you know what I mean?"

"Yes," said Wallander. "That nothing was missing."

"Precisely. No suitcase, no clothes, no purses, not even her passport. That was still in the drawer where Sofia knew she kept it."

"What about her cell phone?"

"That was charging in the kitchen. When I discovered that, I became really worried."

Wallander thought it all over. He would never have thought that Håkan von Enke's disappearance would be followed by another one.

"It's worrying," he said eventually. "Is there a plausible explanation?"

"Not as far as I can see. I called all her closest friends, but nobody has seen or heard from her since Sunday, when she called a friend named Katarina

Lindén and asked about her experience at a mountain hotel in Norway where she'd stayed. According to Katarina Lindén, she sounded exactly the same as she always does. Nobody's spoken to her since then. We'll consult the team dealing with her husband's disappearance. I just wanted to call you first. To get your reaction, to be honest."

"My first thought is that she knows where Håkan is and went to join him. But of course the passport and the cell phone tend to argue against that."

"I thought something similar myself. But I'm doubtful, just like you."

"Could there be a plausible explanation despite everything? Could she be ill? Could she have collapsed in the street?"

"The hospitals were the first places I checked. According to what Sofia has told us, and we have no reason to doubt her, Louise always carried an ID in her jacket or overcoat. Since we haven't found it in the apartment, there's no reason to believe she didn't have it with her when she went out, so the hospitals should be able to identify her."

Wallander wondered why Louise hadn't told him that she had a cleaning woman come in three times a week. Hans hadn't mentioned her either. But that didn't necessarily mean anything. The von Enke family belonged to the upper class, and to them household help were taken for granted. You didn't need to talk about them; they were simply there.

Ytterberg promised to keep him informed. They were just about to end their conversation when Wallander asked if Ytterberg had contacted Atkins, whom he had met in Stockholm.

"Does he have any useful information?" Ytterberg sounded doubtful.

Wallander thought it was odd that Ytterberg evidently didn't know how close the two families were. Or had Atkins told him a different story?

"What time is it in California?" Ytterberg asked. "There's not much point in waking people up in the middle of the night."

"The difference between us and the east coast of the U.S.A. is six hours," said Wallander, "but I don't know about California. I can find out and give him a call."

"Do that," said Ytterberg. "Order the call and we'll pay for it."

"My official telephone hasn't been blocked yet," said Wallander. "I don't think the police lose money on unpaid phone bills. Things haven't gone quite that far yet."

Wallander called directory assistance and was informed that the time difference was nine hours. That meant it was six in the morning in San Diego, so he decided to wait a couple of hours before calling Atkins. Instead he called Linda. She had already had a long conversation with Hans in Copenhagen.

"Come over," she said. "I'm just sitting around, and Klara is asleep in her stroller."

"Klara?"

Linda laughed lightly at his confusion.

"We decided last night. She's going to be named Klara. She's already named Klara."

"Like my mother? Your grandma?"

"I never met her, as you know. Don't get upset, but we chose it basically because it's a nice name. And it goes well with both last names. Klara Wallander and Klara von Enke."

"What will her full name be?"

"For now it will be Klara Wallander. She can make up her own mind eventually. Are you coming? You can have a cup of coffee and we can have a provisional baptism celebration."

"Are you going to have her baptized? Properly?"

She didn't answer that. And Wallander was sensible enough not to push the issue.

Fifteen minutes later he pulled up outside Linda's house. The garden was aflame with color. Wallander thought about his own neglected garden, in which he planted almost nothing. When he lived in Mariagatan he had always envisioned an entirely different environment, with him crawling around on his hands and knees inhaling all the earthy smells, weeding the flower beds.

Klara was asleep in her stroller in the shade of a pear tree. Wallander observed her little face behind the mosquito net.

"Klara's a pretty name," he said. "What made you think of it?"

"We saw it in a newspaper. Someone named Klara behaved heroically in connection with a major fire in Östersund. We made up our minds more or less on the spot."

They wandered around the garden talking about what had happened. The disappearance of Louise was as big a surprise for Linda and Hans as for everybody else. There had been no indications, nothing to suggest that Louise had been hatching a plan.

"Could it be another act of violence?" Wallander wondered. "If we assume that Håkan was attacked in some way?"

"You mean someone wanted to get rid of the pair of them?" Linda said. "But why? What could the motive possibly be?"

"That's the sixty-four-thousand-dollar question," said Wallander, contemplating a bush covered in flame-red roses. "Could they both have been involved in something the rest of us know nothing about?"

They continued their tour of the garden in silence. Linda was considering his question.

"We know so little about people," she said in the end, when they had returned to the front of the house and she had checked on Klara behind the net.

Klara was fast asleep, her hands gripping a quilt.

"You could say that I know no more about that couple than this little girl does," she said.

"Did you find Louise and Håkan mysterious?"

"Not at all. On the contrary! They were always frank and straightforward with me."

"Some people can leave false tracks," Wallander said thoughtfully. "Frankness and straightforwardness could be a sort of invisible lock protecting a reality they'd prefer not to reveal."

They sat in the garden drinking coffee until Wallander checked his watch and saw that it was time for him to call Atkins. He went back to the police station and dialed the number from his office. After four rings

Atkins answered with a grunt that sounded as if he were waiting to receive an order. Wallander told him what had happened. When he finished there was such a long silence that he began to wonder if they had been cut off. Then Atkins reacted in a loud voice.

"It's not possible," he said.

"Nevertheless, she's been missing since Monday or Tuesday."

Wallander could hear that Atkins was shocked. He was breathing heavily. Wallander asked when he had last spoken to her. There was a pause while Atkins thought it over.

"Friday afternoon. Her afternoon, my morning."

"Who made the call?"

"She did."

Wallander frowned. That was not the answer he had expected.

"What did she want?"

"She wanted to wish my wife a happy birthday. Both my wife and I were surprised. Neither of us bothers about birthdays."

"Could there have been some other reason why she called?"

"We had the impression that she was feeling lonely, and wanted to talk to somebody. That's not so difficult to understand."

"If you think carefully, looking back, was there anything she said that could be tied to her disappearance?"

Wallander didn't trust his bad English, but Atkins understood what he meant. There was a pause before he answered.

"Nothing," he said eventually. "She sounded exactly the same as always."

"But there must be something going on," said Wallander. "First he disappears, and then she does."

"It's sort of like the poem about the ten little Indians," said Atkins. "They disappear one after the other. Half the family has vanished now. There's only the two children left."

Wallander gave a start. Had he heard wrong?

"But there's only one who could disappear," he said tentatively. "You're not including Linda, surely?"

"We shouldn't forget the sister," said Atkins.

"Sister? Does Hans have a sister?"

"Oh yes. She's named Signe. I don't know if I'm pronouncing it correctly. I can spell it if you like. She didn't live with her parents. I don't know why. You shouldn't dig into other people's lives unnecessarily. I've never met her. But Håkan told me he had a daughter."

Wallander was too astonished to ask any more questions, and they hung up. He stood by the window and contemplated the water tower. **There was a sister named Signe.** Why had nobody said anything about her?

That evening Wallander sat at his kitchen table and worked through all his notes from the day Håkan von Enke had disappeared. But nowhere did he discover any hint at all of a daughter in the family. There was no mention of a Signe. It was as if she had never existed.

PART 2

Incidents Under the Surface

11

Wallander was annoyed. So, unusually for him, he decided to launch a direct attack. He felt duped by this family in which two members had disappeared and a third had just been discovered. He thought he'd been a victim of the lies that come naturally to the upper classes, concerning family details that must be hidden at any cost from the rest of the world, which probably wouldn't be particularly interested anyway. After the phone call to Atkins and the long evening spent going over yet again everything that had happened and been said since Håkan von Enke's seventy-fifth birthday party, he slept soundly until shortly after seven the next morning, when he called Linda. He had hoped to talk to Hans, but Hans had already left, at about six.

"What can he find to do at that time?" Wallander asked, irritated. "Surely there aren't any banks open now, nor any dealers buying and selling shares."

"What about Japan?" Linda suggested. "Or New Zealand? There's a lot of movement in the exchanges all over Asia. It's not unusual for Hans to leave for work this early. But it's unusual for you to call at seven o'clock. Don't take it out on me. Did something happen?"

"I want to talk about Signe," Wallander said.

"Who's she?"

"Your boyfriend's sister."

He could hear her heavy breathing. Every breath a new thought.

"But he doesn't have a sister."

"Are you sure about that?"

Linda knew her father, and she realized right away that he was serious. He wouldn't call her this early to play a cruel joke.

Klara started crying.

"You'd better come over," Linda said. "Klara just woke up. She tends to be difficult in the morning. I wonder if she inherited that from you?"

An hour later Wallander pulled up on the gravel drive outside her house. By then Klara had been fed and was content, and Linda was up and dressed. Wallander thought she still looked pale and out of sorts, and he wondered if she was ill. But he didn't ask. She took after him, and didn't like people interfering in her affairs.

They sat down at the kitchen table. Wallander recognized the tablecloth. He remembered it from his childhood, then from his father's house in Löderup, and now here it was again. As a small boy he had often traced the complicated pattern in the border, running his finger over the red thread.

"Explain," she said. "I repeat what I said before: Hans doesn't have a sister."

"I believe you," said Wallander. "I'm sure you're not aware of any sister, just as I wasn't. Until now."

He told her about his conversation with Atkins and

the sudden reference to a sister called Signe. Presumably it was pure coincidence that the secret sister was mentioned. If the conversation had been slightly different, her existence would still be totally unknown. Linda listened intently to what he had to say, her frown growing more pronounced the whole time.

"Hans has never said anything to me about a sister," she said when Wallander had finished.

Wallander pointed at the phone.

"Call him and ask a simple question: Why haven't you told me that you have a sister?"

"Is she older or younger?"

Wallander thought for a moment. Atkins had said nothing about that. Nevertheless he felt sure that she must be an older sister. If she'd been born after Hans it would have been more difficult to keep her secret.

"I don't want to call him," Linda said. "I'll take it up with him when he gets home."

"No," said Wallander. "We have two missing persons we have to track down. This is not a private matter, but police business. If you don't call him, I will."

"That might be best," she said.

Wallander dialed the number she gave him for the office in Copenhagen. Classical music was playing when he got through. Linda leaned forward in order to listen.

"It's his direct line," she said. "I chose the music. Before, he had some awful American country junk. Somebody named Billy Ray Cyrus. I forced him to change it by threatening to stop calling. He'll probably answer soon."

She had hardly finished the sentence when Wallander heard Hans's voice. He sounded harassed, almost out of breath. Wallander wondered what on earth had been happening on the Asian stock exchanges.

"I have a question for you that can't wait," he said. "I'm sitting at your kitchen table, by the way."

"Louise," said Hans. "Or Håkan? Have you found them?"

"I wish we had. But this is about an entirely different person. Can you guess who?"

Wallander could see that Linda was annoyed by what she probably saw as an unnecessary cat and mouse game. He conceded that she was right. He should get straight to the point.

"It's about your sister," he said. "Your sister, Signe."

There was silence at the other end of the line, and a pause before Hans spoke again.

"I don't know what you're talking about. Is this some kind of joke?"

Linda had leaned forward over the table, and Wallander held up the receiver so she could hear. He could tell that Hans was telling the truth.

"It's not a joke," he said. "Are you seriously telling me you don't know anything about a sister called Signe?"

"I don't have any brothers or sisters. Can I speak to Linda?"

Wallander handed the receiver over to Linda, who repeated what her father had told her.

"When I was a kid I used to ask my parents why I didn't have any brothers or sisters," Hans said. "They always told me they thought one child was enough. I've never heard of anyone named Signe, never seen any photographs of her. I've always been an only child."

"It's difficult to believe," said Linda.

Hans exploded and yelled at the phone.

"What the hell do you think it's like for me?"

Wallander took the receiver out of Linda's hand.

"I believe you," he said. "So does Linda. But you must understand that it's important to find out how this fits in, assuming it does. Your parents vanish. And now an unknown sister suddenly turns up."

"I don't understand it," said Hans. "I feel sick."

"Whatever the explanation is, I'll find it."

Wallander handed the receiver back to Linda. He listened to her trying to calm Hans down. He didn't want to hear exactly what they said to each other. Since the conversation seemed set to continue for a while, he scribbled a few words on a scrap of paper and put it on the kitchen table in front of her. She nodded and handed him a bunch of keys from the windowsill. He left the house after taking a look at Klara, lying asleep on her stomach in her crib. He gently stroked her cheek with one of his fingers. Her face twitched, but she didn't wake up.

When Wallander got back to the police station he called Sten Nordlander even before he had taken off his jacket. He immediately received the confirmation he had been hoping for.

"Oh yes, there's certainly another child," Nordlander said. "A girl who was severely handicapped from birth. Completely helpless, if I understood Håkan correctly. There was no possibility of them keeping her at home; she needed special care from the very first day of her life. They never spoke about her, and I thought I had to respect that."

"Is her name Signe?"

"Yes."

"Do you know when she was born?"

Nordlander thought for a moment before answering.

"She must be nearly ten years older than her brother. I think her handicap was such a shock to them that it was a long time before they dared to try again."

"So she must be over forty now," said Wallander. "Do you know where she lives? The name of the home or institution?"

"I think Håkan once said it was somewhere near Mariefred, but I never heard a name."

Wallander rushed to end the call. Finding Signe felt urgent, despite the fact that the case was none of his business. He knew that he should contact Ytterberg first, but his curiosity got the better of him. He searched through his hopelessly messy address book until he found the phone number he was looking for. It belonged to a woman who worked for the Ystad Social Welfare Board. She was the daughter of a former civilian secretary at the police station. Wallander had met her in connection with a pedophile ring a few years back. Her name was Sara Amander, and she answered almost immediately. They exchanged a few pleasantries before Wallander came to the point.

"I'm looking for an institution for the handicapped

not far from Mariefred. Maybe there's more than one? I need addresses and phone numbers."

"Can you give me any more information? Are you talking about congenital brain damage, for instance?"

"It's mainly physical, as I understand it. A child who needed care from the day she was born. But it's also possible that she has mental limitations. No doubt it would be an advantage for a person that handicapped not to be fully aware of what an awful life she was condemned to lead."

"We have to be careful when we talk about other people's lives," said Sara Amander. "There are severely handicapped people whose lives are filled with much happiness. But I'll see what I can find out."

Wallander hung up, went to get some coffee, and exchanged a few words with Kristina Magnusson, who reminded him that her colleagues were going to have a casual summer party in her garden the following evening. Wallander had forgotten all about it, of course, but he said he'd be there. He went back to his office and wrote a reminder in large letters that he placed by the phone.

A couple of hours later Sara Amander called back. She had two possibilities for him. One was a private care home called Amalienborg, on the very edge of Mariefred. The other was a state-run home, Niklasgården, not far from Gripsholm Castle. Wallander made a note of the addresses and phone numbers and was about to call the first one when Martinsson appeared in the half-open door. Wallander replaced the receiver and waved him in. Martinsson pulled a face.

"What's the matter?"

"A poker party that ran off the rails. An ambulance just took a man to the hospital with stab wounds. We have a car there, but you and I should go too."

Wallander grabbed his jacket and followed Martinsson out of the room. It took the rest of the day and part of the night for them to figure out what caused the poker party to collapse into chaos and violence. It was only when Wallander returned to the police station at about eight o'clock that he was able to call the numbers from Sara Amander. He began with Amalienborg. A friendly woman answered the phone. Even as he asked his question about Signe von Enke he realized his mistake. He wouldn't get an answer, of course. An institution that took care of severely handicapped people naturally couldn't hand out information to any old Tom, Dick, or Harry. And that was the reply he was given. He didn't even receive a reply to his other questions about whether they had residents of varying ages or if the home was only for adults. The friendly woman continued to inform him patiently that she wasn't allowed to tell him anything. Unfortunately, she couldn't help him at all, no matter how much she would like to. Wallander hung up and thought he should give Ytterberg a call. But he decided against it. There was no reason to disturb his evening. The conversation could wait until the following day.

Since it was a pleasant evening, warm and calm, he ate dinner outside in the garden. Jussi lay at his feet, and snapped up everything that fell off Wallander's fork. In the surrounding fields the oilseed rape was now a sea of gleaming yellow.

But the thought of that sister wouldn't go away. He tried to understand the silence that surrounded her, and thought about how he and Mona would have reacted if they'd had a child that needed the expert care of outsiders from birth. He shuddered at the thought, which was impossible for him to come to grips with. He was sitting lost in thought when eventually he noticed that the phone was ringing. Jussi pricked up his ears. It was Linda. She spoke in a low voice and explained that Hans was asleep.

"He's completely shattered," she said. "The worst thing, he says, is that now he has nobody he can ask about her."

"I'm trying to track her down," said Wallander. "Give me another couple of days and I should know where she is."

"Do you understand how Håkan and Louise could do something like this?"

"No. But maybe it's the only way they could cope with having such a severely handicapped child—to pretend she simply didn't exist."

Then Wallander described the view of the oilseed rape fields and the distant horizon for her.

"I'm looking forward to when Klara can run around here," he said eventually.

"You should get yourself a woman."

"You don't 'get yourself' a woman!"

"You won't find one if you don't make an effort!

Loneliness will eat you up from the inside. You'll become an unpleasant old man."

Wallander sat outside until after ten o'clock, thinking about what Linda had said. But despite everything, he slept soundly and woke up fully rested soon after five. He was in his office by six-thirty. A thought had begun to develop in his mind. He checked his calendar for the period between now and Midsummer, and established that nothing compelled him to stay in Ystad. Somebody else could take charge of the poker case. Since Lennart Mattson was an early bird, Wallander knocked on his door. Mattson had just arrived when Wallander came to ask for four days' leave, starting the next day.

"I'm aware that this request comes out of the blue," he said. "But I have a personal reason. And I can make myself available during the Midsummer holiday, even though I'm down for a week's vacation then."

Mattson didn't protest. Wallander was granted four days off. He went back to his office and looked up on the Internet the exact locations of Amalienborg and Niklasgården. The information he found about the two institutions wasn't enough to help him decide which was the right one. Both of them seemed to care for people with a wide variety of serious disabilities.

He handed Jussi over to his neighbors, who would look after him for the next few days. The dog's kennel was deserted. Wallander lay down on top of the bed, set the alarm clock for three, and slept for a few hours.

It was four o'clock when he got into his car and set off northward. Dawn was enveloped by a diaphanous mist, but that meant it would be a fine day. He arrived in Mariefred shortly after noon. After lunch in a roadside restaurant, he dozed in his car for a while, then set off for Amalienborg, a former college with an annex that had been turned into a nursing home. At the front desk Wallander produced his police ID and hoped that would be sufficient for him to find out whether he had come to the right place. The receptionist wasn't sure what to do and got her supervisor, who studied Wallander's ID carefully.

"Signe von Enke," he said in a friendly tone. "That's all I need to know. Is she here or not? It's really about her parents, who have disappeared."

The supervisor's badge indicated that her name was Anna Gustafsson.

She listened to Wallander, then studied him for a moment before answering.

"A naval commander?" she said. "Is that him?"

"Yes, that's him," said Wallander, making no attempt to conceal his surprise.

"I've read about him in the newspapers."

"I'm talking about his daughter," said Wallander. "Is she here?"

Anna Gustafsson shook her head.

"No," she said. "We don't have anyone named Signe. None of our patients is the daughter of a naval commander. I can promise you that."

. . .

On the way to his next port of call, Wallander ran into a violent thunderstorm. The rain was so heavy that he was forced to stop, unable to see anything through the windshield. He drove down a side road and switched off the engine. As he sat there, enclosed in a kind of bubble, with the rain pelting against the car roof, he tried yet again to work out what had happened to the two missing persons. Even if Håkan von Enke was the first to run away, or to be the victim of a crime or an accident, that didn't necessarily mean that Louise's disappearance was a direct consequence of what had happened to him. That was an elementary pearl of wisdom from Rydberg during his time as Wallander's mentor. Often an incident that happened or was discovered last was actually the beginning rather than the conclusion of a sequence of events. He thought about the messy state of one of Håkan von Enke's desk drawers. The compass inside his head was whirling around without settling on a direction in which to point.

The bottom line was that anything was possible. Not even the perception that Håkan von Enke was worried was necessarily fact. Wallander had seen ghosts before, even if he usually managed to stay immune to illusions. He had also tried to trace lots of missing persons during his career. Nearly always there were indications from the very beginning that there was either a natural explanation or there were grounds for being worried. But in the case of Håkan and Louise, he simply didn't know. Everything was very unclear, he thought as he sat in his car, waiting for the cloudburst to subside. A state of mental fog to match the lack of real-life visibility.

When the rain eventually stopped, he made his way to Niklasgården, attractively located on the shore of a lake that his map told him was called Vångsjön. The white-painted wood buildings were on a slope dotted with clumps of tall trees, and beyond them extensive cornfields and pastureland. Wallander got out of the car and took deep breaths of air made invigorating after the rain. It was like looking at one of the old posters that decorated the walls of his classroom at school in Limhamn: biblical landscapes, always Palestine with shepherds and flocks of sheep, and Swedish agricultural landscapes in all their variations. For a moment he was overcome by a nostalgic longing to be back in the days when those posters had dominated his thoughts, but he shrugged it off. He knew that sentimentality about the past only drew attention to the fact that he was getting old, and made the process even more painful and frightening.

He took a pair of binoculars from his backpack and scanned the buildings and their park-like grounds. Wallander couldn't help smiling at the thought that he was surveying this pretty, summery scene as a sort of periscope in the guise of an old, scratched Peugeot. He noticed several wheelchairs standing in the shade of some trees. He adjusted the focus and tried to hold the binoculars steady. There were people sitting in the wheelchairs with their heads drooping. One of them, a woman whose age he found impossible to guess, was resting her chin on her chest. In another wheelchair was a man, a young man as far as Wallander could make out, with his head leaning back as if his neck was incapable of supporting it. Wallander lowered his binoculars. He felt uneasy about what lay in store for him. He returned to his car and drove up to the main building, where signs informed him that the Södermanland county council welcomed him and told visitors where various paths led. Wallander went into the reception area. He rang a bell and waited. He could hear a radio somewhere in the background. A woman emerged from an adjacent room. She was in her forties, and Wallander was immediately struck by her beauty. She had short black hair and dark eyes, and she greeted him with a smile. When she spoke, he could hear that she had a foreign accent. Wallander guessed that she came from an Arab country. He showed her his ID and asked his question. He didn't receive a direct answer. The beautiful woman continued to smile at him.

"This is the first time a police officer has visited us," she said. "And you've come from so far away! But I'm afraid I can't give you any names. Everybody living here has a right to privacy."

"I understand that, of course," said Wallander. "But if necessary I will get a warrant that will give me the right to go through every single room you have here and all your records, for every single patient. I would rather not do that. It would be sufficient for you to simply nod or shake your head. Then I promise to go away and never come back."

She thought for a moment before answering. Wallander was still taken by how beautiful she was.

"Ask your question," she said eventually. "I see your point."

"Is there somebody living here named Signe von Enke? She's about forty years old and handicapped from birth."

She nodded. Just once, but that was enough. Now Wallander knew where Signe was. Before going any further he must talk to Ytterberg.

He had managed to tear his eyes away from the woman and turn away, when it occurred to him that there was another question she might be prepared to answer. He looked at her again.

"One more thing," he said. "When did Signe last have a visitor?"

She thought for a moment before answering. With words this time, not a movement of the head.

"That was a few months ago," she said. "Sometime in April. I can check if it's important."

"It's extremely important," Wallander said. "It would be a great help."

She disappeared into the room she had emerged from earlier. A few minutes later she came back with a sheet of paper in her hand.

"April tenth," she said. "That was her latest visit. Nobody has been here since then. She has become a very lonely person."

Wallander thought for a moment. **The tenth of April. The day before Håkan von Enke set out on his walk. And never came back.**

"I assume it was her father who visited her on that occasion," he said slowly.

She nodded.

Wallander left Niklasgården and drove to Stockholm. He parked outside the building in Grevgatan and unlocked the apartment with the keys Linda had given him.

He realized he would have to go back to the beginning. But the beginning of what?

He stood in the middle of the living room for a long time, trying to understand. But he couldn't think of anything that would further his understanding of the case.

He was surrounded by silence. At submarine depth, where the restless movement of the ocean was undetectable.

12

Wallander spent the night in the empty apartment.

Because it was warm, almost oppressively so, he left some windows ajar and watched the thin curtains swaying gently. He could occasionally hear people shouting in the street below. Wallander had the feeling that he was listening to phantoms, as you always do in recently vacated houses or apartments. But it wasn't to save the cost of a hotel room that he had asked Linda for the keys to the apartment. Wallander knew from experience that first impressions are often the most important ones in a criminal investigation. A return visit rarely produces anything new. But this time he knew what he was looking for.

Wallander tiptoed around in his socks to avoid making the neighbors suspicious. He went through Håkan's study and Louise's two chests of drawers. He also searched the big bookcase in the living room, and any closets and shelves he could find. By about ten o'clock, when he slipped cautiously out of the apartment to find somewhere to eat, he was as sure as he could be. All trace of the handicapped daughter had been carefully removed.

Wallander ate at what claimed to be a Hungarian restaurant, despite the fact that all the waiters and other staff in the open-plan kitchen spoke Italian. As he returned to the third-floor apartment in the slow-moving elevator, he wondered where he should sleep. There was a sofa in Håkan's study, but he eventually lay down under a tartan blanket on a couch in the living room, where he had drunk tea with Louise.

He was woken up at about one by a particularly noisy group of merrymakers, and as he lay in the dark room, he was suddenly wide awake. It was absurd for there to be absolutely nothing at all in the apartment to mark the existence of the woman who was now living at Niklasgården. It almost made him physically ill not to find any pictures or even documents, the bureaucratic identification indicators that surround all Swedes from birth. He got up and tiptoed around once more. He was carrying a penlight, and he occasionally used it to illuminate the darkest corners. He avoided turning on more than a single lamp here and there in case someone in the apartment building across the street might react, but at the same time he also thought of the lamps that Håkan von Enke always used to leave burning all night. Wasn't the invisible line between reality and lies in the von Enke family unusually easy to cross? He stood in the middle of the kitchen and thought it over yet again. Then he carried on indefatigably, becoming the bloodhound he could sometimes arouse within himself, and resolved not to allow it to rest until it picked up the trail of Signe; it had to be here somewhere.

He succeeded at about four in the morning. In the bookcase, hidden behind some big art books, he found a photo album. It did not contain many pictures, but they were carefully mounted, most of them in faded color, a few in black and white. There was no written commentary, only pictures. There was no picture of the two siblings together, but then he hadn't expected to find one. When Hans was born, Signe had already vanished, been whisked away, rubbed out. Wallander counted less than fifty photos. Signe was alone in most of them, lying in various positions. But in the last picture Louise was holding her, looking away from the camera. Wallander felt sad to note that the picture made it clear that Louise would have preferred not to have to sit there, holding the child in her arms. The photograph exuded an atmosphere of intense desolation. Wallander shook his head, feeling very uncomfortable.

He lay down on the sofa again. He was exhausted but also relieved, and he fell asleep immediately. He woke up with a start at about eight o'clock when a car in the street below sounded its horn loudly. He had been dreaming about horses. A herd had come galloping over the sand dunes at Mossby and raced straight into the water. He tried to figure out what the dream meant, but he failed. It hardly ever worked; he had no idea how to do it. He ran a bath, drank some coffee, and called Ytterberg at about nine. He was in a meeting. Wallander asked the receptionist to pass on a message and received a text in response saying that Ytterberg could meet him at ten-thirty at city hall, on the side overlooking the water. Wallander was waiting there when Ytterberg arrived on his bicycle. There was a café nearby, and before long they were sitting at a table, each with a cup of coffee.

"What are you doing here?" asked Ytterberg. "I thought you preferred little towns or rural areas."

"I do. But sometimes you have no choice."

Wallander told him about Signe. Ytterberg listened intently without interrupting. Wallander finished by mentioning the photo album he had discovered during the night. He had brought it with him in a plastic bag, and he placed it on the table. Ytterberg slid his coffee cup to one side, wiped his hands on a paper napkin, and leafed carefully through the album.

"How old is she now?" he asked. "About forty?"

"Yes, if I understood Atkins correctly."

"There aren't any pictures of her in here after the age of two, or three at the most."

"Exactly," said Wallander. "Unless there's another album. But I don't think so. After the age of two she's been expunged."

Ytterberg pulled a face and carefully slid the album back into the plastic bag. A white-painted passenger boat chugged past along Riddarfjärden. Wallander moved his chair into the shade.

"I thought of going back to Niklasgården," Wallander said. "After all, I'm now a member of this girl's family. But I need the go-ahead from you. You should be aware of what I'm doing."

"What good do you think it would do, meeting her?"

"I don't know. But her father visited her the day before he disappeared. And she hasn't had any visitors since then."

Ytterberg thought for a while before replying.

"It's remarkable that Louise hasn't been to see her the entire time since he disappeared. What do you make of that?"

"I don't make anything of it. But I wonder just as much as you do. Maybe we should go there together?"

"No, you go on your own. I'll give them a call and tell them you have the right to see her."

Wallander walked down to the edge of the quay and gazed out over the water while Ytterberg made his call. The sun was high in the clear blue sky. It's full summer now, he thought. After a while Ytterberg came and stood beside him.

"All set," he said. "But there's something you should know. The woman I spoke to said that Signe von Enke doesn't speak. Not because she doesn't want to, but because she can't. I don't know if I understood everything correctly, but she seems to have been born without vocal cords. Among other things."

Wallander turned to look at him.

"Among other things?"

"She's evidently extremely handicapped. Lots of essential parts are missing. I have to say I'm glad it's not me going there. Especially not today."

"What's special about today?"

"It's such lovely weather," said Ytterberg. "One of the first summer days this year. I'd rather not be upset if I can avoid it."

"Did she speak with a foreign accent?" Wallander asked as they walked away from the quay. "The woman at Niklasgården, I mean."

"Yes, she did. She had a lovely voice. She said her name was Fatima. I would guess she's from Iraq or Iran."

Wallander promised to get in touch later that day. He had parked outside the main entrance to city hall, and he just managed to drive off before an alert parking attendant turned up. He drove out of town and pulled up outside Niklasgården about an hour later. When he entered the reception area he was received by an elderly man who introduced himself as Artur Källberg—he was on duty in the afternoons until midnight.

"Let's start at the beginning," Wallander said. "Tell me about Signe's condition."

"She's one of our most severely affected patients," Artur Källberg informed him. "When she was born, nobody thought she would live very long. But some people have a will to live that few ordinary mortals can begin to comprehend."

"Can you be more precise?" Wallander asked. "What exactly is wrong with her?"

Källberg hesitated before answering, as if weighing whether Wallander would be able to cope with hearing all the facts; or possibly if he was worthy of hearing the full truth. Wallander became impatient.

"I'm listening," he said.

"She's missing both arms. And there's something wrong with her vocal cords, which means that she can't talk, plus congenital brain damage. She also has a malformation of the spine. That means her movements are incredibly limited."

"Meaning what, exactly?"

"She has a small amount of mobility in her neck and head. For instance, she can blink."

Wallander tried to envisage the horrific possibility that Linda might have given birth to a child with such severe disabilities. How would he have reacted? Could he imagine what this tragedy must have meant for Håkan and Louise? Wallander was unable to decide how he would have coped with it.

"How long has she been here?" he asked.

"During the early years of her life she was cared for in a home for severely handicapped children," said Källberg. "It was on Lidingö, but it closed in 1972."

Wallander raised his hand.

"Let's be exact," he said. "Assume that the only thing I know about this girl is her name."

"Then perhaps we should stop calling her a girl," said Källberg. "She's about to turn forty-one years old. Guess when."

"How on earth should I know?"

"It's her birthday today. Under normal circumstances, her father would have come and spent the afternoon here with us. But as things stand, no one is coming."

Källberg seemed troubled by the thought that Signe von Enke might be forced to endure a birthday without a visit.

One question was more important than any other, but Wallander decided to wait and do everything in order. He took his battered notebook out of his pocket.

"So," said Wallander, "she was born on June 6, 1967, is that right?"

"Yes, that's right."

"Did she ever spend any time at home with her parents?"

"According to the case notes I've been through, she was taken directly from the hospital to the Nyhaga home on Lidingö. When it became necessary to expand the home, the neighbors were scared that their properties would go down in value. I don't know exactly what they did in order to put a wrench in the works, but they not only prevented the expansion, they managed to get the home closed down completely."

"So where was she transferred?"

"She ended up on a sort of nursing-home merry-go-round. She went from one place to another, and spent a year in a home on Gotland, just outside Hemse. But she came here twenty-nine years ago, and she's been here ever since."

Wallander noted it all down. The image of Klara without any arms kept cropping up in his mind's eye with macabre obstinacy.

"Tell me about her capabilities," Wallander said. "You've done that already to an extent, but I'm thinking about how much she understands. Just how much is she aware of?"

"We don't know. She only expresses herself by means of basic reactions, and even that is done via body language that can be hard to interpret for anyone who isn't used to her. We regard her as a sort of infant with a long experience of life."

"Is it possible to figure out what she's thinking?"

"No. But nothing suggests that she's aware of how great her suffering is. She never gives any indication of pain or despair. And if that is a reflection of the facts, it's obviously something we can be grateful for."

Wallander nodded. He thought he understood. But now he was ready to ask the most important question.

"Her father came to visit her," he said. "How often?"

"At least once a month. Sometimes more. They weren't short visits—he never stayed for less than several hours."

"What did he do? If they couldn't talk?"

"**She** can't talk. He sat there and talked to her. It was

very moving. He would sit there and tell her about everything, about everyday things, about life in their own little world and also in the world at large. He spoke to her just as you would speak to another adult, without ever tiring."

"What about when he was at sea? For many years he was in charge of submarines and other naval vessels."

"He would always explain that he was going to be away. It was touching to hear him telling her all about it."

"And who came to visit Signe when he was away? Her mother?"

Källberg's answer was clear and cold, and it came without hesitation.

"She has never been here. I've been working at Niklasgården since 1994. She has never been to visit her daughter during that time. The only visitor Signe ever had was her father."

"Are you saying that Louise never came here to see her daughter?"

"Never."

"Surely that must be unusual?"

Källberg shrugged.

"Not necessarily. Some people simply can't cope with the sight of suffering."

Wallander put his notebook back in his pocket. He wondered if he would be able to interpret what he had scribbled down.

"I'd like to see her," he said. "Assuming that wouldn't upset her, of course."

"There's something I forgot to mention," said Källberg. "She sees very badly. She perceives people as a sort of blur against a gray background. At least, that's what the doctors say."

"So she recognized her father by his voice?" Wallander wondered.

"Presumably, yes. That seemed to be the case, judging by her body language."

Wallander stood up, but Källberg remained seated.

"Are you absolutely certain you want to see her?"

"Yes," said Wallander. "I'm absolutely certain."

That wasn't true, of course. What he really wanted to see was her room.

They went out through the glass doors, which closed silently behind them. Källberg opened the door to a room at the end of a hallway. It was a bright room with a plastic mat on the floor. It held a couple of chairs, a bookcase, and a bed, on which Signe von Enke lay hunched up.

"Leave me alone with her," Wallander requested. "Wait outside."

After Källberg left, Wallander took a quick look around the room. **Why is there a bookcase here when the occupant is blind and unaware of what is going on around her?** He took a step closer to the bed and looked at Signe. She had fair, short-cropped hair and looked a bit like Hans, her brother. Her eyes were open but staring vacantly out into the room. She was breathing irregularly, as if every breath caused her pain. Wallander felt a lump in his throat. Why did a human being have to suffer like this? With no hope of a life

with even an illusory glimmer of meaning? He continued looking at her, but she seemed unaware of his presence. Time stood still. He was in a strange museum, he
thought, a place where he was forced to look at an immured person. The girl in the tower. Immured inside
herself.

He looked at the chair next to the window. **The
chair Håkan von Enke usually sat in when he visited
his daughter.** He moved over to the bookcase and
squatted down. There were children's books, picture
books. Signe von Enke had not developed at all; she
was still a child. Wallander went carefully through the
bookcase, taking out books and making sure there was
nothing hidden behind them.

He found what he was looking for behind a row of
Babar the Elephant books. Not a photo album this
time, but then he hadn't expected to find that. He
hadn't been at all sure of what exactly he was looking
for, but there was something missing from the apartment in Grevgatan, he was convinced of that. Either
somebody had weeded out documents, or Håkan had
done it himself. And if it had been him, where could
he have hidden something but in this room? Among
the Babar books, which he and Linda had both read
when they were children, was a thick file with hard
black covers, held closed by two thick rubber bands.
Wallander hesitated: should he open it here and now?
Instead he slipped off his jacket and fit the book into
the capacious inside pocket. Signe was still lying there
with her eyes open wide, motionless.

Wallander opened the door. Källberg was poking a finger into the soil of a potted plant that badly needed watering.

"It's very sad," said Wallander. "Just looking at her makes me break into a cold sweat."

They went back to reception.

"A few years ago we had a visit from a young art school student," said Källberg. "Her brother lived here, but he's dead now. She asked permission to sketch the patients. She was very good—she had brought drawings with her to show what she could do. I was in favor of it, but the board of trustees decided it would be a breach of the patients' privacy."

"What happens when a patient dies?"

"Most of them have a family. But one or two are buried quietly with no family present. On such occasions as many of us as possible try to attend. There's not a lot of turnover among the staff here. We become a sort of new family for patients like that."

After taking his leave, Wallander drove to Mariefred and had a meal in a pizzeria. There were a few tables on the sidewalk, and he sat outside over a cup of coffee after he had finished eating. Thunderclouds were building up on the horizon. A man was playing an accordion in front of a little store not far away. His music was hopelessly out of tune—he was obviously a beggar, not a street musician. When Wallander couldn't put up with it anymore, he drained his coffee and returned to Stockholm. He had just stepped in through the door of the apartment in Grevgatan when the phone rang. The ringing echoed through the empty rooms. Nobody left

a message on the answering machine. Wallander listened to the earlier messages, from a dentist and a
seamstress. Louise had been given a new appointment
after a cancellation—but when was that? Wallander
noted the dentist's name: Sköldin. The seamstress simply said, "Your dress is ready." But she left no name, no
time.

It suddenly started pelting down rain. Wallander
stood by the window, looking into the street. He felt
like an intruder. But the disappearance of the von
Enkes had significance for other people's lives, people
close to him. That was why he was standing there now.

After an hour or more the rain eased up—it had
been one of the heaviest downpours to affect the capital that summer. Basements were flooded, traffic lights
were out of order due to shorts in the electric cables.
But Wallander noticed none of that. He was fully occupied with the ledger Håkan von Enke had hidden in
his daughter's room. It was clear after only a few minutes that he was faced with a hodgepodge of documents. There were short haiku poems, photocopied
extracts from the Swedish supreme commander's war
diary from the fall of 1982, more or less obscure apho-
risms Håkan von Enke had formulated, and much
more—including press clippings, photographs, and
some smudged watercolors. Wallander turned page
after page of this remarkable diary, if you could call it
that, with the growing feeling that it was the last thing
he would have expected of von Enke. He started by
leafing through the book, trying to get an overall sense
of it. Then he started again at the beginning, reading

more carefully this time. When he finally closed it and stretched his back, it struck him that it had thrown no new light on anything at all.

He went out for dinner. The heavy rain had passed. It was nine o'clock by the time he returned to the empty apartment. He turned once again to the pages inside the black covers, and started working his way through the contents for the third time.

He told himself he was searching for the **other** contents, the invisible writing between the lines.

It must be there somewhere. He was sure of that.

13

It was nearly three in the morning when Wallander got up from the sofa and walked over to the window. It had started raining again, but only a drizzle now. He forced his weary brain to return to that party in Djursholm when Håkan had told him about the submarines. Wallander felt sure that even then there were documents hidden among Signe's Babar books. It was Håkan's secret room, safer than a bank vault. What made Wallander so sure was that von Enke had dated some of the papers. The last date was the day before his seventy-fifth birthday party. He had visited his daughter at least once more after that, the day before he disappeared. But he hadn't written anything then.

I can't go any farther, he had written that last time. **But I've come far enough.** Those were his last words. Apart from one final word that had evidently been added later, written with a different pen. **Swamp.** That was all. Just one word.

That was probably the last word he ever wrote, Wallander thought. He couldn't be sure, and for the moment he had no suspicion that it might be important. Other things he had found in the collection of documents said much more about the man behind the pen.

What impressed him most of all were the photocopies of Supreme Commander Lennart Ljung's war diaries. It wasn't the diary itself that was important, but von Enke's margin notes. They were often written in red ink, sometimes crossed out or corrected, with additions sometimes many years after the first notes were written, containing completely new lines of thought. Sometimes he also drew little matchstick men between the lines, little devils with axes or red-hot pokers in their hands. At one point he had pasted in a reduced-size sea chart of Hårsfjärden. He had marked various points in red, sketched in the progress of unknown vessels, and then crossed everything out again and started from the beginning once more. He had also noted down the number of depth charges laid, various underwater minefields, and sonar contacts. At times everything merged to form an incomprehensible mush before Wallander's weary eyes. So he would go into the kitchen, rinse his face in cold water, and start again.

Von Enke had often pressed so hard that he made holes in the paper. The notes suggested an entirely different temperament, almost an obsession, in the old submarine commander. There was none of the calm he had displayed in delivering his monologue in that windowless room.

Wallander remained at his post by the window, listening to a group of young men yelling out obscenities as they staggered home through the night. The ones shouting are the ones who failed to pick up a partner, he thought, the ones forced to go home alone. That's what often happened to me forty years ago.

Wallander had read the extracts from the war diaries so carefully that he thought he could probably recite every sentence by heart. **Wednesday, September 24, 1980.** The supreme commander visited an air force regiment not far from Stockholm, noted that they were still having difficulty in recruiting officers despite the investment of large sums of money in refurbishing the barracks to make them more attractive. Von Enke hadn't made a single margin note in this section. It wasn't until much farther down on the page that his red pen leaped into action, a sort of bayonet charge on the document. **The question of foreign submarines in Swedish territorial waters has arisen once more today. Last week a submarine was discovered off Utö, well inside Swedish territory. Parts of the submarine were seen on the surface and identified it beyond doubt as a Misky class vessel. The Soviet Union and Poland have submarines of this type.**

The notes suddenly became difficult to read. Wallander borrowed a magnifying glass from von Enke's desk and eventually managed to work out what the notes said. He wondered what "parts" they claimed had been seen. Periscope? Conning tower? How long had the submarine been visible? Who saw it? What was its course? He was irritated by the lack of detail in the diary. Von Enke had commented on the term "Misky class": **NATO and whiskey. The West European designation of the submarine in question.** He had underlined in red the last few lines on the page. **Snap shots and depth charges were fired, but the submarine could not be forced to surface. It is assumed that it then left Swedish territorial waters.** Wallander sat for a while wondering what snap shots were, but he could find no explanation from either his own experience or the book he had in front of him. A margin note announced: **You don't force a submarine up to the surface with warning shots, only with volleys for effect. Why did they let the submarine get away?**

The notes continued until September 28. That was when Ljung had talks with the head of the navy, who had been on a visit to Yugoslavia. From then on Håkan von Enke was no longer interested. No more notes, no matchstick men, no exclamation points. But farther down the page Ljung is dissatisfied with a press release from the navy's information service. He calls on the head of the navy to take whoever was responsible to task. The red pen comments in the margin: **It would be more appropriate to clamp down on other blunders.**

The submarine off Utö. Wallander recalled having heard about that during the party in Djursholm. **That**

was when it all began, he seemed to remember Håkan von Enke saying. Or something like that. He didn't remember the exact words.

The other extract from the war diaries was significantly longer. It covered the period from October 5 to October 15, 1982. That was the big gala performance, Wallander thought. Sweden was at the center of the world's attention. Everybody was watching as the Swedish navy and its helicopters tried to pin down the foreign submarines or possible submarines or non-submarines. And while all this was happening, there was a change of government in Sweden. The supreme commander had great difficulty keeping both the outgoing and incoming governments informed. At one point Thorbjörn Fälldin seemed to forget that he was on his way out, and Olof Palme angrily expressed his surprise that he had not been kept fully informed of what was happening out at Hårsfjärden. The supreme commander wasn't allowed a moment's rest. He was traveling back and forth like a yo-yo between Berga and the two governments that were treading on each other's toes. And in addition, he had to answer sarcastic questions from the leader of the Swedish Conservative Party, Ulf Adelsohn, about why it had not been possible to make the intruding submarines surface. Håkan von Enke commented ironically that for once a politician was asking the same questions he was.

Wallander now started writing names and times in his battered notebook. He wasn't sure why. Perhaps just to keep the mass of details in some sort of order so that he could try to begin to understand von Enke's increasingly bitter notes more clearly.

He sometimes had the impression that von Enke was trying to rewrite history. He's like that lunatic in the asylum who spent forty years reading the classics and changing the endings when he thought they were too tragic. Von Enke writes what he thinks **should** have happened. And in doing so asks the question: Why didn't it happen?

Wallander had long since taken off his shirt and, sitting half-naked on the sofa, eventually began to wonder if Håkan von Enke was paranoid. But he soon dismissed the thought. The notes in the margins and between the lines were angry, but at the same time clear and logical, as far as Wallander could understand.

At one point a few simple words were inserted into the text, almost like a haiku.

> **Incidents under the surface**
> **Nobody notices**
> **What is happening.**

> **Incidents under the surface**
> **The submarine sneaks away**
> **Nobody wants it to be forced up.**

Is that how it was? Wallander wondered. Had everything been a show? Had there never been any real desire to identify the submarine? But for Håkan von Enke there was another, more important question. He was involved in a different hunt, not for a submarine but for a person. It kept recurring in his notes, like a stubbornly repeated drumroll. Who makes the decisions? Who changes them? Who?

At another point von Enke makes a comment: **In order to identify the person or persons who actually made these decisions, I have to answer the question why. Assuming it hasn't been answered already.** He didn't sound angry, or agitated, but totally calm. He hadn't made any holes in the paper here.

By this stage Wallander no longer found it difficult to understand Håkan von Enke's version of what had happened. Orders had been given, the chain of command had been followed—but suddenly somebody had intervened, changed course, and before anybody realized what was happening, the submarines had vanished. Von Enke mentioned no names, or at least didn't point an accusing finger at anybody. But sometimes he referred to people as **X** or **Y** or **Z**. He's hiding them, Wallander thought. And then he hides his diary among Signe's Babar books. And disappears. And now Louise has disappeared as well.

Studying the photocopies of the war diaries took up most of Wallander's time that night; but he also examined the rest of the material in great detail. There was an overview of Håkan von Enke's life, from the day he first decided to become a naval officer. Photographs, souvenirs, picture postcards. School reports, military examination results, appointments. There were also wedding photographs of him and Louise, and pictures of Hans at various ages. When Wallander finally stood up and gazed out the window into the summer night and the drizzle, he thought: I know more than I did; but I can't say that anything has become any clearer. Not why he's been missing for nearly two months now, or why Louise has vanished as well. But I know more about who Håkan von Enke is.

Those were his final thoughts before he lay down on the sofa at last, pulled the blanket over himself, and fell asleep.

When he woke up the next morning he had a slight headache. It was eight o'clock; his mouth was as dry as if he'd been boozing the night before. But as soon as he opened his eyes he knew what he was going to do. He made the phone call before he'd even tasted his coffee. Sten Nordlander answered after the second ring.

"I'm back in Stockholm," said Wallander. "I need to see you."

"I was just about to go out for a little trip in my boat—if you'd called a couple of minutes later you would have missed me. If you want to, you can come with me. We could chat to our hearts' content."

"I don't have much in the way of boating gear with me."

"I can supply everything. Where are you?"

"In Grevgatan."

"I'll pick you up in half an hour."

Sten Nordlander was wearing shabby gray overalls with the Swedish navy emblem when he met Wallander. On the backseat of his car was a large basket with food and thermoses. They drove out toward Farsta, then turned off onto small roads and eventually came to the little marina where Nordlander kept his boat. Nordlander had noticed the plastic bag and the file with the black covers, but he made no comment. And Wallander preferred to wait until they were in the boat.

They stood on the dock admiring the gleaming, newly varnished wooden boat.

"A genuine Pettersson," said Nordlander. "Authentic through and through. They don't make boats like this anymore. Plastic means less work when you need to make your boat ready for launching in the spring, but it's impossible to fall in love with a plastic boat the way you can a wooden boat. One like this smells like a bouquet of flowers. Anyway, let's go take a look at Hårsfjärden."

Wallander was surprised. He had lost his sense of direction once they had left town, and assumed that the boat was moored by an inland lake, or perhaps Lake Mälaren. But now he could see that he was looking out toward Utö and the Baltic Sea, as Nordlander pointed out their location on a sea chart. To the northwest were Mysingen and Hårsfjärden, and the legendary Muskö naval base.

Sten Nordlander gave Wallander a pair of overalls similar to the ones he was wearing, and also a dark blue peaked cap.

"Now you look presentable," Nordlander said when Wallander had changed into the borrowed gear.

The boat had a diesel engine. Wallander started it

like a pro. He hoped there wouldn't be too much of a wind once they came out into the navigable channels.

Nordlander concentrated on the route ahead, one hand on the attractively carved wooden steering wheel.

"Ten knots," he said. "That's about right. Gives you the opportunity to enjoy the sea rather than race off as if you were in a hurry to reach the horizon. What was it you wanted to talk about?"

"I went to see Signe yesterday," Wallander said. "In her nursing home. She was lying curled up in bed, like a little child, even though she's forty years old."

Sten Nordlander raised a hand demonstratively.

"I don't want to hear. If Håkan or Louise had wanted to tell me about her, they would have."

"I won't say another word about her."

"Is that why you called me? To tell me about her? I find that hard to believe."

"I found something. Something I'd like you to take a closer look at when we get a chance."

Wallander described the folder, without going into detail about the contents. He wanted Nordlander to discover that for himself.

"That sounds remarkable," he said when Wallander had finished.

"Why? What surprises you about it?"

"That Håkan kept a diary. He wasn't the writing type. We went on a trip to England once, and he didn't send any postcards—he said he had no idea what to write. His logbooks weren't exactly compelling reading either."

"He even seems to have written what look like poems."

"I find that very hard to believe."

"You'll see for yourself."

"What's it all about?"

"Most of it is about the place we're heading for."

"Muskö?"

"Hårsfjärden. The submarines. He seems to have been obsessed with all those events at the beginning of the eighties."

Nordlander stretched out an arm and pointed in the direction of Utö.

"That's where they were searching for submarines in 1980," he said.

"In September," Wallander elaborated. "They thought it was one of the so-called Whiskey class, as NATO calls them. Probably Russian, but it could also have been Polish."

Nordlander gave him an appraising look.

"You've been doing your homework, haven't you?"

Nordlander gave Wallander control of the wheel and produced coffee cups and a thermos. Wallander maintained their course by aiming at a spot on the horizon that the skipper had pointed out to him. A coast guard ship heading in the opposite direction caused a swell as it passed by. Nordlander switched off the engine and allowed the boat to drift while they drank coffee and ate sandwiches.

"Håkan wasn't the only one who was upset," he said. "A lot of us wondered what on earth was going on. It was several years after the Wennerström affair, but there were a lot of rumors going around."

"About what?"

Nordlander cocked his head, challenging Wallander to say what he should already know.

"Spies?"

"It simply wasn't plausible for the submarines that were definitely present under the surface of Hårsfjärden always to be one step ahead of us. They acted like they knew what tactics we were adopting, and where our mines were laid. It was as if they could hear all the discussions our superiors were having. There were rumors about a spy even better placed than Wennerström. Don't forget that this was the time when a spy in Norway, Arne Treholt, was moving in Norwegian government circles, and Willy Brandt's secretary was spying for East Germany. The suspicions didn't lead anywhere. Nobody was exposed. But that doesn't mean there wasn't somebody high up in the Swedish military who was spying."

Wallander thought about the letters X, Y, and Z in von Enke's margin notes.

"There must have been individuals you suspected?"

"There were naval officers who thought a lot of facts suggested that Palme himself was a spy. I always thought that was nonsense. But the truth is, nobody was above suspicion. And we were being attacked in different ways."

"Attacked?"

"Cutbacks. All the available money was being spent

on guided missiles and on the air force. The navy was being squeezed more and more. Quite a few journalists at the time spoke dismissively about our 'budget submarines.' They figured the alleged invaders had been invented as part of a plan for the navy to get more and better resources."

"Were you ever doubtful?"

"What about?"

"About the existence of the submarines."

"Never. Of course the Russian submarines existed."

Wallander produced the black file from its plastic bag. He felt sure Sten Nordlander had never seen it before. His surprised expression didn't seem put on. He dried his hands and placed the open file on his knee. There was hardly any wind, barely a ripple on the surface of the sea.

Nordlander leafed slowly through the pages. He occasionally looked up to check where the boat was drifting, then looked back down at the file. When he came to the end, he closed it, handed it back to Wallander, and shook his head.

"I'm astonished," he said. "But then, I knew Håkan was looking into these matters. I just didn't realize he was doing it in so much detail. What would you call it? A diary? A private memoir?"

"I think it can be read in two ways," said Wallander. "Partly just as it stands. But also as an incomplete investigation into what happened."

"Incomplete?"

He's right, Wallander thought. Why did I say that?

The book is presumably just the opposite. Something completed and closed.

"You're probably right," Wallander said. "He must have finished it. But what did he think he would achieve?"

"It was a long time before I realized how much time he was spending in archives, reading reports, investigation accounts, books. And he spoke to everybody you could think of. Sometimes people would call me and ask what Håkan was up to. I just told them I thought he wanted to know the truth about what had happened."

"And what he was doing wasn't popular, I gather? That's what he told me."

"I think that in the end he was seen as unreliable. That was tragic. Nobody in the navy was more honest and conscientious than Håkan. He must have been deeply hurt, even if he never said anything."

Nordlander lifted the hatch and took a look at the engine.

"A real beauty, like a beating heart," he said as he closed the hatch again. "I once worked as chief engineer on one of our two Halland class destroyers, the **Småland.** Just being in her engine room was one of the greatest experiences of my life. There were two de Laval turbines that produced almost sixty thousand horsepower. She was a thirty-five-hundred-ton vessel, but we could shift her through the water at thirty-five knots max. That was something special. It was good to be alive."

"I have a question," Wallander said. "It's extremely important. Is there anything in the stuff you've just looked through that shouldn't be there?"

"Something secret, you mean?" said Nordlander, frowning. "Not that I could see."

"Did anything surprise you?"

"I didn't read in detail. I could barely decipher the margin comments. But nothing gave me pause."

"Then can you explain to me why he hid the stuff away?"

Nordlander hesitated before answering. He contemplated a sailboat passing some distance away.

"I don't understand what could have been secret about it," he said eventually. "Who was he hiding it from?"

Wallander pricked up his ears. Something the man sitting beside him had said was important. But he couldn't pin it down. He memorized both sentences.

Nordlander started the engine again and revved up to ten knots, heading for Mysingen and Hårsfjärden. Wallander stood beside him. Over the next few hours Sten Nordlander took him on a guided tour of Muskö and Hårsfjärden. He pointed out where the depth charges had been sunk, and where the submarines might have been able to escape through minefields that had not been activated. The whole time, Wallander was following their route on a sea chart, noting all the deep and hidden depressions. He understood that only a very well-trained crew could negotiate Hårsfjärden under the surface.

When Nordlander decided they had seen enough,

he changed course and headed for a cluster of islets and skerries in the narrows between Ornö and Utö. Beyond was the open sea. He skillfully guided the boat into an inlet in one of the skerries, and moored at the bottom of a cliff.

"Not many people know about this inlet," he said as he shut down the engine. "So I always have it to myself. Enjoy!"

Wallander jumped ashore and secured the mooring rope, then collected the basket and placed it on a convenient rock. It smelled like the sea and the vegetation that filled the crevices. He felt like a child again, on a journey of exploration on an unknown island.

"What's the island called?" he asked.

"It's not much more than a rocky outcrop. It doesn't have a name."

Without further ado Nordlander undressed and jumped into the water. Wallander watched his head bobbing up before disappearing again under the surface. He's like a submarine, Wallander thought. Practicing diving and surfacing. He's not worried about how cold the water is.

Nordlander clambered back up onto the rocks and took a large red towel from the picnic basket.

"You should give it a try," he said. "It's cold, but it does you good."

"Some other time perhaps. What's the water temperature?"

"There's a thermometer behind the compass. You can take a measurement while I get dried off and serve up the food."

Wallander found the thermometer attached to a little rubber ball. He let the ball float in the water, then pulled it out and took the reading.

"Fifty-two degrees," he said when he came back to where Nordlander was laying out the food. "Too cold for me. Do you go swimming in the winter as well?"

"No. But I've thought about it. We can eat in ten minutes. Go for a walk around the little island. You might find a message in a bottle from a capsized Russian submarine."

Wallander wondered if there was something behind Nordlander's words, but he didn't think so. Sten Nordlander wasn't a man who dealt in obscure subtexts.

He sat down on a large flat rock with an unobstructed view of the horizon, picked up a few stones, and threw them into the water. When had he last played ducks and drakes? He recalled a visit to Stenshuvud with Linda when she was a teenager and reluctant to take trips with him. They had played ducks and drakes then, and she was much better at it than he was. And now she's as good as married, he thought. She found the right man. If she hadn't, I wouldn't be standing here on this rocky outcrop, staring out to sea and wondering about his vanished parents.

One day he would teach Klara to skim flat stones over the water and watch them jump along like frogs before sinking.

He was just about to stand up and go—Sten Nordlander had shouted for him—but he remained seated with the last stone in his hand. Small, gray, a fragment of Swedish rock. A thought struck him, vague at first, but becoming clearer all the time.

He remained seated for so long that Nordlander had to shout for him again. Then he stood up and walked over to the picnic, but with the thought firmly lodged in his mind.

After he had been dropped off back at Grevgatan that evening by Sten Nordlander and watched him drive away, he hurried up the stairs to the apartment.

His suspicion was confirmed. The little gray stone that had been lying on Håkan von Enke's desk was missing.

14

The sea trip had tired Wallander out. It had also stimulated many thoughts. Not just about why the stone was missing. Something inside him had clicked when Sten Nordlander said: "Who was he hiding it from?" Håkan von Enke could have had only one reason for hiding his book. **There was still something going on.** He wasn't simply rooting around in the past; he wasn't trying to bring a sleeping or mummified truth to life. What had happened in the 1980s was linked to what was happening today.

It must have something to do with people. People

who were still alive. At one point in the book von Enke had written a list of names that had meant nothing to Wallander—with one exception, that of a man who often appeared in the media during the hunt for the submarines, a man highly placed in the Swedish navy: Sven-Erik Håkansson. Beside that name von Enke had written a cross, an exclamation point, and a question mark. What could that mean? The notes were not haphazard; everything was calculated, even if much of it was in a secret language that Wallander had only partially been able to interpret.

He took out the file again and examined the names once more, wondering if they were people involved somehow or other in the battle against the intruders, or if they were suspects. And if so, suspected of what?

He took a deep breath. **Håkan von Enke had been on the trail of a Russian spy.** Somebody who had given the Russian submarines sufficient information for them to fool their pursuers, even to dictate what weaponry they would need. Somebody who was still out there, who still hadn't been exposed. That was the person from whom von Enke had concealed his notes, the person he was afraid of.

The man outside the fence in Djursholm, Wallander thought. Was that someone who didn't like the idea of Håkan von Enke hunting down a spy?

Wallander adjusted the floor lamp next to the sofa and worked his way through the thick file yet again. He paused every time he came to notes that could possibly indicate traces of a spy. Perhaps that was also the answer to another question, the feeling that somebody had removed documents from the archive in von Enke's study. The person responsible for removing the papers was probably Håkan von Enke himself. It was all like some sort of Russian nesting doll. He had not only hidden his notes, but he had also hidden from outsiders what they actually meant. He had laid a smoke screen. Or perhaps rather a minefield that could be activated whenever he wanted, if he noticed that someone was getting close to him, someone who had no business being there.

Wallander eventually turned off the light and went to bed. But he couldn't get to sleep. On a sudden impulse, he got up, dressed, and went out. Earlier in his life when he was feeling especially lonely he had tried to improve the situation by going for long nocturnal walks. There wasn't a single street in Ystad that he hadn't become familiar with. Now he walked along Strandvägen and then turned left toward the bridge to Djurgården. It was a warm summer night and there were still people out and about, many of them drunk and boisterous. Wallander felt like a furtive stranger as he wandered through the shadows. He continued past the amusement park at Gröna Lund, and didn't turn back until he came to the Thielska art gallery. He wasn't thinking about anything in particular, just strolling around in the night instead of sleeping. When he arrived back at the apartment he fell asleep right away; his excursion had achieved its desired effect.

The following day he drove home. He was back in Skåne by midafternoon and stopped to stock up on provisions before tackling the final stretch and picking up Jussi, who was overjoyed to see him and left muddy paw prints on his clothes. After eating and sleeping for an hour or two, he sat down at the kitchen table with the file in front of him. He had taken out his strongest magnifying glass. His father had given it to him many years ago, when he had displayed a sudden interest in tiny insects crawling around in the grass. It was one of the few presents he had ever received, apart from the dog, Saga, and he treasured it. Now he used it to examine the photographs between the black covers, leaving the texts and margin notes in peace for a change.

One of the photos seemed to stick out like a sore thumb. It hadn't occurred to him before, but there was something too **civilian** about the picture. He was quite sure that nothing in the book was there by accident. Håkan von Enke was a careful and very dedicated hunter.

The photo, which was in black and white, had been taken at some sort of harbor. In the background was a building with no windows, presumably a warehouse. With the aid of the magnifying glass, Wallander was able to make out two trucks and some stacks of fish crates in a blurred area at the edge of the picture. The photographer had aimed the camera at two men standing by a fishing boat, an old-fashioned trawler. One of the men was old, the other very young, no more than a boy. Wallander guessed that the picture had been taken sometime in the sixties. The fashion was still wool sweaters and leather jackets, sou'westers and oilskins. The boat was white, and scraped up. Behind and between the older man's legs Wallander could just make out the registration plate. The last letter was **G.** The first letter was almost completely hidden, but the middle one could be an **R** or a **T.** The numbers were easier to read: **123.** Wallander sat down at his computer and Googled various search words in an attempt to find out where the trawler was registered. He soon established that there was only one possibility: the combination of letters had to be **NRG.** The trawler was based on the east coast, in the neighborhood of Norrköping. After a little more searching Wallander found the home pages of the National Administration of Shipping and Navigation and the National Board of Fisheries. He noted down the phone numbers on a scrap of paper and returned to the kitchen table. The phone rang. It was Linda, wondering why he hadn't been in touch.

"You just vanished into thin air," she said. "I think we have enough missing persons to contend with."

"You don't have to worry about me," said Wallander. "I came home an hour or so ago. I was planning to call you tomorrow."

"No," she said, "now! I—not to mention Hans—want to know what you've found out."

"Is he at home?"

"He's at work. I told him off this morning because he's never here. I tried to hammer it into him that one of these days I'll start working again. What will happen then?"

"Well, what will happen?"

"He'll have to help. Anyway, tell me all about it."

Wallander started to describe his visit to Signe, the

lonely, hunched-up creature with the blond hair, but before he had hit his stride, Klara started crying and Linda was forced to hang up. He promised to call her the following day.

The first thing he did when he arrived at the police station the next morning was to find Martinsson and figure out whether or not he would be on duty over the Midsummer holiday. Martinsson was, of all his colleagues, best acquainted with the constantly changing work schedule, and he was able to answer within a couple of minutes. Despite so many officers being on leave, Wallander would not be required to work over Midsummer. As for Martinsson, he had arranged to take his youngest daughter to a yoga camp in Denmark.

"I don't really know what it involves," he said, trying to hide his concern. "Is it normal for a thirteen-year-old to be so crazy about yoga?"

"Better that than a lot of other things."

"My two older children were into horses. Much less stressful. But this girl is different."

"We're all different," said Wallander mysteriously, and left the room.

He dialed the number he had tracked down the previous evening and soon discovered that NRG123 belonged to a fisherman by the name of Eskil Lundberg on Bokö in the Gryt southern archipelago. He made another call and, when an answering machine came on, he left a message saying it was urgent.

Then he called Linda and finished the conversation they had begun the previous evening. She had spoken to Hans, and as soon as possible they would go visit Signe. Wallander wasn't surprised, but he wondered if they really understood what was in store for them. What had he himself expected to find?

"We've decided to celebrate Midsummer," she said. "In spite of everything that's happened, and all the anguish over his parents' disappearance. We thought we'd cheer you up by coming to visit you."

"By all means," said Wallander. "I'm looking forward to it. What a nice surprise!"

He got a cup of coffee from the machine, which was actually working for once, and exchanged a few words with one of the forensic officers who had spent the night in a swamp where a confused woman appeared to have committed suicide. When the officer eventually arrived home at dawn, he had produced a frog from one of the many pockets in his uniform. His wife had been less than overjoyed.

Wallander returned to his office and managed to find yet another number in his overloaded address book. It was the last call he planned to make that morning before abandoning the missing von Enkes and returning to his routine police work. Earlier he had left a message on an answering machine. Now he was about to dial the cell phone number of that same person. This time he got through.

"Hans-Olov."

Wallander recognized the almost childish voice of the young professor of geology he had met in the course of duty several years ago. He could hear an announcement in the background about a flight departure.

"Wallander here. I gather you're at an airport?"

"Yes, Kastrup. I'm on my way back home after a geology congress in Chile, but my suitcase seems to have been lost."

"I need your help," said Wallander. "I'd like you to compare some stones."

"Sure thing. But can it wait until tomorrow? I'm always a wreck after a long flight."

Wallander remembered that Uddmark had no less than five children, despite his youth.

"I hope your presents for the children weren't in the missing bag."

"It's worse than that. It contains some beautiful stones I brought home with me."

"Is your office address the same as it was the last time we worked together? If it is I can send you the stones later today."

"What do you want me to do with them, apart from establishing what kind of rock they are?"

"I want to know if any of them might have originated in the U.S.A."

"Can you be more precise?"

"In the vicinity of San Diego in California, or somewhere on the east coast, near Boston."

"I'll see what I can do, but it sounds difficult. Do you have any idea how many different species of rock there are?"

Wallander told him that he didn't know, sympathized with him once again about the missing suitcase, hung up, and then hurried to join a meeting he should have been at. Someone had left a note on his desk saying it was important. He was the last person to enter the conference room, where the window was wide open because the forecast said it was going to be a hot day. He couldn't help thinking about all the times he had been in charge of these kinds of meetings. During all the years when it had been his responsibility, he had often dreamed of the day when the burden would no longer be on his shoulders. But now, when it was often somebody else in charge of investigations, he sometimes missed not being the driving force sorting through proposals and telling people what to do.

The man in charge today was a detective by the name of Ove Sunde. He had arrived in Ystad only the previous year, from Växjö. Somebody had whispered in Wallander's ear that a messy divorce and a less than successful investigation that led to a heated debate in the local newspaper, **Smålandsposten**, had induced him to request a transfer. He came from Gothenburg originally, and never made any attempt to disguise his dialect. Sunde was considered to be competent, but a bit on the lazy side. Another rumor suggested that he had found a new companion in Ystad, a woman young enough to be his daughter. Wallander distrusted men his own age who chased after women far too young for them. It rarely ended happily, but often led to new, heart-rending divorces.

It was doubtful, though, that his own constant loneliness was a better alternative.

Sunde began his presentation. It was about the case of the woman in the swamp, which was probably not just a suicide but also a murder. Her husband was found lying dead in their home in a little village not far from Marsvinsholm. The situation was complicated by the fact that a few days earlier the man had gone to the police station in Ystad and said that he thought his wife was planning to kill him. The officer who spoke to him hadn't taken him seriously because the man seemed confused and made a lot of contradictory claims. They needed to figure out as quickly as possible what had actually happened, before the media caught on to the fact that the man's complaint had been shelved. Wallander was annoyed by Sunde's excessively officious tone. He considered this fear of the opinion of the mass media sheer cowardice. If a mistake was made, it should be acknowledged and the consequences accepted.

He thought he should point that out, calmly and objectively, firmly but without losing his temper. But he said nothing. Martinsson was sitting at the other side of the table, watching him. He knows exactly what's going on inside my head at the moment, Wallander thought, and he agrees with me, whether I speak up now or hold my tongue.

After the meeting they drove out to the house where the dead man had been found. With photographs in their hands and plastic bags over their shoes, he and Martinsson went from room to room in the company of a forensic officer. Wallander suddenly experienced déjà vu, feeling like he had already visited this house at some point in the past and made an "ocular inspection" (as Lennart Mattson would no doubt have described it) of the crime scene. He hadn't, of course; it was simply that he had done the same thing so many times before. A few years ago he bought a book about a crime committed on the island of Värmdö off Stockholm in the early nineteenth century. As he read it, he became increasingly involved, and had the distinct feeling that he could have entered the story and together with the county sheriff and prosecutor worked out how the victims, man and wife, had been murdered. People have always been the same, and the most common crimes are more or less repeats of what happened in earlier times. They are nearly always due to arguments about money, or jealousy, sometimes revenge. Before him, generations of police officers, sheriffs, and prosecutors had made the same observations. Nowadays they had superior technical means of establishing evidence, but the ability to interpret what you see with your own eyes was still the key to police work.

Wallander stopped dead and broke off his train of thought. They had entered the couple's bedroom. There was blood on the floor and on one side of the bed. But what had caught Wallander's attention was a painting hanging on the wall above the bed. It depicted a capercaillie in a woodland setting. Martinsson materialized by his side.

"Painted by your father, right?"

Wallander nodded, but also shook his head in disbelief.

"I never cease to be amazed."

"Well, at least he didn't need to worry about forgeries," said Martinsson thoughtfully.

"Of course not," said Wallander. "From an artistic point of view, it's crap."

"Don't say that," protested Martinsson.

"I'm only calling a spade a spade," said Wallander. "Where's the murder weapon?"

They went out into the yard. A plastic tent had been erected over an old ax. Wallander could see blood high up on the shaft.

"Is there a plausible motive? How long had they been married?"

"They celebrated their golden wedding anniversary last year. They have four grown children and goodness knows how many grandchildren. Nobody can understand what happened."

"Is there money involved?"

"According to the neighbors they were both thrifty and stingy. I don't know yet how much they have stashed away. The bank's looking into it. But we can assume that there's a fair amount."

"It looks as if there was a fight," Wallander said after a few minutes' thought. "He resisted. Until we recover the body, we can't say what sort of injuries she had."

"It's not a big swamp," said Martinsson. "They expect to pull her out today."

They drove back from the depressing scene of the crime to the police station. It seemed to Wallander that just for a moment, the summer landscape had been transformed into a black-and-white photograph. He spent some time swiveling back and forth in his desk chair, then dialed Eskil Lundberg's number. His wife answered, and she said her husband was out in his boat. Wallander could hear young children playing in the background. He guessed that Eskil Lundberg was the boy he had seen in the photograph.

"I assume he's out fishing," said Wallander.

"What else? He has nearly a mile of nets out there. Every other day he delivers fish to Söderköping."

"Eel?"

She sounded almost offended when she replied.

"If he'd been after eels he'd have taken eel traps with him," she said. "But there are no eels anymore. Before long there won't be any fish left at all."

"Does he still have the boat?"

"Which boat?"

"The big trawler. NRG123."

Wallander noticed that she was becoming less and less cooperative, almost suspicious.

"He tried to sell it ages ago. Nobody wanted it, it was such a wreck. It rotted away. He sold the engine for a hundred kronor. What exactly do you want?"

"I want to speak to him," Wallander said, in as friendly a tone as he could manage. "Does he have a cell phone with him?"

"There's not much of a signal out there. You'd be better off calling him when he gets back home. He should be here in about two hours."

"I'll do that."

He managed to bring the call to a close before she had another chance to ask him what he wanted. He leaned back and put his feet on his desk. Now he had no meetings, no tasks that required his immediate attention. He grabbed his jacket and left the police station—to be on the safe side, he left via the basement garage, so that nobody could catch him at the last moment. He walked down the hill into town, and felt a spring in his step. He wasn't yet so old that nothing affected him anymore. Sun and warm weather made everything more tolerable.

He had lunch in a café just off the square, read **Ystads Allehanda** and one of the evening newspapers. Then he sat on a bench in the square. He had another quarter of an hour to kill. He wondered where Håkan and Louise were at that moment. Were they still alive, or were they dead? Had they made some kind of pact regarding their disappearance? He was reminded of the turmoil caused by the spy Stig Bergling, but he had trouble finding any similarities between the serious submarine commander and the conceited Bergling.

Wallander also considered another factor that he reluctantly conceded could be of vital significance. Håkan von Enke had visited his daughter regularly. Was he really prepared to let her down by going underground? The inevitable conclusion was that von Enke must be dead.

There was an alternative, of course, Wallander thought as he watched people rummaging through old LP records at one of the market stands. Von Enke had been scared. Could it be that whoever he was afraid of had caught up with him? Wallander had no answers, only questions that he must try to formulate as clearly and precisely as possible.

When the time came he called Bokö just as a somewhat drunk man sat down on the other end of the bench. A man's voice eventually answered. Wallander decided to put all his cards on the table. He said his name, and explained that he was a police officer.

"I found a photograph in a file that belongs to a man called Håkan von Enke. Do you know him?"

"No."

The answer came quickly and firmly. Wallander had the impression that Lundberg was on his guard.

"Do you know his wife? Louise?"

"No."

"But your paths must have crossed somehow. Why else would he have a photo of you and a man I assume is your father. And of the boat NRG123. That's your boat, isn't it?"

"My father bought it in Gothenburg sometime in the early 1960s. Around the time when they started building bigger boats and no longer used wood as the main material. He got it cheap. There was no shortage of herring in those days."

Wallander described the photo, and wondered where it had been taken.

"Fyrudden," said Lundberg. "That's where the boat was berthed. **Helga,** she was named. She was built in a yard in the south of Norway. Tønsberg, I think."

"Who took the picture?"

"It must have been Gustav Holmqvist. He ran a marine joinery business and was always taking pictures when he wasn't working."

"Could your father have known Håkan von Enke?"

"My father's dead. He never mixed with that crowd."

"What do you mean, 'that crowd'?"

"Noblemen."

"Håkan von Enke is also a seafarer. Like you and your father."

"I don't know him. Neither did my dad."

"Then how did he get ahold of that photograph?"

"I don't know."

"Maybe I should ask Gustav Holmqvist. Do you have his phone number?"

"He doesn't have a phone number. He's been dead for fifteen years. And his wife is dead. Their daughter too. They're all dead."

Wallander obviously wasn't going to get any further. There was nothing to suggest that Eskil Lundberg wasn't telling the truth. Yet at the same time, Wallander had the feeling that something didn't add up. He couldn't put his finger on it.

Wallander apologized to Lundberg for disturbing him, and remained sitting with his cell phone in his hand. The drunken man on the other end of the bench had fallen asleep. It suddenly dawned on Wallander that he recognized him. Several years ago Wallander had arrested him and some accomplices for a series of burglaries. The man had spent some years in jail, and then left Ystad. Evidently he was back again.

Wallander stood up and began walking to the police station. He repeated the conversation to himself, word for word. Lundberg hadn't displayed any curiosity at all. Was he really as uninterested as he seemed to be? Or did he know what I was going to ask about? Wallander continued rehashing the conversation until he

was back in his office. He hadn't reached any clear conclusion.

His thoughts were interrupted by Martinsson, who
appeared in the doorway.

"We've found the old woman," he said.

Wallander stared at him. He didn't know what Martinsson was talking about.

"Who?"

"The woman who killed her husband with an ax.
Evelina Andersson. The woman in the swamp. I'm
going to drive out there again. Do you want to come
with me?"

"Yes, I'll come."

Wallander racked his memory in vain. But he didn't
have the slightest idea what Martinsson was talking
about.

They took Martinsson's car. Wallander still didn't
know where they were going, or why. He was feeling
increasingly desperate. Martinsson glanced at him.

"Are you feeling all right?"

"I'm fine."

It was only after they had left Ystad that his memory
became unblocked. It's that shadow inside my head,
Wallander thought, furious with himself. Everything
came back to him now, with full force.

"Something just occurred to me," he said. "I forgot
that I have a dentist appointment."

Martinsson braked.

"Should I turn around?"

"No. One of the others can drive me back."

Wallander didn't bother to take a look at the woman they had just lifted out of the swamp. A patrol car took him back to Ystad. He got out at the police station and thanked the driver for the lift, then sat in his own car. He felt cold and worried. The gaps in his memory were scaring him.

After a while he went up to his office. He had decided to talk to his doctor about the sudden spells of darkness that filled his head. He had just sat down when his cell phone gave a chime: he had received a text. It was short and precise. **Both stones Swedish. Neither from U.S.A.'s coasts. Hans-Olov.**

Wallander sat motionless in his chair. He couldn't decide immediately what that meant, but now he knew for sure that something didn't add up.

He felt that this was a sort of breakthrough. But exactly what the implications were he didn't know.

He couldn't decide if the von Enkes were gliding farther away from him or if they were slowly getting closer.

15

A few days before Midsummer, Wallander drove north along the coast road. Shortly after Västervik he nearly ran into an elk. He pulled onto the shoulder, his heart racing, and thought of Klara before he could bring himself to continue. His journey took him past a café where, many years ago, he had stopped, exhausted, and been allowed to sleep in a back room. Several times over the years he had thought with a sort of melancholy longing about the waitress who had been so kind to him. When he came to the café he slowed down and drove into the parking area. But he didn't leave the car. He sat there, hesitating, his hands clamped to the steering wheel. Then he continued on his way.

He knew why he didn't go in, of course. He was afraid of finding somebody else behind the counter, and being forced to accept that here too, in that café, time had moved on and that he would never be able to return to what now lay so far away in the past.

He came to the harbor at Fyrudden at eleven o'clock. When he got out of the car he saw that the warehouse in the photo was still there, even though it had been converted and now had windows. But the fish boxes were gone, as was the big trawler alongside the quay. The harbor was now full of pleasure boats. Wallander parked outside the red-painted coast guard building, paid the required entrance fee at the chandler's, and wandered out to the farthest of the jetties.

He acknowledged to himself that the whole journey was like a game of roulette. He hadn't warned Eskil Lundberg that he would be coming. If he'd called from Skåne he had no doubt that Lundberg would have refused to meet him. But if he was standing here on the quay? He sat on a bench outside the chandler's shop and took out his cell phone. Now it was sink or swim. If he had been a von Wallander, with a coat of arms and a family motto, those were the words he would have chosen: **sink or swim.** That's the way it had always been throughout his life. He dialed the number and hoped for the best.

Lundberg answered.

"It's Wallander. We spoke about a week ago."

"What do you want?"

If he was surprised, he concealed it well, Wallander thought. Lundberg was evidently one of those enviable people who are always prepared for anything to happen, for anybody at all to call them out of the blue, a king or a fool—or a police officer from Ystad.

"I'm in Fyrudden," Wallander informed him, and took the bull by the horns. "I hope you have time to meet me."

"Why do you think I'd have any more to tell you now than I did when we last spoke?"

That was the moment when Wallander's long experience as a police officer told him that Lundberg **did** have more to tell him.

"I have the feeling we should talk," he said.

"Is that your way of telling me that you want to interrogate me?"

"Not at all. I just want to talk to you, and show you the photo I found."

Lundberg thought for a few moments.

"I'll pick you up in an hour," he said eventually.

Wallander spent the time eating in the café, where

he had a view of the harbor, the islands, and in the distance the open sea. He had consulted a sea chart in a glass case on one of the café walls and established that Bokö was to the south of Fyrudden; so it was boats coming from that direction he kept an eye on. He assumed that a fisherman would have a boat at least superficially reminiscent of Sten Nordlander's wooden gig, but he was completely wrong. Lundberg came in an open plastic boat with an outboard motor. It was filled with plastic buckets and net baskets. He berthed at the jetty and looked around. Wallander made himself known. It was only when he had clambered awkwardly down into the boat and almost fallen over that they shook hands.

"I thought we could go to my place," said Lundberg. "There are far too many strangers around here for my taste."

Without waiting for an answer, he pulled away from the jetty and headed for the harbor entrance at what Wallander thought was far too fast a speed. A man in the cockpit of a berthed sailboat stared at them in obvious disapproval. The engine noise was so loud that conversation was impossible. Wallander sat in the bow and watched the tree-clad islands and barren rocks flashing past. They passed through a strait that Wallander recognized from the map on the wall of the café as Halsösundet, and continued south. The islands were still numerous and close together; only occasionally was it possible to glimpse the open sea. Lundberg was wearing calf-length pants, turned-down boots, and a top with the somewhat surprising logo "I burn my own trash." Wallander guessed he was about fifty, possibly slightly older. That could well fit in with the age of the boy in the photograph.

They turned into an inlet lined with oaks and birches and berthed by a red-painted boathouse smelling of tar, with swallows flying in and out. Next to the boathouse were two large smoking ovens.

"Your wife said there weren't any eels left to catch," Wallander said. "Are things really that bad?"

"Even worse," said Lundberg. "Soon there won't be any fish left at all. Didn't she say that?"

The red-painted two-story house could just be seen in a dip about a hundred yards from the water's edge. Plastic toys were scattered about in front. Lundberg's wife, Anna, seemed just as cautious when they shook hands as she had on the phone.

The kitchen smelled of boiled potatoes and fish, and a radio was playing almost inaudible music. Anna Lundberg put a coffeepot on the table, then left the room. She was about the same age as her husband, and in a way they were quite similar in appearance.

A dog came bounding into the kitchen from some other room. A handsome cocker spaniel, Wallander thought, and stroked it while Lundberg was serving coffee.

Wallander laid the photo on the table. Lundberg took a pair of glasses from his breast pocket. He glanced at the picture, then slid it to one side.

"That must have been 1968 or 1969. In the fall, if I remember correctly."

"I found it among Håkan von Enke's papers."

Lundberg looked him straight in the eye.

"I don't know who that man is."

"He was a high-ranking officer in the Swedish navy. A commander. Could your father have known him?"

"It's possible. But I doubt it."

"Why?"

"He wasn't all that fond of military men."

"You're in the picture as well."

"I can't answer your questions. Even if I'd like to."

Wallander decided to try a different tack and started again from the beginning.

"Were you born here on the island?"

"Yes. So was my dad. I'm the fourth generation."

"When did he die?"

"In 1994. He had a heart attack while he was out in the boat, dealing with the nets. When he didn't come home, I called the coast guard. Our neighbor Lasse Åman found him. He was lying in the boat and drifting toward Björkskär. But I figure that was how the old man would have preferred to go."

Wallander thought he could detect a tone of voice that suggested the father-son relationship was less than perfect.

"Have you always lived here on the island? While your father was alive?"

"That would never have worked. You can't be a hired hand for your own father. Especially when he makes all the decisions, and is always right. Even when he's completely wrong."

Eskil Lundberg burst out laughing.

"It wasn't only when we were out fishing that he was

always right," he said. "I remember we were watching a TV show one evening, some kind of quiz show. The question was: Which country shares a border with the Rock of Gibraltar? He said it was Italy and I said it was Spain. When it turned out that I was right, he switched off the television and went to bed. That's the way he was."

"And so you moved away?"

Eskil Lundberg pulled a face.

"Is it important?"

"It might be."

"Tell me again, one more time, so that I understand. Somebody disappeared, is that right?"

"Two people, a man and his wife. Håkan and Louise von Enke. I found this photo in a diary belonging to the husband, the naval commander."

"They live in Stockholm, you said? And you're from Ystad? What's the connection?"

"My daughter is going to marry the son of the missing couple. They have a child. The couple who have vanished are her future parents-in-law."

Lundberg nodded. He suddenly seemed to be looking at Wallander less suspiciously.

"I left the island as soon as I finished school," he said. "I found a job in a factory just outside Kalmar. I lived there for a year. Then I came back home and worked with my dad as a fisherman. But we couldn't get along. If you didn't do exactly as he said, he was furious. I left again."

"Did you go back to the factory?"

"Not that one. I traveled east, to the island of Gotland. I worked in the cement factory at Slite for twenty years, until Dad got sick. It was on Gotland that I met my wife. We had two children. We came back here when Dad couldn't keep the business going any longer. Mom had died and my sister lives in Denmark, so we were the only ones who could help out. We own farmland, fishing waters, thirty-six little islands, countless rocky outcrops."

"So that means you weren't here in the early 1980s?"

"The occasional week in the summer, but that's all."

"Could it be that around that time your father was in touch with a naval officer?" Wallander asked. "Without you knowing about it?"

Lundberg shook his head energetically.

"That wouldn't fit at all with the way he was. He thought there should be a bounty on the head of every member of the Swedish navy. Especially if they were captains."

"Why?"

"They were far too gung-ho during their maneuvers. We have a jetty on the other side of the island where the trawler used to be berthed. Two years in a row the swell from the navy boats wrecked it—the stone caissons were dragged loose. And they refused to pay for repairs. Dad wrote letters, protested, but nothing happened. And the crew often threw slops from the kitchen into wells on the islands—if you know what a freshwater well means to island dwellers, you don't do things like that. There were other things too."

Lundberg seemed to hesitate again. Wallander waited, didn't nudge him.

"Shortly before he died, he told me about something that happened at the beginning of the 1980s," Lundberg said eventually. "You could say that he'd become less malevolent, finally reconciled to the fact that I was going to take over everything, no matter what."

Lundberg stood up and left the room. Wallander was beginning to think that he wasn't going to say any more when he came back, carrying a few old diaries.

"September 1982," he said. "These are his diaries. He noted down catches, and the weather. But also anything unusual that happened. And something unusual happened on September 19, 1982."

He passed the diary over the table to Wallander and pointed out the appropriate place. It said, in very neat handwriting: **Almost pulled down.**

"What did he mean by that?"

"He told me about it once. At first I thought he was confused and sinking into senility, but what he said was too detailed to be imagined."

"Tell me all about it, from the beginning," said Wallander. "I'm especially interested in what happened in the fall of 1982."

Lundberg moved his cup to one side, as if he needed the extra space in order to tell his story.

"He was drifting off the east coast of Gotland, fishing, when it happened. The boat seemed to come to a sudden stop. Something was tugging at the nets, and the boat nearly capsized. He had no idea what had happened, apart from the obvious fact that something heavy had become caught in the nets. He was very careful because in his younger days he had occasionally fished up gas shells. He and the two assistants he had on board tried to cut themselves loose—but then they realized that the boat had turned and the trawl had worked itself free. They managed to haul it in, and found they had caught a steel cylinder about three feet long. It wasn't a shell or a mine; it looked more like a part of a ship's engine. It was heavy, and it didn't seem to have been lying in the water very long. They tried to decide what it was, but to no avail. When they got back home Dad continued examining the cylinder, but he couldn't work out what it had been used for. He put it aside and continued repairing the trawl. He had always been cheap, and it went against the grain to throw anything away. But there's a sequel to the story."

Lundberg slid the diary back toward himself and leafed forward a few days, to September 27. Once again he showed Wallander the open page. **They are searching.** Three words, no more.

"He'd almost forgotten about the cylinder when navy vessels suddenly started turning up at the precise spot where he'd found it. He often used to fish there, off the east coast of Gotland. He knew it wasn't a routine maneuver—the ships were moving in such strange ways. They would stay still for a while, then start moving in ever-decreasing circles. It wasn't long before he figured out what was going on."

Lundberg closed the diary and looked at Wallander.

"They were looking for something they had lost. But Dad didn't have the slightest intention of returning the steel cylinder. It had ruined his trawl. He continued fishing and took no notice of them."

"What happened then?"

"The navy had ships and divers deployed there during the fall and on until December. Then the last of the ships moved away. There were rumors that a submarine had sunk there. But the place where they were searching wasn't deep enough for a submarine. The navy never got its cylinder back, and Dad never really understood what it was. But he was pleased to have gotten back at them for destroying his jetty. I honestly can't believe that he was in close touch with a naval officer."

They sat there without speaking. Wallander was trying to work out how von Enke could have fit in to what he had just been told.

"I think it's still there," said Lundberg.

Wallander thought he must have misheard, but Eskil Lundberg had already gotten to his feet.

"The cylinder," he said. "I think it's still in the shed."

They left the house, the dog scampering around at their feet sniffing for tracks. A wind was blowing up. Anna Lundberg was hanging wash on a line suspended between two old cherry trees. The white pillowcases were smacking in the wind. Behind the boathouse was a shed balancing precariously on the uneven rocks. There was just one lightbulb hanging from the ceiling. Wallander entered a space full of smells. An ancient-looking eel spear hung from one of the walls. Lundberg squatted down and rummaged around in one corner of the shed among tangled ropes, broken bailers, old cork floats, and tattered nets. He poked and prodded with a degree of violence that suggested he shared his father's anger at the trouble caused by the navy. He eventually stood up, took a step to one side, and pointed. Wallander could see a cylindrical object, in gray steel, like a large cigar case with a diameter of about eight inches. At one end was a half-open lid, revealing a mass of electric cords and switching relays.

"We can take it outside," said Lundberg, "if you give me a hand."

They lifted it down onto the jetty. The dog ran up immediately to examine it. Wallander tried to imagine what the cylinder's function could be. He doubted it was part of an engine. It might have something to do with radar equipment, or with the launching of torpedoes or mines.

Wallander squatted down and searched for a serial number or a place of manufacture, but found nothing. The dog was licking his face until Lundberg shooed her away.

"What do you think it is?" he asked when he stood up again.

"I don't know," said Lundberg. "Neither did my dad. He didn't like that. That's one way in which I'm like him. We want answers to our questions."

Lundberg paused for a few moments before continuing.

"I don't need it. Maybe it's of some use to you?"

Wallander didn't realize at first that Lundberg was referring to the steel cylinder at their feet.

"Yes, I'd be happy to take it," he said, thinking that Sten Nordlander might be able to explain what the cylinder was used for.

They put it in the boat and Wallander unfastened

the line. Lundberg turned east and headed for the strait between Bokö and Björkskär. They passed a small island with a building at the edge of a clump of trees.

"An old hunting lodge," said Lundberg. "They used to use it as a base when they were out shooting seabirds. My dad sometimes stayed there for a few nights when he wanted to spend some time drinking and be on his own. It's a good hiding place for anybody who wants to disappear from the face of the earth for a while."

They docked at the pier. Wallander reversed the car to the water's edge, and they lifted the steel cylinder into the backseat.

"There's one thing I'm wondering about," said Lundberg. "You said that both husband and wife vanished. Am I right in thinking that they didn't disappear at the same time?"

"Yes. Håkan von Enke disappeared in April, and his wife only a few weeks ago."

"That's strange. The fact that there's no trace of them at all. Where could he have gone to? Or they?"

"We simply don't know. They might be alive, they might be dead."

Lundberg shook his head.

"There's still the question about the photograph," said Wallander.

"I don't have an answer for you."

Was it because Lundberg's reply came too quickly? Wallander wasn't sure, but he did wonder, purely intuitively, if what Lundberg said was true. Was there something he didn't want to tell Wallander about, despite everything?

"Maybe it will come to you," said Wallander. "You never know. A memory might rise to the surface one of these days."

Wallander watched him backing away from the quay, then they both raised their hands to say goodbye, and the boat shot off at high speed toward the strait and Halsö.

Wallander took a different route home. He wanted to avoid passing that little café again.

When he arrived he was tired and hungry, and he didn't pick up Jussi from the neighbor's. He could hear the rumble of thunder in the distance. It had been raining; he could smell it in the grass under his feet.

He unlocked the door and went into the house, took off his jacket and kicked off his shoes.

He paused in the hall, held his breath, listened intently. Nobody there. Nothing had been disturbed, but even so he knew that somebody had been in the house while he was away. He went into the kitchen in his socks. No message on the table. If it had been Linda, she would have scribbled a note and left it there. He went into the living room and looked around.

He'd had a visitor. Somebody had been there and had left.

Wallander pulled on his boots and walked around the outside of the house.

When he was sure that nobody was observing him, he went to the dog kennel and squatted down.

He felt around inside. What he had stashed was still there.

16

He had inherited the tin box from his father. Or rather, he had found it among all the discarded paintings, tins of paint, and paintbrushes. When Wallander cleared out the studio after his father's death, it brought tears to his eyes. One of the oldest paintbrushes had a maker's mark indicating that it had been manufactured during the war, in 1942. This had been his father's life, he thought: a constantly growing heap of discarded paintbrushes in the corner of the room. When he was cleaning up and throwing everything into big paper bags before losing patience and ordering a Dumpster, he had come across the tin box. It was empty and rusty, but Wallander could vaguely remember it from his childhood. At one time in the distant past his father had used it to store his old toys—well-made and beautifully painted tin soldiers, parts of a Meccano set.

Where all these toys had disappeared to he had no idea. He had looked in every nook and cranny of both the house and the studio without finding them. He even searched through the old trash heap behind the house, dug into it with a spade and a pitchfork without finding anything. The tin box was empty, and Wallander regarded it as a symbol, something he had inherited and could fill with whatever he pleased. He cleaned it up, scraped away the worst of the rust, and put it in the storeroom in the basement in Mariagatan. It was only when he moved into his new house that he rediscovered it. And now it had come in handy, when he was wondering where to hide the black file he had found in Signe's room. In a way it was her book, he thought; it was Signe's book and might contain an explanation for her parents' disappearance.

He decided the best place to hide the tin box was under the wooden floor of the kennel in which Jussi slept. He was relieved to find that the book was still there. He decided to pick up Jussi without further ado. The neighboring farm was at the other side of several oilseed rape fields that had been harvested while he was away. He walked until he came to where his neighbor was repairing a tractor and collected Jussi, who was leaping around and straining at his chain at the back of the house. When they arrived home he dragged in the cylinder, spread some newspapers out on the kitchen table, and started to examine it. He was being very cautious since alarm bells were ringing deep down inside him. Perhaps there was something dangerous inside it? He carefully disentangled all the cords and disconnected the various relays and plugs and switches. He could see that some sort of fastening device on the underside of the cylinder had been torn off. There was no serial number or any other indication of where the cylinder had been made, or who its owner had been. He took a break to make dinner, an omelette that he filled with the contents of a can of mushrooms and ate in front of the television while failing to be enthused by a soccer match as he tried to forget all about the cylinder and missing persons. Jussi came and lay down on the floor in front of him. Wallander gave him the rest of the omelette, then took him for a walk. It was a lovely summer evening. He couldn't resist sitting down on one of the white wooden chairs on the western side of the house, where he had a superb view of the setting sun as it sank below the horizon.

He woke with a start, surprised to realize that he had fallen asleep. He had been oblivious to the world for nearly an hour. His mouth was dry, and he went back inside to measure his blood sugar. It was much higher than normal, 274. That worried him. The only conclusion he could draw was that it was time to increase yet again the amount of insulin he injected into his body at regular intervals.

He remained seated for a while at the kitchen table, where he had pricked his finger when checking his blood sugar level. Once again he was overcome by feelings of dejection, resignation, awareness of the curse of old age. And by worry about the blackouts when his memory and sense of time and place disappeared completely. I'm sitting here, he thought, messing around with a steel cylinder when I should be visiting my daughter and getting to know my grandchild.

He did what he always did when he was feeling dejected. He poured himself a substantial glass of schnapps and downed it in one go. Just one big glass, no more, no refill, no topping up. Then he messed around with the cylinder one more time before deciding that enough was enough. He took a bath, and was asleep before midnight.

Early the next day he called Sten Nordlander. He was out in his boat but said he should be on land in an hour and promised to call back then.

"Has anything happened?" he shouted in an attempt to make himself heard above all the interference.

"Yes," shouted Wallander in return. "We haven't found the missing persons, but I've found something else."

Martinsson called at seven-thirty and reminded Wallander of the meeting due to take place later in the morning. A member of a notorious Swedish gang of Hells Angels was in the process of buying a property just outside Ystad, and Lennart Mattson had called a meeting. Wallander promised to be there at ten o'clock.

He didn't intend to tell Sten Nordlander exactly where he'd found the cylinder. After discovering that somebody had invaded his house while he was away, he had decided not to trust anyone—at least not without reservations. Obviously, whoever the intruder was might have had reasons for breaking in that had nothing to do with Håkan and Louise von Enke, but what could they possibly be? The first thing he did that morning was make a thorough search of the house.

One of the windows facing east, in the room where he had a guest bed that was never used, was ajar. He was quite certain he hadn't left it open. A thief could easily have entered through that window and left again the same way without leaving much in the way of traces. But why hadn't he taken anything? Nothing was missing, Wallander was sure of that. He could think of only two possibilities. Either the thief hadn't found what he was looking for, or he had left something behind. And so Wallander didn't simply look for something that was missing, but also for something that hadn't been there before. He crawled around, looking under chairs, beds, and sofas, and searched among his books. After almost an hour, just before Nordlander called, he concluded his search without having discovered anything at all. He wondered if he should talk to Nyberg, the forensic expert attached to the Ystad police force, and ask him to look for possible hidden microphones. But he decided not to—it would raise too many questions and give rise to too much gossip.

Sten Nordlander explained that he was sitting with a cup of coffee at an outdoor café in Sandhamn.

"I'm on my way north," he said. "My vacation route is going to take me up to Härnösand, then across the gulf to the Finnish coast, then back home via Åland. Two weeks alone with the wind and the waves."

"So a sailor never gets tired of the sea?"

"Never. What did you find?"

Wallander described the steel cylinder in great detail. Using a yardstick—his father's old one, covered in paint stains—he had measured the exact length, and he'd used a piece of string to establish the diameter.

"Where did you find it?" Nordlander asked when Wallander had finished.

"In Håkan and Louise's basement storeroom," Wallander lied. "Do you have any idea what it might be?"

"No, not a clue. But I'll think about it. In their basement, you said?"

"Yes. Have you ever seen anything like it?"

"Cylinders have aerodynamic qualities that make them useful in all kinds of circumstances. But I can't recall having seen anything like what you describe. Did you open up any of the cables?"

"No."

"You should. They could provide some clues."

Wallander found an appropriate knife and carefully split open the black outer casing of one of the cords. Inside were even thinner wires, no more than threads. He described what he had found.

"Hmm," said Nordlander. "They can hardly be live electricity cables. They seem more likely to have some kind of communications function. But exactly what, I can't say. I'll have to mull it over."

"Let me know if you figure it out," said Wallander.

"It's odd that it doesn't say where it was made. The serial number and place of manufacture are usually engraved in the steel. I wonder how it came to be in Håkan's basement, and where he got ahold of it."

Wallander glanced at his watch and saw that he had to head to the police station or he would be late for the meeting. Nordlander ended the call by describing in critical terms a large yacht on its way into the harbor.

The meeting about the motorbike gang lasted for nearly two hours. Wallander was frustrated by Lennart Mattson's inability to steer the meeting efficiently and his failure to reach any practical conclusions. In the end, Wallander became so impatient that he interrupted Mattson and said that it should be possible to stop the purchase of the house by directly contacting the present owner. Once that was done they could develop strategies to put obstacles in the way of the gang's activities. Mattson refused to be put off. However, Wallander had information that nobody else in the room knew about. He had been given a tip by Linda, who had heard about it from a friend in Stockholm. He requested permission to speak, and spelled it out.

"We have a complication," he began. "There is a notorious medical practitioner whose contribution to the well-being of Swedish citizenry includes providing doctor's certificates for no less than fourteen members of one of these Hells Angels gangs. All of them have been receiving state benefits because they are suffering from severe depression."

A titter ran through the room.

"That doctor has now retired, and unfortunately he's moved down here," he went on. "He bought a pretty little house in the center of town. The risk is, of course, that he will continue writing sick notes for these poor motorcyclists who are so depressed that they are unable to work. He's being investigated by the social services crowd, but as we all know, they can't be relied on."

Wallander stood up and wrote the doctor's name on a flip chart.

"We should be keeping an eye on this fellow," he said, and left the room.

As far as he was concerned, the meeting was now over.

He spent the rest of the morning brooding over the cylinder. Then he drove to the library and asked for help looking up all the literature they had about submarines, naval ships in general, and modern warfare. The librarian, who had been a classmate of Linda's, produced a large pile of books. Just before he left he also asked her for Stig Wennerström's memoirs.

Wallander went home, stopping on the way to do some shopping. When he left the house that morning he had fixed little pieces of tape discreetly on doors and windows. None had been disturbed. He ate his fish stew and then turned to the books he had piled up on the kitchen table. He read until he couldn't go on any longer. When he went to bed at about midnight, heavy rain was pummeling the roof. He fell asleep immediately. The sound of rain had always put him to sleep, ever since he was a child.

When Wallander arrived at the police station the next morning he was soaking wet. He had decided to walk partway to work, and parked at the railroad station. The high blood sugar reading of the other night was a challenge. He must get more exercise, more often. Halfway there he had been caught in a heavy shower. He went to the locker room, hung up his wet pants and took another pair out of his locker. He noticed that he had put on weight since he wore them last. He slammed the door in anger, just as Nyberg entered the room. He raised an eyebrow at Wallander's extreme reaction.

"Bad mood?"

"Wet pants."

Nyberg nodded and replied with his own personal mixture of jollity and gloom.

"I know exactly what you mean. We can all cope with getting our feet wet. But getting your pants wet is much worse. It's like pissing yourself. You feel pleasantly warm but then it gets uncomfortably cold."

Wallander went to his office and called Ytterberg, who was out and hadn't said when he would be back. Wallander had already tried calling his cell phone, without getting an answer. When he went to get a cup of coffee, he bumped into Martinsson, who felt he needed some fresh air. They went to sit down on a bench outside the police station. Martinsson talked about an arsonist who was still on the run.

"Are we going to catch him this time?" Wallander asked.

"We always catch him," said Martinsson. "The question is whether we can keep him or if we'll have to let him go. But we have a witness I believe in. This time we might be able to nail him at last."

They went back inside, each to his own office. Wallander stayed for several hours. Then he went home, still not having managed to contact Ytterberg. But he had scribbled down the most important points on a scrap of paper and intended to keep on trying to make contact during the evening. Ytterberg was the man in charge of the investigation. Wallander would hand over the material he had, the file inside the black covers and the steel cylinder. Then Ytterberg could draw the necessary and the possible conclusions. The investigation had nothing to do with Wallander. He was not a member of the investigating team, he was merely a father who didn't like the idea of his daughter's future parents-in-law disappearing without a trace. Now Wallander would concentrate on celebrating Midsummer, and then taking a vacation.

But things didn't turn out as planned. When he got home he found an unknown car parked outside his house, a beat-up Ford covered in rust. Wallander didn't recognize it. He wondered whose it could be. As he approached the house he saw that on one of the white chairs, the one he had dozed on the night before, there was a woman.

There was an open bottle of wine on the table in front of her. Wallander could see no trace of a glass.

Reluctantly he went up to her and said hello.

17

It was Mona, his ex-wife. It had been many years since they last met—fleetingly, when Linda graduated from the police academy. Since then they had spoken briefly on the phone a few times, but that was it.

Late that night, when Mona had fallen asleep in the bedroom and he had become the first person to make up the bed in his own guest room, he felt ill at ease. Mona's emotional state had been changing from one minute to the next, and she had boiled over several times, angry and emotional outbursts that he found difficult to deal with. She was already drunk by the time he arrived at home. When she stood up to give him a hug, she stumbled and nearly fell over, but he managed to catch her at the last moment. He could see that she was tense and nervous at the prospect of seeing him again, and had put on far too much makeup. The girl Wallander had fallen in love with forty years ago used hardly any makeup; she didn't need it.

She had come to visit him that evening because she was wounded. Somebody had treated her so badly that Wallander was the only person she felt she could turn to. He had sat down beside her in the garden, swallows swooping down over their heads, and he'd had a strange feeling that the past had caught up with him and was repeating itself. At any moment a five-year-old Linda would come bounding up out of nowhere and demand their attention. But he managed to come up with only a few words of greeting before Mona burst into tears. He felt embarrassed. This was exactly how it had been during their last awkward times together. He had found it impossible to take her emotional outbursts seriously. She became more and more of an actress, and cast herself in a role for which she was unsuited. Her talents were not appropriate for tragedy, perhaps not for comedy either: she embodied a normality that didn't accommodate emotional outbursts. Nevertheless, there she was, weeping copiously, and all Wallander could think to do was bring her a roll of toilet paper to dry her tears. After a while she stopped crying and apologized, but she had trouble talking without slurring her words. He wished Linda were there; she had a different way of dealing with Mona.

At the same time, he was affected by another emotion, one he had trouble acknowledging, but which kept nagging at him. He had a desire to take her by the hand and lead her into the bedroom. Her very presence excited him, and he was close to testing how genuine the feeling was. But of course, he did nothing. She staggered over to the dog kennel, where Jussi was jumping up and down in excitement. Wallander followed her, more like a bodyguard than a consort, ready to pick her up if she fell over. Soon the dog was no longer of interest to her, and they went inside since she was feeling cold. She made a tour of the house, and asked him to show her **everything**, stressing the word, as if she were visiting an art gallery. He had decorated the place **magnificently**, she said; she couldn't find words to express how **fabulous** it was, even if he should have thrown out long ago that awful sofa they'd had in their apartment just after they were married. When she noticed their wedding photo on a bureau, she burst out crying again, this time in such an obviously fake way that he was tempted to throw her out. But he let her indulge herself, made a pot of coffee, hid a bottle of whiskey that had been sitting out, and eventually persuaded her to sit down at the kitchen table.

I loved her more than any other woman in my life, Wallander thought as they sat there with their cups of coffee. Even if I were to fall head over heels in love with another woman today, Mona will always be the most important woman in my life. That is a fact that can never be changed. New love might replace an earlier love, but the old love is always there, no matter what. You live your life on two levels, probably to avoid falling through without a trace if a hole appears in one of them.

Mona drank her coffee, and unexpectedly began to sober up. That was another thing Wallander remembered: she had often acted more drunk than she really was.

"I'm sorry," she said. "I've been acting like a fool, busting in on you. Do you want me to leave?"

"Not at all. I just want to know why you came here."

"Why are you so dismissive? You can't claim that I disturb you often."

Wallander backed off immediately. The last year with Mona had been a constant battle, with him trying not to be drawn into her nonstop complaints and threats. She of course thought that was exactly how he was behaving toward her, and he knew she was right. They were both culprits and victims in the confusion that could be stopped only by drastic action: divorce, with each of them going their separate ways.

"Tell me what's wrong," he said cautiously. "Why are you so depressed?"

What followed was a long, drawn-out lament, a dirge with what seemed to be an endless number of verses. Mona's own variation of the **Lamentations**, or of **Elvira Madigan**, Wallander thought. A year ago she had met a man who, unlike the previous one, was not a golf-playing retiree who Wallander was convinced had acquired his money by plundering shell companies. By contrast, the new man was the manager of a co-op store in Malmö, about her own age and also divorced. But it was not long before Mona discovered to her horror that even an honest grocer could display psychopathic traits. He had tried to dominate her, made veiled threats, and eventually subjected her to physical violence. Foolishly enough, she had convinced herself that it would pass, that he would get over his jealousy, but that didn't happen, and now she had cut all ties with him. The only person she could turn to was her former husband, who she thought could protect her from the persecution she was sure the grocer would subject her to. In short, she was scared—and that was why she had come to him.

Wallander wondered how much of what she told him was true. Mona was not always reliable; she sometimes told lies without any malicious intent. But he thought he should believe her in this case, and he was naturally upset to hear that she had been beaten.

When she had finished telling her story, she felt sick and rushed to the bathroom. Wallander stood outside the door and heard that she really was sick—it wasn't just for show. Then she lay down on the sofa she thought he should have thrown out, cried again, and then fell asleep with a blanket over her. Wallander sat in his easy chair and continued reading the books he had borrowed from the library, although he was unable to concentrate, of course. After almost two hours she woke with a start. When she realized that she was in Wallander's house, she almost started crying again, but Wallander told her enough was enough. He could make her some food if she wanted to eat, then she could spend the night and the next day she could talk to Linda, who would doubtless be able to give her better advice than he could. She wasn't hungry, so he just made some soup and filled his own stomach with many slices of bread. As they were sitting across from each other at the table, she suddenly started talking about all the good times they had enjoyed in the old days. Wallander wondered if this was the real reason for her visit, if she was going to start pursuing him again. If she had tried a year or so earlier, he thought, she might have succeeded. I still felt then that we'd be able to live together again—but later I realized that was an illusion. All of it was behind us, and it wasn't something I wanted to go through again.

After the meal she wanted something to drink. But he said no, he wasn't going to give her another drop as

long as she was in his house. If she didn't like that she
could call a taxi and spend the night at a hotel in Ystad.
She started to argue, but she gave up when it became
clear that Wallander was serious.

When she went to bed at midnight, she made a ten-
tative effort to embrace him. But he resisted, merely
stroked her hair and left the room. He listened outside
the door, which was ajar; she was awake for a while,
but eventually fell asleep.

Wallander went out, let Jussi out of his kennel, and
sat down on the garden hammock that used to be his
father's. The summer night was bright, windless, and
filled with scents. Jussi came to sit at his feet. Wallander
suddenly felt uneasy. There was no going back in life,
even if he were naïve enough to wish that was possible.
It was not possible to take even one step backward.

When he finally went to bed, he took half a sleeping
pill in the hope of avoiding a restless night. He simply
didn't want to think anymore, neither about the
woman asleep in his bed nor the thoughts that had tortured him when he'd been sitting in the garden.

When he woke up the next morning he was astonished
to find that she had left. He was normally a very light
sleeper, but he hadn't heard her get up and slip quietly
out of the house. There was a note on the kitchen
table: "Sorry for being here when you came home."
That was all, nothing about what she actually wanted
to be forgiven for. He wondered how many times during their marriage she had left similar notes, apologiz-

ing for what she'd done to him. A vast number that he neither could nor even wanted to count.

He drank coffee, fed Jussi, and wondered if he should call Linda and tell her about Mona's visit, but since what he needed to do above all else was talk to Ytterberg, that would have to wait.

It was a breezy morning, with a cold wind blowing from the north; summer had gone away for the time being. The neighbor's sheep were grazing in their fenced-off field, and a few swans were flying east.

Wallander called Ytterberg in his office. He picked up right away.

"I heard that you were asking for me. Have you found the von Enkes?"

"No. How are things going for you?"

"Nothing new worthy of mention."

"Nothing at all?"

"No. Do you have anything to report?"

Wallander had been planning to tell Ytterberg about his visit to Bokö and the remarkable cylinder he had found, but he changed his mind at the last minute. He didn't know why. Surely he could rely on Ytterberg.

"Not really."

"I'll be in touch again."

When the short and basically pointless call was over, Wallander drove to the police station. He needed to devote the whole day to going through a depressing assault case in connection with which he'd been called as a witness. Everybody blamed everybody else, and the victim, who had been in a coma for two weeks, had no memory of the incident. Wallander had been one of the first detectives to arrive at the scene, and would therefore have to testify in court. He had great difficulty recalling any details. Even the report he'd written himself seemed unfamiliar.

Linda suddenly appeared in his office. It was about noon.

"I hear you had an unexpected visit," she said.

Wallander slid the open files to one side and looked at his daughter. Her face now seemed less puffy than it had been, and she might even have lost a few pounds.

"Mona's been knocking on your door, has she?"

"She called from Malmö. She complained that you'd been nasty to her."

Wallander reacted in astonishment.

"What did she mean by that?"

"She said you only reluctantly let her in despite the fact that she was feeling sick. Then you gave her hardly anything to eat, and locked her in the bedroom."

"None of that is true. The bitch is lying."

"Don't call my mom that," said Linda, her face darkening.

"She's lying, whether you like it or not. I welcomed her, I let her in, I dried her tears, and I even made up the bed with clean sheets for her."

"She wasn't lying about her new man, at least. I've met him. He's just as charming as psychopaths usually are. Mom has an odd talent for choosing the wrong man."

"Thank you."

"I don't mean you, of course. But that lunatic golf player wasn't much better than the guy she's with now."

"The question is: What can I do about it?"

Linda thought for a moment before answering. She rubbed her nose with the index finger of her left hand. Just like her grandfather used to do, Wallander thought. He'd never noticed that before, and now he burst out laughing. She looked at him in surprise. He explained. Then it was her turn to laugh.

"I have Klara in the car," she said. "I just wanted to have a quick word about this business with Mom. We can talk later."

"You mean you left the baby alone in the car?" Wallander was upset. "How could you do such a thing?"

"I have a friend with me; she's looking after Klara. How could you think I'd leave her alone?"

She paused in the doorway.

"I think Mom needs our help," she said.

"I'm always here," said Wallander. "But I'd prefer her to be sober when she visits. And she should call in advance."

"Are you always sober? Do you always call before you visit somebody? Have you never felt sick?"

She didn't wait for a reply but vanished into the hallway. Wallander had just started reading his report again when Ytterberg called.

"I'm taking a few days off," he said. "I forgot to mention that."

"Going anywhere interesting?"

"I'll be staying in an old cottage in a lovely location by a lake just outside Västerås. But I wanted to tell you a few of my thoughts about the von Enkes. I was a bit curt when we spoke a few minutes ago."

"I'm all ears."

"Let me put it like this. I have two theories about their disappearance, and my colleagues agree with me. Let's see if you're thinking along the same lines. One possibility is that they planned their disappearance in advance, but for some reason they decided to vanish at different times. There could be various explanations for that. For instance, if they wanted to change their identity, he might have gone ahead to some unknown place in order to prepare for her arrival. Meet her on a road filled with palm fronds and roses, to use a biblical image. But there could be other reasons, of course. There's really only one other plausible possibility: that they've been subjected to some sort of attack. In other words, that they're dead. It's hard to find a reason why they might have been exposed to violence, and if so, why it should happen at different times. But apart from those two alternatives, we have no idea. There's just a black hole."

"I think I'd have reached the same conclusions as you."

"I've consulted the leading experts in the country about possible circumstances associated with missing persons, and our job is simple in the sense that there's only one way for us to approach this."

"Find them, you mean."

"Or at least understand why we can't find them."

"Have there been any new details at all?"

"None. But there is one other person we have to take into account."

"You mean the son?"

"Yes. We can't avoid it. If we assume that they engi-neered their disappearance, we have to ask why they'd subject him to such horrors. It's inhuman, to put it mildly. Our impression is that they are not cruel peo-ple. You know that yourself; you've met them. What we've dug up about Håkan von Enke indicates that he was a well-liked senior officer, unassuming, shrewd, fair, never temperamental. The worst we've heard about him is that he could occasionally be impatient. But can't we all? As a teacher, Louise was well liked by her pupils. Uncommunicative, quite a few said. But re-fraining from speaking nonstop is hardly grounds for suspicion—you have to listen now and then too. Any-way, it doesn't seem credible that they could have lived double lives. We've even consulted experts in Europol. I've had several phone conversations with a French po-licewoman, Mlle. Germain in Paris, who had a lot of sensible things to say. She confirmed my own thought, that we also need to look at the matter in a radically different light."

Wallander knew what he was getting at.

"You mean what role Hans might have played?"

"Exactly. If there was a large fortune at stake, that might have provided us with a lead. But there isn't. All in all, the Enkes have about a million kronor—plus their apartment, which is probably worth seven or eight million. You could argue that it's a lot of money for an ordinary mortal. But given contemporary circum-stances, you could say that a person with no debts and the assets I've referred to is well off, but hardly rich."

"Have you spoken to Hans?"

"About a week ago he was in Stockholm for a meeting with the Financial Supervisory Authority. He was the one who took the initiative and got in touch with me, and we had a chat. I have to say that he seemed genuinely worried, and that he simply couldn't understand what had happened. Besides, he earns a pretty substantial salary."

"So that's where we are, is it?"

"Not exactly a strong position to be in. But we'll keep digging, even if the ground seems very hard."

Ytterberg suddenly put down the receiver. Wallander could hear him cursing in the background. Then he picked up the receiver again.

"I'm leaving in two days," said Ytterberg. "But you can always contact me if there's an emergency."

"I promise to call only if it's important," said Wallander, and hung up.

After that phone call Wallander went down to sit on the bench outside the entrance to the station. He thought through what Ytterberg had said.

He stayed there for a long time. Mona's sudden visit had tired him out. This was not the way he wanted things to be; he didn't want her turning his life upside down by making new demands on him. He would have to make this clear to her if she turned up on his doorstep again, and he must persuade Linda to be his ally. He was prepared to help Mona—that wasn't a problem—but the past was the past. It no longer existed.

Wallander walked down the hill to a sausage stand across from the hospital. A lump of mashed potato fell off his tray, and a jackdaw swooped down immediately to steal it.

He suddenly had the feeling that he'd forgotten something. He felt around for his service pistol. Or could he have forgotten something else? He wasn't sure if he'd come to the hot dog stand by car, or walked down the hill from the police station.

He dumped the half-eaten sausage and mashed potatoes into a trash can and looked around one more time. No sign of a car. He slowly started to trudge back up the hill. About halfway there, his memory returned. He broke into a cold sweat and his heart was racing. He couldn't put off consulting his doctor any longer. This was the third time it had happened within a short period, and he wanted to know what was going on inside his head.

He called the doctor he had consulted earlier when he'd returned to duty. He was given an appointment shortly after Midsummer. When he put the receiver down, he checked to make sure that his gun was locked up where it should be.

He spent the rest of the day preparing for his court appearance. It was six o'clock when he closed the last of his files and threw it onto his guest chair. He had stood up and picked up his jacket when a thought suddenly struck him. He had no idea where it came from. Why hadn't von Enke taken his secret diary away with him when he visited Signe for the last time? Wallander could see only two possible explanations. Either he intended to go back, or something had happened to make a return impossible.

He sat down at his desk again and looked up the number for Niklasgården. It was the woman with the melodious foreign voice who answered.

"I just wanted to check that all is well with Signe," he said.

"She lives in a world where very little changes. Apart from that which affects all of us—growing older."

"I don't suppose her dad has been to visit her, has he?"

"I thought he went missing. Is he back?"

"No. I was just wondering."

"Her uncle was here yesterday on a visit. It was my day off, but I noticed it in the ledger where we keep a record of visits."

Wallander held his breath.

"An uncle?"

"He signed himself in as Gustaf von Enke. He came in the afternoon and stayed for about an hour."

"Are you absolutely certain about this?"

"Why would I make it up?"

"No, as you say, why would you? If this uncle comes back to visit Signe, could you please give me a call?"

She suddenly sounded worried.

"Is something wrong?"

"No, not at all. Thanks for your time."

Wallander replaced the receiver but remained seated. He was not mistaken; he was sure of that. He had studied the von Enke family tree meticulously, and he was certain there was no uncle.

Whoever the man was that had visited Signe, he had given a false name and relationship.

Wallander drove home. The worry he had felt earlier had now returned in spades.

18

The following morning, Wallander had a fever and a sore throat. He tried hard to convince himself that it was his imagination, but in the end he got a thermometer, which registered 102. He called the police station and told them he was sick. He spent most of the day either in bed or in the kitchen, surrounded by the books from the library he still hadn't read.

During the night he'd had a dream about Signe. He'd been visiting Niklasgården, and suddenly noticed that it was in fact somebody else curled up in her bed. It was dark in the room; he tried to switch the light on, but it didn't work. So he took out his cell phone and used it as a flashlight. In the pale blue glow he discovered that it was Louise lying there. She was an exact copy of her daughter. He was overcome by fear, but when he tried to leave the room he found that the door was locked.

That was when he woke up. It was four o'clock and already light. He could feel a pain in his throat, but he felt warm and soon dropped off to sleep again. When he eventually woke up he tried to interpret his dream, but he didn't reach any conclusions. Apart from the fact that everything seemed to be a cover-up for everything else when it came to the disappearance of Håkan and Louise von Enke.

Wallander got out of bed, wrapped a towel around his neck, and looked up Gustaf von Enke on the Internet. There was nobody by that name. At eight o'clock he called Ytterberg, who would be going on vacation the following day. He was on his way to what he expected to be an extremely unpleasant interrogation of a man who had tried to strangle his wife and his two children, probably because he had found another woman he wanted to live with.

"But why did he have to kill the children?" he wondered. "It's like a Greek tragedy."

Wallander didn't know much about the dramas written more than two thousand years ago. Linda had once taken him to a production of **Medea** in Malmö. He had been moved by it, but not so much that he became a regular theatergoer. His last visit hadn't exactly increased his interest either.

He told Ytterberg about his call to Niklasgården the previous day.

"Are you sure?"

"Yes," said Wallander. "There is no uncle. There's a cousin in England, but that's it."

"It certainly sounds odd."

"I know you're about to go away. Maybe you can send somebody else out to Niklasgården to try to get a description of the man?"

"I have a very good cop named Rebecka Andersson," he said. "She's phenomenal with assignments like this, even though she's very young. I'll speak to her."

Wallander was just about to end the call when Ytterberg asked him a question.

"Do you ever feel like I do?" he asked. "An almost desperate longing to get away from all this shit that we're chest-deep in?"

"It happens."

"How do we manage to survive it all?"

"I don't know. Some sort of feeling of responsibility, I suspect. I once had a mentor, an old detective named Rydberg. That's what he always used to say. It was a matter of responsibility, nothing more."

Rebecka Andersson called at about two o'clock from Niklasgården.

"I understood that you wanted the information as soon as possible," she said. "I'm sitting on a bench on the grounds. It's lovely weather. Do you have a pencil handy?"

"Yes, I'm ready to go."

"A man in his fifties, neatly dressed in suit and tie, very friendly, light curly hair, blue eyes. He spoke what is usually called standard Swedish, in other words, no particular dialect and certainly without any trace of a foreign accent. One thing was obvious from the start: he'd never been here before. They had to show him which room she was in, but nobody seems to have thought that was at all remarkable."

"What did he have to say?"

"Nothing, really. He was just very friendly."

"And the room?"

"I asked two members of the staff, separately, to check the room and see if anything had been moved. They couldn't find any changes. I had the impression that they were very sure about that."

"But even so, he stayed for as long as an hour?"

"That's not definite. Assessments varied. They're evidently not all that strict when it comes to entering visits and times in their ledger. I'd say he was there for at least an hour, an hour and a half at most."

"And then what happened?"

"He left."

"How did he get there?"

"By car, I assume. But nobody saw a car. Then suddenly he simply wasn't there anymore."

Wallander thought it all over, but he had no more questions, so he thanked her for her help. He looked out the window and caught a glimpse of the yellow mail van driving away. He went out to the mailbox in his robe and a pair of wooden clogs. There was just one letter, postmarked Ystad. The sender was somebody by the name of Robert Åkerblom. The name sounded vaguely familiar, but Wallander couldn't remember the circumstances in which he had met the man. He sat down at his kitchen table and opened the envelope. It contained a photo of a man and two young women. When Wallander saw the man, he knew immediately who it was. A painful memory, over fifteen years old, rose up to the surface. At the beginning of the 1990s Robert Åkerblom's wife had been brutally murdered, an incident linked to remarkable events in South

Africa and an attempt to murder Nelson Mandela. He turned the photo over and read what it said on the reverse side: "A reminder of our existence, and a thank-you for all the support you gave us during the most difficult period of our lives."

Just what I needed, Wallander thought. Proof that despite everything, what we do has significance for a lot of people. He pinned up the photo on the wall.

The following day would be Midsummer's Eve. Although he didn't feel great, he decided to go shopping. He didn't like being in crowded supermarkets, didn't really like shopping at all; but he had made up his mind that his Midsummer table would be full of appropriate goodies. Sensibly, he had already stocked up on alcohol. He wrote out a shopping list and set off.

The following day he felt better, and his temperature was back to normal. It had rained during the night, but Wallander scanned the horizon and decided that they would be able to sit outside. When Linda and her family arrived at five o'clock, everything was ready. She congratulated him on his efficiency, and took him to one side.

"There'll be one extra guest."

"Who?"

"Mom."

"No. I don't want her here. You know what happened the last time."

"I don't want her to be alone on a night like this."

"You can take her home."

"Don't worry. Try to remember that you'll be doing your good deed for the day by letting her be here."

"When's she coming?"

"I said five-thirty. She'll be here any minute."

"It's your responsibility to make sure she doesn't drink herself silly."

"Fair enough. Don't forget that Hans likes her. Besides, she has a right to see her grandchild."

Wallander said nothing more. But when he was briefly alone in the kitchen, he took a large swig of whiskey to calm himself down.

Mona arrived, and all went well at the beginning. She had dressed up and was in a good mood. They ate, drank moderately, and enjoyed the fine weather. Wallander noted how nicely Mona played with her grandchild. It was almost like seeing her with Linda again. But the peace didn't last. At about eleven o'clock Mona suddenly started going on about all the injustices she had suffered in the past. Linda tried to calm her down, but evidently Mona had drunk more than they had realized. Maybe she had a little bottle hidden in her purse. Wallander said nothing at first, merely listened to what she had to say. But there came a point when he couldn't stand it anymore. He banged his fist on the table and told her to leave. Linda, who wasn't completely sober either, yelled at him to calm down, saying it wasn't a big deal. But for Wallander it was a big deal. Now, after all this time, he finally noticed that he no longer missed Mona, and the realization turned into an accusation. It was Mona's fault that all those years had gone by without his being able to find another woman to live with. He left the table, took Jussi, and stormed off.

When he came back half an hour later, the party was breaking up. Mona was already in the car. Hans, who had drunk only one glass of wine, would drive.

"It's a shame it turned out this way," said Linda. "It was a lovely evening. But now I know that Mona's drinking will always lead to something like this."

"So I was right after all?"

"If that's how you want to put it. Maybe she shouldn't have come. But now we know that she needs help. I didn't realize until now that my mother is drinking herself to death."

She stroked his cheek, and they embraced.

"I'd never have survived if it hadn't been for you," he said.

"Klara will soon be able to spend time on her own here with you. In a year or so. Time passes quickly."

Wallander saw them off and cleared away the leftovers and dirty dishes. Then he did something he did only once or twice a year: he dug out a cigar, sat down in the garden, and lit it.

It was starting to get chilly. He began reminiscing. He thought about his former classmates, the ones he'd been at school with in Limhamn. What had they made of their lives? There had been a reunion a few years ago, but he hadn't made the effort to attend. He regretted it now. It would have put his own life in perspective, seeing what had happened to them.

He sat outside until two. At one point he heard a snatch of music in the distance—it might have been that Swedish Midsummer favorite "Calle Schewen's Waltz," but he wasn't sure. Then he went to bed and slept until late the next morning. He stayed in bed, reading through the books he'd borrowed from the library. He suddenly sat up with a start. He had come to some black-and-white photographs in a book about American submarines and their constant trials of strength with their Russian counterparts during the Cold War.

He stared at the picture and could feel his heart beating faster. There was no doubt about it. The picture was an exact likeness of the cylinder he had taken home with him from Bokö. Wallander leaped out of bed and dragged the cylinder out from behind a bookcase he used for storing old shoes.

He grabbed an English-Swedish dictionary to make sure he didn't misunderstand anything in the chapter that contained the photograph. It was about James Bradley, who was in charge of submarine command in the U.S. Navy at the beginning of the 1970s. He was known for spending whole nights in his office in the Pentagon, working out new methods of dealing with the Russians. One night, when the building was more or less deserted except for the security guards patrolling the hallways, he had an idea. It was so daring that he knew immediately he would need to go directly to President Nixon's security adviser, Henry Kissinger. There was a rumor circulating at the time that Kissinger seldom listened to anybody for more than five minutes and never for more than twenty. Bradley spoke for over forty-five minutes. When he drove back to the Pentagon he was convinced he would get the money he needed for the equipment he had in mind. Kissinger had promised nothing, but Bradley had seen that he was deeply impressed.

It was soon decided that the submarine **Halibut** would be used for this top secret project. It was one of the biggest in the U.S. submarine fleet. Wallander was astonished when he read about the weight, the length, the armaments, and the number of officers and crew. There was no reason it couldn't be operational year-round, provided it could surface occasionally to load up with fresh air and provisions. The food stores could be refilled in less than an hour in open water, but in order to fulfill its new assignment it needed to be refitted. It had to be provided with a pressure chamber for divers, who would perform the most difficult part of the assignment, deep down at the bottom of the sea.

Bradley's idea was basically very simple. In order to maintain communications between command bases on the mainland and the submarines armed with nuclear weapons out on patrol from bases in Petropavlovsk on the Kamchatka Peninsula, the Russians had laid a cable over the Okhotsk Sea. Bradley's plan was to attach a listening device to it.

But there was a big problem. The Okhotsk Sea was over two hundred thousand square miles in area; how would they ever locate the cable? The solution was just as improbably simple as the whole idea.

One night in the Pentagon, Bradley remembered the summers he used to spend as a child by the Mississippi River. That childhood memory solved his problem. At regular intervals along the bank there were notices saying: "Anchoring Forbidden. Underwater Cable." Apart from the town of Vladivostok, eastern Russia was pure wilderness, so there couldn't be very many places where an underwater cable could be laid. They have warning notices even in the Soviet Union.

Halibut set off and crossed the Pacific Ocean under-surface. After an adventurous voyage with several sonar contacts with Russian submarines, they managed to enter Russian territory. Then came one of the most risky moments of the operation, when they needed to sneak into one of the channels between the Kuril Islands. Thanks to the fact that the **Halibut** had been fitted with the most advanced equipment for detecting minefields and sonar links, they succeeded. They located the cable relatively quickly. The problem then was to connect the bugging device to the cable without the Russians' notic-ing. After several attempts they finally succeeded, and on board the submarine they could listen in on all mes-sages from the mainland to the Russian submarine cap-tains, and vice versa. As thanks, Bradley was granted an interview with President Nixon, who congratulated him on the success of the operation.

Wallander went outside and sat down in the garden. There was a cold wind blowing, but he found a shel-tered spot next to the house. He had released Jussi, who disappeared behind the back of the house. The questions he now asked himself were few and straight-forward. How had one of those bugging cylinders found its way into a Swedish shed behind a boathouse? How was it linked with Håkan and Louise von Enke? This whole business is bigger than I ever imagined, he thought. There is something behind their disappearance that I don't have the information to understand. I need help.

He hesitated, but not for long. He went back inside and called Sten Nordlander. As usual the connection was bad, but with some effort they were able to understand each other.

"Where are you?" Wallander asked.

"Just off Gävle, in the Gävlebukten. Southwesterly breeze, light cloud cover—it's spectacular! Where are you?"

"At home. You need to come here. I found something you should look at. Take a flight."

"It's that important, is it?"

"I'm as certain as it's possible to be. It's somehow connected with Håkan's disappearance."

"I must say I'm curious."

"There's a chance I'm wrong, of course. But in that case you can be back on your boat tomorrow. I'll pay for all your tickets."

"That's not necessary. But don't count on seeing me before late tonight. It'll take me a while to sail back to Gävle."

It was six o'clock when Nordlander called back. He'd gotten as far as Arlanda, and would be catching a flight from Stockholm to Malmö an hour later.

Wallander got ready to pick him up. He let Jussi stay

in the house—his presence would no doubt deter any possible intruders.

The flight landed on time. Wallander was waiting in the arrivals hall when Nordlander emerged. They drove back to Wallander's house to examine the mysterious steel cylinder.

19

Sten Nordlander recognized immediately the steel cylinder Wallander had lifted up onto the kitchen table. He hadn't seen the genuine article before, but he had seen a lot of sketches, plans, and pictures that enabled him to identify it.

He made no attempt to disguise the fact that he was astonished. Wallander decided there was no longer any reason to maintain the cat-and-mouse game with him. If Nordlander had been Håkan von Enke's best friend while he was alive, and if the worst-case scenario turned out to be reality, he could also be his best friend in death. Wallander served coffee and told his guest the full story of how he had obtained the cylinder. He left nothing out, beginning with the photo of the two men and the fishing boat and finishing only when he explained how he had been able to identify the cylinder they had dragged out of the dark shed on Bokö.

"I don't know what you think," Wallander said in the end. "Whether it was worth the trip from Gävle."

"It certainly was," said Nordlander. "I'm as mystified as you are. This isn't a dummy. Maybe I can see some sort of connection."

It was past eleven. Nordlander declined the offer of a full meal and said he'd be satisfied with a cup of tea and some cookies. Wallander had to spend some time ransacking the pantry before he finally found a packet of oatcakes. Most of them had crumbled and were not much more than a heap of crumbs.

"It's tempting to keep talking now," said Nordlander, "but my doctor tells me I must go to bed at a decent hour, whether or not alcohol is involved. I'm afraid we'll have to continue tomorrow. Let me just have a look through the book where you found the photograph before I go to sleep."

The next day was warm, with no wind. A hawk hovered over the edge of a neighboring field. Jussi was fascinated and sat motionless, watching the bird. Wallander had been up since five o'clock, impatient to hear what Sten Nordlander had to say.

At seven-thirty Nordlander emerged from the guest room. He gazed out the window at the garden and the vista beyond, obviously impressed.

"The myth is that Skåne is a flat and rather lifeless landscape," he said. "But this strikes me as much more than that. It feels to me like a gentle swell out at sea. And beyond it the waves."

"I see it in much the same way," Wallander said. "Dark, dense forests scare me to death. This openness makes it hard to hide. We all need to hide sometimes, no doubt, but some people do it too often."

"Have you been thinking along the same lines as I have? That maybe, for reasons we know nothing about, Håkan and Louise have gone into hiding?"

"That is always a possibility when you are looking for missing persons."

After breakfast Nordlander suggested they go for a walk.

"I have to do some exercise every morning. It's the only way to get my digestive juices flowing."

Jussi raced off in a flash toward the trees, where little pools always seemed to have something interesting for a dog to sniff at.

"There were times at the beginning of the seventies when we seriously thought the Russians were as strong from a military point of view as they appeared to be," Nordlander began. "Their October parades were telling the truth, or so it seemed. Thousands of military experts sat watching television images of armored vehicles rolling past the Kremlin, and the most important question they were asking themselves was: What is it that we **can't** see? That was when the Cold War was at its height, you could say. Before the spell broke."

They stopped at a ditch where an improvised footbridge had collapsed. Wallander found another plank that was less rotten, and put it in place so that they could continue on their way.

"'The spell broke,'" Wallander repeated. "My old

colleague Rydberg used to say that when a line of inquiry turned out to be completely wrong."

"In this case it was our realization that the Russian defense forces were not as strong as we'd thought. It was a worrying insight that gradually dawned on those whose job it was to solve jigsaw puzzles using all the pieces of information gathered from spies, U-2 planes, or even everyday television. The Russian military, at all levels, was worn-out and in many cases nothing more than an impressive-looking but empty shell. Don't misunderstand what I'm saying, there was a very real and powerful threat of a possible nuclear attack. But just as the whole economic setup was rotting away, so was the incompetent bureaucracy. The party no longer believed in what it was doing, and the defense forces were also disintegrating. That naturally gave the top brass in the Pentagon and NATO, and even in Sweden, a lot to think about. What would happen if it became public knowledge that the Russian bear was in fact no more than an aggressive little polecat?"

"Presumably the threat of doomsday would be reduced?"

Nordlander seemed almost impatient when he answered.

"Military men have never been especially philosophical by nature. They are practical people. Hiding inside every competent general or admiral is nearly always a pretty good engineer. Doomsday wasn't the most important question as far as they were concerned. What do you think it was?"

"Defense expenditure?"

"Right. Why should the Western world continue to be on a war footing if their main enemy was no longer a threat? You can't find a new enemy of similar proportions just like that. China and to some extent India were next in line. But at that time China was still a nonstarter in military terms. The core of their armed forces was still an apparently endless supply of soldiers to deploy at any given moment. But that wasn't sufficient motivation for the Western world to continue developing advanced weapons designed exclusively for the arms race with Russia. So there was suddenly a major problem. It simply wasn't appropriate to reveal what everybody knew, that the Russian bear was now limping badly. It was essential to make sure the spell didn't break."

They came to a little hillock with a view of the sea. The previous year Wallander and Linda had carried there an old wooden bench she had bought at an auction for practically nothing. Now he and Nordlander sat down. Wallander shouted for Jussi, who clearly didn't want to join them.

"What we're talking about took place when Russia was still a very real enemy," Nordlander went on. "It wasn't only at ice hockey that we Swedes were convinced we'd never be able to beat them. We were certain that our enemies always came from the east, and hence we needed to be very aware of whatever they were up to in the Baltic Sea. It was around that time, at the end of the 1960s, that rumors started flying."

Nordlander looked around, as if he were afraid that somebody might be listening to their conversation. A combine was busy close to the main road to Sim-rishamn. Now and then the distant buzz of traffic drifted up to the hillock.

"We knew that the Russians had a big naval base in Leningrad. And they had quite a few more bases, more or less secret, dotted around the Baltic Sea and in East Germany. We in Sweden weren't the only ones blasting our way down into the rocks underneath the Baltic Sea. The Germans had been doing it even during the Hitler period, and the Russians continued in the same tradition after the swastika had been replaced by the red flag. A rumor spread that there was a cable over the bottom of the Baltic Sea, between Leningrad and their Baltic satellites, that handled most of their important electronic messages. It was considered safer to lay your own cables than to risk your messages being intercepted by others listening in to radio traffic. We shouldn't forget that Sweden was deeply involved in what was going on. One of our reconnaissance planes was shot down at the beginning of the fifties, and nowadays nobody has any doubt that they were spying on the Russians."

"You say the cable was a rumor?"

"It was supposedly laid at the beginning of the 1960s, when the Russians really believed that they could match the Americans and maybe even outdo them. Don't forget how put out we were when the first **Sputnik** started cruising around up there in space and everybody was amazed that it wasn't the Yanks who had launched it. There was some justification for the Russian view. It was a time when they nearly caught up with the West. Looking back, if you want to be cynical, you could say that was when they should have attacked. If they had wanted to start a war and bring about the doomsday scenario you talked about. In any case, it's rumored that there was a defector from the East German security forces, a general with a chest full of medals who had acquired a taste for the good life in London, and he is supposed to have revealed the existence of the cable to his British counterpart. The British then sold the information for a staggering amount to their American friends, who were always sitting at the ready with their hand held out. The problem was that they couldn't send the really advanced U.S. submarines through the Öresund because the Russians would have detected them immediately. So they had to find less conspicuous methods—mini-submarines and so on. But they didn't have precise information. Where exactly was the cable? In the middle of the Baltic Sea, or had they chosen the shortest route from the Gulf of Finland? Perhaps the Russians had been even more cunning and laid it near Gotland, where nobody would have expected to find it. But they kept on looking, and the intention was to attach to it the sister of that bugging cylinder they had already placed off Kamchatka."

"You mean the one that's now lying on my kitchen table?"

"But is that the one? There could well be several."

"Even so, it's all so strange. Russia no longer exists as a great power. The Baltic states are free again; the former East Germans are now united with the West Germans. Shouldn't a bugging device like that be relegated to some museum of the Cold War?"

"You would think so. I'm not capable of answering that question. All I can do is confirm what the thing is that's come into your possession."

They continued their walk. It was only when they were back in the garden again that Wallander asked the most important question.

"Where does this leave us with regard to the disappearance of Håkan and Louise?"

"I don't know. For me, it's just becoming odder and odder. What are you going to do with the cylinder?"

"Get in touch with the CID in Stockholm. The bottom line is that they are in charge of the investigation. What they do next in conjunction with Säpo has nothing to do with me."

At eleven o'clock Wallander drove Nordlander back to Sturup Airport. They said their good-byes outside the yellow-painted terminal building. Yet again, Wallander tried to pay Nordlander's travel expenses. But Sten Nordlander shook his head.

"I want to know what happened. Never forget that Håkan was my best friend. I think about him every day. And about Louise."

He picked up his bag and went into the terminal. Wallander walked back to his car and drove home.

When he entered the house he felt exhausted and wondered if he was getting sick again. He decided to take a shower.

The last thing he remembered was having difficulty closing the plastic shower curtain.

· · ·

When he woke up he was in a hospital room. Linda was standing at the foot of the bed. Fixed to the back of his hand was an IV supplying him with fluid. He had no idea why he was there.

"What happened?"

Linda told him, objectively, as if she were reading from a police report. Her words awoke no memories, merely filled the vacuum in his mind. She had called him at about six o'clock but there was no answer, even when she tried again repeatedly. By ten o'clock she was so worried that she left Klara with Hans, who was at home for once, and drove out to Löderup. She had found him in the shower, soaking wet and unconscious. She had called an ambulance, and was able to give the doctor who examined him some background information. It wasn't long before it was established that Wallander had gone into insulin shock. His blood sugar level had become so low that he had lost consciousness.

"I remember being hungry," he said slowly when Linda finished her account. "But I didn't actually eat anything."

"You could have died," said Linda.

He could see that she had tears in her eyes. If she hadn't driven to his house, hadn't suspected that something was wrong, his life could have ended there, with him naked on a tiled floor. He shuddered.

"You neglect yourself, Dad," she said. "One of these days you'll do it once too often. I want you to let Klara have a grandfather for at least another fifteen years. Then you can do whatever you want with your life."

"I don't understand how it could have happened. It's not the first time my blood sugar has been too low."

"You'll have to discuss that with your doctor. I'm talking about something different. Your duty to stay alive."

He merely nodded. Every word he uttered was a strain. He was filled with a strange feeling of echoing exhaustion.

"What's in the fluid I'm getting?" he asked.

"I don't know."

"How long am I going to have to lie here?"

"I don't know that either."

She stood up. He could see how tired she was, and realized with a sort of misty insight that she might have been sitting at his bedside for a long time.

"Go home now," he said. "I'll manage."

"Yes," she said. "You'll manage. This time."

She leaned over him and looked him in the eye.

"Greetings from Klara. She also thinks it's good that you survived."

Wallander was left alone in the room. He closed his eyes and tried to sleep. What he wanted most of all was to wake up with the feeing that what had happened was not his fault.

But later in the day Wallander was visited by his own doctor, who was not on duty but had come to the hospital to see him anyway, and told him that the time was now past when he could be careless about keeping tabs on his blood sugar readings. Wallander had been Dr. Hansén's patient for nearly twenty years, and there were no excuses that would impress this decidedly unsentimental physician. Dr. Hansén told him over and over again that as far as he was concerned, Wallander was welcome to walk the tightrope and not take his illness seriously, but the next time anything like this happened he should expect consequences that he was really too young to suffer.

"I'm sixty years old," Wallander said. "Isn't that old?"

"A couple of generations ago that was old. But not now. The body gets older; there's nothing we can do about that. But nowadays we can expect to live for another fifteen or twenty years."

"What's going to happen now?"

"You'll stay in the hospital until tomorrow so that my colleagues can make sure that your blood sugar readings have stabilized, and that you haven't suffered any damage. Then you can go home and continue in your sinful ways."

"But I don't lead a sinful life, do I?"

Dr. Hansén was a few years older than Wallander and had been married no less than six times. Local gossip in Ystad suggested that his maintenance payments to his former wives forced him to spend his vacations working in Norwegian hospitals way up inside the Arctic circle, where nobody would volunteer unless they had to.

"Maybe that's what's missing from your life. A little pinch of refreshing sinfulness—a detective breaking the rules."

It was only after Dr. Hansén had left that it really dawned on him how close to death he had been. For a brief moment he was overcome by panic and fear, stronger than ever before. In situations not connected with his professional duties, that is. There was a sort of fear that police officers felt, and a different sort that was experienced by a civilian.

He was reminded yet again of the time he had been stabbed when he was a young constable on foot patrol in Malmö. On that occasion the final darkness had been only a hair's breadth away. Now death had been breathing down his neck once again, and this time it was Wallander himself who had opened the door and let him in.

That evening, lying in his hospital bed, Wallander made a series of decisions that he knew he would probably never be able to stick to. They were about eating habits, exercise, new interests, a renewed battle with loneliness. Above all he must make the most of his vacation, not work, not keep hunting for Hans's missing parents. He must take it easy, rest, catch up on sleep, go for long walks along the beach, play with Klara.

He made a plan. Over the next five years he would walk the whole length of the Skåne coastline, from the end of Hallandsåsen in the west to the Blekinge border in the east. He doubted he would ever make it happen, but it made him feel a bit better, letting a dream form then watching it slowly fade away again.

A few years earlier he had attended a dinner party at Martinsson's house and spoken to a retired high school teacher, who told him about his experiences walking to Santiago de Compostela, the classic pilgrimage. Wallander had immediately wanted to make that pilgrimage himself, divided into installments, perhaps over a five-year period. He even started to train, carrying a backpack full of stones—but he overdid it and succumbed to bone spurs in his left foot. His pilgrimage came to an end before it had even started. The bone spurs were cured now, thanks to treatment that included painful cortisone injections into his heel. But perhaps a number of well-planned walks along Scanian beaches might be within the bounds of possibility.

The following day he was discharged and sent home. He picked up Jussi, who had once again been looked after by his neighbor, and declined Linda's offer to drive to Löderup to make him dinner. He felt he needed to come to terms with his situation without her help. He was on his own, so he had to accept personal responsibility.

Before going to bed that night he wrote a long e-mail to Ytterberg. He didn't mention having been ill, merely that he had to take a vacation since he was feeling burned out, and he needed to give Håkan and Louise von Enke a rest for a while. **For the first time, I have to acknowledge the limitations imposed by my age and my depleted strength,** he ended the message. **I've never done that before. I'm not forty years old anymore, and I have to reconcile myself to the fact that time past will never return. I think that's an illusion I share with more or less everyone—that it's possible to step into the same river twice.**

He read through what he had written, clicked on Send, then switched off his computer. As he went to bed, he could hear the rumble of thunder in the distance.

The storm was approaching, but the summer evening sky was still light.

20

Wallander woke the next day to find that the thunderstorm had moved on without affecting his house. The front had veered away to the east. Wallander felt fully rested when he got up at about eight o'clock. It was chilly, but even so he took his breakfast with him into the garden and ate it at the white wooden table. As a way of celebrating his vacation, he snipped a few roses from one of the bushes and laid them on the table. He had just sat down again when his cell phone rang. It was Linda, wanting to know how he was feeling.

"I've had my warning," he said. "Everything's fine at the moment. But I'm going to make sure my cell phone is always within reach."

"That's exactly what I was going to advise you to do."

"How are you all?"

"Klara has a bit of a cold. Hans took this week off."

"Because he wanted to, or against his will?"

"Because I wanted him to! He didn't dare do anything else. I gave him an ultimatum."

"What?"

"Me or his work. We don't negotiate where Klara is concerned."

Wallander ate the rest of his breakfast, thinking that it was becoming more and more obvious how much Linda took after her grandfather. The same caustic tone of voice, the same ironic, slightly mocking attitude to the world around her. But also a tendency to anger lurking just under the surface.

Wallander put his feet up on a chair, leaned back, and closed his eyes. At last his vacation had begun.

The phone rang.

"Ytterberg here. Did I wake you?"

"You'd have had to call a few hours ago to do that."

"We found Louise von Enke. She's dead."

Wallander held his breath, and slowly rose to his feet.

"I wanted to call you right away," said Ytterberg. "We might be able to keep the news quiet for another hour or so, but we need to inform her son. Am I right in thinking the only other family member is the cousin in England?"

"You're forgetting the daughter at Niklasgården. The staff there should be informed. But I can take care of that."

"I suspected you would want to—but if you'd rather not, which I would understand perfectly, I'll call them myself."

"I'll do it," said Wallander. "Just tell me the most important details that I need to know."

"The whole thing is absurd, to be honest," said Ytterberg. "Last night a senile woman went missing from a nursing home on Värmdö island. She usually went out for walks in the evening—they'd fitted her with some sort of GPS tag that would make it easier to track her down, but she somehow managed to take it off. So the police had to organize a search party. They eventually found her; she wasn't in too bad a state. But two of the searchers got lost—can you believe it? The batteries in their cell phones were so low that another search party had to be sent out to find them. Which they did. But on the way back they happened to come across somebody else."

"Louise?"

"Yes. She was lying at the side of a woodland path, a couple of miles from the nearest road. The path went through a clear-cut area, and I just got back from there."

"Was she murdered?"

"There's no sign of violence. In all probability she committed suicide. We found an empty bottle of sleeping pills. If the bottle was full, she would have swallowed a hundred tablets. We're waiting to see what the forensic boys have to say."

"What did she look like?"

"She was lying on her side, a bit hunched up, wearing a skirt, socks, a gray blouse, and an overcoat. Her shoes were next to her body. There was also a purse with various papers and keys. Some animal or other had been sniffing around, but the body hadn't been nibbled at."

"No sign of Håkan?"

"None at all."

"But why would she choose that particular place? An open area where all the trees had been cut down?"

"I don't know. It wasn't to die in idyllic surroundings. The spot is full of dry twigs and dead tree stumps. I'll send you a map. Call if you have any comments."

"What about your vacation?"

"It's not the first time in my life that a vacation has been shot down."

The map arrived a few minutes later. With his hand on the phone, it occurred to Wallander that this was something he shared with every other police officer he knew: the reluctance to be the one to inform relatives about a death. That was never routine.

Death always causes havoc, no matter when it comes.

He dialed the number, and noticed that his hand was shaking. Linda answered.

"You again? We just hung up. Is everything all right?"

"I'm fine. Are you alone?"

"Hans is busy changing a diaper. Didn't I tell you I gave him an ultimatum?"

"Yes, you did. Listen carefully now—you might want to sit down."

She could hear from his voice that this was serious. She knew he never exaggerated.

"Louise is dead. She committed suicide several days ago. She was found last night or this morning at the side of a woodland path where they'd been clear-cutting in the Värmdö forests."

She was dumbstruck.

"Really?" she asked eventually.

"There doesn't seem to be any doubt. But there's no trace of Håkan."

"This is awful."

"How will Hans take it?"

"I don't know. Are they completely certain?"

"I wouldn't have called if Louise hadn't been identified, obviously."

"I mean that she committed suicide. She wasn't like
that."

"Go and talk to Hans now. If he wants to speak to
me he can call me direct. I can also give him the number of the police in Stockholm."

Wallander was about to hang up, but Linda wasn't
finished.

"Where has she been all this time? Why did she take
her life only now?"

"I know as little about that as you do. Let's hope, in
the midst of all the tragedy, that this can help us to find
Håkan. But we can talk about that later."

Wallander hung up, then called Niklasgården. Artur
Källberg was on vacation, and so was the receptionist,
but Wallander eventually managed to get ahold of a
temp. She knew nothing about Signe von Enke's background, and he had the uncomfortable feeling that he
was talking to a brick wall. But maybe that was an advantage under the circumstances.

Wallander had barely finished the conversation
when Hans von Enke called. He was shaken, and close
to tears. Wallander answered all his questions patiently,
and promised to let him know as soon as any more information became available. Linda took the phone.

"I don't think it's sunk in yet," she said quietly.

"That goes for all of us."

"What did she take?"

"Sleeping pills. Ytterberg didn't say what kind.
Maybe Rohypnol? Isn't that what it's called?"

"She never took sleeping pills."

"Women often use sleeping pills when they want to take their own life."

"There's something you said that makes me wonder."

"What?"

"Did she really take her shoes off?"

"According to Ytterberg, yes."

"Don't you think that sounds odd? If she was indoors I could have understood it. But why take your shoes off if you're going to lie down and die outside?"

"I don't know."

"Did he say what kind of shoes they were?"

"No. But I didn't ask."

"You have to tell us absolutely everything," she said after a pause.

"Why would I hold anything back?"

"You sometimes forget to mention things, possibly because you're trying to be considerate when you don't need to be. When will the press get ahold of this?"

"At any moment. Check teletext—they're usually the first to know."

Wallander waited, phone in hand. She came back a minute later.

"They've got it already. 'Louise von Enke found dead. No trace of her husband.'"

"We can talk again later."

Wallander switched on his own television and saw that the news had been given prominence. But if nothing else happened to change or complicate the situation, Louise von Enke's death would no doubt soon fade into the background again.

Wallander tried to devote the rest of the day to his
garden. He had bought a pair of hedge clippers on sale
in a DIY store, but he soon discovered that they were
more or less unusable. He trimmed a few bushes and
cut back some branches on various old, parched fruit
trees, well aware that they shouldn't be pruned in the
middle of summer. But the whole time, he was thinking about Louise. He'd never gotten close to her. What
did he actually know about who she was? That woman
who listened to the conversations taking place around
the dinner table with the trace of a smile on her lips,
but very rarely said anything herself? She taught German, and maybe other foreign languages as well. He
couldn't remember offhand, and had no desire to go
inside and search through his notes.

And she gave birth to a daughter, he thought. When
she was still in the maternity ward she had been told
about the child's severe handicaps. The daughter they
named Signe would never lead a normal life. She was
their first child. What effect does something like that
have on a mother? He wandered around with his useless hedge clippers in his hand and failed to find an answer. But he didn't feel much genuine sorrow. You
couldn't feel sorry for the dead. He could understand
what Hans and Linda felt. And there was also Klara,
who would never get to know her grandmother.

Jussi limped up with a thorn in one of his front
paws. Wallander sat down at the garden table, put on
his glasses, and with the aid of a pair of tweezers managed to pull it out. Jussi displayed his thanks by racing
off like a flash of black lightning into the fields. A

glider flew low over Wallander's house. He watched its progress, squinting. He simply couldn't feel like he was on vacation. He could see Louise in his mind's eye, lying on the ground next to a path that meandered through a clear-cut area of the forest. And by her side a pair of shoes, neatly on parade.

He threw the clippers into the shed and lay down on the garden hammock. Tractors were hard at work in the distance. The buzz from the main road came and went in waves. Then he sat up. This was pointless. He wouldn't be able to relax until he had seen it all with his own eyes. He would have to go to Stockholm again.

Wallander flew to Stockholm that same evening, having handed over Jussi once again to his neighbor, who asked somewhat ironically if Wallander was beginning to get tired of his dog. He called Linda from the airport; she said she wasn't surprised—she had expected no less of him.

"Take lots of photos," she said. "There's something here that doesn't add up."

"Nothing adds up," said Wallander. "That's why I'm going to Stockholm."

His flight was ruined by a screeching child in the seat behind him. He spent nearly the entire journey with his fingers in his ears. He managed to find a room in a little hotel not far from the Central Station. As he walked in the door, the skies opened. He looked out the window of his room and watched people scurrying to find shelter from the heavy rain. Can loneliness get any worse than this? he suddenly found himself thinking. Rain, a hotel room, me at sixty years old. If I turn around, there's nobody else there. He wondered how things were going for Mona. She's probably just as lonely as I am, he thought. Probably even more so, as she tries to conceal all the turmoil that's bubbling away inside her.

When the rain stopped, Wallander went back to the Central Station and bought a map of Stockholm. Then he got on the phone and booked a car for the following day. Because it was summer, rental cars were in high demand, and the best deal he could find was much more expensive than he'd hoped for. He ate dinner in the Old Town. He drank red wine, and was reminded of a summer many years ago, shortly after his divorce from Mona, when he had met a woman. Her name was Monika, and she had been visiting friends in Ystad. Their first encounter was at a less than enjoyable dance, and they arranged to see each other again in Stockholm for dinner. Even before they'd finished their appetizers, he realized that it was a disaster. They had nothing to talk about; the silences became longer and longer, and he got very drunk. He now drank a toast to her memory, and hoped that she had achieved happiness in her life. He was tipsy when he left the restaurant and wandered through the alleys and cobbled streets before returning to his hotel. That night he dreamed once again about horses running into the sea. When he woke up the next morning he dug out his blood sugar meter and stuck the needle into his finger: 100. What it should be. The day had begun well.

Thick clouds covered the sky over Stockholm when he reached the place on Värmdö where Louise von Enke's body had been found. It was ten o'clock. Police tape was still scattered around. The ground was waterlogged, but Wallander could see traces of the marks the police had made where the body had been lying.

He stood there motionless, held his breath, listened. The first impression was always the most important. He looked around in a slow circle. They had found Louise in a shallow depression, with outcrops of rock and low mounds on both sides. If she had lain down here so as not to be seen, she had chosen the right place.

Then he thought about the roses. Linda's words, the first time she told him about her future mother-in-law. **A woman who loves flowers, who always dreamed of having a beautiful garden, a woman with a green thumb.** That's what Linda had said. He remembered very clearly. But this was as far from a beautiful garden as you could get. Was that why she had chosen this place? Because death was not beautiful, had nothing to do with roses and a well-tended garden? He walked around the site, viewing it from different angles. She must have walked a short way, he thought. From the same direction as where my car is. But how did she get there? By bus? By taxi? Had somebody driven her?

He walked over to an old hunting stand in the middle of the cleared area. The steps were slippery. He climbed up cautiously. The floor was littered with a few cigarette butts and some empty beer cans. A dead mouse was lying in one corner. Wallander climbed down again and continued walking around. He tried to imagine himself as the person about to commit suicide. A lonely spot, ugly and covered in scrub, a bottle of sleeping pills. He stopped dead. **A hundred sleeping pills.** Ytterberg had said nothing about a bottle of water. Was it possible to swallow that many pills without anything to drink? He retraced his steps to see if there was something he'd missed. As he studied the ground, he tried to channel Louise. The silent woman who was always willing to listen to what other people had to say.

That was the moment Wallander really and truly began to comprehend that he was on the periphery of a world he knew nothing about. It was Håkan and Louise von Enke's world, a world he had never thought about before. He didn't know what he saw and felt during the time he spent in the clear-cut area; it wasn't something tangible, nor was it a kind of revelation. It was more a feeling of being close to something he had no qualifications for understanding.

He left the place, drove back to town, parked in Grevgatan, and walked up the stairs to the apartment. He wandered silently through the deserted rooms, collected the mail lying on the floor next to the door, and picked out the bills Hans would need to pay. The mail forwarding wasn't yet working. He examined the letters to see if there was anything unexpected among them, but found nothing. The apartment was stuffy and stifling, and he had a headache, probably due to the poor-quality red wine he'd drunk the night before, so he carefully opened a window overlooking the street. He glanced at the answering machine. The red light was flashing, indicating new messages. He listened. **Märta Hörnelius wonders if Louise von Enke is interested in joining a book club that will start this fall, to discuss works of classical German literature.** That was all. Louise von Enke won't be joining any book club, Wallander thought. She has closed her last book for good.

He made some coffee in the kitchen, checked that there was nothing in the refrigerator starting to smell, then went into the room where she had two large closets. He didn't bother with the clothes but took out all the shoes, carried them into the kitchen, and stood them on the table. By the time he had finished there were twenty-two pairs in total, plus two pairs of Wellingtons, and he'd been forced to use a counter and the draining board as well. He put on his glasses and started to work methodically through them all, one shoe at a time. He noticed that she had large feet and bought only exclusive brands. Even the rubber boots were an Italian make that Wallander suspected was expensive. He didn't know what he was looking for, but both he and Linda had been surprised to hear that she had taken off her shoes before she died. She wanted everything to be neat and tidy, Wallander thought. But why?

It took him half an hour to go through the shoes. Then he called Linda and told her about his visit to Värmdö.

"How many shoes do you have?" he asked.

"I don't know."

"Louise has twenty-two pairs, in addition to the ones the police have. Is that a lot or a little?"

"It seems about right. She cared what she looked like."

"That was all I wanted to know."

"Do you have anything else to tell me?"

"Not now."

Despite her protests, he hung up and called Ytterberg. To Wallander's surprise a small child answered. Then came Ytterberg.

"My granddaughter loves answering the phone. I have her with me in my office today."

"I don't want to disturb you, but there's something I've been wondering about."

"You're not disturbing me. But aren't you supposed to be on vacation? Or did I misunderstand?"

"I am on vacation."

"What do you want to know? I don't have any new information about Louise von Enke's death. We're waiting to see what the pathologist has to tell us."

Wallander suddenly remembered his doubts about the water.

"I have two questions, basically. The first one is simple. If she swallowed so many pills, surely she must have drunk something as well?"

"There was a half-empty liter bottle of mineral water next to the body. Didn't I mention that?"

"No doubt you did. I probably wasn't listening carefully enough. Was it Ramlösa?"

"No, Loka, I think. But I'm not sure. Is it important?"

"Not at all. Then there's that matter of the shoes."

"They were standing by the side of the body, very neatly."

"Can you describe the shoes?"

"Brown, low heels, new, I think."

"Does it seem reasonable that she would wear shoes like that in the woods?"

"They weren't exactly party shoes."

"But they were new?"

"Yes. They looked new."

"I don't think I have any more questions."

"I'll be in touch as soon as the pathology report is in. But it might take some time, now that it's summer."

"Do you have any idea how she got out to Värmdö?"

"No," said Ytterberg. "We haven't figured that out yet."

"I was just wondering. Many thanks yet again."

Wallander sat in the silent apartment, gripping the phone tightly, as if it were the last thing he possessed in this life. **Brown shoes. New. Not party shoes.** Slowly, deep in thought, he moved the shoes back into the closets.

Early the next day he flew back to Ystad. That afternoon he returned the faulty hedge clippers to the store he had bought them from, and explained how useless they were. Because he made a fuss, and because one of the managers knew who he was, he was given a better pair at no extra charge.

When he got back home he saw that Ytterberg had called. Wallander dialed his number.

"You made me think," Ytterberg said. "I had to take another look at those shoes. As I said, they were almost brand-new."

"You didn't need to do that for my sake."

"It's not really the shoes I'm calling about," said Ytterberg. "While I was at it I took another look at her purse, and I discovered a sort of inner lining. You could even call it a secret pocket. There was something very interesting in it."

Wallander held his breath.

"Papers," said Ytterberg. "Documents. In Russian. And also some microfilm. I don't know what it is, but it's remarkable enough for me to phone our Säpo colleagues."

Wallander found it difficult to grasp what he had just heard.

"You're saying she was carrying secret material around in her purse?"

"We don't know that. But microfilm is microfilm, and secret pockets are secret pockets. And Russian is Russian. I thought you should know. It might be best to keep this to ourselves for now. Until we know what it actually means. I'll call again when I have more to tell you."

After the call Wallander went out and sat in the garden. It was warm again. It would be a pleasant summer evening.

But he had begun to feel very cold.

PART 3

The Sleeping Beauty's Slumber

21

Wallander had no intention of keeping his promise. He decided immediately that he would talk to Linda and Hans. When it came to a choice between respecting his family and respecting the Swedish security services, he didn't hesitate. He would tell them, word for word, what he had heard. It was his duty to them.

Wallander sat thinking for a long time after his conversation with Ytterberg. His first reaction was that something didn't make sense. Louise von Enke a Russian agent? Even if the police had discovered classified documents in her purse, even in a hidden compartment, he couldn't believe it.

But why would Ytterberg tell him things that weren't true? After having met him briefly on a couple of occasions, Wallander had every confidence in him. He would never have called if he hadn't been sure about what he was going to say.

Wallander knew what he had to do. Trying to protect Linda by withholding facts wouldn't help her. He must take seriously what Ytterberg had said. Whatever eventually emerged as the truth, it would not show that Ytterberg's account of the facts was wrong; rather there would—or must—be different conclusions to draw.

He got into his car and drove to Linda and Hans's

house. Klara's stroller was standing in the shade of a tree; her parents were sitting side by side in the garden hammock, cups of coffee in their hands.

Wallander sat down on one of the garden chairs and told them what he had heard. Both Hans and Linda reacted with furrowed brows and incredulous expressions. While Wallander was speaking, he thought of Stig Wennerström—the colonel who had sold Sweden's defense secrets to the Russians nearly fifty years previously. But it was impossible for him to link Louise von Enke with this man who had been active as a spy for so many years, displaying so much greed and cunning.

"I don't doubt that I was told the facts," he concluded. "But nor do I have any doubt that there is a plausible explanation for those papers in her purse."

Linda shook her head, turned to her partner, then looked her father in the eye.

"Is this really true?"

"I wouldn't give you anything other than an exact account of what I've just heard myself."

"Don't get annoyed. We have to be able to ask you questions."

"I'm not annoyed. But don't start asking me unnecessary questions."

Both Wallander and Linda realized that a quarrel was about to break out, and they managed to smooth things over. Hans didn't appear to notice anything amiss.

Wallander turned to him and could see the dejection in his face.

"Do you have any thoughts?" he asked cautiously. "After all, you knew her better than any of us."

"Absolutely none. I recently discovered that I have a sister I knew nothing about. And now this. It feels as if my parents are becoming more and more like strangers. The telescope is turned around. They are disappearing from my view."

"No distant memories? Words that were said, people who came to visit?"

"Nothing. All I feel is a stomachache."

Linda took Hans's hand. Wallander stood up and walked over to the stroller under the apple tree. A bumblebee was buzzing around the mosquito net. He carefully wafted it away and observed the sleeping bundle. Remembered Linda in her stroller, Mona's constant anxiety, and his own joy at having a child.

He returned to his chair.

"She's asleep."

"Mona says I used to cry at night."

"You did. I was usually the one who got up to comfort you."

"That's not how Mona remembers it."

"She has never been too concerned about the truth."

"Klara hardly ever wakes us up."

"Then you are truly blessed. You used to give us some absolutely awful nights with all your screaming and yelling."

"And you were the one who used to carry me around and hush me?"

"Sometimes with cotton balls in my ears. But yes, I was the one who used to carry you around. Any other suggestion is untrue, no matter what Mona says."

Hans slammed his cup onto the table so hard that

coffee sloshed over onto the cloth. He didn't seem to have been listening.

"Where has Mom been all this time? And where is Håkan?"

"What do you think? What's the first thought that comes into your mind? Now, when everything is changing?"

It was Linda who asked the questions. Wallander looked at her in surprise. He had been formulating the same words, but she got them out first.

"I can't answer that. But something tells me my father is alive. Strangely enough, at the same time I was told my mother is dead, I had a strong feeling that he's alive."

Wallander took over and asked more questions.

"Why? Something must make you think that."

"I don't know."

Wallander hadn't really expected Hans to have much to say this soon after hearing the shattering news. He had come to see that the distance between individual members of the von Enke family was vast.

Wallander paused, since it struck him that this in itself was something to think more closely about. What had Håkan and Louise actually known about each other? Had there been just as much secrecy between them as in their relations with other members of the family? Or was it just the opposite? Was it possible that the relationship between the two of them was extremely close?

He couldn't answer those questions at the moment. Hans stood up and went into the house.

"He needs to call Copenhagen," Linda said. "We had just made the decision when you arrived."

"What decision?"

"That he should stay home another day."

"Does that man never have any time off?"

"Stock exchanges all over the world are very restless at the moment. Hans is worried. That's why he works all the time."

"With Icelanders?"

She looked doubtfully at him.

"Are you trying to be funny? Don't forget you're talking about the father of my child."

"When he showed me his office there were Icelanders sitting around. Why should my recalling that be funny?"

Linda waved her hand dismissively. Hans returned to the hammock. They spoke briefly about Louise's funeral. Wallander was unable to tell them when they could expect to receive the body after the pathologists had completed their work.

"It's odd," said Hans. "Only yesterday I received a large envelope with photographs from Håkan's seventy-fifth birthday party."

"Do you want us to look at them?" Linda asked.

"Not right now." Hans shrugged.

"I've put them together with the lists of guests and other papers connected with the party. Including copies of all the bills."

Wallander had been lost in his own thoughts and only heard, as if from a distance, what Hans said to Linda. He suddenly woke up.

"Did I hear right? Did you mention guest lists?"

"Everything was very efficiently organized. My father wasn't an officer for nothing. He checked off the names of all those who actually attended, those who sent their apologies, and those who went against convention and neither turned up nor explained why they couldn't come."

"How is it that you have the lists?"

"Because neither my father nor my mother was much good when it came to computers. I helped them create the documents. The idea was that I should write in my father's comments. God only knows why. But it never happened."

Wallander bit his lip as he thought that over. Then he stood up.

"I'd like to see those lists, if I may. And the photographs. I can take them home with me if you have other plans."

"How can we have other plans when we have a little baby?" Linda wondered aloud. "Have you forgotten that? She'll wake up soon. And that will put an end to the heavenly peace we're enjoying now. In any case, I think it would be best if you went home now and took the stuff with you."

Hans went indoors and soon reappeared with several files full of papers and photographs. Linda accompanied Wallander to his car. They could hear thunder in the distance. She stood in front of the car door as he was about to open it.

"Could they have gotten it wrong? Could it be murder?"

"There's nothing to suggest that. Ytterberg is a competent police officer, very experienced. He sees what there is to see. He would react if there was the slightest trace of a suspicion."

"Tell me again what she looked like when they found her."

"Her shoes were standing neatly beside the body. She was lying on her side, in her stocking feet. Her clothes were all in place—in other words, she hadn't fallen down, she'd lain down."

"But her shoes?"

"Isn't that something that used to be normal, but we don't think about it anymore nowadays? You always take your shoes off before you die."

Linda shook her head.

"What was she wearing?"

Wallander tried to remember what Ytterberg had said. Skirt, blouse, knee socks.

Linda shook her head.

"I never saw her in knee socks. She either wore tights or nothing at all."

"Are you sure?"

"Absolutely certain. She would wear special thick socks when she went skiing, but that's irrelevant in this context."

Wallander tried to assess the significance of this. He had no doubt that Linda knew what she was talking about. When she was as sure as she seemed to be now, she was nearly always right.

"I have no sensible answer. I'll pass your comments on to the police in Stockholm."

She moved to one side and closed the door once he had settled in behind the wheel.

"Louise wasn't the type of woman who would commit suicide," Linda said.

"But that's what she did."

Linda shook her head without speaking. Wallander realized she had told him something that she wanted him to take into account. They didn't need to discuss it right now. He started the engine and drove away. When he came to the main road, he surprised himself by turning away from Ystad and instead taking the coast road toward Trelleborg. He felt the need to get some fresh air. He came to Mossby Strand, where several mobile homes and campers enjoyed sea views. He parked at the side of the road and walked down to the beach. Every time he came back to this place he had the feeling that this stretch of coast, not very remarkable in itself, certainly not all that pretty, was nevertheless one of the central points in his life. This was where he had taken Linda for walks when she was a little girl; this was where he had tried to make peace with Mona when she told him she wanted a divorce. This was also where, ten years ago, Linda had told him about her ambition to become a police officer, and that she had already been offered a place at the police academy. And it was here that Linda had told him she was pregnant.

Wallander set off along the beach, banishing the stiffness that had possessed his body after all that sitting around. He thought about what Linda had said. But people do commit suicide, whether we believe it or not, he told himself. Several people who I would never have imagined would take their own lives had in fact done so, in most cases after careful planning. How many people have I watched being taken down from nooses they used to hang themselves, how many bits and pieces have I gathered together after somebody placed the barrel of a shotgun in their mouth and pulled the trigger? And I can count on the fingers of one hand the number of relatives who told me they **weren't** surprised.

Wallander walked so far that he was tired when he got back to his car. He sat behind the wheel and opened one of the files. He picked out several photographs at random. He thought he recognized some of the faces, but others he couldn't remember at all. He put the photos back into the file and drove home. If the material was going to be of any use, he needed to work his way through it carefully, not haphazardly.

It was evening before he sat down at the kitchen table with the files. This is where I'll begin, he thought. With the pictures of a large and well-organized party for a man celebrating his seventy-fifth birthday. He examined the photos one at a time. The dining tables could almost always be seen in the background, so he could judge, roughly, if the picture had been taken before, during, or after the meal. There were 104 in total, many of them blurred and with no obvious focus. Either Håkan or Louise was in 64 of them, and both were in 12. In 2 of the pictures they were looking at each other; she was smiling. Wallander laid the photos out in a row, grouped according to when they were probably taken. He was struck by how serious Håkan looked in all the pictures. Is he just being an austere naval officer, or is it a reflection of the worry he will soon begin talking to me about? Wallander wondered.

On the other hand, Louise was smiling virtually all the time. He found one exception, but then she was unaware that her picture was about to be taken. Only one true picture, Wallander thought—or was it just a coincidence? He moved on to the pictures containing a large number of guests. Friendly, elderly people, giving an impression of general well-being. No down-and-outs had come to celebrate Håkan von Enke's birthday, he muttered to himself. These people can afford to look happy and contented.

Wallander slid the photos to one side and moved on to the two lists of guests. He counted 102. The names were in alphabetical order, and a lot of the guests were married couples.

The phone rang while he was studying the first list. It was Linda.

"I'm curious," she said. "Have you found anything?"

"Nothing that I didn't know already. Louise is smiling. Håkan looks serious. Did he never smile?"

"Not very often. But Louise's smile is genuine. She never pretended to be something she wasn't. And I think she was also pretty good at judging other people."

"I've just started looking at the guest lists. A hundred and two names. Nearly all of them unknown to me. Alvén, Alm, Appelgren, Berntsius—"

"I remember him," Linda said. "Sten Berntsius. A high-ranking naval officer. A couple of years ago, I went to an unpleasant dinner party at Håkan and Louise's place when he was a guest. He had his wife with him, a timid little creature who just sat there blushing, and she drank too much wine as well. But Berntsius was awful."

"How?"

"Palme hatred."

"Are you seriously telling me that you attended a dinner party at which the guests said bad things about a Swedish prime minister who had been murdered twenty years earlier?"

"That's exactly what I'm saying. Hatred lives on for a long time. Sten Berntsius started going on about how Palme was a spy for the Soviet Union, a cryptocommunist, a traitor, and God only knows what else."

"What did Louise and Håkan have to say?"

"I'm afraid Håkan at least tended to agree. Louise didn't say much; she tried to smooth things over. But the atmosphere was unpleasant."

Wallander tried to think back. For him, Olof Palme was above all else an example of the most dramatic failure of the Swedish police. He could hardly remember him as a politician. A man with a shrill voice and a smile that was occasionally far from friendly? He couldn't recall which of the memories were genuine. He hadn't been interested in politics in Palme's day. That was when he was trying to get his own life in order, and also dealing with his intractable father.

"Palme was prime minister when those submarines were snorkeling in Swedish waters," he said. "I suppose that's the context in which his name cropped up?"

"Not really, no. If I remember correctly it was mostly about defense cuts that they claimed had begun during his time. He alone was responsible for the fact that Sweden was no longer capable of defending itself. Berntsius maintained it was a big mistake to believe that Russia would always be as peaceful as it is now."

"What were the political views of the von Enkes?"

"They were both extremely conservative, of course. Louise always tried to give the impression that she was contemptuous about politics, but that wasn't true."

"So she did have a mask, despite what you said earlier."

"Perhaps. Let us know if you find anything important."

Wallander went out to feed Jussi. The dog was looking disheveled and tired. Wallander wondered if it was true that dogs and their owners grew to look like each other. If so, old age really had gotten its claws into him. Was he already getting close to his devastating dotage, when he would become increasingly helpless? He shuddered at the thought and went back inside. But, about to sit down at the kitchen table again, he realized that it was pointless. There was nothing in either the guest lists or the photos that could throw light on the missing persons. There must be some other explanation for what had happened. He was wasting his time. He wasn't looking for a needle, he was looking for a haystack.

Wallander picked up everything he'd spread out over the kitchen table and put it all on the table in the hall. He would give it back the next day and then try to stop thinking about the dead Louise and the missing Håkan. Soon enough they would all go to Kristberg church, prettily located with a view over Lake Bören in

Östergötland. The von Enkes had a family grave there over a century old, and that is where Louise would be buried. Hans had told him that his parents had written a joint will in which they had stated that they did not wish to be cremated. Wallander sat in his armchair and closed his eyes. What did he want to happen to his own body? He didn't have a family grave, no sepulchral rights. His mother was buried in a memorial grove in Malmö, his father in one of Ystad's cemeteries. He didn't know what his sister, Kristina, who lived in Stockholm, planned to do.

He fell asleep in the chair and woke up with a start. He had been dragged out of sleep by a dog barking. He stood up. His shirt was wet through; he must have been dreaming. Jussi didn't usually bark for no reason. When he started moving, he discovered that his legs were numb. He shook them into life while continuing to listen for sounds out there in the darkness of the summer night. Jussi was quiet now. Wallander opened the door and stood on the threshold. Jussi immediately started jumping against the fence of his kennel, yelping. Wallander looked around. Perhaps there's a fox on the prowl, he thought. He walked over to Jussi. There was a strong smell of grass. But no wind; everything was still. He tickled Jussi behind the ears. "What were you barking at?" he asked quietly. "Can dogs also have nightmares?" He gazed out over the field. Shadows everywhere, a faint hint of morning light in the east. He checked his watch. A quarter to two. He had been asleep for nearly four hours. His sweaty shirt was making him shiver. He went back inside and lay down in bed. But he couldn't get to sleep. "Kurt Wallander is lying in his bed, thinking of death," he said aloud to himself. It was true. He really was thinking of death. But he often did that. Ever since he was a young police officer, death had always been present in his life. He saw it in the mirror every morning. But now, when he couldn't sleep, it crept up very close to him. He was sixty years old, a diabetic, slightly overweight. He didn't pay as much attention to his health as he should, didn't exercise enough, drank too much, ate what he shouldn't, and at irregular times. Sometimes he tried to discipline himself, but it never lasted long. He would lie there in the dark and become panic-stricken. There was no leeway left. Now he had no choice. Either he must change his lifestyle or die early. Either make an effort to reach at least seventy or assume that death would strike at any moment. Then Klara would be robbed of her maternal grandfather, just as she had been robbed of her paternal grandmother for reasons that were not yet clear.

He lay awake until four o'clock. Fear came and went in waves. When he finally fell asleep, his heart was full of sorrow at the thought that so much of his life was now over and could never be relived.

He had just woken up, shortly after seven, still feeling tired and with a headache, when the phone rang. At first he thought he would ignore it. Presumably it was Linda, who wanted to satisfy her curiosity. She could wait. If he didn't answer, she would know that he was asleep. But after the fourth ring he got out of bed and reached for the receiver. It was Ytterberg, who sounded lively and full of energy.

"Did I wake you up?"

"Nearly," said Wallander. "I'm trying to be on vacation, but I'm not doing too well."

"I'll keep it brief. But I suspect you'd like to know about what I'm holding in my hand. It's a report from the pathologist—Dr. Anahit Indoyan. She analyzed the chemicals found in Louise von Enke's body and discovered something she thinks is odd."

Wallander held his breath and waited for what was coming next. He could hear Ytterberg sorting through his papers.

"There's no doubt that the pills Louise took could be classified as sleeping pills," said Ytterberg. "Dr. Indoyan can identify some of the chemical ingredients. But there are some things she doesn't recognize. Or rather, she's not able to describe the substances in question. She has no intention of giving up, of course. She allows herself a very interesting comment at the end of her preliminary report. She thinks she has found similarities, more or less vague, with substances used during the DDR regime."

"DDR?"

"Are you sure you're awake?"

Wallander didn't get the connection.

"East Germany. All those athletic miracles—remember them? The outstanding swimmers and track athletes breaking all those records. We know now that they were drugged up to the eyeballs. There's no doubt that everything was connected—what the Stasi did and what went on in the sports laboratories were two branches of the same tree. And so," concluded Ytterberg, "our friend Anahit suspects that she might have discovered substances that can be linked to the former East Germany."

"That no longer exists. And hasn't existed for twenty years."

"Not quite. But almost. The Berlin Wall was smashed to pieces in 1989. I remember the date because I got married that fall."

Ytterberg had nothing more to say. Wallander tried to think.

"It sounds very odd," he said eventually.

"Yes, it does. But I thought you'd be interested. Shall I send a copy of the report to the police station in Ystad?"

"I'm on vacation. But I can stop in and pick it up."

"There'll be more to come," said Ytterberg. "But now I'm going for a walk through the woods with my wife."

Wallander hung up and thought about what Ytterberg had said. Something had already occurred to him. He knew what he was going to do next.

Shortly after eight o'clock he was in his car, heading northwest. His destination was just outside Höör, a little house that was long past its prime.

22

On the way to Höör Wallander picked up the report from the reception desk at the police station. Then he did something he very rarely permitted: he pulled over just north of Ystad and picked up a hitchhiker. It was a woman in her thirties with long, dark hair and a small backpack over one shoulder. He didn't really know why he stopped; perhaps it was just pure curiosity. Over the years he noticed that hitchhikers had largely disappeared from the roads. Cheap buses and flights had made that way of traveling almost obsolete.

As a young man, first when he was seventeen and then the following year, he had hitchhiked his way through Europe, despite his father's stern opposition to such hazardous undertakings. On both trips he had succeeded in getting as far as Paris, and then back home again. He still recalled desperate roadside waits in the rain, his backpack far too heavy, and the drivers who picked him up but bored him stiff. But two occasions stood out from all the rest. The first time he had been standing in pouring rain just outside Ghent in Belgium—with hardly any money left and on his way home. A car had stopped and taken him all the way to Helsingborg. He had never forgotten that feeling of happiness, of getting back to Sweden with a single ride. The other memory was also from Belgium. One Saturday evening, this time on the way to Paris, he had been marooned in a tiny village off the beaten track. He had indulged in a bowl of soup in a cheap café, and then gone out in search of a viaduct he might be able to sleep under. He had noticed a man standing by the side of the road, in front of a war memorial. The man raised a trumpet to his lips and beat a mournful tattoo in memory of all the soldiers who had been killed during the two world wars. Wallander was deeply touched by the moment, and he'd never forgotten it.

But now, early in the morning, there was a woman standing at the side of the road, thumbing a lift. It was almost as if she had materialized from a different era. She ran to catch up with the car as he pulled over, jumped in and sat in the passenger seat beside him. She seemed to be pleased with the prospect of getting as far as Höör—she would then continue her journey up toward Småland. She smelled strongly of perfume and seemed very tired. She kept pulling her skirt down over her knees, and he thought he could see traces of stains on it. Even as he pulled over he regretted stopping. Why on earth should he pick up somebody he had never met before? What could he talk to her about? She said nothing, and neither did Wallander. There was a ringing noise inside her backpack. She dug out a cell phone and read the display, but didn't answer it.

"They're disruptive," said Wallander. "Cell phones."

"You don't need to answer if you don't want to."

She spoke with a broad Scanian accent. Wallander guessed that she was from Malmö, from a working-class family. He tried to imagine her work, her life. She wasn't wearing a ring on her left hand, and he noticed that she had bitten her nails down to the quick. Wallander rejected the idea that she was some kind of caregiver, or a hairdresser. She could hardly be a waitress either. She also seemed restless. She was biting her lower lip, almost chewing it.

"Were you standing there long?" he asked.

"Fifteen minutes or so. I had to get out of the previous car. The driver was making a nuisance of himself."

She sounded preoccupied, unwilling to talk. Wallander decided not to disturb her anymore. He would drop her off in Höör and they would never meet again. He toyed with the idea of giving her a name: Carola, who came from nowhere.

He asked where she would like to be dropped.

"I'm hungry," she said. "Somewhere near a café."

He stopped at a roadside restaurant. She smiled rather shyly, thanked him, and headed for the entrance. Wallander reversed—then suddenly had no idea what to do next. Where was he going? His mind was a blank. He was in Höör, he'd just dropped off a hitchhiker— but why was he here? He became increasingly panic-stricken. He tried to calm himself down, closed his eyes and waited for normality to return.

It was more than a minute before he remembered where he was going. Where did it come from, this sudden emptiness that overcame him? What was wiping his mind clean? Why couldn't his doctors tell him what was happening to him?

Although it was five or six years since he had last visited the man he was on his way to see, he remembered how to get there. The road meandered through some woods, passed a few paddocks with Iceland ponies, then sank down into a hollow. The redbrick house was still standing, just as tumbledown as he remembered it from the last time. The only thing that seemed to have changed was that there was a shiny new mailbox beside the open gate, with space for post office vans and garbage trucks to turn around. The name "Eber" was written in large red letters on the box. Wallander switched off the engine but remained sitting at the wheel. He recalled the first time he had met Hermann Eber. It was more than twenty years ago, 1985 or 1986, on police business; Eber had entered Sweden illegally from East Germany. He had requested political asylum, and it had eventually been granted. Wallander was the first to interview him when he turned up at the police station in Ystad and claimed to be a refugee. Wallander could still recall their faltering conversation in English, and his suspicions when Hermann Eber said he was a member of the Stasi, the East German secret police, and feared for his life. Somebody else had taken over the case, and it was only later, when Eber had been granted a residence permit, that he contacted Wallander on his own initiative. He had become almost fluent in Swedish in an astonishingly short time, and he came to see Wallander in order to thank him. Thank me for what, Wallander had asked. Eber had explained how surprised he had been to discover that a police officer could be as friendly as Wallander was to a man from a foreign country. He had slowly realized that the malicious propaganda directed by East Germany toward neighboring countries was not reciprocated in those lands. He felt he had to thank somebody, he said. And Wallander was the person he had chosen for his symbolic gratitude. They started meeting socially now and then, because Hermann Eber's great passion was Italian opera. When the Berlin Wall came down, Eber sat

in Wallander's apartment in Mariagatan, his eyes over-
flowing with tears, and watched the historical events
unfolding on television. He had confessed to Wallander in a series of long conversations that he was no
longer a passionate enthusiast of the political system in
East Germany. He had begun to hate himself. He had
been one of the men who had bugged, persecuted, and
pestered his fellow citizens. He himself had been privi-
leged, and had even shaken the hand of Erich Honecker
at one of the sumptuous banquets put on by the state.
He had felt so proud to have shaken the hand of the
great leader. But afterward he wished he had never
done it. In the end, his doubts about what he had been
doing and an increasing conviction that East Germany
was a political project condemned to death had become
so great that he decided to defect. He chose Sweden
merely because he felt his chances of fleeing there were
good. He could easily acquire false ID papers and board
one of the ferries to Trelleborg.

Eber's worries about his past eventually catching
up with him were very strong. Despite the fact that
East Germany no longer existed, the people he had tar-
geted were still there. It had become clear to Wallander
that nobody could assuage Eber's fear; it was a constant
presence and would probably never disappear completely. As the years passed, Eber became increasingly
reserved and withdrawn; their meetings became less
frequent and eventually ceased altogether.

The last time they had seen each other was because
Wallander had heard that his friend was ill. One Sunday afternoon he drove out to Höör in order to see

how things were. Eber was the same as ever, possibly a bit thinner. He was about the same age as Wallander but seemed to be aging more quickly. Wallander had thought a lot about Hermann Eber's fate on his drive back home after the failed visit, when they had sat and looked at each other without being able to think of anything to say.

The door of the redbrick house had been opened slightly. Wallander got out of his car.

"It's only me," he shouted. "Your old friend from Ystad."

Hermann Eber appeared in the doorway. He was wearing an ancient tracksuit that Wallander suspected was one of the few garments he'd had with him when he fled from East Germany. The garden was full of trash. He wondered fleetingly if Eber had set up cunning man-traps around his house.

"You," he said. "How long is it since you last came to visit me?"

"Many years. But when have you been to visit me? Do you even know that I've moved to the country?"

Eber shook his head. He was almost completely bald. His wandering eyes convinced Wallander that he was still afraid of a possible revenge attack.

Eber pointed at a decrepit-looking garden table and some rickety chairs. Wallander realized that Eber didn't want to let him into the house. His place had always been a mess, but in the past he had invited Wallander inside anyway. Perhaps it's in an even worse state now, Wallander thought. He sat down carefully on the chair that seemed least likely to collapse. Eber remained

standing, leaning against the house. Wallander wondered if he still retained the acuity that had been his
most characteristic trait. Eber was an intelligent man,
even if he led a life that seemed at odds with his intel-
lectual capacity. Several times he had surprised Wallander by turning up to meetings unwashed and smelly.
He dressed oddly, and in the middle of winter often
wore summer clothes. But Wallander had realized at an
early stage that beneath this confusing and often repulsive surface was a clear head. The way he analyzed what
was no longer an East German miracle had given Wallander insight into a social system and a view of politics
that had previously been beyond his comprehension.

Hermann Eber had often reacted with reluctance
and irritation when Wallander asked him questions
about the work he did for the Stasi. It was still difficult,
hurtful, a pain he was unable to shake off. But at times
when Wallander had been sufficiently patient, Eber
had eventually begun to talk about it. One day he
had admitted, matter-of-factly, that for a while he had
worked in one of the secret departments concerned exclusively with killing people. That was why Wallander
had thought of him when Ytterberg called and told
him about Louise von Enke's pathology report.

When Eber appeared in the doorway he was carrying a bundle of papers, and behind both ears were pencils. All the years he had lived in Sweden, Eber had
earned a living by writing crossword puzzles for various
German newspapers. He specialized in very difficult
puzzles, aimed at the most advanced solvers. Creating
crosswords was an art—it wasn't just a matter of fitting

words into a grid with as few black squares as possible; there was always another dimension: a theme hard to detect, possibly associations with various historic figures. That is how he had described his work to Wallander.

He nodded at the papers Eber had in his hand.

"Some more brainteasers?"

"The most difficult I've done. A crossword puzzle in which the most elegant clues are linked with Classical philosophy."

"But surely you must want people to solve your puzzles?"

Eber didn't reply. It occurred to Wallander that the man sitting opposite him in the shabby old tracksuit dreamed of creating a crossword puzzle that nobody would ever manage to solve. Wallander wondered for a moment if Eber's fear had driven him crazy, despite everything. Or perhaps it was living here in this hollow where the hills on all sides could be perceived as walls closing in on him.

He didn't know. Hermann Eber was still at his core a complete stranger as far as Wallander was concerned.

"I need your help," he said, putting the pathology report on the table and proceeding to explain calmly and thoroughly everything that had happened.

Eber put on a pair of dirty glasses. He studied the papers for a few minutes, then suddenly stood up and disappeared into the house. Wallander waited. Eber still hadn't returned after fifteen minutes. Wallander wondered if he had gone to bed, or perhaps started to prepare a meal and forgotten about the guest waiting for him on the rickety garden chair. But he continued to wait, his impatience growing. He decided to give Eber five more minutes.

At that moment Eber reemerged. He had some yellowed documents in his hand and a thick book under his arm.

"This stuff belongs to a different world," Eber said. "I had to search for it."

"But you appear to have found something."

"It was clever of you to come to me. I'm probably the only person who can give you the help you need. At the same time, I must tell you that this aroused many nasty memories. I started crying as I was searching. Did you hear that?"

Wallander shook his head. He thought Eber was exaggerating. There were no signs of tears in his face.

"I recognize the substances," Eber resumed. "They have woken me up out of a Sleeping Beauty slumber that I would have preferred to remain in undisturbed for the rest of my life."

"So you know what it is?"

"I think so. The ingredients, the synthetically produced chemical substances mentioned in the report, are exactly what I used to work with."

He paused. Wallander waited. Eber didn't like being interrupted. He had once told Wallander, when under the influence of several glasses of whiskey, that it had to do with all the power he once had as a high-ranking officer in the Stasi. Nobody in those days dared to contradict him.

Eber cradled the thick book in his hands, as if it were

a holy writ. He seemed hesitant. Wallander would have to be careful. A blackbird perched on the rim of a plastic kiddie pool nearby. Eber immediately slammed the heavy book down onto the table. The blackbird flew off. Wallander remembered that Eber suffered from a mysterious fear of birds.

"Let's hear it, then," said Wallander. "What are these substances?"

"I dealt with them a thousand years ago. I thought they were out of my life for good. Now you turn up one lovely summer's day and remind me of something I don't want to remember."

"What is it you want to forget?"

Eber sighed and scratched at where his hair used to be. Wallander knew it was important to keep a grip on him, otherwise he might disappear to spend endless hours composing his crossword puzzles.

"What is it you want to forget?" Wallander repeated.

Eber began rocking back and forth on his chair, but he said nothing. Wallander's patience was stretched thin.

"I want to know if you can identify these substances," he said sharply.

"I've dealt with them in the past."

"That's not a good enough answer. 'Dealt with'? You have to be clearer than that! Don't forget you once promised me you'd do me a favor when I asked for one."

"I haven't forgotten."

Eber shook his head, and Wallander could see that he was tortured by the situation.

"Take your time," he said. "I need your answer, your

views, and your thoughts. But there's no hurry. I can come back later if you prefer."

"No, no, stay! I just need time to find my way back into the past. It's as if I'm being forced to dig out a tunnel that I've already refilled carefully."

Wallander stood up.

"I'll go for a walk," he said. "I'll take a closer look at the Icelandic horses."

"Half an hour, that's all I need."

Hermann Eber wiped the sweat from his brow. Wallander walked out of the hollow and back to the nearest paddock.

After half an hour, it had started to get windy, and a bank of clouds was building up from the south. Hermann Eber was sitting motionless in the garden chair when Wallander opened the rusty gate. Now there was another book lying on the table, an old diary with brown covers. Eber started talking the moment Wallander sat down. When he was agitated, as he was now, his voice became shrill, almost strident. Wallander had several times wondered with distaste what it would have been like to be interrogated by Hermann Eber when he was still convinced that East Germany was a paradise on earth.

"Igor Kirov," Eber began, "also known as 'Boris.' That was his stage name, the alias he used. A Russian citizen, the official liaison with one of the KGB's special divisions in Moscow. He came to East Berlin a few months before the Wall went up. I met him several times, though I had no direct contact with him. But there was no doubt about his reputation: Boris knew his stuff. He had zero tolerance for irregularities or slapdash procedures. It was no more than a couple of months before several of the highest officials in the Stasi had been transferred or demoted. You could say he was the Russian star, the much-feared center of the KGB's operations in East Berlin. Before he had been with us for six months, he had cracked Great Britain's most efficient spy ring. Three or four of their agents were executed after secret and summary trials. They would normally have been exchanged for Soviet or East German agents imprisoned in London, but Boris went straight to Ulbricht and demanded that the British agents be executed. He wanted to send an unambiguous warning not only to foreign agents, but also to any East German citizens who might be contemplating treason. Boris had turned himself into a universally feared legend after less than a year in East Berlin. He apparently led a simple life. Nobody knew if he was married, if he had any children, if he drank, or even if he played chess. The only thing that could be said about him with any certainty was that he had a unique ability to organize effective cooperation between the Stasi and the KGB. When the end came, we in the Stasi were stunned. The whole of East Germany would have been, if events had been made public. But everything was hushed up, of course."

"What happened?"

"One day he simply vanished. A magician had draped

a cloth over his head and presto, he was no longer there! But obviously, nobody applauded. The big hero had sold his soul to the English, and of course to the U.S.A. as well. I don't know how he managed to conceal the fact that he had been responsible for the execution of British agents. Perhaps he didn't need to. Security organizations have to be cynical in order to operate efficiently. It was a slap in the face for both the KGB and the Stasi. Heads rolled. Ulbricht was summoned to Moscow and came back crestfallen, even though it was hardly his fault that Boris hadn't been unmasked. Markus Wolf, the head of the Stasi, was very close to being left out in the cold. No doubt he would have been if he hadn't issued an order that brings us back to why you're sitting here today. An order that was given the highest priority."

Wallander could guess what was coming next.

"Boris had to die?"

"Exactly. But not only that, it would have to look as if he had been stricken by remorse. He would have to kill himself and leave a suicide note in which he described his treachery as unforgivable. He would have to praise both the Soviet Union and East Germany, and with a large dose of self-contempt and an equally large dose of our doctored sleeping pills, he would have to lie down and die."

"How was it done?"

"At that time I was working at a lab just outside Berlin—interestingly enough at a place not far from Wannsee, where the Nazis had assembled in order to decide how to solve the Jewish problem. One day a new man showed up."

Eber broke off and pointed to the notebook with the brown covers.

"I saw you noticed it. I had to look up his name. My memory let me down, which it doesn't normally. How's your memory nowadays?"

"It's okay," said Wallander noncommittally. "Go on."

Eber appeared to have quietly registered Wallander's reluctance to talk about his memory. It seemed to Wallander that the perception of tone of voice and subtexts must be especially well developed in people who at some stage in their life have worked in the security services, where overstepping the mark or making an incorrect assessment could result in an appointment with a firing squad.

"Klaus Dietmar," said Eber. "He had been transferred directly from the women swimmers, I know that for certain, even though he had never been their official coach. He was one of those behind the sports miracle. He was a small, slim man who moved without making a sound and had hands like a girl's. People who misjudged him might have interpreted his bearing as a sort of apology for existing at all, but he was a fanatical Communist who no doubt prayed every night to Walter Ulbricht before switching off the light. He was the leader of a group to which I belonged. Our only task was to produce a substance that would kill Igor Kirov but leave no trace apart from what seemed to be that of an ordinary sleeping pill."

Eber stood up and disappeared into his house. Wallander couldn't resist the temptation to peer in through a window. He had been right in his assumptions. The room was in a state of absolute chaos. Every square inch was filled with newspapers, clothes, trash, dirty plates, and half-eaten meals. Some sort of path through all the mess could just about be discerned. The stench from inside the room seeped through the windows. The sun had disappeared behind a bank of clouds. Eber reappeared, adjusting his tracksuit pants. He sat down and scratched his chin, as if plagued by a sudden itch. Wallander had the distinct impression that he was sitting opposite somebody he would hate to change identity with. Just for a moment, he was endlessly grateful for being who he was.

"It took us about two years," said Eber, contemplating his filthy nails. "Many of us thought the Stasi was committing far too many resources to the effort to nail Igor Kirov. But the Kirov affair was all about prestige. He had sworn allegiance to the holiest dogmas of the Communist church and would not be allowed to die in a state of sin. It didn't take us all that long to find a chemical combination that corresponded to the most commonly prescribed sleeping pills available in England at that time. The problem was finding a moment when it would be possible to circumvent all the security protecting him. The most difficult part, of course, was getting past his own vigilance. He knew what he had done and was well aware of all the hounds baying for his blood."

Eber suffered a sudden attack of coughing. There was a wheezing and rasping in his bronchial tubes.

Wallander waited. The wind was getting stronger, and the back of his neck felt cold.

"Any agent knows that the most important thing in his or her life is to keep changing routines," Eber continued once he had recovered. "That's what Kirov did, of course. But he overlooked one tiny detail. And that mistake cost him his life. Every Saturday, at three o'clock, he went to a pub in Notting Hill and watched soccer on the television. He always sat at the same table, drinking Russian tea. He would arrive at ten to three, and leave as soon as the match was over. Our cat burglar, who could break into any building you care to name, kept him under constant surveillance for quite a while, and eventually he came up with a plan for how to eliminate Igor Kirov. The weak link was two waitresses who were sometimes replaced by temporary stand-ins. We could replace them with some of our own. The execution took place in December 1972. The waitresses we supplied served him the poisoned tea. In the report I read it was stated specifically that the last match Kirov watched was Birmingham City versus Leicester City. The result was a draw, one to one. He returned to his apartment and died an hour or so later in his bed. The British security service had no doubt that it was suicide. The letter they found seemed to be in his own handwriting, and his fingerprints were on it. There was great rejoicing in the East German secret police; Igor Kirov had finally met his fate."

Hermann Eber asked a few questions about the dead woman. Wallander answered in as much detail as he could. But he was growing increasingly impatient.

He didn't want to sit here answering Eber's questions. Eber seemed to detect his irritation.

"So you think that Louise died after swallowing the same substance that killed Igor Kirov all those years ago?"

"It seems so."

"Which would mean that she was murdered? And that the assumed suicide was an illusion?"

"If the pathologist's report is correct, that could be the case."

Wallander was skeptical and shook his head. Such things simply couldn't happen in the world as he knew it.

"Who makes stuff like this nowadays? Neither the Stasi nor East Germany exists any longer. You're living here in Sweden, thinking up crossword puzzles."

"Secret police organizations never die. They change names, but they are always there. Anybody who thinks there's less spying in the world today just doesn't get it. Don't forget that quite a few of the old masters are still around."

"Old masters?"

Eber seemed to be almost offended when he answered.

"Irrespective of what we did, no matter what people say about us, we were specialists. We knew what we were doing."

"But why should Louise von Enke of all people be subjected to something like this?"

"That's not a question I can answer."

Wallander was feeling both tired and uneasy. He stood up and shook Hermann Eber's hand.

"I'll be back; you can count on that," he said by way of good-bye.

"So I gather," said Eber. "In our world, we are used to meeting again at the most unlikely times."

Wallander went to his car and drove home. It started raining just as he came to the roundabout at the turnoff to Ystad. It was pouring by the time he ran from the car to his front door. Jussi was barking from his kennel. Wallander sat down at his kitchen table and watched the rain pattering on the windowpane. Water was dripping from his hair.

He had no doubt that Hermann Eber was right. Louise von Enke had not committed suicide. She had been murdered.

23

Wallander took a piece of meat out of the refrigerator. Together with half a head of cauliflower, that would be his meal. When he sat down at the table and opened the newspaper he'd bought on the way home, he thought how, for as long as he could remember as an adult, he had always derived deep satisfaction from eating undisturbed while leafing through a newspaper. But on this occasion he had barely opened the paper when an enlarged photograph stared him in the face, with a dramatic headline. He wondered if he was imagining it—

but no, it really was a picture of the hitchhiker he'd picked up. His astonishment increased as he read that the previous day she had killed her parents in the center of Malmö, in a residential block just off Södra Förstadsgatan, and had been on the run ever since. The police had no idea of her motive. But there was no doubt that she was the killer—her name was not Carola at all, but Anna-Lena. A police officer whose name Wallander thought he recognized described the murder as exceptionally violent, a frenzied attack culminating in a bloodbath in the little apartment the family had lived in. The police were now searching for the woman and had issued an APB. Wallander slid both the newspaper and his plate to one side. He asked himself once again if it could possibly be the same woman. Then he reached for the phone and dialed Martinsson's home number.

"Come right away," Wallander said. "To my house."

"I'm bathing my grandchildren," said Martinsson. "Can't it wait?"

"No. It can't wait."

Exactly thirty minutes later Martinsson drove up to Wallander's house. Wallander was standing at the gate, waiting for him. It had stopped raining and was looking much brighter. Martinsson was well acquainted with Wallander's methods and had no doubt that something serious had happened. Jussi had been let out of his kennel and was leaping around Martinsson's feet. With considerable difficulty, Wallander succeeded in making him lie down.

"I see you've taught him how to behave at last," said Martinsson.

"Not really. Let's go and sit in the kitchen."

They went inside. Wallander pointed at the picture in the newspaper.

"I picked her up and drove her to Höör this morning," he said. "She said she was on her way to Småland, but that might not be true, of course. The probability is that with a picture like this in the newspapers, somebody will have recognized her already. But the police should start looking there."

Martinsson stared at Wallander.

"I seem to recall that as recently as last year we talked about the fact that we never pick up hitchhikers, you and I."

"I made an exception this morning."

"On the way to Höör?"

"I have a good friend there."

"In Höör?"

"It's possible that you don't know where all my friends live. Why shouldn't I have a good friend there? Don't you have a good friend in the Hebrides? Every word I say is true."

Martinsson nodded. He took a notebook out of his pocket. His pen wouldn't write. Wallander gave him one that did, and placed a towel over his plate—several flies had settled on his food. Martinsson made a note of what the woman had been wearing, what she'd said, the exact times. He already had his cell phone in his hand when Wallander held him back.

"Maybe it would be best to say that the police received an anonymous tip?"

"I've already thought of that. We'd better not say that it was a well-known police officer from Ystad who gave a woman a lift and helped her to escape."

"I didn't know who she was."

"But you know as well as I do what the papers will write. If the truth comes out. You'd be an excellent news item to liven up the summer."

Wallander listened as Martinsson called the police station.

"The call was anonymous," Martinsson said in conclusion. "I have no idea how he got my home number, but the man who called was sober and very credible."

He hung up.

"Who isn't sober at lunchtime?" wondered Wallander sarcastically. "Was that necessary?"

"When we catch that woman she'll say that she thumbed a ride with an unknown man. That's all. She won't know it was you. Nor will anybody else."

Wallander suddenly remembered something else his passenger had said.

"She said the driver of the car that had taken her to where I picked her up had been making a nuisance of himself. I forgot to mention that."

Martinsson pointed at the photo in the newspaper.

"She looks good, even if she's a murderer. Did you say she was wearing a short yellow skirt?"

"She was very attractive," said Wallander. "Apart from her bitten nails. I can't think of a bigger turnoff than that."

Martinsson smiled at Wallander.

"We've more or less stopped all that," he said. "Discussing women. There was a time when we never stopped talking about them."

Wallander offered Martinsson coffee, but he declined. Wallander saw him off, then resumed his interrupted meal. It tasted good, but it didn't fill him. He took Jussi for a long walk, trimmed a hedge at the back of the house, and reattached his mailbox to the gatepost, where it had been hanging askew. The whole time, he was chewing over what Hermann Eber had said. He was tempted to call Ytterberg but decided to wait until the following day. He needed time to think. A suicide was developing into a murder, in a way he didn't understand. He began to feel once again that there was something he'd overlooked. Not only him, but all the others who were involved in the investigation. He couldn't put his finger on it. It was just his intuition at work yet again, and he had become increasingly skeptical about its reliability.

Until now he had assumed that Håkan was the main character. But what if it was Louise? That's where I have to start, he thought. I need to go through everything again, this time from a different perspective. But first he needed to sleep for a few hours in order to clear his mind. He undressed and got into bed. A spider scuttled along a beam in the ceiling. Then he fell asleep.

He had just finished breakfast at eight o'clock when Linda drove up to the gate. She had Klara with her. Wallander was annoyed at her coming so early in the morning. Now that he was on vacation, a rare occurrence, he wanted to spend his morning in peace.

They sat down in the garden. Wallander noticed that she had blue streaks in her hair.

"Why the blue streaks?"

"I think they're attractive."

"What does Hans say?"

"He also thinks they're pretty."

"Allow me to disagree. Why can't he look after the baby if he's home from work?"

"He felt compelled to go to the office today."

She suddenly looked anxious; a shadow passed quickly over her face.

"Why is he worried?"

"There are things going on in the global finance sector that he doesn't understand."

"I don't understand what you're saying either. 'Things going on in the global finance sector'? But I don't need to know any more about things that are beyond me."

Wallander got up to pour a glass of water. Klara was crawling around happily on the grass.

"How's Mona?"

"She's lying low, doesn't answer the phone. And when I ring her doorbell she doesn't open up, even though I know she's at home."

"Is she still drinking?"

"I don't know. Right now I don't think I can take on responsibility for another child. I have enough on my plate with this one."

A low-flying plane came roaring overhead, descending into Sturup Airport. When the noise had subsided, Wallander told Linda about his visit to Hermann Eber. He repeated their conversation in detail, and the thoughts that had occurred to him as a result. While he was becoming more convinced than ever that Louise had been murdered, he was at a complete loss as to why anyone would want to kill her. Could this quiet, retiring woman have had some sort of link with East Germany? A country that was dead and buried now?

Wallander paused. Klara was crawling around her mother's legs. Linda shook her head slowly.

"I don't doubt any of what you've told me—but what does it mean?"

"I don't know. Right now I have only one question: Who was Louise von Enke? What is there about her that I don't know?"

"What does anybody ever know about another person? Isn't that what you're always reminding me of? Telling me never to be surprised? Anyway, there is a connection with the former East Germany," Linda said thoughtfully. "Haven't I mentioned it?"

"You've only said that she was interested in classical German culture, and taught German."

"What I'm thinking of goes further back than that," Linda said. "Nearly fifty years. Before Hans was born, before Signe. You really should speak to Hans about this."

"Let's start with what you know," said Wallander.

"It's not a lot. But Louise was in East Germany at the beginning of the 1960s with a group of promising young Swedish swimmers and divers. It was some kind of sporting exchange. Louise used to coach up-and-coming young girls. Apparently she was a diver herself in her younger days, but I don't know much about that. I think she went to East Berlin and Leipzig several times over a few years. Then it suddenly stopped. Hans thinks there's a reason why."

"What is it?"

"Håkan simply made it clear to her that the trips to East Germany had to stop. It wasn't good for his military career to have a wife who kept visiting a country regarded as an enemy. You can well imagine that the Swedish top brass and politicians regarded East Germany as one of Russia's nastiest vassals."

"But you say you don't know this for sure?"

"Louise always did what her husband told her to do. I think the situation in the early sixties simply became untenable. Håkan was on his way to the very top in the navy."

"Do you know anything about how she reacted?"

"No, not a thing."

Klara scratched herself on something lying on the ground and started screaming. Wallander couldn't stand the sound of children screeching and went over to the dog kennel to stroke Jussi. He stayed there until Klara had quieted down.

"What did you used to do when I started crying?" Linda asked.

"My ears were more tolerant in those days."

They sat in silence watching Klara investigate a dandelion growing in the middle of some stones.

"I've obviously been doing some thinking during

the time the von Enkes have been missing," Linda said then. "I've been ransacking my memory, trying to recall details of conversations and how they treated each other. I've tried to wheedle out of Hans everything he knows, everything he assumed I knew as well. Only a few days ago I had the impression that something didn't add up, that he hadn't told me the whole truth."

"About what?"

"The money."

"What money?"

"There is presumably a lot more money hidden away than I had known about. Håkan and Louise led a good life without any ostentatious luxury or excesses. But they could have lived in grand style if they'd wanted to."

"What kind of sums are we talking about?"

"Don't interrupt me," she snapped. "I'm coming to that, but I'll do it at my own speed. The problem is that Hans hasn't told me everything he should have. That annoys me, and I know I'll have to have it out with him sooner or later."

"Does this mean you think the money has become vitally important in some new way?"

"No, but I don't like Hans not telling me things. We don't need to discuss it right now."

Wallander raised his hands to signal an apology and asked no more questions. Linda suddenly discovered that Klara was trying to eat the dandelion and wiped her mouth clean, which set the baby off crying again. Wallander gritted his teeth and stayed where he was. Jussi paced up and down in his kennel, keeping an eye on things and looking as if he felt he'd been abandoned. My family, Wallander thought. We're all here, apart from my sister, Kristina, and my former wife, who's drinking herself to death.

The commotion was soon over, and Klara went back to crawling around on the grass. Linda was rocking back and forth on her chair.

"I can't guarantee that it won't collapse," Wallander said.

"Granddad's old furniture," she said. "If the chair breaks, I'll survive. I'll just fall into your overgrown and untended flower bed."

Wallander said nothing. He could feel himself getting annoyed at the way she was always scrutinizing what he did and pointing out his shortcomings.

"When I woke up this morning there was one question I couldn't get out of my head," she said. "It can't wait, no matter how important this business of Louise and Håkan is. I don't understand how I could have avoided asking it all these years. Not asking either you or Mom. Maybe I was scared of what the answer might be. Nobody wants to be conceived by accident."

Wallander was on his guard immediately. Linda very rarely used the word "Mom" in connection with Mona. Nor could he remember the last time she had called him "Dad," apart from when she was angry or being ironic.

"You don't need to be frightened," Linda went on. "I can see that I've worried you already. I only want to know how you met. The very first time my parents met. I simply don't know."

"My memory's bad," said Wallander, "but not **that** bad. We met in 1968 on a boat between Copenhagen and Malmö. One of the slow ferries, not a hovercraft, late one evening."

"Forty years ago?"

"We were both very young. She was sitting at a table. The ferry was crowded, and I asked if I might join her, and she said yes. I'd be happy to tell you more another time. I'm not in the mood to root around in my past. Let's get back to that money. What kind of sums are we talking about?"

"A few million. But you're not going to avoid telling me about what happened when the ferry docked in Malmö."

"Nothing happened then. I promise to tell you, later. Are you saying they had put aside a million or more? Where did they get it from?"

"They saved it."

He frowned. That was a lot of money to put aside. He could never dream of saving such an amount.

"Could there be tax evasion or some other fraud?"

"Not according to Hans, no."

"But you say he hasn't been open with you about this money?"

"There's no reason why he should have been. Until a couple of months ago it was up to his parents to decide what to do with their savings."

"What did they do?"

"They asked Hans to invest it for them. Cautiously, no risky ventures."

Wallander thought for a moment. Something told

him that what he had just heard could be of considerable significance. Throughout his life as a police officer he had been reminded over and over again that money was the cause of the worst and most serious crimes people could commit. No other motive cropped up so often.

"Who oversaw their financial affairs? Both of them, or just Håkan?"

"Hans will know."

"Then we must talk to him."

"Not we. I. If I discover anything, I'll let you know."

Klara was yawning. Linda nodded to Wallander. He picked her up and laid her carefully on the garden hammock. She smiled at him.

"I try to picture myself in your arms," said Linda. "But it's hard."

"Why?"

"I don't know. But I don't mean it negatively."

A pair of swans came flying over the fields toward them. Father and daughter followed their progress and listened to the swishing sound they made.

"Is it really possible that Louise was murdered?" Linda wondered.

"The investigation will have to continue, of course. But I think there's a lot of evidence now that suggests it is true."

"But why? By whom? All that stuff about her having Russian secrets in her purse surely must be nonsense."

"She had **Swedish** secrets in her purse. Intended for Russia. Listen properly to what I say."

He expected her to be angry, but she merely nodded, acknowledging that he was right.

"There's still an unanswered question," said Wallander. "Where's Håkan?"

"Dead or alive?"

"As far as I'm concerned, Håkan has become more
alive now that Louise has been found dead. It's not logical, I know; there's no plausible explanation for my
thinking that. Possibly my considerable experience as a
police officer. But the indications are not clear, not
even in that context. Nevertheless, I believe he's alive."

"Is he the one who killed Louise?"

"There's nothing to suggest that."

"But nothing to suggest that he didn't, either?"

Wallander nodded. That was exactly what he had
been thinking. She was following his train of thought.

Linda drove off with Klara half an hour later.

Wallander felt that **one** thing at least had become crystal clear. No matter what had happened, it had all
begun with Håkan von Enke. And it was with him
that everything would eventually come to a conclusion. Louise was a side issue.

But what it all meant, he had no idea. The only thing
that struck him right now as being an incontestable fact
was that Håkan von Enke had stood face-to-face with
him in a side room during a birthday party on Djursholm, and seemed to be deeply troubled.

That's where it all began, Wallander thought. It
began with the troubled man.

24

One night in July.

Wallander sat there, pen in hand. The first line of the letter he had begun writing sounded like a bad film from the 1950s. Or perhaps a much better novel from a few decades earlier. The kind he recalled from his childhood home. From the library that had belonged to his maternal grandfather, who had died long before he was born.

Otherwise, the description was correct. It was now July, and it was nighttime. Wallander had gone to bed, then suddenly remembered that it would be his sister Kristina's birthday in a few days' time. It had become his custom to enclose with the birthday card the one letter he sent her every year. So he got out of bed—he wasn't tired, after all, and this was a good excuse to avoid tossing and turning. He sat down at the kitchen table with stationery and a fountain pen, the latter a present from Linda for his fiftieth birthday. The opening words could stay as they were—"One night in July"—he wasn't going to change a thing. It was a short letter. Once he had described his delight at Klara's birth, he didn't think he had much else to write about. His letters became shorter and shorter every year, he noticed grimly. It wasn't much of a letter, but it was the best he could do. His contact with Kristina had culminated during the last few years of their father's life.

Since then they had never met, apart from once when he was in Stockholm and remembered to call her. They were totally different people, and had totally different memories of their childhood. After a short time the conversation would dry up and they'd stare at each other uncomprehendingly: did they really have nothing more to say to each other?

Wallander sealed the envelope and went back to bed. The window was ajar. In the distance he could hear the faint sound of music and a party in progress. There was a rustling sound from the grass outside the window. He had done the right thing in leaving Mariagatan, he thought. Out here in the countryside he could hear sounds he had never heard before. And smell country smells, even more of a novelty.

He lay awake, thinking about his visit to the police station earlier that evening. He hadn't planned to go in, but since his computer wasn't working he drove into Ystad at about nine o'clock. In the hope of avoiding on-duty colleagues, he used the basement entrance. He tapped in the entry code and reached his office without bumping into anybody. Voices could be heard from one of the offices he sneaked past. One of the speakers sounded very drunk. Wallander was glad he wasn't the officer doing the interrogating.

Just before going on vacation he had made a big effort and reduced the piles of paper on his desk. It now looked almost inviting. He threw his jacket onto the guest chair and switched on the computer. While he waited for it to boot up he took out two folders he'd locked away in one of the desk drawers. One was labeled "Louise," the other "Håkan." The pen he'd used was faulty, and the names were smudged and unclear. He slid the first file to one side and concentrated on the second. He also thought about the conversation he'd had with Linda a few hours earlier. She had called while Klara was asleep and Hans had gone out to buy some diapers. Without going into unnecessary detail she had reported on what Hans had said when she asked him about his parents' money, about his mother's links with East Germany, and whether there was anything else he hadn't told her about. He had been offended at first, thinking she didn't trust him. She eventually succeeded in convincing him that all she was interested in was trying to find out what had happened to his parents. After all, it was looking very much as if murder might be involved. Hans had calmed down, understood her motivation, and answered as best he could.

Wallander took a folded sheet of paper out of his back pocket and smoothed it out to look over his notes.

It was only when Hans had started his present job that his parents had asked him to oversee their financial affairs. The amount of money involved was a bit less than 2 million kronor, which had now grown to more than 2.5 million. He was told that the money was their savings plus an inheritance from one of Louise's relatives. He didn't know how much was inherited and how much was saved. The relative in question was Hanna Edling, who died in 1976 and had owned a chain of ladies' clothing shops in the west of Sweden. There were no tax irregularities, even though

Håkan had moaned and groaned about what he considered to be the Social Democrats' outrageous capital gains tax. Now that it had been abolished, Hans regretted that he hadn't been able to tell Håkan that a few more kronor had been saved.

"Hans said his parents had a philosophy about money," Linda had explained. "'You shouldn't talk about money, it should simply be there.'"

"If only," Wallander had said. "That sounds like something well-heeled upper-class folk would say."

"They **are** upper-class," said Linda. "You know that. We don't need to waste time discussing it."

Hans used to give them an investment report twice a year, informing them about gains and any losses. Occasionally Håkan would read something in the newspapers about attractive investment options, and he'd call Hans to pass on the tip. But he never checked on whether Hans had followed up. Louise displayed even less interest in what Hans was doing with their money—but on one occasion the previous year she had asked to withdraw 200,000 kronor from the invested capital. Hans was surprised, since it was very unusual for them to take out such a large sum. And it was mostly Håkan who wanted to withdraw money, for such things as a cruise, or a trip to the French Riviera for a few weeks. Hans asked what she wanted the money for, but she didn't tell him, merely insisted that he do what she had requested.

"She also told Hans not to say anything about it to Håkan," Linda added. "That was the strangest part. I mean, he'd have been bound to notice it sooner or later."

"But there might not necessarily have been anything sinister about it," Wallander suggested. "Maybe she wanted to surprise him?"

"Could be. But Hans also said it was the only time she ever spoke to him in a threatening tone of voice."

"Is that the word he used? 'Threatening'?"

"Yes."

"Isn't that a bit odd? Such a strong word?"

"I have no doubt that he chose the word carefully."

Wallander made a note: **threatening**. If it was true, it threw new light on the woman who was always smiling.

"What did Hans have to say about East Germany?"

Linda stressed that she had tried in several ways to jog his memory, but without success. He vaguely remembered that when he was very young his mother had brought him some wooden toys from East Berlin. Nothing else. He couldn't recall how long she had been away, nor why she had gone abroad. In those days they had a housekeeper, Katarina, and he often spent a lot more time with her than he did with his parents. Håkan had been at sea, and Louise had been teaching German at the French School and at one of Stockholm's grammar schools—he couldn't remember which one. It could well have been that they had occasionally been guests at a dinner party in a home where German was the first language. He had a vague memory of a man in uniform singing drinking songs in a foreign language at the dinner table.

"He really doesn't remember anything else," Linda said. "Which either means that there was nothing else for him to remember, or that Louise went out of her way to hide her East German adventures from him. But why would she want to do that?"

"Why indeed," said Wallander. "It was never against the law for Swedes to visit East Germany. We did business with them just as we did with every other country. But on the other hand, it was much harder for East German citizens to visit Sweden. The Berlin Wall was built to prevent defections."

"That was before my time. I can remember the wall being pulled down, but not when it was built."

That was the end of the call. Wallander heard a door opening and closing somewhere in the background. He began working his way methodically through the material he had gathered concerning the disappearance of Håkan von Enke, and it seemed to him there was one conclusion. Experience indicated that von Enke had been missing for so long that in all probability he was dead, like his wife. But Wallander decided nevertheless to regard him as still alive, at least for the time being.

After a while Wallander slid the file to one side and leaned back in his chair. Perhaps when we were talking in that windowless room in Djursholm he already knew that he would soon go missing. Did he hope that I would read between the lines of what he said?

Wallander sat up straight. Everything was standing still. He was impatient; he wanted to move forward. He opened an Internet browser and began searching.

He wasn't really sure what he was looking for. He scrolled through all the information on the navy Web site. Step-by-step he followed Håkan von Enke's career. He had climbed the ladder steadily, but more slowly than many of his contemporaries. After about an hour of surfing, Wallander came across a photograph taken at a reception at the office for foreign military attachés. There were a number of young officers in the picture, including Håkan. He was smiling directly at the camera. A confident, open smile. Wallander contemplated the old picture, trying to see something that would tell him who the troubled man he had met in Djursholm really was.

He stood up and opened the window slightly, then resumed his Internet research. He tried to use his imagination to find unexpected ways of getting information about Håkan von Enke's life: he read about East Germany, and their naval maneuvers in the southern Baltic Sea that both Sten Nordlander and Håkan von Enke had talked about. He spent the most time on submarine incidents in the early 1980s. He occasionally noted down a name, an event, a thought; but he was unable to find any blots on Håkan von Enke's record. Nor did he find anything out of the ordinary about Louise when he visited the Web site of the French School in Stockholm. Linda had chosen a man whose parents were prime examples of bourgeois decency and uprightness. On the surface, at least.

It was almost eleven-thirty when he started yawning. His surfing had taken him to the very limits of what might be interesting. But he suddenly paused and leaned toward the screen. There was an article from one of the evening papers, dating from early 1987. A journalist had dug up information about a private location in Stockholm where parties and receptions often took place, frequented by high-ranking naval officers. The parties were evidently shrouded in secrecy; only a few people were allowed to attend, and none of the officers the journalist had contacted was prepared to comment. But one of the waitresses, Fanny Klarström, had. She talked about the unpleasant, hate-filled conversations about Olof Palme that had taken place, and about the arrogance of the officers, and said that she had stopped working there because she was not prepared to put up with it any longer. Among those who used to attend the gatherings was Håkan von Enke.

Wallander printed out the two newspaper pages. There was also a photograph of Fanny Klarström. Wallander judged her to be about sixty at the time, which meant that she could still be alive. He also wrote down the name of the journalist, and noted that this was the second banquet hall he had come across in connection with Håkan von Enke. He folded the article and put it in his pocket.

There were occasionally rumors in circulation about secret associations and parties in certain police circles. Wallander had never been invited to anything of the sort, however. The nearest he could think of was an occasion a long time ago when Rydberg proposed that they meet once a month for good food and drink in the restaurant at Svaneholm Castle; but nothing had come of it.

Wallander switched off the computer and left the room. Halfway down the hall he turned, went back, and turned off the light. He left the police station the same way he had arrived, through the basement. He collected some dirty towels and shirts from his locker and took them home to wash.

He paused in the parking lot and breathed in the summer night. He was going to live for a long time yet. His will to live was still strong.

He drove home, slept, dreamed uneasily about Mona, but woke up refreshed. He got out of bed immediately, eager to make use of the unexpected energy he seemed to be filled with. It was barely eight o'clock by the time he picked up the telephone to try to track down the journalist who had written about the naval officers' secret meetings over twenty years ago. After several failed attempts via directory assistance, he glanced ruefully at his broken computer and wondered whom to disturb, Linda or Martinsson. He chose the latter. One of the grandchildren answered. Wallander didn't have much sensible conversation with the little girl before Martinsson took the phone.

"You've just been speaking to Astrid," he said. "She's three years old, has blazing red hair, and likes nothing better than to pull at the remaining few tufts of hair that I possess."

"My computer has broken down. Can I ask you to look something up for me, please?"

"I'll call you back in a couple of minutes."

Five minutes later the phone rang. It was Martinsson. Wallander gave him the journalist's name, Torbjörn Setterwall. It didn't take Martinsson long to trace him.

"Three years too late," said Martinsson.

"What do you mean by that?"

"That Torbjörn Setterwall has died. In some strange kind of accident in an elevator, it seems. He was fifty-four years old, and left a wife and three children. How can you die in an elevator?"

"Maybe it dropped down to the bottom of the shaft? Or he could have been squashed?"

"I wasn't able to be of much assistance, I'm afraid."

"I have another name," said Wallander. "This one could be more difficult. And there's a chance she could be dead as well."

"What's her name?"

"Fanny Klarström."

"Another journalist?"

"A waitress."

"Hmm. As you say, it could be more difficult. But her name isn't among the most common, neither Fanny nor Klarström."

Wallander waited while Martinsson began the search. He could hear him humming a tune as he tapped away at the keyboard. Martinsson was usually on the melancholy side, but he was obviously in a good mood. Let's hope he stays that way, Wallander thought.

"I'll get back to you," Martinsson said. "This is going to take a while."

In fact it took Martinsson less than twenty minutes. When he called back he was able to inform Wallander that eighty-four-year-old Fanny Klarström lived in Markaryd in Småland. She had an apartment of her own in a retirement home called Lillgården.

"How did you do it?" Wallander asked. "Are you sure it's the right person?"

"Absolutely certain."

"How can you be so sure?"

"I've spoken to her," said Martinsson, to Wallander's astonishment. "I called her, and she told me she'd been a waitress for nearly fifty years."

"Amazing. One of these days you must explain what you do that I can't do."

Wallander wrote down Fanny Klarström's address and phone number. According to Martinsson, her voice had sounded old and rough, but she was clear in the head.

After the call he went out. The sun was blazing down from a clear blue sky. Kites were soaring in the up-winds, searching for prey at the edge of the fields. Wallander wondered what he wanted, apart from what he had already. Nothing, he thought. Perhaps to be able to afford to travel south when winter was at its coldest. A little apartment in Spain. But he dismissed that thought immediately. He would never feel comfortable there, surrounded by people he didn't know speaking a language he would never be able to learn properly. In one way or another, Skåne would be his terminus. He would stay in his house for as long as possible. When he couldn't manage that anymore, he hoped the end would come quickly. What scared him more than anything else was an old age spent simply waiting to die, a time when nothing of what had been his life was still possible.

He made a decision. He would drive to Markaryd and pay a visit to the waitress. He didn't know what good a conversation might do, but he couldn't shake off the curiosity that had been aroused by that newspaper article. He took out his old school atlas. Markaryd was only a few hours' drive away.

He set off the next day, after speaking to Linda on the phone. She listened carefully to what he had to say. When he finished, she announced that she would like to go with him. He was annoyed and asked how she thought Klara would be able to cope with a car journey on what seemed set to become one of the summer's hottest days.

"Hans is at home today," she said. "He can look after his daughter. But you don't want me to come. I can hear it."

"What makes you say that?"

"The fact that it's true."

It **was** true. Wallander had been looking forward to a drive all on his own, heading north toward the Småland forests. It was one of his simple pleasures, going for drives without company. He liked the freedom it gave him, being alone in the car, without the radio on, and with the possibility of stopping whenever it suited him.

He accepted that Linda had seen through him.

"Are we still on speaking terms?" he asked.

"Of course we are," she said. "But sometimes you're a bit weird for my taste."

"You don't choose your parents. If I'm weird, it's because I inherited it from your grandfather, who really was a strange person."

"Good luck. Let me know how it went. I must say, in all honesty, that you never give up."

"Do you?"

She laughed softly.

"Never. I don't even know how to spell those words."

It was eleven o'clock when Wallander set off. By one he had gotten as far as Älmhult, where he had lunch in a crowded Ikea restaurant. The long line at the counter made him nervous and irritated. He ate far too quickly, and afterward took a wrong turn, so that he reached Markaryd an hour later than planned. The attendant at a gas station explained the best route to the sheltered accommodation at Lillgården. When he got out of the car, he was struck by how similar it looked to Niklasgården. The thought made him wonder if the man who had claimed to be Signe's uncle had made another visit. He would find out about that as soon as he had time.

An elderly man in blue overalls was crouching over a

lawn mower that had been turned upside down. He was poking at it with a stick, removing large chunks of compressed grass from the blades. Wallander asked about Fanny Klarström. The man stood up and stretched his back. He spoke with a broad Småland accent that Wallander found difficult to understand.

"Her apartment is right at the far end, on the ground floor."

"How is she?"

The man looked at Wallander with an expression that was both searching and suspicious.

"Fanny is old and tired. Who are you?"

Wallander produced his police ID, and regretted it immediately. Why should he risk exposing Fanny to gossip about a policeman coming to visit her? But it was too late now. The man in the blue overalls studied the ID card carefully.

"You're from Skåne, I can hear that. Ystad?"

"As you can see."

"And you've come all the way here, to Markaryd?"

"I'm not actually on police business," Wallander explained in as friendly a tone as he could muster. "It's more of a personal visit."

"That's good for Fanny. She hardly ever has any visitors."

Wallander nodded at the lawn mower.

"You should wear earplugs."

"I don't hear a thing. My ears were ruined when I worked as a miner as a young man."

Wallander entered the building and set off along the hallway to the left. An old man was standing by a window, staring out at the back of a tumbledown building. Wallander shuddered. He stopped outside a door with a nameplate, beautifully painted with flowers in pastel shades.

Just for a moment he considered turning on his heel and leaving. Then he rang the bell.

25

When Fanny Klarström opened the door—immediately, as if she had been standing there for a thousand years, waiting for him—she gave him a broad smile. He was the longed-for visitor, he just had time to think before she ushered him into her room and closed the door.

Wallander felt as if he were entering a lost world.

Fanny Klarström smelled as if somebody had just lit a fire of alder wood right next to him. It was a smell Wallander remembered from the short time he had spent as a Boy Scout. His troop had gone for a hike. They had set up camp on the shore of a lake, probably Krageholm Lake, where Wallander had experienced several depressing happenings later in life, and lit a campfire made from newly sawn alder. But then, do alders really grow by lakes in Skåne? Wallander thought that was a question to answer later.

Fanny Klarström had wavy blue hair, and was tastefully made up—perhaps she was always ready to receive an unexpected visitor. When she smiled she displayed a beautiful set of teeth that made Wallander jealous. His own teeth had begun to need filling when he was twelve, and since then he had been fighting a constant battle with dental hygiene and dentists who seemed always to be tearing a strip off him. He still had most of his own teeth, but his dentist had warned him that they would soon start to fall out if he didn't brush them more often and more efficiently. At the age of eighty-four, Fanny Klarström had all her teeth, and they shone brightly as if she were still a teenager. She didn't ask who he was or what he wanted, but invited him in to her little living room, where the walls were covered in framed photographs. Well-tended potted plants and climbers stood on windowsills and shelves. There's not a single grain of dust in this apartment, Wallander thought. He sat down on the sofa she had gestured toward, and said he would be delighted to accept a cup of coffee.

While she was in the little kitchen he wandered around the room, examining all the photographs. There was a wedding photo dated 1942: Fanny with a man with slicked-down hair in a formal suit. Wallander thought he recognized the same man in another photo, this time in overalls and standing on a ship, the picture being taken from the quay. He deduced from other photos that Fanny had only one child. When he heard the clinking of china approaching, he sat down on the sofa again.

Fanny served coffee with a steady hand; she retained

the skill she had acquired during many years as a waitress and didn't spill a drop. She sat down opposite him in a rather worn armchair. A speckled gray cat appeared from nowhere and settled on her knee. She raised her cup, and Wallander did the same before tasting the coffee, which was very strong. It went down the wrong way and made him cough so violently that tears came to his eyes. When he recovered, she handed him a napkin. He dried his eyes and noticed that "Billingen Hotel" was embroidered on it.

"Perhaps I should begin by telling you why I'm here," he said.

"Friendly people are always welcome," said Fanny Klarström.

She spoke with an unmistakable Stockholm accent. Wallander wondered why she had chosen to grow old in a place as far off the beaten track as Markaryd.

Wallander placed a printout of the newspaper article on the embroidered cloth that covered the table. She didn't bother to read it, merely glanced at the two pictures. But she seemed to remember even so. Wallander didn't want to jump in at the deep end, and began by expressing a polite interest in all the photos hanging on the walls. She had no hesitation in telling him about them, and in doing so summarized her whole life in a few words.

In 1941, Fanny—whose surname then was Andersson—met a young sailor by the name of Arne Klarström.

"We were madly in love," she said. "We met on one of the Djurgården ferries, on the way back from the Gröna Lund amusement park. As I was going ashore at Slussen, I stumbled and fell. He helped me up. What would have happened if I hadn't fallen? Anyway, you could say that I literally stumbled into the love of my life. Which lasted for exactly two years. We got married, I became pregnant, and Arne dithered and dallied and wondered if he dared to continue working on the convoy traffic, given the circumstances. It's easy to forget how many Swedish sailors died when their ships were mined during those years, even though we were not directly involved in the war. But Arne no doubt felt he was invulnerable, and I could never imagine that anything would happen to him. Our son, Gunnar, was born in January 1943—the twelfth, at six-thirty in the morning. Arne was on shore leave at the time, and so he saw his son just the once. Nine days later his ship was blown up by a mine in the North Sea. Nothing was ever found—no wreckage of the ship and no bodies of those on board."

She paused, and looked at the photographs on the wall.

"Anyway," she began again after a while, "there I was on my own, with a son to look after and the love of my life gone forever. I suppose I tried to find another man to live with. I was still young. But nobody could compare with Arne. He was my true love, my husband, no matter whether he was alive or dead. Nobody could ever replace him."

She suddenly started crying, almost silently. Wallander felt a lump in his throat. He slid the napkin she had just given him toward her.

"I sometimes long to have somebody to share my sorrow with," she said, still with tears in her eyes. "Maybe that's why loneliness can feel so oppressive. Just think, having to invite a total stranger into your house so that you have somebody to cry with."

"What about your son?" Wallander asked tentatively.

"He lives in Abisko. That's a long way from here. He comes to see me once a year, sometimes alone, sometimes with his wife and some of his children. He keeps trying to persuade me to move there, but it's too far north for me, too cold. Old waitresses get swollen feet and can't cope with cold temperatures."

"What does he do in Abisko?"

"Something to do with forestry. I think he counts trees."

"But you have settled here in Markaryd?"

"I used to live here when I was a child, before we moved to Stockholm. I didn't really want to leave. I moved back here to prove that I'm still just as obstinate as I always was. And it's cheap. A waitress isn't in a position to save up a fortune."

"And you were a waitress for a long time, weren't you?"

"For all those years, yes. Cups, glasses, plates, in and out, a conveyor belt that never stopped. Restaurants, hotels, and once even a Nobel Prize banquet. I remember having the great honor of serving Ernest Hemingway his meal. He actually looked at me once.

I longed to tell him that he should write a book about the terrible fate of so many sailors during the Second World War, but of course I didn't say a word. I think it was 1954. In any case, Arne had been dead for a long time by then. Gunnar was practically a teenager."

"But sometimes you also worked in private banquet halls, is that right?"

"I liked to have a bit of variety. And I wasn't the type to keep quiet when a restaurateur didn't behave as he should. I used to speak out on behalf of my fellow workers, not just for myself, and of course, that meant I got the sack now and then. I was very active as a trade unionist in those days."

"Let's talk about this particular private party facility," said Wallander, judging that the right moment had now arrived.

He pointed to the newspaper article. She put on a pair of glasses that had been hanging on a ribbon around her neck, glanced through the article, then slid it to one side.

"Let me start by defending myself," she said with a laugh. "We were paid very well to serve those unpleasant officers. A poor waitress like me could earn as much for one evening there as I was normally paid for a whole month, if things turned out well. They were all drunk by the time they went home, and some of them used to hand out hundred-krona notes like a farmer spreading muck in his fields. It could add up to a considerable sum."

"Where was this place?"

"On Östermalm—doesn't it say that in the article? It was owned by a man who had previously been associated with Per Engdahl's Nazi movement. Despite his disgusting political views, he was a very good cook. He'd made a small fortune working as a chef for some high-ranking German officers who had fled to Argentina. They paid him well, he served them whatever food they asked for, said 'Heil Hitler' now and again, and at the end of the 1950s returned home and was able to buy that place on Östermalm. Everything I've just told you is what I was told by reliable sources."

"And who might they be?"

She hesitated for a moment before answering.

"People who had been members of the Engdahl movement, but left," she said.

Wallander was beginning to realize that he had not really understood Fanny Klarström's background properly.

"Would I be correct in thinking that you weren't only active in trade union circles, but that you also had political interests?"

"I was an active Communist. I suppose I still am, in a way. The idea of a world in which everybody has a common cause with everybody else is still the only ideal I can believe in. The only political truth that can't be questioned, in my opinion."

"Did that have anything to do with you applying for a job waiting on those officers?"

"I was asked to apply by the party. It was of some interest to know what conservative naval officers talked about among themselves. Nobody suspected that a waitress with swollen legs would remember what they said."

Wallander tried to assess the significance of what he had just heard.

"Wasn't there a risk that repeating what you had heard could be regarded as an impropriety?"

The tears had dried up now. She regarded him with some amusement.

"'Impropriety'? Fanny Klarström has never been a spy, if that's what you mean. I don't understand why police officers always have to express themselves in such a complicated way. I spoke about it to my comrades in the party group, and that was all. Just as other people might talk about the attitudes of bus drivers or sales-clerks. In the 1950s it wasn't only the nonsocialists who regarded us Communists as potential traitors. The Social Democrats thought so as well. But of course, we weren't anything of the sort."

"Let's forget that question, then. But I am a police officer, and justified in thinking along those lines."

"It was over fifty years ago. Whatever was said and happened in those days must surely be out of date and of no interest now."

"Not quite," Wallander said. "History isn't just something that's behind us, it's also something that follows us."

She made no comment. He wasn't sure whether she had understood what he meant. Wallander steered the conversation back to the newspaper article. He realized that Fanny Klarström had a pent-up need to talk to somebody, which meant there was a serious risk that their conversation could go on for a very long time.

Was his own future going to be similar? An aging, lonely old man who grabbed ahold of anybody he happened to come across and held on to them for as long as possible?

Fanny the waitress had a good memory. She remembered most of the men in uniform with their various insignia, gathered together on the fuzzy printout. Her comments were needle sharp, often malicious, and it was obvious to Wallander that she considered every word justified. There was, for instance, a Commander Sunesson who was always telling dirty jokes, which she described as "not funny, just coarse." He had also been one of the most extreme Palme-haters, and the one who proposed quite openly various ways of liquidating the "Russian spy."

"I have a horrible memory of Commander Sunesson," she said. "Two days after Palme was shot down in a Stockholm street, these officers were booked for one of their dinners. Sunesson stood up and proposed a toast in gratitude for the fact that Olof Palme had finally had the sense to disappear from the land of the living and could no longer poison the air for all upright citizens. I recall his exact words, and I came close to pouring something over him. It was a terrible evening."

Wallander pointed at Håkan von Enke.

"What do you remember about him?"

"He was one of the better ones. He didn't drink too

much, seldom said anything, just listened most of the time. He was also one of the most polite. He actually saw me, if I can put it like that."

"What about the hatred of Palme? The fear of Russia?"

"They all shared that. They thought of course Sweden should be a member of NATO—it was a scandal that we steered clear of it. Many of them also thought that Sweden should acquire atomic weapons right away, that if only we could arm a few submarines with those weapons, it would be possible to defend the Swedish borders. All conversations were about the fight between God and the devil."

"The devil came from the east?"

"And God the Father was also known as the U.S.A. There was evidently some kind of secret agreement in the 1950s between the government and the top military brass that American planes could cross Swedish borders whenever they liked. Our air-traffic controllers had certain codes that the Americans knew about and used. So all the Yanks needed to do was to take off from their bases in Norway and head for the Soviet Union. I recall discussing this with my friends and being upset about it."

"But what about the submarines?"

"We talked about them all the time."

"Including the one trapped in the shallows off Karlskrona? And the ones in the Hårsfjärden channel?"

Her reply surprised him.

"They were two entirely separate incidents."

"How could that be?"

"A Russian submarine had run aground off Karl-skrona. But there was never any confirmation of what was lurking under the surface at Hårsfjärden. That was no doubt intentional."

"What do you mean by that?"

"They drank a few toasts to the poor captain—what was his name?"

"Gushchin."

"Yes, that was it. Poor old Gus, they said. He was so drunk that his submarine got stuck on a Swedish rock. So at last they had the Russian submarine they'd always wanted to capture. Right? This proved beyond doubt that it was the Russians who were playing hide-and-seek inside Swedish territorial waters. But with regard to Hårsfjärden, there was nobody there who wanted to drink a toast to any Russian captain—do you get my meaning?"

"Are you suggesting that there weren't any Russians lurking around under the surface at Hårsfjärden?"

"It was impossible to prove anything, one way or the other."

Fanny Klarström continued talking enthusiastically about things Wallander didn't know much about. He had never tried to conceal his extremely limited knowledge of history. Earlier in his life he simply hadn't been all that interested. But now he was listening closely to what Fanny Klarström had to say.

"So Russia was the enemy," Wallander said.

"None of our military men thought otherwise. Whenever the officers met they would talk to each other as if we were already at war with the Russians.

Nobody gave a thought to the possibility that the U.S.A. could be just as big a threat."

"What was the point of those dinners?"

"To eat and drink well, and to criticize the politicians who 'represented a threat to Swedish sovereignty.' Those were the precise words they always used. The main enemy was the Social Democrats. Even though everybody knew that Olof Palme was a staunch Democrat, he was always referred to in these circles as a 'Communist.'"

Despite Wallander's protests, Fanny went to make more coffee. He already had a stomachache. When she came back he explained the real reason for his visit to Markaryd.

"Wasn't there something in the papers about that couple's disappearance?" she asked when he had finished his account.

"The woman, Louise, was recently found dead just outside Stockholm."

"Poor woman. What happened?"

"She was probably murdered."

"Why?"

"We don't have an answer to that yet."

"And the man is that officer in the picture there?"

"Yes, Håkan von Enke. If you can remember anything else about him, I'd like to hear it."

She thought hard, studying the photograph.

"He's difficult to remember," she said eventually. "I think I've already told you everything I can recall. Maybe that in itself says something about him? He hardly ever made a fuss, just sat there quietly. He wasn't one of those who drank a lot and couldn't stop talking. I remember him always having a smile on his face."

Wallander frowned. Could her memory be completely wrong?

"Are you sure he was always smiling? My impression is that he was a very serious man."

"I may be wrong. But I'm quite certain he wasn't one of the awful warmongers. On the contrary, my memory is that he was one of the tiny minority who sometimes spoke up for peace. I no doubt remember that because it interested me."

"What did?"

"Peace. I was one of those who demanded that Sweden renounce nuclear weapons as early as the 1950s."

"So Håkan von Enke spoke up for peace?"

"As I recall, yes. But it was a long time ago."

Wallander could see that she really was doing her best. He sipped at his coffee, trying to avoid actually drinking any, and nibbled on a cookie. And then he lost a filling. The tooth started hurting immediately. He wrapped the filling in a paper napkin and put it in his pocket. It was the middle of summer; his dentist would no doubt be on vacation and Wallander would be referred to some emergency center. He was irritated by the thought that his body was starting to fall to pieces. Once the most important parts stopped working, it would be all over.

"America." Fanny Klarström interrupted his train of thought. "I knew there was something else."

There was an incident that had stuck in her memory and made a deep impression; that was why she remembered it so clearly.

"It was one of the last times I worked at those banquets. There was evidently a request to see young ladies in short skirts rather than old ones with swollen legs. It didn't bother me because I couldn't have coped much longer with serving drinks and meals to those people. They used to have their meetings on the first Tuesday of every month. It must have been 1987, in March. I remember that because I'd broken the little finger of my left hand and wasn't able to work for quite a while. I started again that very evening. They always used to finish up with coffee and brandy or whatever in a drab little room with leather chairs and dark bookcases. I remember because I've always enjoyed reading. Sometimes when I arrived early for one of the banquets, before starting to set the tables I would go to that room and look at the books. I soon discovered to my surprise that they were fakes—just covers with nothing inside. The owner or maybe the interior designer he'd hired had evidently bought them from some stage props supplier. I remember that my respect for those people suffered another significant blow."

She sat up straight in the armchair, as if in an attempt to prevent herself from losing the thread again.

"Suddenly one of the officers started talking about spies," she continued. "I was going around with a bottle of very expensive cognac at the time, filling their glasses. It wasn't unusual for them to talk about spies. Wennerström was a popular topic. Several of them announced that they would willingly kill him with their own hands, once the liquor got them talking. I recall an admiral, von Hartman I think his name was, suggesting that Wennerström be throttled slowly with a balalaika string. Then Håkan von Enke started talking. He asked why nobody seemed to be worried that spies for the U.S.A. might be active in Sweden. That aroused a furious reaction. It deteriorated into a very unpleasant argument, during which several of the officers called his loyalty into question. Of course they were all drunk, with the possible exception of von Enke. In any case, he was so angry that he stood up and stormed out of the room. That had never happened before, during all the years I had been serving them. I don't know if he ever came back, because the young, attractive waitresses took over. I remember the incident well because my friends and I had always thought the same. If the Russians had spies in Sweden, which they doubtless did, you could be sure that the Americans were active as well. But these officers refused to believe that. Or at least, if they did, they preferred not to say so."

She stood up in order to serve him more coffee. Wallander smiled and placed his hand over his cup. When she sat down again, he couldn't help seeing her swollen legs and varicose veins. He could just imagine her, serving the officers in the banquet hall.

"Anyway, that's what I remember," she said. "Could it be of some use?"

"Definitely," said Wallander. "Every piece of information increases the possibility of our being able to work out what happened."

She took off her glasses and studied him.

"Is he dead as well?"

"We don't know."

"Could he be the one who killed her?"

"We don't know that either. But of course, anything is possible."

"That's what usually happens," she said with a sigh. "Men kill their wives. They sometimes claim they intended to kill themselves as well, but there are a lot who don't have the courage."

"Yes," said Wallander. "That often happens. Men can prove to be very cowardly when the chips are down."

She suddenly started crying again, a trickle of almost invisible tears running down her cheeks. Wallander felt a lump in his throat once again. Loneliness is not a pretty thing, he thought. She sits here among all her silent photos, and her only company is her memories.

"It's never happened before, me crying like this," she said, drying her cheeks. "But he keeps coming back to me, my husband, more and more often, the older I get. I think he's waiting for me down there in the depths; he's tugging at me. I'll soon be going to accompany him. I get the feeling that I've lived my life now. But it keeps going nevertheless. A tired old heart, still beating away; but my dark night is somebody's day."

"That rhymes," said Wallander.

"I know," she said, then burst out laughing. "An old woman thinking poetic thoughts in her hours of loneliness."

Wallander stood up and thanked her for her hospitality. She insisted on accompanying him to his car, despite the fact that he could see her legs were hurting. The man with the lawn mower was no longer there.

"Summer brings longing," she said as they shook hands. "My husband has been gone for over sixty years, but I can still feel an intense longing for him, just like when we first met. Can a policeman experience anything like that?"

"Oh yes," said Wallander. "He most certainly can."

She waved as he drove away. That's a person I will never see again, he thought. He left the village and shook off the melancholy of his visit to Fanny Klarström, but he couldn't stop thinking about her comment that men kill their wives and then are too cowardly to kill themselves. That Håkan von Enke might have killed Louise was one of the first thoughts Wallander had had after his meeting with Hermann Eber. There was no obvious motive, no proof, no clues. It was just a possibility among many others. But he had the feeling that, having heard Fanny Klarström say what she did, he should take another look at that fragile hypothesis. As he drove through the Småland forests, he tried to think of a series of events that would lead to Louise's being killed by her husband.

He arrived home without having made any real progress.

But that night he lay awake for a long time thinking about Fanny Klarström before finally falling asleep.

26

Wallander was still asleep when the phone rang. It was his father's old phone that he had rescued for sentimental reasons when the old man's house in Löderup had been cleared out before being sold. He considered letting it ring and ring, but eventually he got up and answered. It was one of the new women in the police station reception; Ebba, who had been there since time immemorial, had now retired and moved with her husband to an apartment in central Malmö, where their children lived. Wallander couldn't recall the new receptionist's name—maybe it was Anna, but he wasn't sure.

"There's a woman here asking for your address," she said. "I only let people have it with your permission. She's from abroad."

"Of course," said Wallander. "All the women I know are from abroad."

He stayed at the phone, and on his third attempt managed to pin down a dentist who could treat him an hour later.

It was almost noon when he got back home from the dentist's. He had started thinking about lunch when there was a knock on the door. When he answered it, he knew immediately who it was, even though she had changed. Baiba Liepa from Riga,

Latvia. There was no doubt she was the one standing on his doorstep, older and paler.

"Good God!" he said. "So you were the lady asking for my address?"

"I didn't want to disturb you."

"How could you ever disturb me?"

He embraced her, and could feel that she had become very thin. It had been over fifteen years since their brief but torrid love affair. And it must have been ten years since they were last in touch. Wallander had been drunk and called her in the middle of the night. Needless to say, he regretted it later, and resolved never to contact her again. But now, with her standing there in front of him, he could feel his emotions bubbling over. Their affair had been the most passionate experience of his life. Being with her had put his protracted relationship with Mona into perspective. He had experienced sensual pleasure with Baiba greater than he had previously thought possible. He had been keen to start a new life and wanted to marry her, but she turned him down. She didn't want to live with another police officer, and risk becoming a widow again, which she had already been through.

Now they were facing each other in his living room. He still found it difficult to believe that it really was her who had reappeared from somewhere far away in time and space.

"I never imagined this would happen," he said. "That we would meet again."

"You never got in touch."

"No. I didn't. I wanted what was over and done with to be over and done with."

He ushered her to the sofa and sat down beside her. He suddenly had the feeling that everything was not as it should be. She was too pale, too thin, too tired and awkward in her movements.

She read his mind, as she always had, and took his hand.

"I wanted to see you again," she said. "You are convinced that people are gone forever, but then you wake up one day and realize that you can never break away entirely from people who have been especially important in your life."

"There's some special reason why you've come here now," said Wallander.

"I'd like a cup of tea," she said. "Are you sure I'm not disturbing you?"

"There's only me and a dog," said Wallander. "That's all."

"How's your daughter?"

"Do you remember her name?"

Baiba looked offended. Wallander recalled how easily she had taken offense.

"Do you really think I've forgotten about Linda?"

"I suppose I thought that you'd erased everything to do with me."

"That was something about you that I never liked— you always made such a drama out of everything. How could anybody possibly 'erase' somebody they'd once been in love with?"

Wallander was already on his way to the kitchen, to make tea.

"I'll come with you," she said, standing up.

When Wallander saw what an effort it was for her, he realized that she was ill.

She filled a saucepan with water and put it on the stove, giving the impression that she was immediately at home in his kitchen. He took out the cups he had inherited from his mother, the only items that remained to preserve her memory. They sat down at the kitchen table.

"This is a lovely house you have here," she said. "I remember you used to talk about moving out to the country, but I didn't believe you'd ever do it."

"I didn't believe it either. Not to mention that I'd ever get myself a dog."

"What's her name?"

"It's a he. Jussi."

Their conversation died out. He eyed her without making it obvious. The bright sunshine coming in through the kitchen window emphasized her emaciated features.

"I never left Riga," she said à propos of nothing. "I've managed to trade up to a better apartment twice, but I could never even think about living out in the country. When I was a child I was sent to live with my grandparents for a few years, in extreme poverty that I always associate with the Latvian countryside. Maybe it's an image that no longer applies today, but I can't shake it off."

"You were working at the university when we were together. What are you doing now?"

She didn't respond, but took a sip of tea and then slid her cup to one side.

"I'm actually a qualified engineer," she said. "Have you forgotten that? When we met I was translating scientific literature for the technical college. But I don't do that anymore. Not now that I'm ill."

"What's the nature of your illness?"

She answered quietly, as if what she was saying wasn't all that important.

"I'm dying. I have cancer. But I don't want to talk about that right now. Do you mind if I lie down for a while? I'm taking painkillers that are so strong, I find it hard to stay awake."

She headed for the sofa, but Wallander ushered her into his bedroom. He had changed the sheets only a couple of days ago. He smoothed out the bed before she lay down. Her head almost disappeared into the pillow. She smiled wanly, as if she had recalled something.

"Haven't I been in this bed before?"

"Of course you have. It's an old bed."

"I'll take a nap. Just an hour. They said at the police station that you were on vacation."

"You can sleep here for as long as you like."

He wasn't sure if she had heard him, or if she had already fallen asleep. Why has she come here to visit me? he wondered. I can't cope with any more death and misery, any more wives drinking themselves to death, any more mothers being murdered. He regretted that thought the moment he had it. He sat down very carefully at the end of the bed and looked at her. The memory of their affair returned and upset him so much that he started shaking. I don't want her to die, he thought. I want her to live. Maybe now she's prepared to give living with a policeman another go.

Wallander went out and sat on one of the garden chairs. After a while he let Jussi out of his kennel. Baiba's car was an old Citroën with Latvian plates. He switched on his cell phone and saw that Linda had called. He called her back, and she sounded pleased when she heard his voice.

"I just wanted to tell you that Hans has been awarded a bonus. Several hundred thousand kronor. That means we can rebuild the house."

"Did he really earn that kind of money?" Wallander wondered, with a trace of cynicism in his voice.

"Why shouldn't he?"

Wallander told her that Baiba had come to visit him. Linda listened to what he said about the woman now lying asleep in his bed.

"I've seen pictures of her," said Linda when he'd finished. "You've spoken about her. But according to Mom she was just a Latvian prostitute."

Wallander was furious.

"Your mother can be a terrible person sometimes. Making a claim like that is shameful. In many ways Baiba has all the qualities that Mona lacks. When did she say that?"

"How do you expect me to remember?"

"I think I'll call her and tell her never to be in touch with me again."

"What good would that do? She was probably jealous. People say things like that when they're jealous."

Reluctantly, Wallander acknowledged that she was right, and calmed down. Then he told her that Baiba was seriously ill.

"Has she come to say good-bye, then?" she asked. "That sounds sad."

"That was my first reaction too. I was surprised and pleased to see her. But it only took a few minutes for me to feel depressed again. I seem to be surrounded by nothing but death and misery nowadays."

"You always have been," Linda said. "That was one of the first things they warned us about at the police academy—the kind of working life that lay ahead. But don't forget that you have Klara."

"That's not what I'm talking about. It's the feeling of old age that's creeping up and sticking its claws into the back of my neck. Wherever I look, my circle of friends is thinning out. When Dad died, I became next in line, if you get my meaning. Klara is at the end of that line, but I'm right at the front."

"If Baiba has come to see you, it's because you mean a lot to her. That's the only important thing."

"Come by," said Wallander. "I want you to meet the only woman who has really meant anything to me."

"Apart from Mona."

"That goes without saying."

Linda thought for a while before speaking.

"I have a friend visiting at the moment," she said. "Rakel—do you remember her? She's a police officer in Malmö. She and Klara get along well."

"Aren't you going to bring Klara with you?"

"I'll come on my own, very shortly."

It was almost three o'clock by the time Linda swung into the drive and had to slam on the brakes in order to avoid running into Baiba's car. Wallander always thought she drove far too fast, but on the other hand he was relieved whenever she didn't use her motorcycle. He frequently told her so, but the only response he ever got was a loud snort.

Baiba had woken up and had a sip of water and another cup of tea. She spent a long time in the bathroom. When she came out she seemed to be less tired than before. Without her knowing, Wallander had watched her injecting herself in the thigh. For a brief moment he glimpsed her nakedness and felt despondency welling up inside him at the thought of all that was now over, never to be repeated, never to be experienced again.

It was an important moment for him when Baiba and Linda greeted each other. It seemed to Wallander that he could now see the Baiba he had met so many years ago in Latvia.

Linda embraced her as if it was the most natural thing in the world, and said she was pleased to meet the love of her father's life at long last. Wallander felt embarrassed but also pleased to see them together. If Mona had been there, despite his current anger with her, and if Linda had been carrying Klara in her arms, the four most important women in his life, in a way the only ones, would have been gathered in his house. A big day, he thought, in the middle of summer, at a time when old age is sneaking up closer and closer.

When Linda heard that Baiba still hadn't had anything to eat, she sent Wallander into the kitchen to make an omelette and went with Baiba out to the garden. He could hear Baiba laughing through the open window. That made his memories even stronger, and his eyes filled with tears. He worried that he seemed to be growing sentimental—a state he had virtually never experienced before, except when he was drunk.

They ate outside, moving with the shade. Wallander spent most of the time listening as Linda asked questions about Latvia, a country she had never visited. Just for a short time, a family is being resurrected, he thought. It will soon be over. And the question, the most difficult question of all to answer, is what will be left?

Linda stayed for just over an hour before announcing that she needed to go home. She had brought a photo of Klara with her, and she showed it to Baiba.

"She might grow up to look just like her grandfather," Baiba said.

"God forbid!" said Wallander.

"Don't believe him," said Linda. "There's nothing he'd wish for more. I hope to see you again," she said as she stood up to go home.

Baiba didn't reply. They hadn't talked about death.

Baiba and Wallander remained in the garden and started talking about their lives. Baiba had a lot of questions to ask, and he answered as best he could. Both of them still lived alone. Some ten years earlier

Baiba had tried to enter into a relationship with a doctor, but she had given up after six months. She had never had any children. Wallander couldn't tell if she regretted that or not.

"Life has been good," she said forcefully. "When our borders finally opened up, I was able to travel. I lived frugally, wrote several newspaper articles, and I was a consultant for a firm that wanted to establish itself in Latvia. I earned the most money from a Swedish bank that is now the biggest in the country. I went abroad twice a year, and I know so much more about the world we live in than I did when we met. I've had a good life. Lonely, but good."

"My torture has always been waking up alone," said Wallander, then wondered if what he had just said was really true.

Baiba laughed as she replied.

"I've always lived alone, apart from that short time with the doctor. But that doesn't mean I've always woken up alone. You don't need to be celibate simply because you're not in a steady relationship."

Wallander felt pangs of jealousy at the thought of strange men lying by Baiba's side in her bed. But he didn't say anything.

Baiba suddenly started talking about her illness. As ever, she was objective.

"It started with my feeling constantly tired," she said. "I soon suspected there was something more ominous behind the weariness. At first the doctors couldn't find anything wrong with me. Burnout, old age; nobody had the right answer. I eventually visited a doctor in Bonn that I'd heard about, a man who specializes in cases that other doctors have failed to diagnose. After a few days giving me various tests and taking samples, he was able to tell me that I had a rare cancerous tumor in my liver. I traveled back to Riga with a death sentence stamped invisibly in my passport. I admit that I leaned on all the contacts I had and was operated on remarkably quickly. But it was too late; the cancer had spread. A few weeks ago I was told that I now have metastases in my brain. It's taken less than a year. I won't last until Christmas; I'll die in the fall. I'm trying to spend the time I have left doing what I want to do more than anything else. There are a few places in the world I want to visit again, a few people I want to see again. You are one of them—perhaps the one I've wanted to see most of all."

Wallander burst into tears, sobbing violently. She took his hand, which made matters even worse. He stood up and walked around to the back of the house. When he had pulled himself together, he returned.

"I don't want to bring you sorrow," she said. "I hope you understand why I was compelled to come here."

"I have never forgotten the time we spent together," he said. "I've often wanted to relive it. Now that you're here, I have to ask you a question. Have you ever had any regrets?"

"You mean that I said no when you asked me to marry you?"

"It's a question I think about all the time."

"Never. It was right then, and it must remain right now, after all these years."

Wallander said nothing. He understood. Why should she have considered marrying a foreign policeman when her husband, also a police officer, had just been murdered? Wallander remembered how he had tried to persuade her. But if the roles had been reversed, how would he have reacted? What would he have chosen to do?

They sat for a long time in silence. In the end Baiba stood up, stroked Wallander's hair, and went back into the house. Since he could see that her pain had started again, he assumed she was giving herself another injection. When she didn't come back, he went inside to investigate. She had fallen asleep on his bed. She didn't wake up until late in the afternoon, and once she had overcome her initial confusion about where she was, her first question was if she could stay the night before catching a ferry to Poland the next morning and driving back to Riga.

"That's too far for you to drive," said Wallander firmly. "I'll go with you, drive you home. Then I can fly back."

She shook her head and said she wanted to go home on her own, just as she had come. When Wallander tried to insist, she became annoyed and shouted at him. But she stopped immediately and apologized. He sat down on the edge of the bed and took her hand.

"I know what you're thinking," she said. "How long does she have? When is Baiba going to die? If I had the least suspicion that my time was up now I wouldn't have stayed. I wouldn't even have come in the first place. When I feel that the end is imminent and unavoidable, I won't prolong the torture. I have access to both pills and injections. I intend to die with a bottle of champagne by my bed. I'll drink a toast to the fact that despite everything, I was able to experience the singular adventure of being born, living, and one day disappearing into the darkness once again."

"Aren't you afraid?"

Wallander immediately wished he could bite his tongue. How could he put a question like that to someone who was dying? But she didn't take offense. He realized with a mixture of despair and embarrassment that she had no doubt long ago grown used to his clumsiness.

"No," said Baiba. "I'm not afraid. I have so little time. I can't waste any of it on thoughts that would only make everything worse."

She got out of bed and made a tour of the house. She paused at the bookcase, noticing a book on Latvia that she had given him.

"Have you ever opened it?" she asked with a smile.

"Lots of times," said Wallander.

It was true.

Afterward, Wallander would remember the time spent in Löderup with Baiba as a room in which all the clocks seemed to have stopped, all movement ceased. She ate very little, spent most of the time in bed with a blanket over her, occasionally injecting herself, and wanted him to be near her. They lay side by side, talked now and then, were just as often silent when she was too tired to converse or had simply fallen asleep. Wallander also dozed off from time to time but woke up with a start after a few minutes, unused to having somebody so close to him.

She told him about the years that had passed, and the astonishing developments that had taken place in her homeland.

"We had no idea in the days you and I were together what was going to happen," she said. "Do you remember the Soviet Black Berets who took potshots all over Riga for no obvious reason? I can admit now that in those days I didn't believe the Soviet Union would ever loosen its grip on us. I imagined the oppression would only increase. The worst of it was that nobody ever knew who could be trusted. Did your neighbors have anything to gain by you being free, or did that frighten them? Which of them were reporting to the KGB, which was everywhere, like a giant ear that nobody could get away from? Now I know I was wrong, and I'm grateful for that. But at the same time, nobody knows what the future holds for Latvia. Capitalism doesn't solve the problems of socialism or the planned economy, nor does democracy solve all the economic crises. I think that right now we are living beyond our resources."

"Isn't there talk of Baltic tigers?" Wallander asked. "States that are as successful as countries in Asia?"

She shook her head with a bitter expression on her face.

"We're living on borrowed money. Including Swedish money. I don't claim to be a particularly knowledgeable or perceptive economist, but I'm quite sure that Swedish banks are lending large sums of money in my country with far too little security. And that can only end one way."

"Badly?"

"Very badly. For the Swedish banks too."

Wallander thought back to the years at the beginning of the 1990s, when they had had their affair. He recalled how scared everybody was. So much had happened in those days that he still didn't understand. Superficially, a major political development had drastically altered Europe, and hence the balance of power between the U.S.A. and the Soviet Union. Until he traveled to Riga to try to solve the case of the dead men in a rubber dinghy that drifted ashore near Ystad, it had never occurred to him that three of Sweden's nearest neighbors were occupied by a foreign power. How could it be that so many of his generation, born in the late 1940s, had never truly comprehended that the Cold War actually was a war, with occupied and oppressed nations as a result? During the 1960s it often seemed that distant Vietnam lay closer to the Swedish border than did the Baltic countries.

"It was difficult to understand for us as well," said Baiba in the middle of the night, when the first light of dawn was beginning to change the color of the sky. "Behind every Latvian was a Russian, we used to say. But behind every Russian there was somebody else."

"Who?"

"Even in the Baltic countries, the way the Russians thought was dictated by what the U.S.A. was doing."

"So behind every Russian was an American, is that right?"

"You could put it like that. But nobody will really know until Russian historians tell us the full truth of everything that happened in those days."

Somewhere during this rambling conversation, their unexpected meeting came to an end. Wallander fell asleep. The last time he'd checked his watch it said five o'clock. When he woke up over an hour later, Baiba had left. He ran outside, but her car was no longer there. Under a stone on the garden table was a photograph. The picture had been taken in 1991, in May, at the Freedom Monument in Riga. Wallander remembered the occasion. Somebody who happened to be passing had taken it for them. They were both smiling, huddled up close, Baiba with her head resting on his shoulder. Next to the photograph was a scrap of paper that seemed to have been torn out of a diary. There was nothing written on it, just a drawing of a heart.

Wallander thought he should drive to Ystad right away, to the quay where ferries to Poland came and went. He was already in the car and had started the engine when he realized that this was the last thing she would want him to do. He went back into the house and lay down on the bed, where he could still smell her body.

He was tired out, and fell asleep. When he woke up a few hours later, he recalled what she had said. Behind every Russian there was somebody else. She had given him something to think about that might be relevant to Håkan and Louise von Enke. **Behind every Russian there was somebody else.**

Who, he wondered, was standing behind them? And which of them was standing behind the other? He didn't know the answer, but could see that it was important.

He went out into the garden, got the ladder the chimney sweep always used, and climbed up onto the roof with a pair of binoculars in his hand. He could see the white ferry heading for Poland. A large part of the most important and happiest time in his life was on board and would never return. He felt a combination of sorrow and pain that he had difficulty coping with.

He was still on the roof when the garbage truck arrived. But the man who collected the bags of trash didn't notice Wallander, perched up there like a crow.

27

Wallander watched the garbage truck drive away. The Poland ferry had vanished in a bank of fog drifting in toward the Scanian coast. His thoughts scared him. Baiba was close to the brink of the abyss at the edge of the unknown. She had said she had a few months, no more.

He suddenly seemed to see himself as he really was. A man filled with self-pity, a thoroughly pathetic figure. He sat there on his roof, and the only truly important thing as far as he was concerned was that Baiba was going to die, not him.

In the end he climbed down and took Jussi for a walk, which was more of an escape. He was who he was, he finally concluded. A man, good at his job, even astute. All his life he had tried to be part of the forces of good in this world, and if he had failed, well, he wasn't the only one. What else could a person do but try his best?

The sky had clouded over. Expecting it to start raining at any moment, he walked with Jussi through fields where the grass had recently been cut, or was lying fallow, or was waiting for the combine. He tried to think a new thought after every fifty strides but couldn't manage it. It was a game he used to play with Linda when she was a child. Now he tried to think thoughts about his life, about Baiba's courage in the face of the inevitable, and about the courage he was sure he lacked himself. He walked slowly along the edge of fields, allowing Jussi to roam freely.

Wallander had worked up a sweat, and he sat down by the side of a small pond surrounded by rusty remains of old agricultural machines. Jussi sniffed at the water, drank, then came to lie down at Wallander's side. The clouds had begun to disperse; it wasn't going to rain after all. Wallander could hear emergency sirens in the distance. Fire engines this time, not an ambulance or some of his colleagues. He closed his eyes and tried to conjure up Baiba. The sirens were coming closer; they were behind him now, on the road leading to Simrishamn. He turned around. The binoculars he'd had with him on the roof were still hanging around his neck. The sirens were very loud and clear now. He stood up. Could one of his neighbors' houses be on fire? He hoped it wasn't the house occupied by the Hanssons, an old couple: Elin was practically immobile, and her husband, Rune, could barely walk with the aid of a walking stick. The sirens were getting closer and closer. He raised the binoculars and saw to his horror two fire engines coming to a halt outside his own house. He started running, with Jussi ahead of him on the path. He occasionally stopped to view his house through the binoculars. Every time, he expected to see flames shooting through the roof, where he had been sitting not long ago, or smoke belching from shattered windows. But there was none of that. Only the fire engines, whose sirens were now silent, and firemen swarming around.

When he arrived at the house, his heart threatening to burst through his chest, fire chief Peter Edler was stroking Jussi, who had arrived first by a large margin. He smiled grimly when Wallander came staggering up. The firemen were preparing to leave. Peter Edler was about the same age as Wallander, a freckled man with a slight Småland accent. They sometimes met in connection with an investigation. Wallander had great respect for him, and appreciated his dry humor.

"One of my men knew you lived here," said Edler, continuing to stroke Jussi.

"What happened?"

"That's what I should be asking you."

"Is the place on fire?"

"Apparently not. But it could easily have been."

Wallander stared uncomprehendingly at Edler.

"I went for a walk about half an hour ago."

Edler nodded toward the house.

"Come in and take a look."

The stench of burned rubber that hit Wallander when he entered the building was strong, almost choking. Edler led him into the kitchen. The firemen had opened a window to let the fumes out. On one of the stove's burners was a frying pan, and next to it a charred rubber place mat. Edler sniffed at the frying pan, from which smoke was still rising.

"Fried egg? Sausage?"

"Egg."

"You went out for a walk without turning off the stove. Not only that, but you left a place mat on a burner. How careless can a detective get?"

Edler shook his head. They went outside again. The firemen were already in the trucks, waiting for their leader.

"It's never happened to me before," said Wallander.

"It had better not happen again."

Edler looked around, admiring the view.

"So you moved out to the country in the end. To be honest, I never thought you'd get around to it. You have a lovely view."

"You haven't moved yourself?"

"We're still in the same house in the middle of town.

Gunnel wants to move out to the country, but I don't. Not as long as I'm still working."

"How long to go?"

Edler shuddered and looked miserable. He smacked the shiny helmet he was holding in his hand against his thigh, as if it were a gun.

"As long as I can, or am allowed to. I might be able to keep going for a few more years, but then I'll be on the scrap heap as well. What I'll do then, I have no idea. I can't just sit at home doing crossword puzzles."

"You could try writing them," said Wallander, thinking of Hermann Eber.

Edler looked at him in surprise, but didn't ask what he meant. It almost seemed as if he hoped Wallander's future would turn out to be as grim as his own.

"Maybe we could form a team? Start a little company and travel around telling people how to protect themselves from burglary and fire?"

"Is it possible to protect yourself from burglary?"

"Hardly. But you can teach people some simple methods of making thieves think twice before targeting your house or apartment."

Edler eyed him doubtfully.

"Do you really believe what you're saying?"

"I'm trying to. But thieves are like children. They learn quickly."

Edler shook his head at Wallander's highly dubious comparison, and climbed into his fire truck.

"Remember to turn off your burners," he said by way of farewell. "But it was smart of you to have a first-rate fire alarm installed that's linked directly to us. Your house could have burned down. Then you'd have had to cope with the nightmare of a smoldering ruin in the middle of summer."

Wallander didn't respond. It was Linda who had insisted on the fire alarm. She had paid for it, given it to him as a Christmas present and made sure it was installed.

He fed Jussi and was just about to start his lawn mower when Linda drove up. She didn't have Klara with her. He could see right away that she was upset. He assumed she had passed the fire engines on the way here.

"What were fire engines doing on your road?" she asked.

"They'd taken a wrong turn," he lied. "There was a short circuit in a neighbor's barn."

"Which barn?"

"The Hanssons'."

"Who are they?"

"What does it matter? You don't know where their house is anyway."

She suddenly threw her purse at him as hard as she could. He managed to duck and was hit only on the shoulder. He picked it up, furious.

"What do you think you're doing?"

"Why the hell do I have to stand here while you tell me boldfaced lies!"

"I'm not telling you lies."

"The fire brigade was here! I stopped and spoke to

your neighbor. He said you were standing next to two fire engines."

"I forgot to switch off one of the burners."

"Did you fall asleep?"

Wallander pointed out into the fields, from where only a few minutes ago he had come racing back; he could still feel the pain in his leg muscles.

"I was out with Jussi."

Without a word, Linda grabbed her purse out of his hand and went into the house. Wallander considered getting into his car and driving off. Linda would go on and on about his lie, and then about his incredible carelessness. She would continue to be upset, and that in turn would make him angry. Indeed, he was already well on the way there. He didn't know what she had in her purse, but it had been heavy, and his shoulder hurt. He felt even more agitated when he thought about the fact that this was the first time she had ever used physical violence toward him.

Linda came out again.

"Do you remember what we talked about a few weeks ago? That day when it was pouring rain, and I was here with Klara?"

"How can I be expected to remember everything we say to each other?"

"We talked about how she could come here and stay with you when she was a bit older."

"Let's stay calm and talk things through," Wallander said. "You arranged the installation of a fire alarm. Now we know it works. The house didn't burn down.

I forgot to turn off a burner. Has that never happened to you?"

She answered without hesitation.

"Not since Klara was born, no."

"I don't think it ever happened to me either when you were little."

The argument died away. They were both good fencers, but neither had the strength to deliver a fatal blow. Linda sat down on one of the garden chairs. Wallander remained standing, afraid her fury might boil over again. She looked at him, clearly worried.

"Are you starting to become forgetful?"

"I've always been forgetful, to a certain extent. Maybe it would be better to say that I'm absentminded."

He sat down, tired of hiding the truth.

"Sometimes whole chunks of time just disappear. Like ice melting away."

"What do you mean?"

Wallander told her about his trip to Höör. But he left out the part about the hitchhiker.

"I suddenly had no idea why I was there. It was like being in a brightly lit room when somebody turns off the light, without warning. I don't know how long I was in pitch darkness. It was as if I didn't even know who I was anymore."

"Has that ever happened before?"

"Not as badly. But I've gone to a doctor, a specialist in Malmö, and she says I'm just overworked. That I think I'm a dashing young thirty-year-old who can still do everything I used to be able to do."

"I don't like what I'm hearing. Go see another doctor."

He nodded but didn't say anything. She stood up and disappeared into the house, emerging eventually with two glasses of water. Wallander suddenly asked if the police had found the woman from Malmö who killed her parents.

"I heard she was arrested in Växjö. Someone had given her a ride and become suspicious. He treated her to a cup of coffee at a roadside café outside the town and called the police. She tried to stab herself through the heart with a knife she had with her, but she didn't succeed."

"Have you ever wanted to kill me?" he asked, relieved to hear that his own part in her flight hadn't come to light. Martinsson had kept his word and said nothing.

"Of course," she said, and burst out laughing. "Plenty of times. Most recently a few minutes ago. I hope the old man doesn't live until he's gaga, I keep thinking. Every child occasionally wishes her parents were dead. How often have you wanted to kill me?"

"Never."

"Do you expect me to believe that?"

"Yes."

"I can console you by telling you that Mona's the one I've had in my sights more often. But naturally, I'm horrified at the thought of one day no longer having you two around. Incidentally, Hans and I managed to persuade Mona to go to a clinic for treatment."

Jussi caught sight of a hare in the field and started

barking. They sat in silence and watched his vain attempts to break out of his kennel. The hare ran off, and Jussi quieted down.

"I came for another reason," she said out of the blue.

"Don't tell me something's happened to Klara?"

"No, she's fine. Hans is at home with her today. I make him accept his responsibilities. I think he enjoys it, actually. Klara is about as far away from the stressful banking world as you can get."

"But something else must have happened?"

"I was in Copenhagen yesterday evening. With a couple of friends. We went to a concert—Madonna, the idol of my youth. It was terrific. Afterward we had a late dinner, then went our separate ways. I was staying at the posh Hotel d'Angleterre—the firm Hans works for gets a corporate rate. I was in a good mood and not all that sleepy, so I went for a walk along Strøget. There were a lot of people out. I sat down on a bench, and that was when I saw him."

"Saw who?"

"Håkan."

Wallander held his breath and stared at her. She was quite certain, he could see that; she had no hesitation.

"It wasn't just his face, which I only caught a glimpse of. It was the way he walked, shoulders back, short rapid strides."

"Describe in detail exactly what you saw."

"I'd sat down on a bench in a little square on Strøget, I don't know what it's called. He was coming from Nyhavn and had already passed me when I noticed him. First I recognized his hair from behind, then the way he walked, and finally his overcoat."

"His overcoat?"

"Yes."

"But there must be thousands of overcoats that look like his?"

"Not Håkan's overcoat. It's a thin, dark blue coat sort of like a sailor's raincoat. I can't describe it any better than that. But that's what I saw."

"So what did you do?"

"Just imagine! A concert with Madonna, two old friends, dinner, a summer night, no squealing baby, no boyfriend—and suddenly I catch sight of Håkan. I sat there transfixed for about fifteen seconds, then I hurried after him. But it was too late. There was no sign of him. There were people everywhere, side streets, taxis, restaurants. I walked all the way along Strøget as far as the city hall at Rådhuspladsen, and then back again. But I couldn't find him."

Wallander emptied his glass of water. Even if what he'd just heard sounded implausible, he knew that Linda was sharp-eyed and was rarely wrong when it came to identifying people.

"Let's take a step back," he said. "If I understood you correctly he'd already passed by the bench where you were sitting before you noticed him. But you said you caught a glimpse of his face. So he must have turned around?"

"Yes, he looked over his shoulder."

"Why would he do that?"

She frowned.

"How would I know?"

"It's a simple question. Did he expect to find somebody following him? Was he worried? Did he do it automatically, or had he heard something?"

"I think he was checking to make sure he wasn't being followed."

"You think?"

"I can't know for sure. But yes, I think he was checking to make sure there wasn't somebody behind him."

"Did he seem scared? Worried?"

"I can't answer that."

Wallander considered her answer. He still had questions.

"Could he have seen you?"

"No."

"How can you be sure?"

"If he had, he'd have looked at the bench. But he didn't."

"Have you told Hans?"

"Yes. He was upset and said that I must have been imagining things."

"Will you make sure that he hasn't been meeting his father in secret?"

She nodded, without speaking.

The sun disappeared behind a cloud, and there was a rumble of thunder in the distance. They went inside. Wallander wanted Linda to stay for a meal, but she said she needed to go home. She was just about to leave when the clouds opened, and it started pouring. The parking area in front of the house was transformed into a mud bath. Wallander decided that before the week was out he would order several loads of gravel so that nobody would need to wade through the mud whenever it rained.

"I'm positive," she said. "It was Håkan. Very much alive in Copenhagen."

"So we know one thing," Wallander said. "Håkan hasn't suffered the same fate as his wife. He's alive. That changes everything."

Linda nodded. They both knew they could no longer rule out the possibility that Håkan had killed his wife. But they shouldn't jump to conclusions. Maybe there was some other reason he had gone into hiding. Was he on the run from something or somebody?

They stood there in silence, each of them lost in thought. The rain died away as quickly as it had started.

"What was he doing in Copenhagen?" Wallander asked. "For me there's only one plausible answer to that question."

"To meet Hans. That's what you're thinking. Maybe to solve money problems? But I'm convinced that Hans isn't lying to me."

"I believe you. But there's no reason to think they've had contact already. That might happen tomorrow."

"In that case he'll tell me."

"Maybe," said Wallander thoughtfully.

"Why shouldn't he?"

"Loyalty. What if his father says he can't breathe a word to anybody, not even to you, about their meeting? And that he gives Hans a reason that he dare not question?"

"I'll notice if he's hiding something from me."

"If there's one thing I've learned," said Wallander, testing the wet and soggy ground with one foot, "it's that you should never believe you know all that much about other people's thoughts and ideas."

"So what should I do?"

"Say nothing for the moment. Ask nothing. I have to think about what this implies. So do you. But I'll talk to Ytterberg."

He accompanied her to the car. She held on to his arm so as not to slip.

"You should do something about this parking area," she said. "Have you thought about spreading some gravel around?"

"It had occurred to me," said Wallander.

She had already gotten into her car when she began talking about Baiba again.

"Is it really that bad? That she's going to die?"

"Yes."

"When did she leave?"

"Early this morning."

"Will you see her again?"

"She came here to say good-bye. She has cancer and will die before long. I think you can work out how that feels without any help from me."

"It must have been awful."

Wallander turned away and walked around the corner of the house. He didn't want to burst out crying—not because he didn't want to display weakness in front of his daughter, but for his own sake. He simply didn't want to think about his own death, which was basically the only thing that frightened him. He remained there until he heard her start the car and drive away. She had realized that he wanted to be left alone.

When he went back into the kitchen, he sat in the chair opposite where he usually sat at mealtimes.

He thought about what Linda had said about Håkan von Enke. They were back to square one.

28

Wallander clambered up the rickety ladder leading to the attic. A musty smell of damp and mold hit him hard. He was aware that one of these days he would have to have the whole roof removed and replaced. But not yet. Maybe in a year or, with a bit of luck, two.

He knew roughly where he had put the cardboard box he was looking for, but another one caught his eye first. In a box supplied by the moving company in Helsingborg was his collection of LPs. During all the years he had lived in Mariagatan, he had a record player on which he could listen to them, but it had finally broken, and he hadn't been able to find anybody to repair it. It had been taken away with the rest of the trash when he moved, but he had kept the records and stored them in the attic. He sat down and thumbed through his old albums. Every sleeve contained a memory, sometimes clear and comprehensive, just as often a flickering image of faces, smells, emotions. In his late teens he had been an almost fanatical fan of The Spotnicks. He had their first four records, and he recognized the title of every song. The music and the electric guitars echoed inside him. Also in the box was a record featuring Mahalia Jackson, which he had once been astonished to receive as a present from one of the silk knights who bought his father's paintings. The man probably spent his life peddling paintings and gramophone records. Wallander remembered carrying a canvas to the man's car and being given the record in return. The gospel songs had made a big impression on him. **Go down, Moses,** he thought, and he could see in his mind's eye his first record player, with the speaker in the lid making a rasping sound.

He suddenly found himself sitting there with an Edith Piaf record in his hands. The album cover, in black and white, was a close-up of her face. Mona, who hated The Spotnicks, had given him that LP—she preferred other Swedish groups such as Streaplers and Sven-Ingvars, but her great favorite was the French chanteuse. Neither she nor Wallander understood a word of what Piaf sang, but her voice fascinated them both.

After Piaf came a record featuring the jazz musician John Coltrane; where had he gotten that one? He couldn't remember. When he took it out of the sleeve he saw that it had barely been played. He tried hard, but the record didn't speak to him. He couldn't hear a single note from Coltrane's saxophone.

Right at the back of the box were two opera LPs: **La Traviata** and **Rigoletto.** Unlike the Coltrane, these records were almost worn out.

He remained there, sitting on the attic floor, wondering if he should take the box downstairs and buy a new record player so that he could listen to them. But in the end he slid the box to one side. The music he listened to nowadays was on cassette or CD. He didn't need those scratchy vinyl LPs anymore. They belonged to the past, and they could stay there in the darkness of the attic.

He found the box he was looking for and brought it down to the kitchen. He took out of it a large number of Legos, and spread them out over the table. He had given the Legos to Linda when she was a little girl— he'd won them in a raffle.

He'd gotten the idea from Rydberg. They'd been sitting at his kitchen table late one evening in spring, not long before Rydberg died. Ystad and the surrounding area had been subjected to a series of robberies by a masked man with a sawed-off shotgun. In order to organize the incidents and in the hope of finding a pattern, Rydberg had produced a pack of cards and used it to trace the robber's movements. The unknown villain had been the jack of spades. It had taught Wallander a way of seeing how a criminal went about his business, possibly even how he thought. When he had tried out the Rydberg method himself a few years later, he used Lego pieces instead of playing cards. But he had never told Rydberg.

He arranged figures to represent Håkan and Louise, various dates, places, and events. A fireman in a red helmet was Håkan; Louise was a little girl Linda had called Cinderella. He placed a group of marching Lego soldiers on one side; they were the unanswered questions he now considered the most important. Who was pretending to be Signe's uncle? Why had her father emerged from the shadows? Where had he been and why had he hidden himself away?

He remembered that he needed to call Niklasgården. He did so and was informed that nobody had been to visit Signe. Neither her father nor some unknown uncle.

He sat there at the kitchen table with a Lego in his hand. Somebody isn't telling the truth, he thought. Of all the people I've spoken to about Håkan and Louise von Enke, there's one who's not being straight with me. He or she is either lying or distorting the truth by holding back information. Who? And why?

The phone rang. He took it out into the garden. It was Linda. She came straight to the point.

"I talked to Hans. He felt like I was pressuring him. He got annoyed, and stormed out. When he comes back, I'll apologize."

"That's something Mona never did."

"What? Storm out or apologize?"

"She often stormed out. That was always the last card she played whenever we had an argument. A slammed door. When she came back she never apologized."

Linda laughed. She's on edge, Wallander thought. They probably argue a lot more often than she wants me to know.

"According to Mona it was the other way around," she said. "It was you who slammed the door, you who never apologized."

"I thought we'd already agreed that Mona sometimes says things that aren't true," Wallander said.

"You do exactly the same. Neither of my parents is a thoroughly honest person."

Wallander reacted angrily.

"Are you? Thoroughly honest?"

"No. But I've never claimed to be."

"Get to the point!"

"Am I interrupting something?"

Wallander decided on the spur of the moment, not without a certain amount of pleasure, to tell a lie.

"I'm cooking."

She saw through him right away.

"In the garden? I can hear birds singing."

"I'm having a barbecue."

"You hate barbecues."

"You don't know everything I hate and don't hate. What is it you want to tell me?"

"Hans has had no contact with his father. Nor have

there been any transactions in the family bank accounts apart from the withdrawals made by Louise before she disappeared. Hans is dealing with all the mail now. No money has been taken out at the bank, nor in any other way."

Wallander suddenly realized that this was more important than he'd first thought.

"So what has Håkan been living on while he's been hidden away? He turns up in Copenhagen, but obviously he doesn't need any money because he doesn't contact his son, nor does he make any withdrawals. That seems to suggest that somebody is helping him. Or could he have bank accounts that Hans doesn't know about?"

"That's possible. Hans has lots of contacts in the banking world; he's looked into it and hasn't found anything. But there are lots of ways of hiding money."

Wallander said nothing. He didn't have any more questions. But he was now beginning to wonder seriously if Håkan von Enke's not needing money might be a significant clue. Klara started crying.

"I have to go now," Linda said.

"I can hear that. So you believe we can rule out any secret contacts between Hans and his father, yes?"

"Yes."

She hung up. Wallander put down the phone and moved over to the garden hammock. He rocked back and forth, with one foot on the ground. In his mind's eye he could see Håkan von Enke walking along Strøget. He was walking fast, stopping now and then to turn around before continuing on his way. And then he disappeared, possibly down a side street, or into the mass of people on Strøget.

Wallander woke up with a start. It had started raining, and drops were falling on his bare foot that was resting on the ground. He stood up and went inside. He closed the door behind him, but then he paused. He could sense some sort of connection, still very vague, but nevertheless something that could shed light on where Håkan von Enke had been since he disappeared. An escape hatch, Wallander thought. When he vanished, he knew what he was going to do. He fled from his walk along Valhallavägen to a place where nobody would be able to find him. Wallander now felt quite sure that Louise had not been prepared for her husband's disappearance; her worry had been genuine. No proof had come to light, no facts, only this feeling that he found persuasive.

Wallander went to the kitchen. The stone floor felt cold under his bare feet. He was moving slowly, as if he was afraid that the thoughts might disappear. The Legos were on the table. He sat down. An escape hatch, he thought again. Everything planned, well organized—a submarine commander knows how to arrange his environment down to the last detail. Wallander tried to envisage the escape hatch. He had the feeling that he knew where Håkan von Enke was hiding. He had been close by, without noticing.

He leaned over the table and arranged a line of

Legos. Everybody who had ever had anything to do with Håkan and Louise. Sten Nordlander; their daughter, Signe; Hans; Steven Atkins in his house near San Diego. But also the others who had been more peripheral. He arranged them in a line, one after the other, and thought about who could have helped von Enke, who might have been able to supply everything needed, including money.

This is what I'm looking for, Wallander thought. An escape hatch. The question is, is Ytterberg thinking along the same lines, or is he playing with different Legos? He picked up his cell phone and dialed the number. It was raining harder now, pelting against the tin-plate windowsills. Ytterberg answered. It was a bad connection. Ytterberg was outside, in the street.

"I'm at an outdoor café," Ytterberg said. "I'm just about to pay. Can I call you back?"

He did so twenty minutes later when he had returned to his office in Bergsgatan.

"I'm the type that thinks it's easy to get back to work again after a vacation," Ytterberg said in response to Wallander's question about how he felt, after being off.

"I can't say I share that view," said Wallander. "Going back to work means being faced with a desk overloaded with files passed on by others who have left cheerful little Post-it notes about how pleased they are to be going on vacation."

He started by reporting on his meeting with Hermann Eber. Ytterberg listened carefully and had several questions. Then Wallander told him about Håkan von Enke's return. He passed on what Linda had told him;

he was even more convinced now that she really saw him.

"Could your daughter have been mistaken?"

"No. But I understand why you ask. It's astonishing."

"So there's no doubt at all that it was him?"

"No. I know my daughter. If she says it was him, it was him. Not a doppelgänger, not somebody who looked like him—it was Håkan von Enke."

"What does your future son-in-law have to say?"

"That his father hadn't gone to Copenhagen in order to visit him. There's no reason not to believe him."

"But is it really plausible to think that he wouldn't make contact with his son?"

"Whether it's plausible or not I can't say. But I don't think Hans is stupid enough to try to mislead Linda."

"Mislead his partner, or mislead your daughter?"

"The mother of his child. If that makes a difference."

They talked for a while about what von Enke's reappearance could imply. As far as Ytterberg was concerned, it meant above all else that he would have to reconsider what role Håkan von Enke might have played in the death of his wife.

"I don't know what you've been thinking," said Ytterberg, "but I always assumed that he was dead as well. Ever since his wife's body was discovered on Värmdö, at least."

"I've had my doubts," said Wallander. "But if I'd been in charge of the investigation I'd probably have thought the same thing."

Wallander told him briefly, but nevertheless in detail, his thoughts about von Enke's escape hatch.

"Those secret documents we found in Louise's purse made me think," Ytterberg said. "Since von Enke was in hiding, it was reasonable to think that he was involved as well, that they were working together."

"As spies?"

"Well, it wouldn't be the first time in Sweden that a man and his wife had been caught spying. Even if only one of them was directly involved."

"I assume you're referring to Stig Bergling and his wife?"

"Are there any others?"

It occurred to Wallander that Ytterberg occasionally assumed an arrogant tone of voice that Wallander would never have tolerated under normal circumstances. If somebody in the police station in Ystad had asked him ironic questions like that he would have been furious. But he let it pass—Ytterberg was probably not always aware of how he sounded.

"Do you know anything about what was on the microfilms? Defense secrets, armaments, foreign policy?"

"I have no idea. But I get the impression that our Säpo colleagues are worried. They're insisting that we hand over every single document linked to this investigation, not that there are very many. I've been summoned to a meeting later today with a Commander Holm, who is evidently a bigwig in the military intelligence service."

"I'd be interested to hear what questions he asks you."

"That's always a good way of finding out what people know already. In other words, you want to know what questions he **doesn't** ask?"

"Exactly."

"I promise to let you know."

The next morning after breakfast he checked all the burners carefully before going out for a walk with Jussi, who ran off like a shot into the lifting mist. He felt clearer in the head than he had in a very long time. Nothing seemed excessively difficult, and his zest for life was strong. He suddenly started running, challenging the lethargy that had filled him for the last few months. He kept running until he was thoroughly out of breath. The sun was warming things up now. He took off his sweaty shirt, made a face when he saw his protruding belly, and decided, as he had so often before, to start dieting.

On the way back to the house his cell phone started ringing. Somebody was speaking in a foreign language, a woman, but her voice was very faint, almost completely drowned out by a veritable storm of crackling and noise. After three or four seconds the line went dead. Wallander thought it could have been Baiba. He thought he recognized her voice, despite the background noise. But whoever it was didn't call back, so he went home and sat out in the garden with a cup of coffee.

· · ·

It was going to be a lovely summer's day. He decided to go for a picnic, all on his own. He had always thought one of the best things in life was settling down among the sand dunes and having a nap in the sunshine after eating the meal he'd brought with him from home. He started packing a basket, which was a souvenir from his childhood home. His mother used to use it for keeping balls of wool, knitting needles, and half-finished sweaters. Now he filled it with sandwiches, a thermos, two apples, and a few copies of the **Swedish Policeman** magazine that he hadn't gotten around to reading. It was eleven o'clock when he once again checked the burners before locking the door. He drove out to Sandhammaren and found a place among the dunes and stunted trees. When he had finished eating and reading the magazines, he wrapped himself in a blanket and was soon fast asleep.

He woke up feeling cold. The sun had gone behind a cloud, the air was chilly, and he had cast off the blanket. He rolled himself up inside it again, and folded his jacket to serve as a pillow. The sun soon reemerged, and he remembered a dream he had had many years ago, a recurring dream that always vanished just as quickly as it had appeared. He was involved in some erotic game with a faceless black woman. He had never had a relationship with a dark-skinned woman, apart from an incident during a visit to the West Indies when he had drunk himself silly one evening and taken a prostitute back to his hotel room. Nor had he particularly lusted after any such relationship. But then that black woman had turned up in his dreams, only to vanish again after a few months.

A storm was brewing on the horizon. He packed everything into the basket and went back to the car. When he came to Kåseberga he drove down to the harbor and bought some smoked fish. He had just gotten back home when his cell phone started ringing again. It was the same woman as before, but this time the reception was much better and he could hear right away that it wasn't Baiba. The woman was speaking broken English.

"Kurt Wallander?"

"Speaking."

"My name is Lilja. You know who I am?"

"No."

The woman suddenly burst out crying. She screamed into his ear. He was scared stiff.

"Baiba," she yelled. "Baiba."

"What about her? I know her."

"She dead."

Wallander was standing with the bag of fish from Kåseberga in his hand. He dropped it.

"She's dead? She was here only a couple of days ago!"

"I know. She was my friend. But now she dead."

Wallander could feel his heart pounding. He sat down on the stool just inside the front door. He eventually managed to piece together the confused and anguished message that Lilja was trying to convey. Baiba had been only a few miles outside Riga when she drove off the road at high speed and crashed into a stone wall, wrecking the car and killing herself. She had died on the spot; that was something Lilja repeated over and over again, as if it might prevent Wallander from sinking into a bottomless pit of sorrow. But it was in vain, of course. The despair welling up inside him was something he had never experienced before.

They were suddenly cut off, without warning, before Wallander could get Lilja's phone number. He waited for her to call him again, still sitting on the stool in the hall. Only when it became clear that she was unable to get through did he move into the kitchen. He left the bag with the smoked fish lying on the floor. He had no idea what to do next. He lit a candle and placed it on the table. She must have been driving nonstop, he thought. From the ferry when it docked in Poland, through Poland, through Lithuania, and then almost all the way to Riga. Had she fallen asleep at the wheel? Or had she driven into the wall on purpose, intending to kill herself? Wallander knew that fatal car accidents involving nobody but the driver were often suicides. A former secretary who used to work in the Ystad police station, a divorcée with a drinking problem, had chosen that way out only a few years ago. But he didn't think Baiba would do anything like that. Somebody who decides to travel around to say good-bye to her friends and lovers would hardly be likely to set up a car crash to bring her life to a close. She must have been tired and lost control; that was the only explanation he could think of.

He picked up his cell phone to call Linda—he didn't feel capable of coping with what had happened on his own. There were times when he needed to have other people on hand. He dialed the number, but then hung up when her phone started ringing. It was too soon; he didn't have anything to say to her. He threw his phone onto the sofa and went out to Jussi, let him out of his kennel, sat down on the ground and started stroking him. The phone rang. He rushed indoors. It was Lilja. She was calmer now. He asked her questions and got a clearer picture of what had happened. There was also something else he wanted to ask about.

"Why are you calling me? How did you know that I exist?"

"Baiba asked me to. "

"Asked you to do what?"

"To call you when she was dead. But I didn't think it would be quickly like this. Baiba thought she would live until Christmas."

"She told me she hoped to live until the fall."

"She said different things to different people. I think she wanted us to have the same uncertainty that she had."

Lilja explained who she was, an old friend and colleague who had known Baiba since they were teenagers.

"I knew about you," she said. "One day Baiba rings and she says: 'Now he is here in Riga, my Swedish friend. I take him to the café in Hotel Latvia this afternoon. Go there and you will see him.' I went there, and I saw you."

"Perhaps Baiba mentioned your name. I think so. But we never met, is that right?"

"Never. But I saw you. Baiba always thought much of you. She loved you."

She burst out crying again. Wallander waited. Thunder was rumbling in the distance. He could hear her coughing, and blowing her nose.

"What happens now?" he asked when she picked up the phone again.

"I don't know."

"Who are her closest relations?"

"Her mother, and brothers and sisters."

"If her mother is still alive she must be very old. I don't remember Baiba ever talking about her."

"She is ninety-five years. But she is clear in the head. She knows her daughter is dead. They had hard relations since Baiba was child."

"I want to know when the funeral will take place," Wallander said.

"I promise to call you."

"What did she say about me?" Wallander asked in the end.

"Not much."

"But she must have said something?"

"Yes. But not much. We were friends, but Baiba never allowed anybody very close."

"I know," he said.

When the call was over, he lay down on the bed and stared up at the ceiling where a patch of damp had appeared a couple of months ago. He lay there for quite a while before returning to the kitchen table.

Shortly after eight he called Linda and told her what had happened. He found it very difficult, and could feel a sense of mounting desperation.

29

On July 14, at eleven o'clock in the morning, Baiba Liepa's funeral took place at a chapel in central Riga. Wallander had arrived the previous day on a flight from Copenhagen. When he disembarked he recognized the airport immediately, even though the terminal had been rebuilt. The Soviet military planes that had been visible all over the place at the beginning of the 1990s were no longer there, and from the windows of the taxi taking him into Riga he noted that there had been a lot of changes. The billboards were different; the façades had been newly painted; the sidewalks had been repaired. But pigs were still rooting around in dunghills next to tumbledown farmhouses, and in the center of town the old buildings were still standing. The main difference was the large number of people in the streets, their clothes, and the cars lining up at red lights and at turnoffs to centrally located parking lots.

Warm rain was falling over Riga the day Wallander returned. Lilja, whose surname was Blooms, had called and given him the details of Baiba's funeral. His only question had been whether his presence might somehow be regarded as inappropriate.

"Why should it be?"

"Perhaps there are circumstances within the family that I don't know about?"

"Everybody knows who you are," said Lilja Blooms. "Baiba told about you. You were never a secret."

"The question is what she said."

"Why are you so worried? I thought you and Baiba were in love? I thought you would be married. We all thought that."

"She didn't want to."

He could tell that what he'd said surprised her.

"We thought it was you who backed out. She said nothing. It was long before we understood it was over. But she never wanted to talk about it."

It was Linda who had persuaded him to go to the funeral. When he called her she had jumped into her car and come over. She was so upset that she had tears in her eyes when she walked through his front door. That helped him to mourn Baiba openly. He sat there for a long time, reminiscing to his daughter about the time he and Baiba had spent together.

"Baiba's husband, Karlis Liepa, had been murdered," he said. "It was a political murder. Tensions between the Russians and the Latvians were running high in those days. That was why I went to Riga, to assist in the murder investigation. Needless to say, I had no idea about the political chasms that opened up the country. Looking back, that could well be the moment when I began to understand what the world looked like during the Cold War. It was seventeen years ago."

"I remember you going," said Linda. "I was in college at the time, and I didn't know what I wanted to do with myself. Although deep down I think I realized that I wanted to become a police officer."

"I seem to recall that you talked about all kinds of possibilities, but never that one."

"That should have made you suspicious. I can't believe you had no idea what I was thinking!"

"Nor did I have any idea about Baiba when Karlis Liepa came to the police station in Ystad."

Wallander remembered the details very clearly. Apart from his chain-smoking, which aroused vehement protests from all the nonsmokers, Karlis Liepa had been a calm, reserved man, and Wallander had gotten along well with him. One evening, during a heavy snowstorm, he had taken Liepa back to his apartment in Mariagatan. He had produced a bottle of whiskey, and to his delight had discovered that Liepa was almost as interested in opera as he was himself. They had listened to a recording of **Turandot** with Maria Callas as the snow whirled about in the strong winds blowing through the deserted streets of Ystad.

But where was that record now? It hadn't been among those he had found in the attic the previous day. The question was solved when Linda told him she had it at home.

"You gave it to me in the days when I was dreaming of becoming an actress," she said. "I thought of putting on a one-woman show depicting the tragic fate of Maria Callas. Can you imagine? If there's anything I'm totally different from, it's a Greek opera singer."

"With bad nerves," Wallander added.

"What was Baiba? A teacher?"

"When I met her she was translating technical literature from English. I think she did a bit of practically everything."

"You must go to her funeral. For your own sake."

It wasn't all that straightforward, but she convinced him in the end. She also made sure that he bought a new dark suit, accompanied him to a tailor's in Malmö, and when he expressed his astonishment at the price she explained that it was a high-quality suit that would last him for the rest of his life.

"You'll be attending fewer weddings," Linda said. "But at your age, the number of funerals increases."

He muttered something inaudible and paid. Linda didn't press him to repeat whatever it was he had said.

He clambered out of the taxi and carried his little suitcase into the reception area at the Hotel Latvia. He noted right away that the café where Lilja Blooms had seen him and Baiba together was no longer there. He checked in and was given room 1516. When he got out of the elevator and stood in front of the door, he had the feeling that this was the very room he'd stayed in the first time he went to Riga. He was quite sure that the figures 5 and 6 had been part of the room number then as well. He unlocked the door and went in. It didn't look at all like what he remembered. But the view from the window was the same, a beautiful church whose name he had forgotten. He unpacked his bag and hung up his new suit. The thought that it was in this hotel, and possibly even in this very room, that he first met Baiba filled him with almost unbearable pain.

He went to the bathroom and rinsed his face. It was only twelve-thirty. He had no plans, but thought he might take a walk. He wanted to mourn Baiba by remembering her as she was when he met her for the first time.

A thought suddenly struck him, a thought he had never dared to confront before. Had his love for Baiba been stronger than the love he had once felt for Mona? Despite the fact that Mona was Linda's mother? He didn't know, and would never be sure.

He went out and strolled through the town, had a meal in a restaurant even though he wasn't especially hungry. That evening he sat in one of the hotel bars. A girl in her twenties came up and asked him if he wanted company. He didn't even answer, merely shook his head. Shortly before the hotel restaurant closed, he had another meal, a spaghetti dish that he hardly touched. He drank red wine, and felt tipsy when he stood up to leave the table.

It had been raining while he ate, but it was clear now. He retrieved his jacket and went out into the damp summer evening. He found his way to the Freedom Monument, where he and Baiba had once had their photograph taken. A few youths on skateboards were practicing their skills on the flagstones in front. He continued his walk, and didn't arrive back at the hotel until very late. He fell asleep on top of the bed without taking off anything but his shoes.

. . .

The next morning he put on his funeral suit and went down to the dining room for breakfast, despite the fact that he wasn't hungry.

He had bought two half-bottles of vodka at Kastrup Airport. He had one of them in his inside pocket. As the elevator conveyed him down to the dining room, he unscrewed the top and took a swig.

When Lilja Blooms came in through the glass doors, Wallander was already in the reception area, waiting for her. She went over to him right away. Baiba must have shown her pictures of him, he thought.

Lilja was short and plump, and her hair was cropped. She didn't look anything like what he had imagined. He thought she would look more like Baiba. When they shook hands, Wallander felt embarrassed, without knowing why.

"The chapel isn't far from here," she said. "It's only a ten-minute walk. I have time for a cigarette. You can wait here."

"I'll come with you," said Wallander.

They stood in the sun outside the hotel, Lilja wearing sunglasses and holding a cigarette in her hand.

"She was drunk," she said.

It was a moment before Wallander realized what she was referring to.

"Baiba?"

"She was drunk when she died. The autopsy made that clear. She had a lot of alcohol in her blood when she crashed her car."

"I find that hard to believe."

"So do I. All her friends are astonished. But then, what do we know about the thoughts of a person who is going to die?"

"Are you saying that she committed suicide? That she crashed the car on purpose? Drove into that stone wall?"

"There's no point in worrying about it—we'll never know for certain. But there were no skid marks on the road. A motorist behind her said that she wasn't driving unusually fast, but that the car was wobbling all over the road."

Wallander tried to picture the last moments of Baiba's life. He couldn't be sure about what had happened, whether it was an accident or suicide. But another thought struck him. Could Louise von Enke's death also have been an accident, and not murder or suicide after all?

He never followed that thought through because Lilja stubbed out her cigarette and announced that it was time to set off. Wallander excused himself, paid a visit to the men's room in reception, and took another swig of the vodka. He examined himself in the mirror. What he saw was a man on his way into old age, worried about what was in store for him in life.

They came to the chapel. The darkness inside was all the more intense because the sunshine had been so

bright. It was some time before Wallander's eyes adjusted.

When they did, he had the feeling that Baiba Liepa's
funeral was a sort of rehearsal for his own. It scared
him, and almost made him stand up and leave. He
should never have gone to Riga; he had nothing to do
there.

But he remained seated nevertheless, and thanks
mainly to the vodka, he didn't even start crying, not
even when he saw how upset Lilja Blooms was by his
side. The coffin was like a desert island, washed up in
the sea—the last resting place for a person he had once
been in love with, Wallander thought.

For some unknown reason, he suddenly saw Håkan
von Enke in his mind's eye. He felt annoyed, and he
brushed aside the thought.

He was beginning to feel drunk. It was as if the funeral
had nothing to do with him. When it ended, and Lilja
Blooms hastened over to express her condolences to
Baiba's mother, Wallander took the opportunity to slip
out of the chapel. He didn't give a backward glance,
but went straight to the hotel and asked the desk clerk
to help him change his flight. He had planned to stay
until the next day, but now he wanted to leave as soon
as possible. There were seats available on an afternoon
flight to Copenhagen. He packed his suitcase, kept his
funeral suit on, and left the hotel in a taxi, afraid that
Lilja Blooms might come looking for him. He sat out-

side the terminal building for nearly three hours before
it was time for him to pass through security.

He continued drinking on the plane. When he came
to Ystad, he took a taxi home and almost fell out of the
car. As usual, Jussi was being looked after by the neighbors, and he decided to leave him there until the next
day.

He collapsed into bed and slept soundly. When he
woke up shortly before nine the next morning, he regretted having fled from the chapel without even having said good-bye to Lilja. He would have to call her
soon and try to make a plausible excuse. But what on
earth would he say?

Although he had slept well, Wallander felt sick. He
couldn't find any aspirin, despite searching through
the bathroom and all the drawers in the kitchen. Since
he couldn't face driving to Ystad, he asked his neighbor
if she had any. She did, and he dissolved one in a glass
of water and drank it in her kitchen. She gave him a
few extra to take home with him.

When he got back, he put Jussi in his kennel. The
light on the answering machine was blinking when he
entered the house. Sten Nordlander had called again.
Wallander got his cell phone and called him. He could
hear the wind howling around Nordlander when he
answered.

"I'll call you back," he said. "I have to find a spot
sheltered from the wind."

"I'm at home."

"Give me ten minutes. Are you okay?"

"Yes, I'm fine."

Wallander sat down at the kitchen table to wait. Jussi wandered around his kennel, sniffing to see if he had been visited by any mice or birds. He occasionally glanced at the kitchen window. Wallander raised his hand and waved to him, but Jussi didn't react; he couldn't see anything, but he knew that Wallander was in the house somewhere. Wallander opened the window. Jussi immediately started wagging his tail and stood up on his hind legs, resting his front paws on the bars.

The phone rang. It was Sten Nordlander. He had found a sheltered spot; there was no sound of any wind.

"I'm on a little island, not much more than a bare rock, not far from Möja," he said. "Do you know where that is?"

"No."

"At the outer edge of the Stockholm archipelago. It's very beautiful."

"I'm glad you called," said Wallander. "Something has happened. I should have contacted you. Håkan has turned up."

Wallander summarized what had happened.

"Amazing!" said Nordlander. "I thought about him when I stepped ashore here on the skerry."

"Any particular reason?"

"He liked islands. He once told me about an ambition he'd had when he was young: he wanted to visit every island in the world."

"Did he ever try to achieve it?"

"I don't think so. Louise wasn't keen on sea voyages."

"Did that cause any problems?"

"Not that I know of. He was very fond of her, and she of him. But dreams can be of value even if you don't have an opportunity to turn them into reality."

The connection was poor; the skerry was at the very limit of the coverage area. They agreed that he would call Wallander again once he was back on the mainland.

Wallander slowly put the phone down on the table and sat motionless. He suddenly had the feeling that he knew where Håkan von Enke was. Sten Nordlander had shown him the direction he should be following.

He couldn't be sure, and he had no proof. Nevertheless, he knew.

He thought about a book he'd seen in Signe von Enke's bookcase, along with the books about Babar. **The Sleeping Beauty.** I've been lost in a deep sleep, Wallander thought. I should have realized long ago where he was. I've only just woken up.

Jussi started barking. Wallander went out and gave him some food.

The following day, early in the morning, he got into his car. The farmer's wife looked surprised when he turned up with Jussi yet again.

She asked how long he was going to be away. He told her the truth.

He didn't know. He had absolutely no idea.

30

The boat he rented was an open plastic craft, barely eighteen feet long, with an Evinrude outboard motor, seven horsepower. The proprietor had also lent him a sea chart. He had chosen that particular boat because it was not so big that it would be difficult to row, which he suspected he would need to do. When he signed the contract he produced his police ID. The man gave a start.

"Everything's fine," Wallander said. "But I need a spare can of gas. I might be able to return the boat to-morrow, but then again, I might need it for a few more days. Anyway, you have my credit card number. You know you'll be paid."

"A police officer," said the man. "Is something wrong?"

"No, it's just that I'm going to surprise a good friend on his fiftieth birthday."

Wallander hadn't prepared his lie in advance. But he was used to inventing excuses, and they came auto-matically now.

The boat was jammed between two big motor cruis-ers, one of them a Storø. There was no electric igni-tion, but it started the moment Wallander pulled the cord. The boat owner, who spoke with a Finnish ac-cent, guaranteed that the engine was reliable.

"I use it myself when I go fishing," he said. "The problem is, there are hardly any fish. But I go fishing even so."

It was four o'clock in the afternoon. Wallander had arrived at Valdemarsvik an hour earlier. He'd eaten at what appeared to be the only restaurant in the village, then found his way to the boat-rental establishment just a couple of hundred yards away, on one side of the long inlet known as Valdemarsviken. Wallander had packed a backpack containing, among other things, two flashlights and some food. He'd also taken warm clothes, despite the fact that it was a warm afternoon.

On the way up to Östergötland he had driven through several downpours of rain. One of them, just outside Ronneby, was so heavy that he'd been forced to pull into a rest stop and wait until it passed. As he listened to the pattering on the car roof and watched the water cascading down his windshield, he began to wonder if he really had judged the situation correctly. Had his instinct let him down, or—as it had so often before—would it turn out to be right after all?

He stayed in the rest stop, lost in thought, for almost half an hour before the rain stopped. He set off again and eventually came to Valdermarsvik. It was clear now, and there was hardly any wind. The water in the inlet was ruffled only occasionally by a light breeze.

There was a smell of mud. He remembered it from the last time he was here.

· · ·

Wallander started the outboard motor and set out. The man who had rented him the boat stood for some time, watching him, before returning to his office. Wallander decided to leave the long inlet before darkness fell. Then he would moor somewhere and enjoy the summer twilight. He had tried to work out the current phase of the moon, without success. He could have called Linda, but since he didn't want to reveal where he was going nor why he was making this trip, he didn't. Once he had left the inlet he would call Martinsson instead. If he decided to call anyone, that is. The task he had set himself wasn't dependent on whether the night was dark or moonlit, but he wanted to know exactly what was in store for him.

When he glimpsed the open sea between the islands ahead of him, he let the engine turn over while he studied the sea chart in its plastic cover. Once he had established precisely where he was, he selected a place not too far from his final destination where he could moor and wait for dusk to fall. But it was already occupied by several boats. He continued and eventually found a small island, not much more than a rock with a few trees, where he could row to the beach, having first detached the outboard motor. He put on his jacket, leaned against one of the trees, and took a drink of coffee from his thermos. Then he called Martinsson. Once again it was a child who answered, possibly the same one as last time. Martinsson took the phone from her.

"You're a lucky man," he said. "My little grand-daughter has become your secretary."

"The moon," said Wallander.

"What about it?"

"You're asking too quickly. I haven't finished yet."

"I'm sorry. But I can't take my eyes off the grand-children; they need watching all the time."

"I understand that, and I wouldn't disturb you unless it was necessary. Do you have a calendar? What phase is the moon in right now?"

"The moon? Is that what you're asking about? Are you out on some sort of astronomical adventure?"

"I could be. But can you answer my question?"

"Hang on a minute."

Martinsson put down the receiver. It was obvious from Wallander's voice that he wasn't going to receive any sort of explanation.

"It's a new moon," he said when he returned to the phone. "A thin little crescent. Assuming you're still in Sweden and not some other part of the world."

"I'm still in Sweden. Thank you for your help," said Wallander. "I'll explain it all one of these days."

"I'm used to waiting."

"Waiting for what?"

"For explanations. Including from my children when they don't do as I tell them. But that was mainly when they were younger."

"Linda was just the same," said Wallander, in an attempt to appear interested. He thanked Martinsson again for his help regarding the moon, and hung up.

He ate a couple of sandwiches, then lay down with a stone as a pillow.

The pains came from nowhere. He was lying there, looking up at the sky and listening to seagulls screeching in the distance, when he felt a stab of pain in his left arm, which then spread to his chest and stomach. At first he thought he must be lying on a sharp edge of stone, but then he realized that the pains were coming from inside his body, and he suspected that what he had always dreaded had now come to pass. He'd had a heart attack.

He lay completely motionless, stiff and terrified, and held his breath, afraid that if he tried to breathe he would use up the rest of his heart's ability to beat.

The memory of his mother's death suddenly came vividly into his mind. It was as if her last moments were being played out by his side. She had been only fifty years old. His mother had never worked outside the home, but had always struggled to maintain her marriage to her temperamental husband, whose income could never be relied on, and look after their two children, Kurt and Kristina. They had been living in Limhamn at the time, sharing a house with a family that Wallander's father couldn't stand. The father was a train conductor who never hurt a fly, but once, in the friendliest possible way, he asked Wallander's father if it might be relaxing to paint some other motif rather than the same old landscape over and over again. Wallander had overheard the conversation. The conductor, whose name was Nils Persson, had used his own working life as an example. After a long period driving back and forth between Malmö and Alvesta, he was very pleased when he was transferred to an express route that went to Gothenburg, and sometimes even as far as Oslo. Wallander's father had naturally reacted furiously. After that it had been Wallander's mother who tried to smooth things over and make living alongside the other family not completely intolerable.

Her death had come suddenly one afternoon in the early fall of 1962. She had been in their little garden, hanging up laundry. Wallander had just come home from school and was sitting at the kitchen table, eating a sandwich. He had looked out of the window and seen her hanging up sheets with a bunch of clothespins in her hand. He had returned to his sandwich. The next time he looked out, she was on her knees, clutching at her chest. At first he thought she had dropped something, but then he watched her fall over onto her side, slowly, as if she were trying hard not to. He ran outside, shouting her name, but she was beyond help. The doctor who performed the autopsy said she had suffered a massive heart attack. Even if she had been in a hospital when it happened, they wouldn't have been able to save her.

Now he could see her in his mind's eye, a series of blurred, jerky images as he tried to keep his own pains at arm's length. He didn't want his life to end early like hers had, and least of all now, all alone on a little island in the Baltic Sea.

He said silent, agitated prayers—not really to any god, but more to himself, urging himself to resist, to not allow himself to be dragged down into eternal silence. And he eventually realized that the pains were not getting any worse; his heart was still beating. He forced himself to remain calm, to act sensibly, to not sink into a desperate and blind panic. He sat up gingerly and felt for his cell phone, which he had left next to his backpack. He started to dial Linda's number but changed his mind. What would she be able to do? If he really had suffered a heart attack, he should be calling the emergency number.

But something held him back. Perhaps it was the feeling that the pain was receding? He carefully moved his left arm and found a position in which the pain was less, as well as other positions where it was worse. That was not in accordance with the symptoms of a serious heart attack. He sat up slowly and took his pulse. It was seventy-four beats per minute. His normal rate was somewhere between sixty-six and seventy-eight. Everything was as it should be. It's stress, he thought. My body is simulating something that can afflict me if I don't take it easy.

He lay down again. The pain faded away even more, even if it was still present, nagging away, a sort of background threat.

An hour later he was convinced that he hadn't in fact suffered a heart attack. It had been a warning. He thought, I should stop kidding myself that I'm an irreplaceable police officer and take a proper vacation. Perhaps he should go home, call Ytterberg and tell him what conclusions he had drawn. But he decided to stay on. He had come a long way, and he was keen to establish if his suspicions were justified or not. No matter what the outcome, he could then hand the matter over to Ytterberg and not bother with it anymore.

He felt very relieved. It was a sort of positive affirmation of life that he hadn't experienced for years. He had an urge to stand up and roar in the direction of the open sea. But he remained seated, leaning against the tree trunk, watching the boats passing and relishing the smell of the sea. It was still warm. He lay down with his jacket draped over him and fell asleep. He woke up after about ten minutes. The pains had almost gone altogether now. He stood up and started walking around the little island. On one side, facing south, the rock formed an almost vertical cliff. It was strenuous, skirting it at the very edge of the water.

He suddenly stopped dead. There was a small, narrow creek about twenty yards ahead. A boat had anchored at its entrance, and a dinghy had been beached on the rocks. A couple was lying at the edge of the water, making love. He pressed himself against the cliff, but he couldn't resist the temptation to watch. They were young—barely twenty years old, he guessed. He stared as if bewitched at their naked bodies before gathering the strength to drag himself away and retrace his steps as quietly as possible. A few hours later, as twilight was at last beginning to creep up on the island, he saw the motor cruiser with the dinghy bobbing along behind it sailing past. He stood up and waved. The couple on board waved back.

In a way he was jealous of them. But his thoughts were far from gloomy. His own earliest erotic experiences had been just like most other people's—uncertain, disappointing, bordering on the embarrassing. He had never really believed his friends' descriptions of their escapades and conquests. It was only after he met Mona that sex had become a serious pleasure as far as he was concerned. During their early years together their sex life was beyond his wildest dreams. He had achieved considerable satisfaction with a handful of other women, but nothing like what he and Mona experienced at the beginning of their relationship. The big exception in his life was, of course, Baiba.

But he had never made love to a woman on a rock by the open sea. The nearest he had been to something as risky as that was when he had been slightly tipsy and managed to entice Mona into a bathroom on a train. But they had been interrupted by angry pounding on the door. Mona had found it embarrassing in the extreme, and insisted angrily that he promise never again to try to engage her in such erotic adventures.

And he never had. Toward the end of their long relationship and marriage, their sexual desire had ebbed— although it returned in spades for Wallander when she told him she wanted a divorce. But she had no longer accepted his advances. Her door was locked, once and for all.

Suddenly he seemed to see his life mapped out before his very eyes. Four decisive moments. The first was when I rebelled against my dominating father and became a police officer, he thought. The second was when I killed a man in the line of duty, and didn't think I could take any more, but in the end decided not to resign from the police force. The third was when I left Mariagatan, moved out to the country, and got Jussi. The fourth was probably when I finally accepted that Mona and I could never live together again. That was probably the most difficult to negotiate. But I've made my choices; I haven't hemmed and hawed and then realized one day that it was too late. I have nobody but myself to thank for that. When I see the bitterness in a lot of people around me, I'm glad I'm not one of them. Despite everything, I've tried to take responsibility for my life, and not merely allowed it to float away at the mercy of whatever current came along.

As dusk fell, so the mosquitoes arrived to plague him. But he had remembered to take mosquito repellent, and he pulled the hood of his anorak over his head. There weren't many motor cruisers to be heard now, plying the surrounding channels and straits. A lone yacht was heading for the open sea.

Shortly after midnight, with the mosquitoes whining around his ears, he left the island. He followed the increasingly dark silhouettes of the islands lining the route he had planned with the aid of his sea chart. He was traveling slowly, constantly checking to make sure he didn't deviate from his course. When he was approaching his goal he reduced his speed still further, and eventually he switched off the engine completely. A gentle evening breeze had begun to blow. He tilted up the motor, set up the oars, and started rowing. He occasionally paused and tried to peer through the darkness, but he couldn't see any light, and that worried him. There should be a light, he thought. It shouldn't be dark.

He rowed up to the beach and climbed cautiously out of the boat. There was a scraping noise as he pulled it over the shingle. He tied the painter around some of the alders growing on the shore. He had taken the flashlights out of his backpack before he beached the boat, and now he put one of them in his pocket. He held the other one in his hand.

But there was something else that he was groping for, among the sandwich wrappings and the spare clothes. He had also packed his service pistol. He had hesitated until the very last moment, but eventually he made up his mind and put it in his backpack, along with a full magazine. He wasn't at all sure why he had done this. There was nothing to suggest that he was exposing himself to immediate physical danger.

But Louise is dead, he had thought. And Hermann Eber convinced me that she was murdered. Until I have more information, I have to assume that the culprit could be Håkan, even if I have neither proof nor motive.

He loaded the pistol and checked that the safety catch was on. Then he switched on the flashlight and checked that the blue filter he had placed over the lens was still in place. The light was very pale, and would be difficult to detect by anybody not on his guard.

He listened through the darkness. The noise from the sea drowned out other sounds. He put his backpack back into the boat, then checked the painter and made sure that the boat was securely moored. He began walking slowly and carefully away from the shore. The brushwood was dense near the water's edge. He had been walking for only a few yards when he stepped into a spiderweb, and he started flailing with his arms when he realized that an enormous spider was clinging to his anorak. He could cope with snakes, but not spiders. Instead of fumbling through the brush, he decided to walk along the shore in the hope of finding somewhere where it was less overgrown. After about fifty yards he came to a place where the remains of an old slipway could be made out. Since he had never been ashore on this island before, and had seen it only from a boat, he was finding it difficult to orient himself. The last time he was here they had passed by on the other side, facing west. This time he had landed on the east side, hoping that this was what you might call the rear of the island.

His cell phone started ringing in one of his pockets. He cursed under his breath as he pulled and tugged at his clothes in an effort to find it, dropping the flashlight in the process. He counted at least six rings before he finally succeeded in switching it off. He could see from the display that it was Linda who had been trying to reach him. He put the phone in his breast pocket and closed the zipper. The ringing had sounded like an alarm in his ears. He listened hard, but there was nothing to be seen or heard in the darkness. Only the surging of the sea.

He continued cautiously on his way until he could make out the outline of the house shrouded in darkness. He stationed himself behind an oak tree, but he couldn't see any trace of a light. I got it wrong, he thought. There's nobody here. My deduction was simply wrong.

But then he noticed a faint gleam of light seeping out from between a lowered blind and a window frame. When he came closer he could see more faint glows from other windows as well.

He walked as quietly as he could around the house. The windows were blacked out, as if it were wartime and all lights had been extinguished in order to confuse the enemy. I am the enemy, Wallander thought.

He pressed his ear against the wooden wall and listened. He could hear the murmur of voices, and occasionally music. From a television set or a radio, he couldn't be sure which.

He withdrew into the shadows again and tried to make up his mind about what to do next. He had planned only as far as the point where he now found himself. Now what? Should he wait until the next morning before knocking on the door and waiting to see who answered?

He hesitated. He was annoyed by his indecision. What was he afraid of?

He had no time to answer that question. He felt a hand on his shoulder, gave a start, and turned around.

Even though this was the reason he had set out on his journey, he was still surprised to see Håkan von Enke standing there in the darkness, wearing a tracksuit jacket over a pair of jeans. He was unshaven and in need of a haircut.

They stared at each other without speaking, Wallander with his flashlight in his hand, von Enke barefoot on the wet soil.

"I suppose you heard the phone ringing?" Wallander said.

Von Enke shook his head. He seemed to be not only scared, but rueful.

"I have alarms set all around the house. I've spent the last ten minutes trying to work out who tracked me to this island."

"It's only me," said Wallander.

"Yes," said Håkan von Enke. "It's only you."

They went into the house. It was only when everything was lit up that Wallander noticed that von Enke was also armed. He was carrying a pistol, tucked into his waistband.

What's he afraid of? Wallander thought. Who is he hiding from?

The surging of the sea could no longer be heard. Wallander contemplated the man who had been missing for such a long time.

They sat down and said nothing for a while. Eventually they began talking, hesitantly. Slowly, approaching each other with maximum caution.

PART 4

The Phantom

31

It was a long night. Several times it seemed to Wallander that it was a direct continuation of the conversation he and von Enke had had nearly six months previously, in a windowless room off a banquet hall just outside Stockholm. What he was now beginning to understand surprised him, but it was a more than sufficient explanation of why von Enke had been so worried on that occasion.

Wallander felt nothing like a Stanley who had now found his Livingstone. He had guessed right, that was all. Once again, his intuition had shown him the path to follow. If von Enke was surprised at his hideaway being discovered, he didn't show it. Wallander thought the old submarine commander was displaying his cold-blooded nature. He didn't allow himself to be surprised, no matter what happened.

The hunting lodge that seemed so primitive from the outside gave quite a different impression once Wallander had crossed the threshold. There were no inside walls, just one large room with an open kitchenette. A small extension containing a bathroom was the only space with a door. In one corner of the room was a bed. It's on the small side, Wallander observed, more like a hammock, or the little bunk that even a commander has to make do with on board a submarine. In the middle of the room was a large table covered in books, files, and documents. On one of the short walls was a shelf containing a radio, and there was a television set and a record player on a little table. Next to it was a dark red old-fashioned armchair.

"I didn't think you'd have electricity here," said Wallander.

"There's a generator sunk in a little basement blasted out of the rock. You can't hear the engine even when the water is dead calm."

Von Enke stood by the stove, making coffee. Neither of them spoke, and Wallander tried to prepare himself for the conversation that would follow. But now that he'd found the man he'd spent so much time looking for, he didn't know what to ask him. All his previous thoughts seemed to be a blurred jumble of unfinished conclusions.

"If I remember correctly," said von Enke, interrupting Wallander's thoughts, "you take neither milk nor sugar?"

"That's right."

"I'm afraid I don't have any bread or cookies to offer you. Are you hungry?"

"No."

Von Enke cleared off part of the big table. Wallander noted that most of the books were about modern warfare and contemporary politics. One that seemed to have been read more than any of the others was titled simply **The Submarine Threat.**

The coffee was strong. Von Enke was drinking tea. Wallander regretted not having chosen the same.

It was ten minutes to one.

"Naturally I understand that you have a lot of questions you want answers to," said von Enke. "I may not be able or willing to answer all of them, but before we come to that I must ask you a few questions. First and foremost: Did you come here alone?"

"Yes."

"Who else knows where you are?"

"Nobody."

Wallander could see that von Enke wasn't sure whether to believe him.

"Nobody," he repeated. "This trip was entirely my own idea. Nobody else has been involved."

"Not even Linda?"

"Not even Linda."

"How did you get here?"

"In a little boat with an outboard motor. If you want I can give you the name of the firm I rented it from. But the man had no idea where I was going. I told him I was going to surprise an old friend for his birthday. I'm sure he believed me."

"Where is the boat?"

Wallander pointed over his shoulder.

"On the other side of the island. Beached, and tied up to some alder trees."

Von Enke sat there silently, staring at his teacup. Wallander waited.

"How did you find me?"

Von Enke seemed tired when he asked the question. Wallander could understand that being on the run was strenuous, even if you weren't on the move all the time.

"When I visited Bokö, Eskil Lundberg mentioned in passing that this cottage was perfect for anybody who wanted to disappear from the face of the earth. We were on the way to the mainland when we sailed past. You know I've been to see him, of course. What he said stayed at the back of my mind, nagging away at me. And then when I heard that you were particularly fond of islands, I realized that this might be where you were."

"Who told you about me and my islands?"

Wallander decided on the spot not to say anything about Sten Nordlander for the time being. He could give von Enke an answer that would be impossible to check.

"Louise."

Von Enke nodded, silently. Then he straightened his back, as if steeling himself for battle.

"We can do this in two ways," Wallander said. "Either you tell me all about it, or I ask questions and you answer them."

"Am I accused of anything?"

"No. But your wife is dead, so you are automatically a suspect."

"I can understand that completely."

Suicide or murder, Wallander thought. You seem to be well aware of the score. Wallander knew he had to proceed cautiously. After all, the man he was talking to was somebody he knew very little about.

"Let's hear it, then," said Wallander. "I'll interrupt you if anything is unclear. You can start at Djursholm, when you had your birthday party."

Von Enke shook his head demonstratively. His tiredness seemed to have evaporated. He walked over to the stove, refilled his cup with hot water, and added a new tea bag. He remained standing, cup in hand.

"I need to begin earlier than that. There can be only one starting point," he said. "It's simple, but absolutely true. I loved my wife, Louise, more than anything else in the world. God forgive me for saying it, but I loved her more than I did my son. Louise embodied the happiness in my life—seeing her come into a room, seeing her smile, hearing her moving around in the next room."

He fell silent and gave Wallander a look that was both piercing and challenging. He demanded an answer, or at least a reaction from Wallander's side.

"Yes," said Wallander. "I believe you."

Von Enke began his story.

"We need to go back a long way. There's no need for me to go into detail. It would take too much time, and it isn't necessary. But we have to go back to the 1960s and '70s. I was still active on board naval vessels then, often in command of one of our most modern minesweepers. Louise was working as a teacher. She spent her free time coaching young divers, and once in a while visited Eastern Europe, mainly East Germany, which in those days was very successful in producing champions. Nowadays we know that this was due to a combination of fanatical, almost slavish training techniques and an advanced use of various drugs. At the end of the 1970s I was transferred to staff duties and promoted to the top operations command of the Swedish navy. That involved a lot of work, much of it done at home. Several evenings every week I used to take home secret documents. I had a gun closet because I occasionally used to go hunting, mainly for deer, but sometimes I used to take part in the annual elk hunt. I had my rifles and ammunition locked away in that closet, and I also used to put my secret documents in there overnight, or when Louise and I went out, either to the theater or to some dinner party."

He paused, carefully removed the tea bag from his cup and put it on a saucer, then continued.

"When exactly do you notice that something is not as it should be? The almost invisible signs that suggest something has been changed, or moved? You are a police officer—I assume you must often find yourself in situations where you catch on to these vague signals. One morning, when I opened the gun closet, I noticed that something was wrong. I can still recall how I felt. I was just going to take out my briefcase when I paused. Had I really left it the way it was now? There was something about the lock, and the position of the handle. My doubts bothered me for about five seconds, no more. Then I dismissed them. I always used to check that all the documents were where they should be, and that morning was no exception. I didn't think any more about it. I think I'm pretty observant and have a good memory. Or at least, that was the case when I was younger. As you grow older, all your faculties deteriorate bit by bit, and there's nothing you can do about it. You are considerably younger than I am, but maybe you've noticed this?"

"Eyesight," Wallander said. "I have to buy new reading glasses every couple of years. And I don't think I hear as well as I used to."

"It's your sense of smell that lasts best as you grow older. That's the only one of my senses that I think is unaffected. The smell of flowers is just as clear and subtle as it ever was."

They sat there in silence. Wallander noticed a rustling sound in the wall behind him.

"Mice," said von Enke. "It was still cold when I first came here. At times there was a hellish rustling and rattling inside the walls. But one of these days I'll no longer be able to hear the mice scampering around under the floorboards."

"I don't want to interrupt your story," Wallander said. "But when you vanished that morning, did you come straight here?"

"I was picked up."

"By whom?"

Von Enke shook his head, didn't want to answer. Wallander didn't press him.

"Let me go back to the gun closet," von Enke continued. "A few months later I had the impression yet again that my briefcase had been moved. I decided I was imagining it. The documents inside the briefcase hadn't been jumbled up or interfered with in any other way. But since this was the second occasion, I was worried. The keys to the gun closet were underneath some letter scales on my desk. The only person who knew where the keys were was Louise. So I did what you have to do when there's something worrying you."

"What?"

"I asked her outright. She was in the kitchen, having breakfast."

"What did she say?"

"She said no. And asked the obvious question: why on earth would she be interested in what was in my gun closet? I don't think she ever liked the idea of my keeping guns in the apartment, even if she never said anything about it. I remember feeling ashamed when I walked down the stairs to the car waiting to take me to general staff headquarters. The job I had then gave me the right to have a chauffeur."

"What happened next?"

Wallander noticed that his questions were disturbing von Enke, who wanted to dictate the pace of his revelations himself. He raised his hands as a sort of apology, indicating that he wouldn't interrupt anymore.

"I'm convinced that Louise told me the truth. But even after that I still had the feeling that my briefcase and my documents had been interfered with. I started to set little traps: I purposely put some of the papers in the wrong order, I left a strand of hair over the lock of my briefcase, a blob of grease on the handle. What was hardest to grasp was why Louise would be interested in my papers. I couldn't believe it had to do with pure curiosity or jealousy. She knew there was no reason at all to suspect anything like that. It was at least a year before I first began to wonder if the unthinkable really was a possibility."

Von Enke paused briefly before continuing.

"Could Louise be in touch with a foreign power? It

seemed highly improbable for a very simple reason. The documents I took home with me were rarely anything that could be of the slightest interest to a foreign intelligence service. But I couldn't help feeling worried. I was starting to distrust my wife, to suspect her of treachery for no reason other than a strand of hair that had been disturbed. In the end—and by then it was the late 1970s—I decided to establish once and for all whether or not my suspicions of Louise were justified."

He stood up and rummaged around in a corner of the room full of maps. He came back with a scroll, which he spread out over the table—a sea chart of the central area of the Baltic Sea. He placed pebbles on the corners to weigh it down.

"Fall 1979," he said. "To be more precise, August and September. We were due for our usual fall maneuvers involving nearly all our naval vessels. There was nothing special about this particular exercise. It was while I was attached to the general staff, and my role was to be an observer. About a month before the maneuvers were to take place, when all the plans and timetables were already drawn up, the navigation routes established, and the vessels assigned to specific areas, I made my own plan. I created a document and labeled it Secret. It was even signed by the supreme commander—although he knew nothing about it, of course. I introduced into the exercise a top secret element featuring one of our submarines being refueled in very advanced fashion by a remotely controlled tanker. It was all a complete fabrication, but something that could just about be regarded as possible. I noted the exact location and the precise time when the exercise would take place. I knew that the destroyer **Små-land,** with the observers on board, would be close to that location at that time. I took the document home with me, locked it in the gun closet overnight, then hid it in my desk when I went to staff headquarters the following day. I repeated the same procedure for several days. The next week I placed the document in a secure bank vault I had rented for this very purpose. I considered tearing it up, but I knew I might need it someday as proof. The month that passed before the maneuvers took place was the worst I have ever endured. I had to make sure that Louise didn't suspect anything, but I had set a trap for her that would shatter both of us if my suspicions turned out to be well founded."

He pointed to a spot on the sea chart. Wallander leaned forward and saw that it was a point just northeast of Gotska Sandön.

"This is where the alleged meeting between the submarine and the nonexistent tanker was supposed to happen. It was on the periphery of the area where the maneuvers would be held. There was nothing unusual about the fact that Russian vessels were keeping track of us. We did the same when Warsaw Pact countries' maneuvers were under way. We used to keep at a discreet distance, avoiding provocation. I chose this location for the fictitious meeting because the supreme commander was due to be dropped off at Berga that same morning, so the destroyer would be in the right place, on its way to where the exercises were in full swing, when my fictional refueling operation was to happen."

"I don't want to interrupt," said Wallander, "but was

it really possible to stick to such a tight schedule when so many vessels were involved?"

"That was part of the point of the whole maneuver. What you need in wartime is not just a lot of money, but also a high degree of punctuality."

Wallander gave a start when there was a loud thud on the roof of the lodge. Von Enke didn't seem to react at all.

"A branch," he said. "They sometimes fall down and hit the roof with quite a bang. I've offered to saw down the dried-out, dead oak tree, but nobody around here seems to have a chain saw. The trunk is enormous. I would guess that the oak dates from the middle of the nineteenth century or thereabouts."

He reverted to his account of what happened at the end of August 1979.

"The fall maneuvers acquired some added spice that nobody had foreseen. The Baltic Sea south of Stockholm was hit by a severe southwesterly gale that the forecasters had failed to predict. One of our submarines, commanded by one of our best young captains, Hans-Olov Fredhäll, suffered rudder damage and had to be towed into Bråviken to wait there until we could take it back to Muskö. Those on board no doubt had a less than enjoyable time during the storm—submarines can roll like nobody's business. And in addition, a corvette sprang a leak off Hävringe. The crew had to be taken off and transferred to another ship, but the corvette didn't sink. Anyway, large parts of the exercise couldn't be carried out as planned. The winds had slackened somewhat by the time we were ready for the last phase of the maneuvers. I must admit, I could hardly sleep for days before the imaginary meeting of the submarine and the tanker, but nobody seemed to notice that I was behaving any differently from usual. We dropped off the supreme commander, who was pleased with what he had seen. The captain on board the **Småland** suddenly and unexpectedly ordered full steam ahead, to check that his vessel was in tip-top condition. I was worried at first that we would pass the spot too soon, but the high waves prevented the destroyer from exceeding the speed I had based my calculations on. I spent the whole morning on the bridge. Nobody thought there was anything odd about that—I was a commander myself, after all. The captain had handed over responsibility for the ship to his deputy, Jörgen Mattsson. At a quarter to ten he handed me his telescope and pointed. It was raining, and very misty, but there was no doubt about what he had detected. There were two fishing boats ahead of us to port, sporting all the aerials and security equipment we were familiar with on Russian naval patrol boats. No doubt they didn't have a single fish in their holds, but we could be certain that there were Russian technicians on board, listening to our radio communications. I should perhaps mention that we were in international waters; they had every right to be where they were."

"So they were waiting for a submarine and a tanker?"

"Mattsson didn't know that, of course. 'What do they think they're doing?' he asked. 'Way outside the area where our maneuvers are taking place?' I still recall what I said in reply. **Perhaps they really are ordinary fishing boats.** But he wasn't convinced. He called down to the captain, who came onto the bridge. The destroyer paused while we reported the presence of the fishing boats. A helicopter came and hovered around for a while before we moved on and left them alone. By then I had left the bridge and gone down to the cabin I used during the maneuvers."

"So now you knew what you didn't want to know?"

"It was an experience that made me feel sick, in a way that no bout of seasickness in the world could have achieved. I threw up when I came to my cabin. Then I lay down, thinking about how nothing could ever be like it had been before. There was no other possibility: the document I had forged had come into the hands of the Warsaw Pact countries. Louise could have had an accomplice, of course; that was what I hoped. I didn't want her to be the direct link to the foreign intelligence services, but rather an assistant to a spy who had all the important contacts. But I couldn't even bring myself to believe that. I had investigated her life in the tiniest detail and knew there was nobody she met regularly. I still had no idea how she operated. I didn't even know how she had copied my forged document. Had she taken a photograph, or written it out? Had she simply memorized it? And how had she passed on the information? Even more important, of course, was where she got all her other secret documents. The sparse contents of my gun closet couldn't be enough. Who was she cooperating with? I didn't know, although I spent all my spare time for more than a year trying to work out what had happened. But I was forced to believe the evidence of my own eyes. I lay there in the cabin, and felt the vibrations from the powerful engines. There was no longer any escape. I had to acknowledge that I was married to a woman I didn't know. Which meant that I didn't know myself either. How could I have misunderstood her so fundamentally?"

Håkan von Enke stood up and rolled up the sea chart. When he had put it back on its shelf, he opened the door and went outside. What Wallander had heard still hadn't sunk in. It was too big. And there were too many unanswered questions.

Von Enke came back in, closed the door, and checked that his fly was closed.

"You're telling me about things that happened almost thirty years ago," Wallander said. "That's a long time. What about what's happening now?"

Von Enke suddenly seemed reluctant, sullen, when he replied.

"What did I say when we began this conversation? Have you forgotten? I said that I loved my wife. I couldn't do anything to change that, no matter what she had done."

"Surely you must have confronted her with what you knew."

"Must I?"

"It was one thing for her to commit an offense against our country, but she had also let you down. Stolen your secrets. You couldn't possibly have kept on living with her without telling her what you knew."

"Couldn't I?"

Wallander could hardly believe what he'd heard. But

the man rolling the empty teacup between his hands seemed convincing.

"Are you telling me you didn't say anything to her?"

"Never."

"Never? That sounds implausible."

"But it's true. I stopped taking secret documents home with me. It wasn't anything sudden or unexplained. When my duties changed, there was every reason for my briefcase to be empty in the evenings."

"She must have noticed something. It's impossible to believe she didn't."

"I never said anything to her. She was exactly the same as before. After a few years I began to think it had all been a bad dream. But of course, I might have been wrong. She might have realized that I'd seen through her. So we carried on sharing a secret without being sure what the other one knew or didn't know. It went on like that until one day, everything changed."

Wallander sensed rather than knew what he was referring to.

"You mean the submarines?"

"Yes. By then there was a rumor going around that the supreme commander suspected there was a spy in the Swedish defense forces. The first warning had come when a Russian defector spoke out in London. There was a spy in the Swedish military that the Russians valued extremely highly. Somebody a cut above the norm who knew how to get at the really significant information."

Wallander shook his head slowly.

"This is difficult to understand," he said. "A spy in the Swedish military. Your wife was a schoolteacher; she coached gifted young divers in her spare time. How could she have access to military secrets if your briefcase was empty?"

"I seem to recall that the Russian defector was called Ragulin. He was one of many defectors at that time; we sometimes found it difficult to tell them apart. Obviously, he didn't know the name of or any details about the person the Russians more or less worshipped. But there was one thing he did know, and it changed the whole picture dramatically. For me as well."

"What?"

Von Enke put down the empty cup. It was as if he were bracing himself. As he did so, Wallander remembered that he had heard Hermann Eber talking about another Russian defector, by the name of Kirov.

"It was a woman," he said. "Ragulin had heard that the Swedish spy was a woman."

Wallander said nothing.

The mice were nibbling away quietly in the walls of the hunting lodge.

32

On one of the windowsills was a half-finished ship in a bottle. Wallander noticed it when von Enke left the table and went outside for the second time. It seemed that he was too distraught to continue, having been forced to admit to somebody else that his wife had been a spy. Wallander saw the tears in his eyes when he suddenly excused himself and left the room. He left the door open. Daylight was beginning to break outside, so there was no longer any risk that anybody might notice lights switched on in the lodge. When von Enke came back, Wallander was still engrossed in imagining the delicate work involved in making the tiny ship.

"The **Santa Maria**," said von Enke. "Columbus's ship. It helps me to keep unwanted thoughts at bay. I learned the art from a sailor—an old naval engineer with alcohol problems. It wasn't possible to allow him on board anymore. Instead he used to wander around Karlskrona, criticizing everybody and everything. But remarkably enough, he was a master of making ships in bottles, despite the fact that you'd have thought his hands shook far too much for that. I've never had the time to attempt anything of the sort until I came here to the island."

"A nameless island," said Wallander.

"I call it Blue Island. It has to be called something. Blue Moon and Blue Ridge are already taken."

They sat down at the table again. By means of some kind of unspoken agreement they had each made it clear to the other that sleep could wait. They had begun a conversation that needed to be continued. Wallander realized that it was his turn now. Håkan von Enke was waiting for his questions. He started with what he considered the beginning.

"When you celebrated your seventy-fifth birthday," Wallander began, "you wanted to talk to me. But I'm still not clear about why you chose to talk about those events with me rather than somebody else. And we never really got to the point. There was a lot I didn't understand. I still don't understand it."

"I thought you should know. My son and your daughter, our only children, will spend the rest of their lives together, we hope."

"No," said Wallander. "There was some other reason, I'm sure. And I have to say that I was very upset to discover you haven't been telling me the whole truth."

Von Enke looked at him in incomprehension.

"You and Louise have a daughter," Wallander said. "Signe, who leads a sort of life at Niklasgården. So you see, I even know where she is. You've never said anything about her. Not even to your son."

Håkan von Enke was staring at him. He had stiffened in his armchair. This is a man who is not often caught off guard, Wallander thought. But right now he is really on the spot.

"I've been there," Wallander went on. "I've seen her. I also know that you visited her regularly. You were even there the day before you disappeared. We can choose to keep on not telling the truth, to turn this conversation into something that doesn't clarify but merely makes what is unclear even more obscure. It's our choice. Or rather, your choice. I've already made mine."

Wallander eyed von Enke, wondering why he seemed to be hesitating.

"You're right, of course," said von Enke eventually. "It's just that I'm so used to denying Signe's existence."

"Why?"

"It was for Louise's sake. She always felt strangely guilty about Signe. Despite the fact that Signe's handicaps weren't caused by something that went wrong during childbirth, or by something Louise had done or eaten or drunk while she was pregnant. We never spoke about Signe. As far as Louise was concerned, she simply didn't exist. But she existed for me. I was always tormented by not being able to say anything to Hans."

Wallander said nothing. It suddenly dawned on von Enke why.

"You told him? Was that necessary?"

"I would have regarded it as shameful if I hadn't told him he had a sister."

"How did he take it?"

"He was upset, which is understandable. He felt cheated."

Von Enke shook his head slowly.

"I'd made a promise to Louise, and I couldn't break that promise."

"That's something you have to talk to him about yourself. Or not. Which leads me to an entirely different question. What were you doing in Copenhagen a few days ago?"

Von Enke's surprise was genuine. Wallander felt that he now had the upper hand; the key was how to exploit that in order to make the man on the other side of the table tell the truth. There were still a lot of questions to be asked.

"How do you know I've been in Copenhagen?"

"I'm not going to answer that question at the moment."

"Why not?"

"Because the answer is of no significance. Besides, I'm the one asking the questions now."

"Am I suppose to interpret that to mean I'm now being subjected to a police interrogation?"

"No. But don't forget that you have subjected your son and my daughter to incredible stress and strain since you went missing. To tell you the truth, I'm furious when I think about how you've behaved. The only way you can keep me calm is to give honest answers to my questions."

"I'll try."

"Did you make contact with Hans?"

"No."

"Did you intend to?"

"No."

"What were you doing there?"

"I went to withdraw some money."

"But you said just now that you hadn't been in touch with Hans. As far as I'm aware, he oversaw your and Louise's savings."

"We had an account with Danske Bank that we kept control of ourselves. After I retired I did some consultancy work for the manufacturers of a weapons system for naval vessels. They paid in U.S. dollars. Obviously, some tax evasion was involved."

"What kind of sums are we talking about?"

"I can't see how that could be of any relevance. Unless you intend to report me for tax evasion?"

"You're suspected of more important things. But answer the question!"

"About half a million Swedish kronor."

"Why did you choose to have an account in a Danish bank?"

"The Danish krone seemed stable."

"And there was no other reason for going to Copenhagen?"

"No."

"How did you get there?"

"By train from Norrköping. I went there by taxi. Eskil, whom you've met, took me to Fyrudden. And he picked me up when I came back."

Wallander found no reason to doubt what he had heard, at least for the time being.

"And Louise knew all about your undeclared money?"

"She had the same access to the account as I did. Neither of us had a bad conscience. We both thought that Swedish taxation rates were disgracefully high."

"Why did you need the money now?"

"Because I'd run out of cash. Even if you live frugally, you're always spending money."

Wallander left Copenhagen for the time being and returned to Djursholm.

"There's one thing I've been wondering about that only you can answer. When we were standing in the conservatory, you noticed a man in the street, behind my back. I'll admit that I've spent ages wondering about this. Who was it?"

"I don't know."

"But you seemed worried when you noticed him."

"I was scared."

The admission came out like a roar. Wallander was on his guard. Perhaps being on the run for such a long time had, after all, taken its toll on the man sitting opposite him. He decided to tread carefully.

"Who do you think it was?"

"I've already said I don't know. And it's not important. He was there to remind me. That's what I think, at least."

"Remind you of what? Don't make me drag every answer out of you."

"Somehow or other Louise's contacts must have realized that I suspected her. Maybe it was she herself who told them I'd discovered her. It wasn't the first time I'd had the feeling I was being watched. But the other occasions were not as clear-cut as that one at Djursholm."

"Are you saying that somebody was shadowing you?"

"Not all the time. But I sometimes noticed that I was being followed."

"How long had that been going on?"

"I don't know. It might have been happening for a long time without my noticing. For many years."

"Let's move on from that conservatory to the windowless room," Wallander said. "You wanted us to be away from the rest of the guests so that we could talk.

But I don't know why you picked me to be your confessor."

"It wasn't planned at all; I acted on the spur of the moment. I sometimes surprise myself with the sudden decisions I make. I expect that happens to you as well. I thought the whole celebration was unpleasant. It was my seventy-fifth birthday, and I was throwing a party that I didn't really want. I was pretty close to panic."

"It seemed to me afterward that there was a hidden message in what you told me. Was I right to suspect that?"

"No. I simply wanted to talk. I suppose I might have wanted to see if I could confide my secret in you later on—the probability that I was married to a traitor."

"Wasn't there anybody else you could talk to? Sten Nordlander, for instance? Your best friend?"

"I was ashamed at the mere thought of revealing my misery to him."

"What about Steven Atkins? You had told him about your daughter, after all."

"I was drunk at the time. We had drunk lots of whiskey. I regretted saying anything afterward. I thought he had forgotten about it. But evidently not."

"He assumed that I knew about her."

"What do my friends say about my disappearance?"

"They're worried. Shaken. The day they discover you've been hiding away, they will be very upset. I suspect you will lose them. Which leads me to the question of why you disappeared."

"I felt I was under threat. The man on the other side of that fence was just a sort of prologue. I suddenly began noticing shadows everywhere, no matter where I went. It wasn't like that before. I received strange phone calls. It was as if they always knew where I was. One day when I was visiting the National Maritime Museum a guard came to tell me there was a phone call for me. A man speaking broken Swedish issued a warning. He didn't say precisely what for, just that I should watch my step. It started to become intolerable. I had never been so scared in all my life. I came very close to approaching the police and reporting Louise. I considered sending an anonymous letter. In the end I couldn't keep going any longer. I made arrangements to rent this hunting lodge. Eskil drove to Stockholm and picked me up when I was outside the stadium on my morning walk. Since then I've been here the whole time, apart from that trip to Copenhagen."

"It's still incomprehensible to me that you never confronted Louise with your suspicions, which had become convictions. How could you live with somebody who was a spy?"

"I did confront her. Twice. The first time was the year Palme was killed. That had nothing to do with it, of course, but they were unsettled times. I was sitting with my colleagues, drinking coffee and talking about my suspicions that there was a spy in our ranks. It was a terrible situation, nibbling on a cookie and talking about a possible spy who I thought might well be my wife."

Wallander had a sudden attack of sneezing. Von Enke waited until it had passed.

"I confronted her in the summer of 1986," he said. "We had gone to the Riviera with some friends of ours, a Commander Friis and his wife—we used to play bridge with them. We were staying at a hotel in Menton. One evening Louise and I went for a walk through the town. Suddenly, I stopped dead in my tracks and asked her outright. I hadn't planned to; I suppose you could say that something snapped inside me. I stood in front of her and asked her. Was she a spy or wasn't she? She was upset, refused to answer at first, and raised a hand as if to hit me. Then she recovered her self-control and replied calmly that of course she wasn't a spy. How on earth could such a ridiculous thought have entered my head? What did she have to say that could be of any interest to a foreign power? I remember her smiling. She didn't take me seriously, and as a result I couldn't do so either. I simply couldn't believe that she was so convincing as a dissembler. I apologized, and made the excuse that I was tired. For the rest of that summer I was convinced I'd been wrong. But in the fall my suspicions returned."

"What happened?"

"The same thing again. Papers in the gun closet, a feeling that somebody had disturbed my briefcase."

"Did you notice any changes in her after you revealed your suspicions in Menton?"

He thought before answering.

"I've asked myself the same question. I sometimes thought she was acting differently, but at other times not. I'm still not sure."

"What happened the second time you put her on the spot?"

"It was the winter of 1996, exactly ten years later. We were at home. We were having breakfast, and it was snowing outside. She suddenly asked me about something I'd shouted at her during the night, while I was asleep. She claimed that I'd accused her of being a spy."

"Had you?"

"I don't know. I do sometimes talk in my sleep, but I never remember anything about it."

"What did you say?"

"I turned her question on its head. I asked her if what I'd been dreaming was true."

"What did she say?"

"She threw her napkin at me and stormed out of the kitchen. It was ten minutes before she came back. I remember checking the clock. Nine minutes and forty-five seconds, to be exact. She apologized and insisted, **once and for all,** as she put it, that she didn't want to hear any more talk about my suspicions. They were absurd. If I ever repeated the accusations, she would be forced to conclude that I was either out of my mind or going senile."

"What happened then?"

"Nothing. But my misgivings were not allayed. And rumors were still circulating about a spy in the Swedish military. Two years later things came to a point when I really did begin to think that I was going out of my mind."

"What happened?"

"I was summoned to an interrogation by the military security services. They didn't make any direct accusations, but it seems that for a while I was one of those suspected of being a spy. It was a grotesque situation. But I recall thinking that if Louise **had** sold military secrets to the Russians, she had found a perfect cover."

"You?"

"Exactly. Me."

"So then what happened?"

"Nothing. The rumors kept circulating, sometimes stronger than at others. Many of us were interrogated, even after we had retired. And as I said, I had the feeling I was being watched."

Von Enke stood up, switched off the lamps that were still on, and opened some of the curtains. A gray dawn and an equally gray sea could be glimpsed through the trees. Wallander went over to one of the windows. A storm was brewing. He was worried about the boat. Von Enke accompanied him when he went to check that the painter was secure. A few eiders bobbed up and down on the choppy waves. The sun was beginning to disperse the night mist. The boat seemed safe enough, but the two men used their combined strength to drag it farther up the pebbly beach.

"Who killed Louise?" Wallander asked when they had finished with the boat.

Von Enke turned to face him. It occurred to Wallander that he must have confronted Louise in Menton in more or less the same way.

"Who killed her? You're asking me? All I know is that it wasn't me. But what do the police think? What do you think?"

"The man in Stockholm who's in charge of the case seems to be good. But he doesn't know. Not yet, perhaps I should say. We tend not to jump to conclusions."

They returned to the hunting lodge in silence, sat down at the kitchen table again, and continued their conversation.

"We must begin at the beginning," said Wallander. "Why did she go missing? The obvious conclusion for third-party observers like me was that the two of you had a pact of some sort."

"That wasn't the case. The first I knew of her disappearance was when I read about it in the papers. It was a shock."

"So she didn't know where you were?"

"No."

"How long did you intend to remain in hiding?"

"I needed to be left in peace, to think. And I'd received death threats. I needed to find a way out."

"I met Louise on several occasions. She was genuinely and deeply concerned about what might have happened to you."

"She fooled you just as she'd fooled me."

"I'm not sure. Could she not have loved you just as much as you loved her?"

Von Enke said nothing, merely shook his head.

"Did you do it?" Wallander asked. "Was that the escape route you hit upon?"

"No."

"You must have spent hours thinking, brooding, lying sleepless in this hunting lodge. I believe you when you say you loved Louise. Nevertheless, you didn't leave your hideaway when she died. One would have thought that the danger to your life was over now that she was dead. But you still stayed in hiding. I can't make sense of that."

"I've lost twenty pounds since she died. I can't eat; I can hardly sleep. I try to understand what has happened, but I can't make heads or tails of it. It's as if Louise has become a stranger to me. I don't know who she used to meet, or what led to her death. I don't have any answers."

"Did she ever give you the impression that she was afraid?"

"Never."

"I can tell you something that hasn't appeared in the newspapers, something the police haven't yet released for public consumption."

Wallander told him about the suspicions that Louise had been killed by a poison that had previously been used in East Germany.

"It seems likely that you've been right all along," Wallander concluded. "Somewhere along the way your wife, Louise, became an agent for the Russian intelligence service. She was who you suspected she was. She was the spy the Russians talked about."

. . .

Von Enke stood up and stormed out of the house. Wallander waited. After a while he began to worry, and he went out to investigate. He eventually found von Enke lying in a gully on the side of the island facing the open sea. Wallander sat down on a rock by his side.

"You must come back," he said. "Nothing will ever be solved if you continue to hide here."

"Perhaps the same poison is lying in wait for me. What will be gained if I die as well?"

"Nothing. But the police have resources to protect you."

"I have to get used to the idea. That I was right after all. I have to try to understand why and how she did what she did. I can't return until I've done that."

"You'd better not take too long," said Wallander, standing up.

He returned to the hunting lodge. Now he was the one making the coffee. He was feeling the strain of the long night. When von Enke returned, he had already emptied his second cup.

"Let's talk about Signe," Wallander said. "I went to see her, and I discovered a folder you'd hidden among her books."

"I loved my daughter. But I made my visits in secret. Louise never knew I'd been there."

"So you're the only one who ever visited her?"

"Yes."

"You're wrong. Since you went missing, somebody else has been there at least once. He claimed to be your brother."

Håkan von Enke shook his head in disbelief.

"I don't have a brother. I have a relative who lives in England, but that's all."

"I believe you," said Wallander. "We don't know who visited your daughter. Which might suggest that everything is even more complicated than either you or I could have foreseen."

Wallander could see that Håkan von Enke's demeanor had suddenly changed. Nothing they had talked about had worried him as much as the news that somebody else had visited Signe at Niklasgården.

It was nearly six o'clock. Their long nocturnal conversation was over. Neither of them had the strength to continue.

"I will leave now," said Wallander. "At the moment, I'm the only one who knows you are here. But you can't wait forever before returning to civilization. Besides, I'll keep on pestering you with questions. Think about who it might have been who visited Niklasgården. Someone must have been on your trail. Who? Why? We must keep this conversation going."

"Tell Hans and Linda that I'm okay. I don't want them to worry. Tell them I sent you a letter."

"I'll say you called. The first thing Linda would do would be to demand to see the letter."

They went to the boat and together shoved it out onto the water. Before leaving the house, Wallander had made a note of von Enke's phone number. But he also established that communications links to Blue Island could be bad. The wind was getting stronger.

Wallander was starting to worry about the journey back. He clambered onto the boat and lowered the outboard motor.

"I have to know what happened to Louise," said von Enke. "I must know who killed her. I need to know why she chose to lead the life of a traitor."

The engine started at the first pull. Wallander waved good-bye and headed for the mainland. Just before rounding the Blue Island promontory he looked back. Håkan von Enke was still standing on the beach.

At that moment Wallander had a premonition that something was wrong. He didn't know what, or why. But the feeling was very strong.

He returned the boat and set off on the long drive back to Skåne. He stopped at a rest stop near Gamleby and slept for a few hours.

When he woke up, feeling stiff, the premonition was still there. After that long night with Håkan von Enke, one thing still nagged away at him.

It was a sort of warning. Something didn't add up, something he had overlooked.

When he pulled into the parking area outside his house many hours later, he still didn't know what it was that he'd missed.

But he thought: Nothing is what it seems to be.

33

The following day, Wallander wrote a summary of his conversation with Håkan von Enke. Once again he went through all the material he had gathered. Louise was still a mystery to him. If it was true that she had sold information to the Russians, she had cleverly hidden herself behind a mask of insignificance. Who was she, really? Wallander asked himself. Perhaps she was one of those people who become comprehensible only after they are dead.

It was a windy, rainy day in Skåne. Wallander observed the dreary weather through his windows, and concluded that this summer promised to be one of the worst he could remember. Nevertheless, he forced himself to go for a long walk with Jussi. He needed to get his blood moving and clear his head. He longed for calm, sunny days when he could lie down in his garden without needing to trouble his brain with the problems that were occupying him now.

When he had returned after the walk and taken off his wet clothes, he sat down by the phone in his shabby old robe and began leafing through his address book. It was full of crossed-out phone numbers, changes, and additions. In the car the day before, he had remembered an old school friend, Sölve Hagberg, who might be able to help him. It was his phone number he was looking for. He'd made a note of it when they bumped into each other by pure chance in a Malmö street a few years ago.

Sölve Hagberg was an odd person even as a child. Wallander recalled with a sense of guilt that he had been one of the students who bullied Sölve, because of his nearsightedness and his determination to actually learn something at school. But all attempts to undermine Sölve's self-confidence had failed. All the scornful abuse, all the punches and kicks had been shaken off, like water off a duck's back.

After leaving school they had not been in contact until one day Wallander was amazed to discover that Sölve Hagberg was going to take part in a TV show called **Double or Quits.** Even more astonishing was that his chosen subject was going to be the history of the Swedish navy. He had been overweight as a child, another reason why he had been bullied. But if he'd been overweight then, he was positively fat now. He seemed to roll up to the microphone on invisible wheels. He was bald, wore rimless glasses, and spoke with the same broad Scanian accent that Wallander remembered from school. Mona had commented disparagingly on his appearance and gone into the kitchen to make coffee, but Wallander stayed to watch him answer all the questions correctly. He won, thanks to precise and detailed replies delivered with complete self-confidence. As far as Wallander could recall, he hadn't hesitated for a moment. He really did know everything about the long, complicated history of the Swedish navy. It had been Hagberg's big ambition to become a naval officer. But thanks to his ungainliness he had been turned down as a recruit and sent back home to his books and model ships. Now he had taken his revenge.

For a short while the newspapers showed an interest in this strange man, who still lived in Limhamn and made a living writing articles for journals and books published by various military institutions. The press wrote about Hagberg's comprehensive archive. He had detailed information about Swedish naval officers from the seventeenth century to the present day, constantly updated. Perhaps Wallander might be able to find something in this archive to tell him more about who Håkan von Enke really was.

He finally found Hagberg's number scribbled in the greasy margin of the letter **H**. He picked up the phone and dialed. A woman answered. Wallander gave his name and asked to speak to Sölve.

"He's dead."

Wallander was dumbstruck. After a few seconds of silence the woman asked if he was still there.

"Yes, I'm still here. I had no idea he was dead."

"He died two years ago. He had a heart attack. He was in Ronneby, addressing a group of retired naval engineers. He collapsed during the dinner following his lecture."

"I take it you are his wife?"

"Asta Hagberg. We were married for twenty-six years. I told him he should lose weight, but all he did was put three sugars in his coffee instead of four. Who are you?"

Wallander explained, and decided to end the call as quickly as possible.

"You were one of the kids who used to torment him," she surprised him by saying. "I remember your name now. One of the bullies at school. He had a list of your names, and kept tabs on how you led your lives. He wasn't ashamed to feel pleased when things went badly for anyone on the list. Why are you calling? What do you want?"

"I'd hoped to be allowed access to his archive."

"I might be able to help you, but I don't know if I should. Why couldn't you leave him alone?"

"I don't think any of us really understood what we were doing. Children can be cruel. I was no exception."

"Do you regret it?"

"Of course."

"Come by, then. Sölve suspected that he wouldn't live much longer, so he taught me all about the archive and how to use it. What will happen to it when I'm gone, I don't know. But I'm always at home. Sölve left a fair amount of money, so I don't need to work."

She laughed.

"Do you know how he made his money?"

"I expect he was much sought-after as a lecturer."

"He never asked to be paid for that. Try again!"

"Then I don't know."

"He played poker. He went to illegal gaming clubs. I suppose that's something you deal with in your work?"

"I thought people turned to the Internet these days for gambling."

"He couldn't be bothered with that. He went to his clubs, and was away for several weeks sometimes. Once in a while he lost a large amount of money, but usually he came home with a suitcase full of cash. He told me to count it and put it in the bank. He would then go to bed and sleep, often for days on end. The police were here now and then, and he was sometimes arrested when they raided a club, but he was never charged. I think he had an understanding with the police."

"What do you mean by that?"

"Can I mean anything but that he sometimes tipped them off? Maybe some wanted persons turned up at the clubs with money they'd stolen? Nobody would ever imagine that nice old Fatman Sölve could be a cop's narc, would they? Anyway, are you coming or aren't you?"

When Wallander wrote down the address he realized that Sölve had always lived on the same street in Limhamn. Wallander and Asta agreed that he would go there at five o'clock that same afternoon. Next he called Linda. He got her answering machine and left a message saying that he was at home. Then he went through the contents of the refrigerator and threw away all the food that had passed its use-by date and wrote a shopping list. The fridge was almost completely empty now. He was just about to leave the house when Linda called.

"I just got back from the drugstore. Klara's not well."

"Is it serious?"

"You don't need to sound as if she were at death's

door every time. She has a temperature and a sore throat. That's all."

"Has the doctor seen her?"

"I called the health center. I think I have everything under control. As long as you don't get all excited and irritate me. Where have you been?"

"I'm not saying at the moment."

"Aha, a woman, in other words. Good."

"Not a woman. But I have an important piece of news. I received a phone call not long ago. From Håkan."

At first she didn't seem to understand. Then she shouted into the receiver.

"What? Håkan called you? What the hell are you saying? Where is he? How is he? What's happened?"

"Stop shouting at me! I don't know where he is. He didn't want to tell me. He just said that he was well. It didn't sound as if there was anything wrong with him."

Wallander could hear her heavy breathing. He felt very uncomfortable lying to her. He regretted having made that promise before he left the island. I'll tell her the facts, he thought. I can't deceive my own daughter.

"It seems so unlikely. Did he say anything about why he ran away?"

"No. But he did say that he had nothing to do with Louise's death. He was just as shocked as the rest of us. He hadn't had any contact with her after he left."

"Were Hans's parents both crazy?"

"I can't comment on that. But in any case, we can be glad that he's still alive. That was the only message he wanted me to pass on to you. That he was well. But he couldn't say when he would return, or why he was in hiding."

"Did he say that? That he was in hiding?"

Wallander realized that he had revealed too much. But it was too late for him to retract.

"I don't remember exactly what words he used. Don't forget that I was astonished by the call as well."

"I have to speak to Hans. He's in Copenhagen."

"I'll be out all afternoon. Call me this evening. Then we can talk more. I want to know how Hans reacts."

"He can hardly be anything but happy."

Wallander replaced the receiver in disgust. When Linda discovered the truth he would have to deal with her fury.

He left for Limhamn. He didn't really know what to expect, but when he arrived he experienced the usual mixture of discomfort and loss that always affected him when he returned to the place where he grew up. He parked the car not far from Asta Hagberg's house, then strolled to the apartment building where he had lived as a child. The façade had been renovated and a new fence had been put up, but nevertheless he remembered everything. The sandbox he used to play in was bigger now than it was in those days, and the two birch trees he used to climb were no longer there. He paused on the sidewalk and watched some children playing. They were dark-skinned, no doubt from the Middle East or North Africa. A woman wearing a hijab was sitting by the entrance door, knitting and keeping an eye on the children. He could hear Arabic music wafting through an open window. This is where I used to live, he thought. In another world, another time.

A man came out of the building and approached the gate. He was also dark-skinned. He smiled at Wallander.

"You looking for someone?" he asked in uncertain Swedish.

"No," said Wallander. "I used to live here many years ago."

He pointed up at a window on the second floor, which in the old days had belonged to their living room.

"This is a nice house," said the man. "We like it here; the children like it. We don't have to feel afraid."

"Good. People shouldn't be afraid."

Wallander nodded and left. The feeling of growing old was oppressive. He quickened his pace, in order to get away from himself.

The garden surrounding the house where Asta Hagberg lived was well tended, but the woman who answered the door was just as fat as he remembered Sölve Hagberg being on the TV show. She was sweaty; her hair was tousled and her skirt much too short. At first he thought she was wearing strong perfume, but then he realized that the whole house reeked of unusual aromas. Does she go around spraying the furniture with perfume? he wondered. Does she drench the potted plants in musk?

She offered him coffee, but he declined. He was already feeling sick, thanks to the overpowering smells streaming into his nose from all over the house. When they went into the living room, Wallander had the feeling that he was entering the bridge of a large ship. Wherever he looked there were ships' wheels, compasses with beautifully polished brass fittings, votive ships hanging from the ceiling, and an old-fashioned hammock attached to one of the walls. Asta Hagberg crammed herself into a captain's chair that Wallander presumed had also come from a seagoing vessel. He sat down on what at first looked like a perfectly normal sofa—but a brass plate proclaimed that it had once belonged to the Swedish American Line's **Kungsholm.**

"How can I help you?" she asked, lighting a cigarette that she had put in a holder.

"Håkan von Enke," Wallander said. "An old submarine commander, now retired."

Asta Hagberg was suddenly stricken by a violent coughing fit. Wallander hoped that this overweight smoker wouldn't collapse and die before his very eyes. He guessed she was his own age, about sixty.

She kept on coughing until tears came to her eyes. Then she continued smoking serenely.

"The Håkan von Enke who's gone missing," she said. "And his dead wife, Louise? Am I right?"

"I know that Sölve had a unique archive. I wonder if there might be something in it that can help me understand why Håkan von Enke has disappeared."

"He's dead, of course."

"In which case it's the cause of his death that I'm looking for," Wallander said noncommittally.

"His wife committed suicide. That suggests the family was struggling with major problems. Doesn't it?"

She went to a table and removed a cloth that had been draped over a computer. Wallander was surprised by how agile her fat fingers were as she tapped away at the keyboard. After a few minutes she leaned back and squinted at the screen.

"Håkan von Enke's career was as normal as can be. He progressed about as far as you might have expected. If Sweden had been dragged into the war, he might have achieved a rank or two higher, but that's doubtful."

Wallander stood up and joined her in front of the computer. The stench of perfume was so strong that he tried to breathe through his mouth. He read what it said on the screen, and looked at the photograph that must have been taken when von Enke was about forty.

"Is there anything at all that's unusual?"

"No. As a young cadet he won a few prizes in Nordic athletics competitions. A good shot, very fit, first place in a few cross-country races. If you consider that unusual."

"Is there anything about his wife?"

Her fat fingers began dancing again. The coughing fit returned, but she carried on until a photograph of Louise appeared on the screen. Wallander guessed that she was about thirty-five, possibly forty. Smiling. Her hair was permed, and she was wearing a pearl necklace. Wallander studied the text. There was nothing that seemed unusual or surprising at first glance. Hagberg tapped away again and produced a new page. Wallander discovered that Louise's mother came from Kiev.

"In 1905 Angela Stefanovich married the Swedish coal exporter Hjalmar Sundblad. She moved to Sweden and became a Swedish citizen. She had four children with Hjalmar, and Louise was the youngest."

"As you can see, everything is normal," said Hagberg.

"Apart from the fact that her roots are in Russia?"

"Ukraine, we would say nowadays, I suppose. Most Swedes have roots outside our borders. We are a mixture of Finns, Dutchmen, Germans, Russians, Frenchmen. Sölve's great-grandfather came from Scotland, and my grandmother had links to Turkey. What about you?"

"My ancestors were farmers in Småland."

"Have you looked into your ancestry? Properly, I mean?"

"No."

"When you do, you may find something unexpected. Mark my words. It's always exciting, but not always pleasant. I have a good friend who's a vicar in the Swedish church. When he retired he decided to do some research into his family roots. He soon discovered two people, direct ancestors, who had been executed within the space of fifty years. One was at the beginning of the seventeenth century. He had been convicted of robbery and murder, and was beheaded. His grandson was conscripted into one of the German armies marching around Europe in the middle of the seventeenth century. He deserted, and was hanged. After that my friend the vicar gave up delving into his roots."

She stood up with considerable difficulty and gestured to Wallander to follow her into an adjacent room. There were rows of file cabinets along the walls. She unlocked one of the drawers.

"You never know what you might find," she said as she started searching through the files.

She took one out and placed it on a table. It was full of photos. Wallander didn't know if she was searching for something specific or just looking through them at random. She stopped when she came to a black-and-white photo and held it up to the light.

"I had a vague memory of having seen this picture. It's not without interest."

She handed it to Wallander, who was surprised by what it depicted. A tall, slim man in an immaculate suit and a bow tie, smiling merrily: Stig Wennerström. He was holding a glass in his hand and talking to none other than Håkan von Enke.

"When was this taken?"

"It says on the back. Sölve was meticulous when it came to recording dates and locations."

Wallander read what was typed on a slip of paper taped to the back of the photograph. **October 1959, Swedish naval delegation visiting Washington, D.C., reception hosted by Military Attaché Wennerström.** Wallander tried to work out what it implied. If it had been Louise standing there it would have been easier to guess a connection, but she wasn't present. All he could see in the background was a group of men and a waitress dressed in white.

"Did the wives usually accompany their husbands on such trips?" he asked.

"Only when the top brass were out and about. Wennerström often took his wife with him on trips and to receptions, but at that time von Enke was well short of top brass. He presumably traveled alone. If Louise had been with him, he would have needed to pay for her himself. And in any case, she certainly wouldn't have been present at a reception given by the Swedish military attaché."

"I'd be interested in knowing if she did make that trip."

Hagberg suffered another coughing fit. Wallander moved to a window and opened it slightly. The smell of perfume was bothering him.

"It will take a while," she said when the fit was over. "I need to do some searching. But obviously, Sölve recorded the details of this and all other journeys made by Swedish military delegations."

Wallander returned to the sofa from the **Kungsholm.** He could hear Hagberg humming to herself in a side room as she hunted for the list of those present on various trips to America at the end of the 1950s. It took her almost forty minutes, with Wallander growing increasingly impatient, before she returned with a look of triumph in her eyes, brandishing a sheet of paper.

"Mrs. von Enke was there," she said. "She is specifically classified as 'accompanying,' with some abbreviations that probably indicate that the armed forces were not paying her fare. If it's important, I can look up the precise meaning of the abbreviations."

Wallander took the sheet of paper. The delegation, led by Commander Karlén, comprised eight people. Among those "accompanying" were Louise von Enke and Märta Auren, the wife of Lieutenant Commander Karl-Axel Auren.

"Can one copy this?" Wallander asked.

"I don't know what 'one' can do, but I have a photocopier in the basement. How many copies do you need?"

"One."

"I usually charge two kronor per copy."

She headed for the basement. So the von Enkes had been in Washington for eight days. That meant that Louise could have been contacted by somebody. But was that really credible? he asked himself. So soon? Mind you, the Cold War was becoming more intense at the end of the fifties. It was a time when Americans saw Russian spies on every street corner. Did something significant happen during this journey?

Asta Hagberg returned with a copy of the document. Wallander placed two one-krona coins on the table.

"I suppose I haven't been as much help as you'd hoped," said Hagberg.

"Looking for missing persons is usually a tedious and very slow process. You progress one step at a time."

She accompanied him to the gate. He was relieved to breathe in unperfumed air.

"Feel free to get in touch again," she said. "I'm always here, if I can be of any help to you."

Wallander nodded, and walked to his car. He was just about to leave Limhamn when he decided to make one more visit. He had often thought about investigating whether a mark he had made nearly fifty years ago was still there. He parked outside the churchyard, made his way to the western corner of the surrounding wall, and bent down. Had he been ten or eleven at the time? He couldn't remember, but he'd been old enough to have discovered one of life's great secrets: that he was who he was, a person with an identity all his own. That discovery had sparked a temptation inside him. He would make his mark in a place where it would never disappear. The low churchyard wall topped by iron railings was the sacred place he had chosen. He had sneaked out one fall evening, with a strong nail and a hammer hidden under his jacket. Limhamn was deserted. He had selected the spot earlier: the stones in the section of wall close to the western corner were unusually smooth. Cold rain had started to fall as he carved his initials, **KW**, into the churchyard wall.

Wallander found those initials without difficulty. The letters had faded and were not as clear now, after all those years. But he had dug deep into the stone, and his mark was still there. I'll bring Klara here sometime, he thought. I'll tell her about the day when I decided to change the world. Even if it was only by carving my initials into a stone wall.

He went into the churchyard and sat down on a bench in the shade of a tree. He closed his eyes and thought he could hear his own childhood voice echoing inside his head, sounding like it did when it was cracking and he was troubled by everything the adult world stood for. Maybe this is where I should be buried when the time comes, he thought. Return to the beginning, be laid to rest in this same soil. I've already carved my epitaph into the wall.

He left the churchyard and went back to his car. Before starting the engine he thought about his meeting with Asta Hagberg. What had it accomplished?

The answer was simple. He had not progressed a single step forward. Louise was just as big a mystery as she had been before. The wife of an officer, not present in any photographs.

But the unease he had felt ever since meeting Håkan von Enke on his island was still there.

I can't see it, he thought. Whatever it is that I should have discovered by now.

34

Wallander drove home. He could cope with the fact that his visit to Asta Hagberg had not produced results, but his sorrow following the death of Baiba weighed heavily on him. It came in waves, the memory of her sudden visit and then her equally sudden departure. But there was nothing he could do about it; in her death he also envisaged his own.

When he had parked the car, released Jussi and allowed him to run off, he poured himself a large glass of vodka and drank it in one swig, standing by the kitchen table. He filled his glass again and took it with him into the bedroom. He pulled down the blinds on the two windows, undressed, and lay down naked on top of the bed. He balanced the glass on his wobbly stomach. I can take one more step, he thought. If that doesn't lead me anywhere, I'll drop the whole thing. I'll inform Håkan that I'm going to tell Linda and Hans where he is. If that means he chooses to remain missing and find himself a new hideout, that's up to him. I'll talk to Ytterberg, Nordlander, and Atkins. Then it's no longer my business—not that it ever was. Summer is almost over, my vacation has been ruined, and I'll find myself wondering yet again where all the time has gone.

He emptied the glass and felt the warmth and the sensation of being pleasantly drunk kick in. One more step, he thought again. But what would it be? He put the glass on the bedside table and soon fell asleep. When he woke up an hour later, he knew what he was going to do. While he was asleep, his brain had formulated an answer. He could see it clearly, the only thing that was important now. Who other than Hans could provide him with information? He was an intelligent young man, if not especially sensitive. But people always know more than they think they know, observations they've made in their subconscious.

He gathered his dirty laundry and started the washing machine. Then he went out and shouted for Jussi.

There was a sound of barking from far away, in one of the neighbors' newly mown fields. Jussi eventually came bounding up. He had been rolling in something that smelled foul. Wallander shut him in his kennel, got the garden hose, and washed him off. Jussi stood there with his tail between his legs, looking pleadingly at Wallander.

"You smell like shit," Wallander told him. "I'm not having a stinky dog in my house."

Wallander went into the kitchen and sat at the table. He wrote down the most important questions he could think of, then looked up Hans's phone number at work in Copenhagen. When he was told that Hans was busy for the rest of the day with important meetings, he became impatient. He told the girl on the switchboard to inform Hans that he should call Detective Chief Inspector Wallander in Ystad within the next hour. Wallander had just opened the washing machine and realized that he'd forgotten to put in any detergent when the phone rang. He made no attempt to conceal his irritation.

"What are you doing tomorrow?"

"I'm working. Why do you sound so angry?"

"It's nothing. When do you have time to see me?"

"It'll have to be in the evening. I have meetings and appointments all day."

"Reschedule them. I'll be arriving in Copenhagen at two o'clock. I need an hour. No more, but no less."

"Did something happen?"

"Something's happening all the time. If it was important, I'd have told you already. I just want answers to a few questions. Some new ones, a few old ones."

"I'd be grateful if it could wait until the evening. The financial markets are in turmoil."

"I'll be there at two," said Wallander.

He replaced the receiver and restarted the washing machine after putting in far too much detergent, though he knew it was childish to punish the washing machine for his own forgetfulness.

He mowed the lawn, raked the gravel paths, lay down in the garden hammock, and read a book about Verdi that he'd bought for himself as a Christmas present. When he emptied the washing machine he discovered that a red handkerchief had been lying unnoticed among the white items, and the color had run, turning everything pink. He started the machine yet again. Then he sat down on the edge of the bed, pricked a fingertip and measured his blood sugar. That was another thing he kept forgetting. But the result was just about acceptable at 146.

While the washing machine was doing its job for the third time, he lay down on the sofa and listened to a newly bought recording of **Rigoletto**. He thought about Baiba; his eyes filled with tears and he imagined her restored to life. But she was gone, and would never return. When the music had finished he heated a fish stew he had taken out of the freezer and washed it down with a glass of water. He eyed a bottle of wine standing on the counter but didn't open it. The vodka he had drunk earlier was enough. He spent the evening watching **Some Like It Hot,** a favorite of his and Mona's, on television. He had seen the film many times before, but it still made him laugh.

He slept well that night, to his surprise.

Linda called the next morning as he was having breakfast. The window was wide open; it was a lovely warm day. Wallander was sitting naked on his kitchen chair.

"What did Ytterberg have to say about Håkan getting in touch?"

"I haven't spoken to him yet."

She was shocked.

"Why not? If anybody should know that Håkan isn't dead, surely it's him."

"Håkan asked me not to say anything."

"You didn't tell me that yesterday."

"I must have forgotten."

She realized immediately that his reply was both hesitant and evasive.

"Is there anything else you haven't told me?"

"No."

"Then I think you should call Ytterberg the moment we finish this conversation."

Wallander could hear the anger in her voice.

"If I ask you a straightforward, honest question, will you give me a straightforward, honest answer?" she asked.

"Yes."

"What's behind all this? If I know you, you have an opinion."

"Not in this case I don't. I'm just as bewildered as you are."

"But the suggestion that Louise was a spy is just ridiculous."

"Whether it's plausible or not is not something I can judge. The police found those items in her purse."

"Somebody must have planted them there. That's the only possible explanation. She certainly wasn't a spy," Linda asserted once more.

She paused. Perhaps she was waiting for him to agree. He heard Klara screaming in the background.

"What's she doing?"

"She's in bed. But she doesn't want to stay there. Incidentally, that's something I've been wondering: What was I like at her age? Did I cry a lot? Have I asked you that before?"

"All babies cry a lot."

"I was just wondering. I think you see yourself in your children. Anyway, you're going to call Ytterberg today, I hope?"

"Tomorrow. But you were a well-behaved child."

"Things got worse later, when I was a teenager."

"Oh yes," Wallander said. "Much worse."

When they hung up, Wallander remained seated. That was one of his worst memories, something he rarely allowed to bubble up to the surface. When she was fifteen, Linda had tried to take her own life. It probably wasn't all that serious, more of a classic cry for help, a desire to attract attention. But it could have ended very badly if Wallander hadn't forgotten his wallet and returned home. He had found her, slurring her words, with an empty jar of pills by her side. The panic he felt at that moment was something he had never experienced again. It was also the biggest failure of his life—not having realized how bad she felt as a vulnerable teenager.

He shook off the painful memory. He was convinced that if she had died, he would have taken his own life as well.

He thought back to their conversation. Her absolute certainty that Louise couldn't have been a spy made him think. It wasn't a matter of proof, but of conviction. But if she's right, Wallander thought, what is the explanation? Despite everything, was it possible that Louise and Håkan were somehow working together? Or was Håkan von Enke such a cold-blooded liar that he talked about his great love for Louise in order to ensure that nobody would think what he said wasn't true? Was he behind her death and now trying to send investigators in the wrong direction?

Wallander scribbled a sentence in his notebook: **Linda is convinced that Louise is innocent.** But deep down he didn't believe it. Louise was responsible for her own death. That had to be the case.

Shortly before two Wallander rang the bell outside the glass front door of the exclusive offices at Rundetårn in

Copenhagen. A busty young lady let him in through the whispering doors. She called for Hans, who appeared in reception without delay. He looked pale and tired. They passed by a conference room where an argument was taking place between a middle-aged man speaking English and two fair-haired young men speaking Icelandic. Their interpreter was a woman dressed entirely in black.

"Hard words," Wallander said as they passed by. "I thought finance people had pretty discreet conversations?"

"We sometimes say that we work in the slaughterhouse industry," Hans said. "It sounds worse than it is. But when you work with money, your hands get covered in blood—symbolically speaking, of course."

"Why are they arguing so vehemently?"

Hans shook his head.

"Business. I can't say what exactly, not even to you."

Wallander asked no more questions. Hans took him to a small conference room made entirely of glass—even the floor—and apparently hanging on the outside wall of the office building. Wallander had the feeling of being in an aquarium. A woman, just as young as the receptionist, came in with a tray of coffee and Danish pastries. Wallander placed his notebook and pencil by the side of his cup as Hans served the coffee. Wallander noticed that his hands were shaking.

"I thought the days of the notebook were past," said Hans when he had filled both cups. "Aren't police nowadays only issued cassette recorders, or perhaps video cameras?"

"Television series are not always a true reflection of our work. I do use a tape recorder sometimes, of course. But this isn't an interrogation; it's a conversation."

"Where do you want to start? I really do have just this one hour. It was extremely difficult to rearrange things."

"It's about your mother," Wallander said firmly. "No work can be more important than finding out what happened to her. I take it you agree with me on that?"

"That isn't what I meant."

"Okay, let's discuss what this is all about. Not what you meant or didn't mean."

Hans stared hard at Wallander.

"Let me say from the start that my mother couldn't possibly have been a spy. Even if she could act a bit secretive at times."

Wallander raised his eyebrows.

"That's something you never said before when we talked about her. That she could be secretive."

"I've been thinking since we last spoke. I do find her increasingly puzzling. Mainly because of Signe. Can you imagine a more outrageous deceit than concealing from a child that he has a sister? I sometimes regretted being an only child. Especially when I was very young, before I'd started school. But there was never anything evasive in her answers. Now it seems to me that she answered my childish longing with ice-cold indifference."

"And your father?"

"He was never at home in those days. At least, I remember him as being mostly absent. Every time he came through the door, I knew he would soon be leaving again. He always brought me presents. But I didn't dare enjoy being with him. When his uniform was taken out to be aired and brushed, I knew what was going to happen. The following morning he would leave."

"Can you tell me more about what you regard as secretive behavior on your mother's part?"

"It's hard to pinpoint. Sometimes she seemed preoccupied, sunk so deep in her own thoughts that she grew angry if I happened to disturb her. It was almost as if I'd caused her pain, as if I'd stuck a pin in her. I don't know if that makes sense to you, but that's how I remember it. Sometimes she would close her notebooks, or quickly slide something over the paper she was working on when I came into the room."

"Was there anything your mother did only when your father wasn't at home? Any routines that suddenly changed?"

"No. I don't think so."

"You're answering too quickly. Think about it."

Hans stood up and gazed out the windows. Through the floor Wallander could see a street musician down below strumming away at a guitar with a hat in front of him on the sidewalk. No sound of music penetrated the glass. Hans returned to his chair.

"What I'm about to say now is nothing I could swear to," he said. "It could be my imagination, my memory playing tricks. But now that I think about it, when Håkan was away she often talked on the phone, always with the door closed. She didn't do that when he was at home."

"Didn't talk on the phone or didn't close the door?"

"Neither."

"Go on."

"There were often papers lying around that she worked on. I have the feeling that when Håkan came home the papers were no longer there—there were flowers on the tables instead."

"What kind of papers?"

"I don't know. But sometimes there were drawings as well."

Wallander gave a start.

"Drawings of what?"

"Divers. My mother was very good at drawing."

"Divers?"

"Various dives, different phases of individual dives. 'German leap with full twist' or whatever they say, that sort of thing."

"Can you remember any other kind of drawings?"

"She sometimes drew me. I don't know where those drawings are, but they were good."

Wallander broke a Danish pastry in two and dunked one half in his coffee. He looked at his watch. The musician under his feet was still playing his silent music.

"I'm not quite finished yet," said Wallander. "Let's talk about your mother's views. Political, social, economic. What did she think about Sweden?"

"Politics were not a topic of conversation in my home."

"Never?"

"One of them might say, 'The Swedish armed forces are no longer capable of defending our country' or

something of the sort. The other might reply to the effect that it was the fault of the Communists. And that
would be it. Either of them could have said either of
those things. They were conservative, of course—we've
spoken about that already. There was no question of
voting for any party other than the Moderates. Taxes
were too high. Sweden was allowing in too many immigrants who went on to cause chaos in the streets. I
think you could say they thought exactly as you would
expect them to."

"There was never any exception to that, then?"

"Never, not that I can recall."

Wallander nodded and ate the other half of the
Danish.

"Let's talk about your parents' relationship with
each other," he said when he'd finished chewing.
"What was that like?"

"It was good."

"Did they ever argue?"

"No. I think they really loved each other. That's
something I thought about afterward—that as a child
I never had the slightest fear that they would divorce.
That thought never even occurred to me."

"But surely no couple ever lives together without the
occasional conflict?"

"They did. Unless they argued when I was asleep
and I didn't hear them. But I find that hard to believe."

Wallander had no more questions. But he wasn't
ready to give up.

"Is there anything else you could say about your
mother? She was kind and she was secretive, perhaps

mysterious, we know that now. But to be perfectly honest, you seem to know surprisingly little about her."

"I've come to see that," said Hans, with something that Wallander interpreted as painful honesty. "There were hardly ever any moments of real intimacy between us. She always kept me at a certain distance. She comforted me if I hurt myself, of course. But with hindsight I can see now that she found that almost troublesome."

"Was there any other man in her life?"

That was not a question Wallander had prepared in advance. But now that he'd asked it, it seemed an obvious one.

"Never. I don't think there was any disloyalty between my parents. On either side."

"What about before they got married? What do you know about that time?"

"I have the feeling that because they met so early in their lives, neither of them ever had anybody else. Not anyone serious. But of course, I can't be certain."

Wallander put his notebook in his jacket pocket. He hadn't written down a single word. There was nothing to write. He knew as little now as he had before he'd arrived.

He stood up. But Hans remained seated.

"My father," he said. "I gather he's called you. So he's alive, but he doesn't want to put in an appearance, is that it?"

Wallander sat down again. The guitar player under his feet had moved on.

"There's no doubt that he was the one who called.

He said he was well. He gave no explanation of his behavior. He just wanted you to know that he was alive."

"He really said nothing about where he was?"

"Nothing."

"What impression did you get? Was he far away? Did he call from a landline or a cell phone?"

"I can't say."

"Because you don't want to, or because you can't?"

"Because I can't."

Wallander stood up again. They left the room made of glass. When they passed by the conference room, the door was closed but the people inside were still arguing loudly. They said their good-byes in reception.

"Did I help at all?" Hans asked.

"You were honest," Wallander said. "That's the only thing I can ask for."

"A diplomatic answer. So I wasn't able to give you what you were hoping for."

Wallander made a resigned gesture. The glass door opened, and he waved as he left. The elevator took him silently down to the lobby. He had parked his car in a side street off Kongens Nytorv. Since it was very hot, he took off his jacket and unbuttoned his shirt.

Suddenly he had the feeling he was being watched. He turned around. The street was full of people, but he didn't recognize any of the faces. After a hundred yards he stopped in front of a shopwindow and contemplated some expensive ladies' shoes. He sneaked a look back along the section of street he'd just come from. A man was standing, looking at his wristwatch. Then he moved his overcoat from his right arm to his left. Wallander thought he remembered him from the first time he'd looked around. He turned back to the ladies' shoes. The man passed behind his back. Wallander recalled something Rydberg had said. **You don't always need to be behind the person you're shadowing. You can just as well be in front of him.** Wallander set off and counted a hundred steps. Then he stopped again and turned around. Now there was nobody who attracted his attention. The man with the overcoat had vanished. When Wallander reached his car he looked around one last time. The people he could see, coming and going, were totally new to him. He shook his head. He must have been imagining things.

He drove back over the long bridge, paused at the Father's Hat roadside café, then headed for home.

When he got out of the car, his mind suddenly went blank. He stood there with the keys in his hand, totally confused. The hood was warm. Once again he was panic-stricken. **Where had he been?** Jussi was barking and jumping up and down in his kennel. Wallander stared at the dog and tried hard to remember. He looked at the car keys, then at the car, hoping they would give him a clue. Almost ten horrifying minutes passed before the blockage crumbled and he remembered what he had been doing. He was drenched in sweat. It's getting worse, he thought. I have to find out what's happening to me.

He collected the mail and sat down at the garden table. He was still shaken by the attack of forgetfulness.

It was only later, after he had fed Jussi, that he discovered the letter lying among the newspapers he had collected from the mailbox. There was no return address, and he didn't recognize the handwriting.

When he opened the letter he saw that it was handwritten, and from Håkan von Enke.

35

The letter had been mailed in Norrköping:

There is a man in Berlin by the name of George Talboth. He's an American, and used to work at their embassy in Stockholm. He speaks fluent Swedish and is regarded as an expert on the relationship between Scandinavia and the Soviet Union and, nowadays, Russia. I got to know him as early as the end of the 1960s when he first came to Stockholm and on several occasions accompanied the then military attaché at various receptions and on various visits, including one to Berga. George and I got along well—both he and his wife played bridge—and we started meeting socially. I eventually realized that he was attached to the CIA, but he never tried to elicit secret information from me that I wasn't authorized to pass on. In about 1974, a year or two later, his wife, Marilyn, was diagnosed with cancer, and died shortly afterward. That was a catastrophe for George. He and his wife had enjoyed an even closer relationship than Louise and I, if that was possible. He started visiting us more frequently, nearly every Sunday, and often during the week as well. In 1979 he was transferred to the legation in Bonn, and he stayed in Germany after he retired, although he moved to Berlin. It's possible of course that in his "spare time" he still serves his country, as you might say. But I know nothing about that.

I spoke to him on the phone as recently as last December. Although he is now seventy-two, he is still lively intellectually. I'm sure he thinks the Cold War is very much alive. When the Russian empire collapsed, a revolution took place that was every bit as shattering as the events of 1917. But according to George it was only a temporary setback. He thinks the current situation confirms that view: Russia is growing stronger and stronger and making ever greater demands on the world around it. I have taken the liberty of writing to him and asking him to contact you. If there is anybody who might be able to help you in your efforts to find out what happened to Louise, he's your man. I hope you are not put out by my attempts to make a

positive contribution to what I'm sure are your
honest efforts to solve this riddle.
    With respectful greetings,
    Håkan von Enke

Wallander put the letter down on the kitchen table. It
was good, of course, that von Enke had put Wallander
in touch with a potentially useful contact. But even so,
he didn't like the letter. Once again he had the impression that there was something going on he hadn't detected. He read the letter one more time, slowly, as if
he were picking his way gingerly through a minefield.
Letters need to be deciphered, Rydberg once said. You
have to know what you're doing, especially if the letter
might be of significance for a crime investigation. But
what was there to decipher? The contents were plain
enough.

He measured his blood sugar and this time was less
pleased with the result: 184. That was too high. He had
forgotten to take his Metformin pills and his insulin.
He checked in the refrigerator and saw that within the
next few days he would need to replenish his insulin.
    Every day he took no fewer than seven different pills,
for his diabetes, his blood pressure, and his cholesterol.
He didn't like doing so; it felt like a sort of defeat. Many
of his colleagues didn't take a single pill—or at least, they
said they didn't. In the old days, Rydberg had been
scornful of all chemical preparations. He didn't even take

anything for the headaches that plagued him. Every day my body is filled with goodness knows how many chemicals that I don't really know anything about, Wallander thought. I trust my doctors and the pharmaceutical companies, without questioning the things they prescribe.

He hadn't even told Linda about all the pills. Nor did she know that he was now injecting himself with insulin. To be on the safe side, he had hidden it behind some jars of mango chutney that he knew she wouldn't touch.

He read the letter a few more times without discovering anything between the lines. Håkan von Enke was not sending him any hidden messages. He was looking in vain for something that wasn't there.

That night he dreamed about his father.

He had just woken up, shortly after seven, when the phone rang. He assumed it was Linda at this hour, especially since she knew he was on vacation. He picked up the receiver.

"Is that Knut Wallander?"

It was a man's voice. His Swedish was perfect, although Wallander could hear a slight foreign accent.

"I take it I'm talking to Mr. Talboth," he said. "I've been expecting to hear from you."

"Call me George. I'll call you Knut."

"Not Knut. Kurt."

"Kurt. Kurt Wallander. I'm always getting names wrong. When are you coming to visit?"

Wallander was surprised by the question. What had Håkan von Enke written to Talboth?

"I wasn't planning on going to Berlin. I didn't even know you existed until I received a letter yesterday."

"Håkan wrote in a letter to me that you would definitely want to come here and talk to me."

"Why can't you come to Skåne?"

"I don't have a driver's license. And I hate traveling by train or flying."

An American without a driver's license, Wallander thought. He must be an extremely unusual person.

"Maybe I can help you," Talboth said. "I used to know Louise. Just as well as I knew Håkan. And she was a good friend of my wife, Marilyn. They often used to go out together for tea. Afterward, Marilyn would tell me what they had been talking about."

"And what was that?"

"Louise nearly always talked politics. Marilyn wasn't as interested, but she listened politely."

Wallander frowned. Wasn't that the opposite of what Hans had said? That his mother never talked about politics, apart from a few brief comments in conversations with her husband?

He was suddenly attracted by the thought of visiting George Talboth in Berlin. He hadn't been there since the collapse of East Germany. He had been to East Berlin twice in the mid-1980s with Linda, when she had been obsessed by the theater and had insisted on seeing performances by the Berliner Ensemble. He could still recall his annoyance when the East German border police burst into their sleeping car in the middle of the night and demanded to see his passport. On both occasions they had stayed in a hotel at Alexanderplatz. Wallander had felt uneasy the whole time.

"I might be able to come see you," he said. "I could take my car."

"You can stay at my place," said Talboth. "I have an apartment in Schöneberg. When should I expect you?"

"When would it suit you?"

"I'm a widower. You're welcome whenever is good for you."

"The day after tomorrow?"

"I'll give you my phone number. Call me when you're approaching Berlin, and I'll guide you through the city. Do you eat fish or meat?"

"Both."

"Wine?"

"Red."

"That's all I need to know. Do you have a pencil handy?"

Wallander wrote down the number in the margin of von Enke's letter.

"I look forward to meeting you," said Talboth. "If I understand correctly, your daughter is married to young Hans von Enke?"

"Not quite. They have a daughter, Klara. But they're not married yet."

"Please bring a photo of your granddaughter."

Wallander ended the call. He had pictures of Klara pinned up all over the house. He took down two photos from the kitchen wall and put them on the table next to his passport. He ate his breakfast while studying a road atlas to establish how far it was to Berlin from the ferry terminal at Sassnitz. A phone call to the ferry company in Trelleborg provided him with the timetable. He noted down the times and found himself looking forward to the impending journey. I will remember this summer for all the car trips I've taken, he thought. It reminds me of when Linda was a little girl and we used to go to Denmark on vacation, sometimes to Gotland, and once even as far as Hammarfest in the north of Norway.

On July 23 he drove along the coast road to Trelleborg to catch a ferry to the Continent. He had told Linda that he planned to spend a few days in Berlin. She hadn't asked any suspicious questions, merely said that she envied him. He saw on the television that high temperatures in Berlin and central Europe were breaking records.

He decided not to try to do the driving nonstop. He would leave the highway at some point and stay overnight in a little hotel. He wasn't in a hurry.

He had a meal on board the ferry, sharing a table with a talkative truck driver who told Wallander he was on the way to Dresden with several tons of dog food.

"Why would German dogs want to eat food from Sweden?" Wallander wondered.

"A good question. But isn't that what they call the free market?"

Wallander went out on deck. He could understand why a lot of people chose to work on board a ship. Like Håkan von Enke, even if he had spent long periods of his life underwater. Why would anyone want to become a submarine captain? he asked himself. But then again, there are doubtless lots of people who wonder why anyone would want to become a police officer. My own father did.

Shortly after driving out of Sassnitz he pulled into a rest stop, changed his shirt, and put on shorts and sandals. Just for a moment he enjoyed the thought of being able to go wherever he wanted, spend the night wherever he wanted, eat wherever he wanted. That's what freedom looks like, he thought, and smiled at how pathetic the observation was. An elderly policeman on the run, having escaped from himself.

He drove as far as Oranienburg, on the outskirts of Berlin, before deciding to stop for the night. He spent some time looking for a suitable hotel and eventually chose the Kronhof.

He was given a corner room on the third floor. It was big, with too much heavy, dreary-looking furniture. But Wallander was satisfied. He was on the top floor, so nobody would be walking around over his head during the night. He put on a pair of pants, then strolled around town for a couple of hours, had a coffee, browsed in an antiques shop, and went back to the Kronhof. It was five o'clock. He was hungry, but he decided to eat later. He lay down on the bed with a crossword puzzle. After solving a few clues he fell asleep. It was seven-thirty when he woke up. He went down to the restaurant and took a seat at a corner table. It was still early, and there weren't many diners. He was given a menu by a waitress who reminded him of Fanny Klarström. He chose Wiener schnitzel and ordered a glass of wine. The restaurant began to fill up; most of the guests seemed to know one another. He had chocolate pudding for dessert, despite knowing that he shouldn't eat anything that sweet. He drank another glass of wine and noticed that he was beginning to feel tipsy. But Martinsson wouldn't be coming here to tell him off.

He asked for the bill at nine o'clock, went up to his room, undressed, and got in bed. But he couldn't sleep. He suddenly felt restless, harassed. The good feeling he'd enjoyed during his solitary meal had gone. In the end he gave up, dressed again, and went back down to the restaurant, which had a separate bar. He went there and ordered a glass of wine. A group of elderly men were standing, drinking beer. All the tables were empty, apart from one almost next to him. A woman in her forties was sitting there, drinking a glass of white wine and keying a text into her cell phone. She smiled at Wallander. He smiled back. They raised their glasses and drank to each other. She continued texting. Wallander ordered another glass of wine, and offered one to the woman. She thanked him with a smile, put her phone away, and moved over to his table. He explained in bad English that he was a Swede, on his way to Berlin. He was uncertain about how to pronounce **Kurt** in English, so he told her his name was James.

"Is that a Swedish name?" she asked.

"My mother came from Ireland," he told her.

He smiled at his lie, and asked her name. Isabel, she told him. She explained that within the next few years Oranienburg would be swallowed up by Berlin. Wallander was studying her face, which was excessively made up. She gave the impression of being ravaged, worn out. He wondered if she was a woman on the prowl, using this bar as her hunting grounds. But she wasn't provocatively dressed, he thought. Besides, I'm not looking for a prostitute.

Who was this Isabel he was now sitting with? She said she was a florist, single, with grown-up children who had flown the nest. She lived in an apartment—**sehr schön,** she insisted it was—in a building overlooking a park that she tried to describe the way to. But Wallander wasn't interested in a park or ways to get there; he had become entranced by her, could already picture her naked in his hotel room, and that was where he intended to lure her. He could see that she was drunk, and he felt he shouldn't have anything more to drink either. It was almost midnight, and the barman announced last call. Wallander asked for the bill, and offered her a glass of wine in his room—that was the first time he'd mentioned that he was staying at the hotel. She didn't seem surprised; perhaps she knew already. Could there be some kind of communications link between reception and the bar? But he didn't worry about that. He paid the bill, adding far too big a tip, and ushered her past the unattended reception desk and up to his room. It was only after he had closed the door that he admitted the sad truth: he had no drinks to offer her. There was no minibar—the hotel didn't have luxuries like that—nor was there any room service. But she knew what was expected of her and suddenly embraced him. He was overcome by a desire that he couldn't control, and they ended up in his bed. He couldn't remember the last time he had slept with a woman, and he tried to imagine that Isabel's body belonged to Baiba or Mona, or to other women he had forgotten about long ago. It all happened very quickly, and she was already asleep when Wallander felt desire welling up inside him once more. It was impossible to wake her. Making love to a woman fast asleep was something he couldn't bring himself to contemplate. He had no option but to go to sleep himself, which he duly did, with one hand between her sweaty thighs.

It was still there when he woke up at dawn. He had a headache, his tongue seemed to be glued to his palate, and he made up his mind on the spot to escape as quickly as possible from the room, and from Isabel, who was still fast asleep by his side. He dressed as quietly as he could; he realized that he wasn't fit to drive, but he couldn't entertain the possibility of staying put. He took his suitcase and went down to reception, where a young man was lying fast asleep on a bunk underneath the old-fashioned key rack. He woke up when Wallander shouted for service, presented the bill, and handed over the change. Wallander put the keys on the counter alongside a ten-euro note.

"There's a woman asleep in my room. I assume that this will cover her as well?"

"**Alles klar,**" said the young man, and yawned.

Wallander hurried to his car and set off for Berlin. But he drove only as far as the first rest stop. He pulled in and moved to the backseat to sleep. He regretted the previous night very much. He tried to convince himself that it was no big deal. After all, she hadn't asked him for money. She couldn't have found him totally repulsive.

He woke up at nine o'clock and continued his journey to Berlin. He stopped at a motel just off the highway and called George Talboth, who had a road atlas handy and soon worked out where Wallander was.

"I'll be there in an hour or so," he said. "Sit out and enjoy the lovely weather."

"How will you get here? I thought you said you didn't have a driver's license."

"We'll get around that."

Wallander bought a coffee served in a cardboard cup and sat down in the shade outside the motel's restaurant. He wondered if Isabel had woken up yet and asked herself where Wallander had disappeared to. He could recall next to nothing of their awkward and uninspired lovemaking. Had it really happened? He could only remember vague fragments, which just embarrassed him.

He topped up his cup of coffee, and bought a pre-made sandwich. It feels like chewing a sponge, he thought. After having forced half of it down, he threw the rest to some pigeons pecking at the ground not far from where he was sitting.

Time passed, but still nobody appeared looking for a Swedish detective. After another fifteen minutes, a black Mercedes pulled up to the motel. It had diplomatic plates. George Talboth had arrived. A man in a white suit wearing sunglasses stepped out of the car, looked around and homed in on Wallander. He came over and removed his sunglasses.

"Kurt Wallander?"

"That's me."

George Talboth was over six feet tall, powerfully built, and his handshake would have throttled Wallander if it had been applied to his neck.

"Sorry I'm late. The traffic was worse than expected."

"I did as you suggested and made the most of the good weather. I haven't even looked at my watch."

Talboth raised his hand and signaled to the Mercedes with the invisible chauffeur. It drove off.

"Shall we go?"

They sat in Wallander's Peugeot. Talboth turned out to be a living GPS and guided Wallander confidently through the increasingly busy traffic. After not much more than an hour they came to an attractive apartment building in the Schöneberg district. It occurred to Wallander that this must be one of the few buildings that had survived World War II, when Hitler shot himself in his bunker and the Red Army fought its way through the city, street by street. Talboth lived on the top floor, in an apartment with six rooms. The bedroom he gave to Wallander was large, with a view over a little park.

"I'll have to leave you to your own devices for an hour or two," Talboth said. "I have a few things to deal with."

"I'll manage."

"When I get back we'll have all the time in the world. There's an Italian restaurant just down the road that serves excellent food, where we can have a leisurely conversation. How long are you planning to stay?"

"Not all that long. I thought I'd go home tomorrow, in fact."

Talboth shook his head vigorously.

"Out of the question. You can't possibly do justice to Berlin in such a short time. It would be an insult to this city, which has been at the center of so much of the world's tragic history."

"We can discuss that later," said Wallander. "But as I'm sure you understand, old men also have jobs to do."

Talboth accepted that response, showed Wallander the bathroom, kitchen, and extensive balcony, then left. Wallander watched through a window as Talboth once again clambered into the black Mercedes. He took a bottle of beer from the refrigerator and swigged it back while standing on the balcony. As far as he was concerned, that was a way of saying good-bye to the woman from the previous evening. She no longer existed, except perhaps as a persistent memory in his dreams. That was the way it usually was. He never dreamed about the women he had really been in love with. But the ones with whom he had engaged in more or less unpleasant experiences frequently turned up.

He thought about remembering what he would prefer to forget, and forgetting what he should remember. There was something fundamentally wrong with his way of life. He didn't know if it was the same for everyone. What did Linda dream about? What did Martinsson dream about? What did his interfering boss, Lennart Mattson, dream about?

He drank another beer, started to feel tipsy, and ran a bath. After a good soak, he felt much better.

George Talboth came back a couple of hours later. They sat out on the balcony and started talking.

That was when Wallander noticed a little stone on the balcony table. A stone he was certain he recognized.

36

There was a question nagging at Wallander during the time he spent with George Talboth. Did he realize that Wallander had noticed the stone? Or didn't he? Wallander still wasn't sure when he left for home the following day. But he had no doubt that Talboth was a sharp-eyed man. Things happen at top speed behind those eyes of his, Wallander thought. He has a brain that doesn't leak, or decline. He may seem uninterested or even apathetic at times, but he is always wide awake.

The only thing Wallander could be sure about was the fact that the stone that had disappeared from Håkan von Enke's desk was now on a table on the balcony of George Talboth's apartment. Either that, or an exact copy of it.

The idea of a copy also applied to the man himself. Even at the motel, Wallander had been struck by the feeling that Talboth was very much like somebody else, that he had a doppelgänger. Not necessarily somebody Wallander knew personally, rather somebody he had seen before, but he couldn't remember who.

It wasn't until the evening that the penny dropped. Talboth looked exactly like the film actor Humphrey Bogart. He was taller, and didn't have the cigarette constantly glued to his lips; but it wasn't only his appearance, there was something about his voice that Wallander seemed to recognize from films like **The Treasure of the Sierra Madre** and **The African Queen**. He wondered if Talboth was aware of the similarity, and assumed that he was.

Before they sat down that afternoon Talboth also demonstrated that he had surprises up his sleeve. He opened one of the doors in his apartment that had been kept closed and revealed an enormous aquarium with a whole shoal of red and blue fish swimming silently behind the thick glass. The room was filled with glass tanks and plastic piping, but what astounded Wallander most was that the bottom of the aquarium was criss-crossed by cleverly constructed tunnels through which miniature electric trains were racing around and around. The tunnels were completely transparent, apparently made of glass, and not a drop of water seeped through into them. The fish seemed to be unaware of this railway line at the bottom of their artificially made seabed.

"The tunnels are almost an exact copy of the one between Dover and Calais," said Talboth. "I used the original plans and certain constructional details when I made this model."

Wallander thought of Håkan von Enke sitting in the remote hunting lodge with his ship in a bottle. There's some kind of affinity between them, in addition to their friendship, he thought. But what that implies, I can't say.

"I enjoy working with my hands," Talboth went on. "Using only your brain isn't good for you. Do you find that too?"

"Hardly. My father was pretty handy, but I inherited none of that."

"What did your father do?"

"He produced paintings."

"You mean he was an artist? Why did you use the word 'produced'?"

"My father really only painted one motif throughout his life," Wallander said. "It's not much to talk about."

Talboth noted Wallander's unwillingness to elaborate, and he asked no more questions. They watched the fish swimming slowly to and fro, and the trains rushing through their tunnels. Wallander noticed that they didn't pass at exactly the same point every time; there was a delay that was hardly noticeable at first. He also noted that at one part of the circuit they used the same stretch of line. He hesitated but eventually asked about what he had observed. Talboth nodded.

"You're right," he said. "I've built a short delay into the system."

He reached up to a shelf and took down an hourglass that Wallander hadn't registered when he entered the room.

"This contains sand from West Africa," said Talboth. "To be more precise, from the beaches of the islands in the little archipelago called Buback. It's just off the coast of Guinea-Bissau, a country most people have never heard of. It was an old English admiral who decided that this was the perfect sand for the English navy in the days when hourglasses were used for telling the time. If I'd turned the glass at the same moment as I switched on the trains, you'd have discovered that one of the trains catches up with the other one after exactly fifty-nine minutes. I make that happen now and then, to check that the sand in the hourglass isn't running more slowly, or that the transformer doesn't need adjusting."

As a child Wallander had always dreamed of owning a model train set, but his father was never able to afford it. Trains like the ones in front of him now still seemed an unattainable luxury.

They sat down on the balcony. It was a hot summer's day. Talboth had brought out a jug of ice water and two glasses. Wallander decided that there was no reason to beat around the bush. His first question formulated itself.

"What did you think when you heard that Louise had disappeared?"

Talboth's bright eyes were firmly fixed on Wallander.

"I suppose I wasn't all that surprised," he said.

"Why not?"

"I don't need to tell you what you already know. Håkan's increasingly intolerable suspicions—I suppose we can call it a certainty now—that he was married to a traitor. Is that what you say? My Swedish isn't always perfect."

"That's correct," said Wallander. "If you're a spy, you are usually a traitor. Unless you deal in more specific things, such as industrial espionage."

"Håkan ran away because he couldn't put up with it anymore," Talboth said. "He needed time to think. Before Louise disappeared he had more or less made a decision. He was going to hand over the proof he had to the military intelligence services. Everything would be done according to the rule book. He didn't intend to spare himself or his own reputation. He realized that Hans would also be affected, but that couldn't be helped. It boiled down to a question of honor. When she disappeared, he was dumbfounded. He became increasingly scared. I began to worry after some of the phone conversations I had with him. He almost seemed to be suffering from paranoia. The only explanation he could think of for Louise's disappearance was that she had managed to read his thoughts. He was afraid she would find out where he was. If not her, one of her employers in the Russian intelligence service. Håkan was convinced that Louise had been and still was so important that they wouldn't hesitate to kill her in order to prevent any revelations. Even if she was too old now to be an active spy, it was important that she not be unmasked. Naturally, the Russians didn't want to reveal what they knew. Or didn't know."

"What did you think when you heard that she had committed suicide?"

"I never believed that. I thought it was obvious she had been murdered."

"Why?"

"Let me answer by asking a question. Why would she commit suicide?"

"Perhaps she was overwhelmed by guilt. Perhaps she realized the torture she had inflicted on her husband. There are lots of possible reasons. In my police work I've come across a lot of people who committed suicide for much less serious reasons."

Talboth considered what Wallander had said.

"You may be right. But I haven't told you my overall impression of Louise. I knew her well. Even though she concealed large parts of her identity, I got to know her intimately. She wasn't the kind of person who commits suicide."

"Why do you think that?"

"Certain people simply don't commit suicide. It's as straightforward as that."

Wallander shook his head.

"That's not my experience," he said. "My feeling is that, under unfortunate circumstances, anybody at all can take their own life."

"I'm not going to start arguing with you. You can interpret my view however you like. I'm convinced that your experience as a police officer is important. But you shouldn't just shrug off the experience I have from working for many years in the American security services."

"We know now that she was in fact murdered. And we also know that there was incriminating evidence in her purse."

Talboth had raised his glass of water. He frowned and put it down again without having drunk. Wallander thought he detected a different kind of alertness in him.

"I didn't know that. I had no idea they'd confiscated secret material."

"You're not supposed to know. I shouldn't have told you. But I did so for Håkan's sake. I trust it will go no further."

"I won't say anything to anybody. You learn how to do that when you work in the intelligence service. The day you resign, nothing is left in your head. You clear out your memory just as other employees clear out their lockers or desks."

"What would you say if I were to tell you that Louise was probably poisoned using methods patented by the East Germans in the good old days? In order to conceal executions and make them look like suicides?"

Talboth nodded slowly. Once again he raised his glass of ice water to his mouth; this time he drank some.

"That also happens in the CIA," he said. "Needless to say, we have often found ourselves in a position that made it necessary to liquidate somebody. In such a way that convinced everybody it was suicide."

Wallander wasn't surprised by Talboth's unwillingness to talk about things not directly connected to Håkan or Louise von Enke; but he'd made up his mind to take this as far as possible.

"Anyway, we can assume that Louise was murdered," Wallander said.

"Could it be the Swedish secret service that liquidated her?"

"That's not the way things work in Sweden. Besides, there's no reason to assume she'd been unmasked. In other words, we don't have a potential perpetrator with a plausible motive."

Talboth moved his wicker chair into the shade. He said nothing for a while, chewing his bottom lip.

"It's tempting to think that it's a sort of crime of passion," he said eventually.

He sat upright on his chair.

"Working in Sweden was naturally never the same as being behind the iron curtain, for as long as it existed," he said. "Anybody who was caught there was almost always executed. Assuming you weren't so important that you could be used in exchange deals. One traitor swapped for another. Spies can get careless when they've been out in the field, always in danger of being exposed. The pressure can become too much. That's why spies sometimes turn against one another. The violence turns in on itself. Somebody's success can give rise to jealousy, and the competitive urge replaces cooperation and loyalty. That is a distinct possibility in Louise's case. For a very special reason."

Now it was Wallander's turn to move his chair into the shade. He leaned forward to pick up his glass of water. The ice had melted.

"As Håkan has already told you, rumors about a Swedish spy had been circulating for a while," said Talboth. "The CIA had known about it for ages. When I worked at the Stockholm embassy, we put a lot of resources into trying to solve this problem. The fact that somebody was selling Swedish military secrets to the Russians was a problem for us and for NATO. Sweden's arms industry was at the cutting edge when it came to technical innovations. We used to have regular meetings with our Swedish colleagues about this worrying situation. And with colleagues from England, France, and Norway, among others. We were faced with an incredibly skillful agent. We also realized that there must be an intermediary, an 'informer,' in Sweden. Somebody passing on information to the agent, who in turn sent it on to Russia. We were surprised that we—or rather, our Swedish colleagues—could never find any clues as to who it was. The Swedes had a short list of twenty names, all of them officers in one service or another. But the Swedish investigators got nowhere. And we didn't manage to help them either. It was as if we were hunting a phantom. Some genius hit on the idea of calling the person we were looking for 'Diana.' Like the Phantom's girlfriend. I thought it was idiotic. Mainly because there was nothing to suggest that a woman was involved. But it would eventually transpire that the nitwit responsible had unknowingly but devastatingly stumbled onto something very relevant. In any case, that was the situation until late March 1987. The eighteenth, to be precise. Something happened on that day that changed the whole situation, sent several Swedish intelligence officers out into the cold, and forced us all to start thinking differently. Has Håkan told you about this?"

"No."

"It began outside Amsterdam at Schipol, the big airport, early in the morning. A man appeared outside the airport police's office. He was wearing a baggy suit, a white shirt, and a tie. He was carrying a small suitcase in one hand and had an overcoat over his arm and a hat in his other hand. He must have given the impression of coming from another age, as if he had climbed out of a black-and-white film with somber background music. He spoke to a police officer who was really far too young for the job, but there was a flu epidemic and he was filling in. The man spoke bad English and announced that he was seeking political asylum in the Netherlands. He produced a Russian passport in the name of Oleg Linde. An unusual surname for a Russian, you might think, but it was correct. He was in his forties, with thinning hair and a scar along one side of his nose. The young police officer, who had never set eyes on a defector from the East before, called in an older colleague who took over. I think his name was Geert, but before he had a chance to ask his first question, Linde began talking. I've listened to the interrogation so many times that I know the most important parts almost by heart. He was a colonel in the KGB, the division dealing with espionage in the West, and was seeking political asylum because he no longer wanted to do work that was propping up the crumbling Soviet empire. Those were his first words. Then he came out with the bait he had prepared in advance. He knew about many of the Soviet spies working in the West, especially a number of very competent agents based in the Netherlands. After that he was handed over to the security services. They took him to an apartment in The Hague, ironically enough not far from the International Court of Justice, where he was interrogated. It didn't take long for Säpo to realize that Oleg Linde was completely genuine. They kept his identity secret, but they immediately began informing colleagues all over the world that they had come across a marvelous 'antique,' which was now standing on a table in front of them. Would they like to come and take a look? To examine it? Reports came in from Moscow to the effect that the KGB was in an uproar; everybody was scuttling around like ants in an anthill poked with a walking stick. Oleg Linde was one of those people who simply couldn't be allowed to go missing. But missing he was. He'd disappeared without a trace, and they feared the worst. Moscow figured out that he must be in the Netherlands when their spy network there collapsed. He had begun his big 'clearance sale,' as we called it. And he was cheap. All he wanted was a new name and a new identity. According to what I've heard, he moved to Mauritius and settled in a town with the wonderful name of Pamplemousse, where he earned a living as a cabinetmaker. Evidently Linde had a background as a joiner before he joined the KGB, but I'm not sure about that part of the story."

"What's he doing now?"

"He's sleeping the eternal sleep. He died in 2006. Cancer. He met a young lady in Mauritius and married her, and they had several children. But I don't know anything about their lives. His story is reminiscent of that of another defector, an agent known as 'Boris.'"

"I've heard of him," said Wallander. "There must have been a constant procession of Russian defectors at that time."

Talboth stood up and went indoors. Down in the street below, several fire engines raced past, sirens wailing. Talboth came back with the jug full to the brim with ice water.

"He was the one who informed us that the spy we'd been looking for in Sweden was a woman," he said when he had sat down again. "He didn't know her name; she was overseen by a group within the KGB that worked independently of the other officers—that was normal practice with especially valuable agents. But he was certain that it was a woman. She didn't work in the military or in the arms industry, which meant that she had at least one, possibly several, informers who provided her with information that she sold. It was never clear whether she was a spy for ideological reasons or if she did it purely as a business venture. The intelligence services always prefer spies who operate as a business. If there is too much idealism involved, the operation can easily go off the rails. We always think that agents with great faith in the cause are never entirely reliable. We are a cynical bunch, and we have to be in order to do our job properly. We repeat the mantra that we might not make the world any better, but at least we don't make it any worse. We justify our existence by claiming that we maintain a sort of balance of terror, which we probably do."

Talboth stirred the ice cubes in the jug with a spoon.

"Future wars," he said thoughtfully, "will be over staples such as water. Our soldiers will fight to the death over pools of water."

He filled his glass, being careful not to spill any water. Wallander waited.

"We never found her," Talboth continued. "We helped the Swedes as much as we could, but she was never identified, never exposed and arrested. We started talking about the possibility that she didn't exist. But the Russians were constantly finding out about things they shouldn't have. If Bofors made some technical advance in a weapons system, the Russians soon knew all about it. We set endless traps, but we never caught anybody."

"And Louise?"

"She was above suspicion, of course. Who would have suspected her of anything?"

· · ·

Talboth excused himself, saying he had to attend to his aquarium. Wallander remained on the balcony. He started writing a summary of what Talboth had said, but then decided he didn't need notes; he would remember. He went to the room he'd been given and lay down on the bed with his arms under his head. When he woke up, he saw that he'd been asleep for two hours. He jumped up, as if he had slept far longer. Talboth was on the balcony, smoking a cigarette. Wallander returned to his chair.

"I think you've been dreaming," Talboth said. "You kept shouting in your sleep."

"My dreams are pretty violent at times," said Wallander. "It comes and goes."

"I'm lucky," said Talboth. "I never remember my dreams. I'm very grateful for that."

They walked to the Italian restaurant Talboth had mentioned earlier. They drank red wine with their food, and spoke about everything under the sun—except for Louise von Enke. After the meal Talboth insisted they try various kinds of grappa, before insisting just as strongly on paying for everything. Wallander felt distinctly tipsy when they left Il Trovatore. Talboth lit a cigarette, being careful to turn his head away when he blew out the smoke.

"So," said Wallander, "many years have passed since Oleg Linde talked about a female Swedish spy. It seems implausible to me that she should still be operating."

"If she is," said Talboth. "Don't forget what we talked about on the balcony."

"But if the spying was in fact still going on, that would exonerate Louise," said Wallander.

"Not necessarily. Somebody else could have picked up the baton. There are no simple explanations in this world. The truth is often the opposite of what you expect."

They continued walking slowly down the street. Talboth lit another cigarette.

"The middleman," Wallander said, "the person you called the **intermediary**. Do you have just as little information about him?"

"He has never been exposed."

"Which means, of course, that 'he' could just as well be a woman too."

Talboth shook his head.

"Women seldom have such influential positions in the military or the arms industry. I'd bet my paltry pension it's a man."

It was a very warm evening, oppressively so. Wallander could feel a headache coming on.

"Is there anything in what I've told you that you find particularly surprising?" Talboth asked halfheartedly, mostly to keep the conversation going.

"No."

"Is there any conclusion you've drawn that doesn't fit in with what I've said?"

"No. Not that I can think of."

"What do the police investigating Louise's death have to say?"

"They don't have any leads. There's no murderer, no

motive. The only clues are the microfilm and documents hidden in a secret pocket in her purse."

"But surely that's proof enough to show that she's
the spy everybody has been looking for? Perhaps something went wrong when she was due to hand over her
material?"

"That's a plausible explanation. I assume that's the
basis on which the police are proceeding. But what
went wrong? Who was it that met her? And why did it
happen just now?"

Talboth stopped and stamped on his cigarette butt.

"It's a big step forward in any case," he said. "She's
obviously guilty. The investigation can concentrate on
Louise now. They'll probably find the middleman
sooner or later."

They continued walking and came to the entrance
door. Talboth tapped in the code.

"I need more fresh air," Wallander said. "I'm a dyed-
in-the-wool night owl. I'll stay out for a bit longer."

Talboth nodded, gave him the entry code, and went
inside. Wallander watched the door closing silently.
Then he stared walking along the deserted street. The
feeling that something was fundamentally wrong
struck him once more. The same feeling he'd had after
leaving the island following the night he'd spent with
Håkan von Enke. He thought about what Talboth had
said, about the truth often being the opposite of what
you'd expected. Sometimes you needed to turn reality
upside down in order to make it stand up.

Wallander paused and turned around. The street was still deserted. He could hear music coming from an open window. A German hit song. He heard the words **leben, eben,** and **neben.** He continued walking until he came to a little square. Some young people were making out on a bench. Maybe I should stand here and shout out into the night, he thought. **I don't know what's going on.** That's what I could shout. The only thing I'm sure about is that there's something I'm not getting. Am I coming closer to the truth, or drifting further away from it?

He strolled around the square for a while, growing more and more tired. When he returned to the apartment, Talboth seemed to have gone to bed. The door to the balcony was locked. Wallander undressed and fell asleep almost immediately.

In his dreams the horses started running again. But when he woke up the next morning, he could remember nothing about them.

37

When Wallander opened his eyes, he didn't know where he was at first. He glanced at his watch: six o'clock. He stayed in bed. He could hear through the wall what he assumed was the noise of the machines adjusting the oxygen level of the water in the gigantic aquarium, but he couldn't hear whether the trains were running. They lived a silent life in their well-insulated tunnels. Like moles, he thought. But also like the people who wormed their way into the places where decisions were made, decisions they then stole and passed on to the other side, which was supposed to be kept in ignorance.

He got out of bed and felt an urge to leave. He didn't bother to take a shower, but simply dressed and emerged into the large, well-lit apartment. The balcony door was open, the thin curtains flapping gently in the breeze. Talboth was sitting there, cigarette in hand. A cup of coffee was on the table in front of him. He turned slowly to face Wallander, who had the impression that Talboth had heard him coming. He smiled. It suddenly seemed to Wallander that he didn't trust that smile.

"I hope you slept well."

"The bed was very comfortable," said Wallander. "The room was dark and quiet. But I think I should thank you for your hospitality now and take my leave."

"So you're not going to give Berlin another day to impress you? There's an awful lot I could show you."

"I'd love to stay on, but I think it's best I set off for home now."

"I take it your dog needs somebody to look after it?"

How does he know I have a dog? Wallander thought. I've never mentioned it. He had a vague impression that Talboth realized immediately he'd said something he shouldn't have.

"Yes," said Wallander. "You're right. I mustn't take too much advantage of my neighbors' willingness to keep an eye on Jussi. I've spent all summer heading off to first one place, then another. And of course I have a grandchild I want to see as often as possible."

"I'm glad that Louise had time to enjoy her," said Talboth. "Children are one thing, but grandchildren are even more meaningful; they are the ultimate fulfillment. Children give us the feeling that our existence has been meaningful, but grandchildren are the confirmation of that. Do you have a photo of her?"

Wallander showed him the two photographs he had brought.

"A lovely little girl," said Talboth, getting to his feet. "But you must have some breakfast before you leave."

"Just a cup of coffee," said Wallander. "I never have anything to eat in the morning."

Talboth shook his head in disapproval. But he came back out onto the balcony with a cup of coffee—black, the way Wallander always drank it.

"You said something yesterday that I've been wondering about," Wallander said.

"No doubt I said all kinds of things that you've been wondering about."

"You said that sometimes one needed to look for explanations in places diametrically opposed to where one was looking at the time. Did you mean that as a general principle, or were you referring to something specific?"

Talboth thought for a moment.

"I don't recall saying what you say I did," he said.

"But if I did, it was no doubt meant as a general principle."

Wallander nodded. He didn't believe a word of what Talboth said. He had meant something specific. It was just that Wallander hadn't caught on to what it was.

Talboth seemed on edge, not as calm and relaxed as he had been the previous day.

"I'd like to take a photo of the two of us together," he said. "I'll get my camera. I don't have a guest book, but I always take photographs when I have visitors."

He came back with a camera, which he balanced on the arm of one of the chairs. He set the timer and came to sit down beside Wallander. When the picture was taken, he took another one himself, this time of Wallander alone. They said their good-byes shortly afterward. Wallander had his jacket in one hand and his car keys in the other.

"Will you manage to find your way out of the city without help?" Talboth asked.

"My sense of direction isn't all that good, but I'll no doubt find the right road sooner or later. Besides, there's a logic in the German road network that puts all the others to shame."

They shook hands. Wallander took the elevator down to street level and waved to Talboth, who was leaning over his balcony railing. As he left the building, Wallander noticed that Talboth's name didn't appear on the name-plate listing all the tenants; it said instead "USG Enterprises." Wallander memorized the name, then got in his car and drove off.

It took him several hours to find his way out of the

city. When he finally emerged onto the highway, he realized too late that he had missed an exit and was now heading for the Polish border. With considerable difficulty he eventually managed to turn and set off in the right direction. When he passed Oranienburg, he shuddered at the memory of what had happened there.

He arrived back home without any problems. Linda came to visit him that evening. Klara had a cold, and Hans was taking care of her. The following day he was due to leave for New York.

It was a warm evening, so they sat out in the garden, and Linda drank tea.

"How's business going for him?" Wallander asked as they swung slowly back and forth in the hammock.

"I don't know," said Linda. "But I sometimes wonder what's going on. He always used to come home and tell me about the fantastic deals he'd closed during the day. Now he doesn't say anything at all."

A skein of geese flew past. They watched the birds flying south.

"Are they migrating already?" Linda wondered. "Isn't it too early?"

"Maybe they're practicing," said Wallander.

Linda burst out laughing.

"That's exactly the kind of comment Granddad would have made. Do you realize that you're getting more and more like him?"

Wallander dismissed the thought.

"We both know he had a sense of humor. But he

could be much more malicious than I ever allow my-self to be."

"I don't think he was malicious," Linda said firmly. "I think he was scared."

"Of what?"

"Maybe of growing old. Of dying. I think he used to hide that fear behind his malevolence, which was often just a front."

Wallander didn't reply. He wondered if that was what she meant when she said they were so similar. That he was also beginning to make it obvious that he was afraid of dying?

"Tomorrow you and I are going to visit Mona," Linda said out of the blue.

"Why?"

"Because she's my mother, and you and I are her next of kin."

"Doesn't she have her psychopath of a businessman-cum-husband to look after her?"

"Haven't you figured out that it's all over?"

"No, I'm not coming with you."

"Why not?"

"I don't want anything more to do with Mona. Now that Baiba's dead, I can't forgive Mona for what she said about her."

"Jealous people come out with jealous stupidities. Mona's told me the kind of things you used to say when you were jealous."

"She's lying."

"Not always."

"I'm not going. I don't want to."

"But I want you to. And I think Mom wants you to. You can't just cut her out of your life."

Wallander said nothing. There was no point in protesting anymore. If he didn't do as Linda wished it would make both his and her existence impossible for a long time. He didn't want that.

"I don't even know where the clinic is," he said in the end.

"You'll find out tomorrow. It'll be a surprise."

An area of low pressure drifted in over Skåne during the night. As they sat in the car driving east shortly after eight in the morning, it had started raining and a wind was blowing up. Wallander felt groggy. He had slept badly and was tired and irritable when Linda came to pick him up. She immediately sent him back indoors to change his old, worn-out pants.

"You don't need to be in your best suit to visit her, but you can't show up looking as scruffy as that."

They turned off onto the road leading to an old castle, Glimmingehus. Linda looked at him.

"Do you remember?"

"Of course I remember."

"We have plenty of time. We can stop and take a look."

Linda drove into the parking lot outside the high castle walls. They left the car and walked over the drawbridge into the castle yard.

"This is among my earliest memories," said Linda. "When you and I came here. And you scared me to death with all your ghost stories. How old was I then?"

"The first time we came I suppose you must have been four or thereabouts. But that's not when I told you the ghost stories. I did that when you were seven, I think. Maybe it was the summer when you were about to start school."

"I remember being so proud of you," said Linda. "My big, imposing dad. I like to think back on moments like that, when I felt so safe and secure, and so happy to be alive."

"I have similar memories," said Wallander, genuinely. "They were the best years of my life, when you were a little girl."

"Where does the time go?" Linda wondered. "Do you think like that too? Now that you're sixty?"

"Yes," he said. "A few years ago I noticed that I've started reading the obituaries in **Ystads Allehanda.** If I came across another daily newspaper, I'd read them there as well. I wondered more and more about what had become of my old classmates from Limhamn. How had their lives turned out, compared to mine? I started looking into that, halfheartedly."

They sat down on the stone steps leading into the castle itself.

"Those of us who started school in 1955 really have lived all kinds of different lives. I think I know what happened to most of my classmates now. Things didn't go well for a lot of them. Several are dead; one shot himself after emigrating to Canada. A few were successful, such as Sölve Hagberg, who won **Double or Quits.** Most of them have led quiet lives. Good for them. And this is how my life has turned out. When you reach sixty, most of your life is behind you. You just have to accept that, hard though it is. There are very few important decisions still to be made."

"Do you feel like your life is coming to a close?"

"Sometimes."

"What do you think at times like that?"

He hesitated before replying, then gave her an honest answer.

"I mourn the fact that Baiba is dead. That we never managed to get together."

"There are other women," said Linda. "You don't have to be on your own."

Wallander stood up.

"No," he said. "There aren't any others. Baiba was irreplaceable."

They went back to the car and drove the remaining couple of miles to the clinic. It was in a mansion with four wings, and the old inner courtyard had been preserved. Mona was sitting on a bench smoking as they approached her over the cobblestones.

"Has she started smoking?" Wallander asked. "She never used to."

"She says she smokes to console herself. And that she'll stop once this is over."

"When will it be over?"

"She'll be here for another month."

"And Hans is paying for it all?"

She didn't reply to that question because the answer

was obvious. Mona stood up as they approached. Wallander noticed with distaste the pale gray color of her face, and the heavy bags under her eyes. He thought she was ugly, something that had never struck him before.

"It was nice of you to come," she said, taking his hand.

"I wanted to see how you were," he mumbled.

They all sat down on the bench, with Mona in the middle. Wallander immediately felt the urge to leave. The fact that Mona was struggling with withdrawal symptoms and anxiety was not sufficient reason for him to be there. Why did Linda want him to see Mona in such a state? Was it an attempt to make him acknowledge his share of the guilt? What was he guilty of? He could feel himself growing increasingly irritated while Linda and Mona talked to each other. Then Mona asked if they wanted to see her room. Wallander declined, but Linda went into the house with her.

Wallander wandered around the grounds while he was waiting. His cell phone rang in his jacket pocket. It was Ytterberg.

"Are you on duty?" he asked. "Or are you still on vacation?"

"I'm still on vacation," said Wallander. "At least, that's what I try to convince myself."

"I'm in my office. I have in front of me a report from our secret service people in the armed forces. Do you want to know what they have to say?"

"We might be interrupted."

"I think a few minutes will be enough. It's an extremely thin report. Which means that most of it isn't considered suitable for me or other ordinary police officers to see. 'Parts of the report are classified as secret,' it says. Which no doubt means that nearly all of it is classified. They've tossed us a few grains of sand. If there are any pearls, they're keeping them for themselves."

Ytterberg was suddenly struck by a fit of sneezing.

"Sorry," he said. "I'm allergic. They use some kind of cleaning substance in the police station that I can't tolerate. I think I'll start scrubbing my office myself."

"That sounds like a good idea," said Wallander impatiently.

"I'll read you a section of the report: 'The material, including microfilm and photographic negatives, and some encrypted text, found in Louise von Enke's purse contains military material classified as secret. Most of it is particularly sensitive, and was classified as secret precisely so as to avoid it coming into the wrong hands.' End of quote. In other words, there's no doubt about it."

"That the material is genuine, you mean?"

"Exactly. And it also says in the report that similar material has come into Russian hands in the past, as they have used Swedish elimination processes to establish that the Russians are in possession of knowledge they should not have had access to. Do you understand what they mean? Much of the report is written in opaque military jargon."

"That's the way our own secret colleagues tend to write—why should the military types be any different? But I think I understand."

"It's not possible to avoid the conclusion that Louise von Enke had been sticking her fingers into the military honeypot. She sold intelligence material. God only knows how she came by it."

"There are still a lot of unanswered questions," Wallander said. "What happened out there at Värmdö? Why was she murdered? Who was she supposed to meet? Why didn't that person or those persons take the set of documents she had in her purse?"

"Perhaps they didn't know it was there?"

"Maybe she didn't actually have it with her," said Wallander.

"We're looking into that possibility. That it might have been planted."

"As far as I can see, that's not impossible."

"But why?"

"To make sure she'd be suspected of spying."

"But she is a spy, isn't she?"

"It feels like we're in a labyrinth," said Wallander. "I can't find my way out. But let me think about what you've told me. How high a priority are you giving this murder just now?"

"Very high. The rumor is that it will feature in some television show about current criminal investigations. The bosses are always nervous when the media turn up with microphones."

"Send them to me," said Wallander. "I'm not afraid."

"Who's afraid? I'm just worried I'll turn nasty if they ask me silly questions."

Wallander sat down on the bench again and thought

about what Ytterberg had said. He tried to find things that didn't add up, without succeeding. He was finding it hard to concentrate.

Mona's eyes seemed glazed over when she and Linda returned. Wallander realized that she'd been crying. He didn't want to know what they had been talking about, but he did feel sorry for Mona. He would like to ask her his question as well: How did your life turn out? She was standing in front of him, gray and dejected, shaking, oppressed by forces stronger than she was.

"It's time for my treatment," she said. "Thank you for coming. What I'm going through isn't easy."

"What does your treatment entail?" Wallander asked in a brave attempt to appear interested.

"Right now I'm meeting with a doctor. His name is Torsten Rosén. He's had alcohol problems himself. I have to hurry or I'll be late."

They said their good-byes in the courtyard. Linda and Wallander drove home in silence. He thought she was no doubt more troubled than he was. Her relationship with her mother had grown stronger once the stormy teenage years were past.

"I'm glad you came with me," Linda said when she dropped him off.

"You didn't give me much choice," he said. "But of course, it was important for me to see how she's doing, what she's going through. The question is, will she get better?"

"I don't know. I can only hope so."

"Yes," said Wallander. "There's only one possibility left: to hope."

He thrust his hand in through the open window and stroked her hair. She turned the car around and drove off. Wallander watched the car disappearing.

He felt heavyhearted. He let Jussi out of his kennel and tickled him behind his ears before unlocking the front door. He noticed right away that somebody had been in the house. One of the traps he had set had produced a result. On the windowsill next to the front door he had placed a candlestick directly in front of the window's handle. Now it was standing closer to the pane, to the left of the handle. He paused and held his breath. Could he be mistaken? No, he was quite sure. When he examined the window more closely, he saw that it had been opened from the outside with a narrow, sharp instrument, probably something similar to the tool used by car thieves to open door locks.

He lifted up the candlestick and examined it carefully: it was made of wood, with a copper ring where the candle was inserted. He put it down again just as carefully, then worked his way slowly through the house. He found no other traces of a break-in. They are careful, he thought. Careful and skillful. The candlestick was an uncharacteristic slip.

He sat down at the kitchen table, contemplating the candlestick. There was only one explanation for unknown people breaking into his house.

Somebody was convinced that he knew something he

didn't know he knew. Something based on his notes, or even some object in his possession.

He sat motionless on his chair. I'm getting closer, he thought. Or somebody is getting closer to me.

38

The next morning he was hustled out of his sleep by dreams that he couldn't remember. The candlestick on the windowsill reminded him that somebody had been close to where he was now. He went out into the garden naked, first to pee, and then to let Jussi out of his kennel. An early fall mist was drifting in over the fields. He shuddered and hurried back indoors. He dressed, made coffee, then sat down at the kitchen table, determined yet again to try to clarify what had happened to Louise von Enke. He knew that he wouldn't be able to establish anything but a highly provisional explanation. But he needed to go through everything once more, very carefully, mainly in the hope of finding a reason for the nagging feeling that there was something he'd overlooked. The feeling was even stronger now that, yet again, somebody had been rummaging around in his house. In brief, he had no intention of washing his hands of it all.

But he found it hard to concentrate. After a few

hours he gave up, gathered his papers, and went to the police station. Once again he chose to enter via the basement garage, and he came to his office without bumping into anybody. After half an hour spent hunched over his papers, he checked that the hallway was empty and went to the coffee machine. He had just filled his mug when Lennart Mattson appeared. Wallander hadn't seen his boss for a while, and he hadn't missed him. Mattson was tanned and had lost weight, something that immediately made Wallander jealous and annoyed.

"Here already?" Mattson asked. "Can't keep away, huh? Can't wait to get back to work? That's how it should be, you can't be a good police officer if you're not passionate about your work. But I thought you weren't due back until Monday."

"I was just on my way home," said Wallander. "I needed to get some papers from my office."

"Do you have a moment? I have some good news that I'd like to share with somebody."

"I have all the time in the world," said Wallander, making no attempt to conceal the irony that he knew would pass over Mattson's head.

They went to the chief of police's office. Wallander sat down on one of the guest chairs. Mattson opened a folder lying on his neat and tidy desk.

"Good news, as I said. Here in Skåne we have one of the best closure rates in the country. We solve more crimes than almost everybody else. We've also improved the most from the previous year. That's just what we need to inspire us to even greater things."

Wallander listened to what his boss had to say. There was no reason to doubt the report. But Wallander knew that interpreting statistics was like pulling rabbits out of a hat. You could always present a statistic as fact even if it was an illusion. Wallander and his colleagues were painfully aware that the closure rate in Sweden was among the lowest in the world. And none of them believed they'd hit rock bottom yet. Things would continue to get worse. Constant bureaucratic upheavals meant an equally constant increase in the negative flow of unsolved crimes. Competent police officers were fired, or diverted into other duties until they were no longer able to make a meaningful contribution. It was more important to check boxes and meet targets than to really get down to investigating crimes and taking crooks to court. Moreover, Wallander and most of his colleagues thought that the priorities were all wrong. The day that police chiefs decreed "minor crimes" must be tolerated, the rug had been pulled out from under the remains of a trusting relationship between the police and the general public. The man in the street was not prepared to shrug his shoulders and merely accept that somebody had broken into his car or his garage or his summer cottage. He wanted these crimes to be solved, or at least investigated.

But that wasn't something Wallander felt like discussing with Lennart Mattson right now. There would be plenty of opportunities for that during the fall.

Mattson slid the report to one side and looked at his visitor with a troubled expression on his face. Wallander could see that he had sweat on his brow.

"How are you feeling? You look pale. Why haven't you been getting some sun?"

"What sun?"

"The summer hasn't been all that bad. I made a trip to Crete, so we'd be sure to have some decent weather. Have you ever visited the palace at Knossos? There are fantastic dolphins on the walls there."

Wallander stood up.

"I feel fine," he said. "But since it's sunny today, I'll take your advice and make the most of it."

"No forgotten guns anywhere, I hope?"

Wallander stared at Lennart Mattson. He came very close to punching him in the nose.

Wallander returned to his office, sat down on his chair, put his feet on his desk, and closed his eyes. He thought about Baiba. And Mona shivering away in her rehabilitation clinic. While his boss gloated over a statistic that was no doubt economical with the truth.

He took down his feet. I'll make another attempt, he thought. Another attempt to understand why I'm always doubtful about the conclusions I reach. I wish I had more insight into political goings-on; then I would probably be less confused than I am now.

He suddenly recalled something he'd never thought about as an adult. It must have been 1962 or 1963, sometime in the fall. Wallander had a Saturday job as an errand boy for a flower shop in central Malmö. He had been instructed to deliver a bouquet of flowers as quickly as possible to the People's Park. The prime minister, Tage Erlander, was giving a lecture, and when he had finished a little girl was supposed to hand him the flowers. The problem was that somebody in the local Social Democratic Party office had forgotten to order the flowers. So now there was an emergency. Wallander pedaled away for all he was worth. The flower shop had warned the People's Park officials that he was on his way, and he was allowed in without delay. The little girl designated to present the flowers received them in time and Wallander received a tip of no less than five kronor. He was offered a glass of soda, and stood with a straw in his mouth, listening to the tall man at the lectern speaking in his strange nasal voice. He used a lot of big words—or at least words that Wallander was unfamiliar with. He spoke about détente, the rights of small countries, the neutrality of Sweden, with its freedom from all kinds of pacts and treaties. Wallander thought he'd understood that, at least, from what the great man had said.

When Wallander came home that evening he went to the room his father used as a studio. He could still remember even now that his father was busy painting in the forest background he used in all his pictures. When he was a teenager Wallander had a good relationship with his father—that might have been the best time in their shared existence. It would be another three, perhaps four years before Wallander came home and announced that he was going to become a police officer. His father had gone through the roof and come close to throwing him out—in any case, he refused to talk to him for quite some time.

Wallander had sat on a stool next to his father and told him about his visit to the People's Park. His father often muttered that he wasn't interested in politics, but Wallander eventually realized that this wasn't the case. His father always voted faithfully for the Social Democrats, was angrily skeptical about the Communists, and always criticized the non-socialist parties for favoring citizens who were already leading a comfortable life.

The conversation with his father that day came back to him now, almost word for word. Earlier, his father had always spoken positively about Erlander, maintaining that he was an honest man you could trust, unlike many other politicians.

"He said that Russia is our enemy," Wallander said.

"That's not completely true. It wouldn't do any harm if our politicians devoted a thought or two to the role America plays nowadays."

Wallander was surprised by what he said. Surely America represented the good guys? After all, they were the ones who had defeated Hitler and the Nazis' Thousand-Year Reich. America produced movies, music, clothes. As far as Wallander was concerned, Elvis Presley was the King, and there was nothing to beat "Blue Suede Shoes." He had stopped collecting everything he could find about Hollywood stars, but still there was nobody to beat Alan Ladd. Now his father was implying that you had to be on your guard where America was concerned. Was there something Wallander didn't know?

Wallander repeated the prime minister's words: the neutrality of **Sweden, with its freedom from all kinds**

of pacts and treaties. "Is that what he said?" his father had commented. "The fact is, American jets fly through Swedish air space. We pretend to be neutral, but at the same time we play along with NATO and more specifically with America."

Wallander pressed his father on what he meant, but he didn't get an answer, only some inaudible mumbling and then a request to be left in peace.

"You ask too many questions."

"But you've always said that I shouldn't be afraid to ask you if there was something I wondered about."

"There has to be a limit."

"Where is it?"

"Right here. I'm making mistakes when I paint."

"How is that possible? You've been painting the same picture every day since long before I was born."

"Go away! Leave me in peace!"

And then, as he stood in the doorway, Wallander said:

"I got a five-kronor tip for getting the flowers to Elander in time."

"**Erlander.** Learn people's names."

And at that precise moment, as if the memory had opened a door for him, Wallander saw that he was totally on the wrong track. He'd been deceived, and he'd allowed himself to be deceived. He'd been following the path dictated by his assumptions instead of reality. He sat motionless at his desk, his hands clenched, and allowed his thoughts to lead him to a new and unexpected explanation of what had happened. It was so mind-boggling that at first he couldn't believe he could be right. The only thing that kept him focused was that his instincts had warned him. He really had overlooked something. He had mixed up the truth and the lies and assumed that the cause was the effect and vice versa.

He went to the bathroom and took off his shirt, which was soaked in sweat. When he had given himself a good wash, he went down to his locker in the basement and put on a clean shirt. He recalled in passing having received it from Linda for his birthday a few years earlier.

When he returned to his office he searched through his papers until he found the photograph he had been given by Asta Hagberg, the one of Colonel Stig Wennerström in Washington talking to a young Håkan von Enke. He studied the faces of the two men. Wennerström was smiling coolly, martini glass in hand, facing Håkan von Enke, who looked serious listening to what Wennerström had to say.

He lined up his Lego pieces in his mind's eye once more. They were all there: Louise and Håkan von Enke, Hans, Signe in her bed, Sten Nordlander, Hermann Eber, Steven Atkins in America, George Talboth in Berlin. He added Fanny Klarström, and then another piece—but he didn't yet know whom it represented. Then he slowly removed piece after piece until there were only two left. Louise and Håkan. It was Louise who fell over. That's how her life came to an end; she was knocked over somewhere on Värmdö. But Håkan, her husband, was still standing.

Wallander recorded his thoughts. Then he put the photograph from Washington in his jacket pocket and left the police station. This time he left through the main entrance, greeted the girl in reception, spoke to a few traffic officers who had just come in, then walked down the hill into town. Anybody watching him might have wondered why he was walking so erratically— now fast, now slow. Occasionally he held out one hand, as if he were talking to somebody and needed to emphasize what he was saying with various gestures.

He stopped at the hot dog stand opposite the hospital and stood there for ages wondering what to order; but then he kept on walking without having eaten anything at all.

The whole time, the same thoughts were running through his mind. Could what he now envisaged really be true? Could he have misinterpreted what had happened so fundamentally?

He wandered around town and eventually went to the marina, walked to the end of the pier, and sat down on his usual bench. He took the photo out of his pocket and examined it yet again, then put it back.

The penny had dropped. Baiba had been right, his beloved Baiba whom he was now longing for more than ever.

Behind every person there's always somebody else. The mistake he had made was to confuse those in the foreground with those lurking in the background.

Everything added up at last. He could see the pattern that had eluded him thus far. And he could see it very clearly.

A fishing boat was on its way out of the harbor. The man at the helm raised a hand and waved to Wallander. He waved back. Thunderclouds were building up on the horizon. At this moment he missed his father. That didn't happen often. For a short while after his father's death, Wallander had been aware of a frightening vacuum, but at the same time it was a relief that he had passed away. But at this moment neither the vacuum nor the relief was still there; he simply missed his father and longed to relive the good times they'd had together, despite everything.

Perhaps I never saw him as he really was, didn't know who he really was, nor what he meant for me and for others. Just as little as I understood until now about Håkan von Enke's disappearance and Louise's death. At last I feel I'm getting closer to a solution, rather than drifting farther and farther away from it.

He realized that he would have to make another journey this summer, which had already involved so much traveling. But he had no choice. He knew now what he needed to do.

Once again he took the photo out of his jacket pocket. He held it in front of him, then tore it in two, right down the middle. Once there had been a world that brought Stig Wennerström and Håkan von Enke together, but now he had torn them apart.

"Was that the case even in those days?" he said out loud to himself. "Or was it something that came about much later?"

He didn't know. But he intended to find out.

Nobody heard him as he sat there, at the very end of the pier, speaking aloud to himself.

39

Looking back, he had only vague and disjointed memories of that day. He eventually left the pier and went back into town, stopped outside a newly opened café in Hamngatan, peered in through the door, then left immediately. He made another tour of the streets before stopping at the Chinese restaurant near Stora Torget that he usually frequented. He sat down at an empty table—there were not many customers at this time in the afternoon—and somewhat absentmindedly chose a dish from the menu.

If anybody had asked him afterward what he had eaten, he probably wouldn't have been able to tell them. His thoughts were elsewhere. He was formulating a plan to confirm his suspicions. He now held different cards in his hand; everything he had believed earlier had been proved wrong.

He sat there for ages, poking at his food with his chopsticks, then suddenly devoured everything, far too quickly, paid the bill, and left the restaurant. He returned to the police station. On the way to his office he was stopped by Kristina Magnusson, who invited him to join her family for dinner that weekend. He could pick the day, Saturday or Sunday. Since he couldn't think of an excuse to turn her down, he told her he'd be delighted to join her on Sunday. He hung his home-made "Do Not Disturb" sign on the handle of his office door, switched off his cell phone, and closed his eyes. After a while he straightened his back, scribbled a few notes in his notepad, and knew that he had now made up his mind. For better or worse, he needed to determine whether things really were as he now thought. To make sure he wasn't mistaken, hadn't allowed himself to be fooled again. In a sudden outburst of anger he hurled his pen at the wall and cursed loudly. Just once, no more. Then he called Sten Nordlander. The connection was poor. When Wallander insisted that it was absolutely vital that they talk, Nordlander promised to call him back. Wallander hung up, and wondered why it was so difficult to call certain parts of the archipelago. Or was Nordlander actually somewhere else?

He waited. He spent the time going over all the thoughts filling his head. His brain was like a tank full to the brim. He was worried that it might start to overflow.

Sten Nordlander called forty minutes later. Wallander had placed his watch on the desk in front of him and noted that the hands pointed to ten minutes past six. The connection was now perfect.

"I'm sorry to have kept you waiting. I'm moored at Utö now."

"Not far from Muskö, then," said Wallander. "Or am I wrong?"

"Not at all. You could say without fear of contradiction that I'm in classic waters. Submarine waters, that is."

"We need to meet," said Wallander. "I want to talk to you."

"Did something happen?"

"Something's always happening. But I want to talk to you about a thought that's occurred to me."

"So nothing's happened?"

"Nothing. But I don't want to discuss this on the phone. What are you doing for the next few days?"

"It must be important if you're thinking of coming here."

"There's something else I need to take care of in Stockholm," said Wallander, as calmly as he could.

"When were you thinking of coming?"

"Tomorrow. I know it's short notice."

Nordlander thought for a moment. Wallander could hear his heavy breathing.

"I'm on my way home," he said. "We could meet in town."

"If you tell me how to get to wherever you'll be, I can make my way there."

"I think that would be best. Shall we meet in the lobby of the Mariners' Hotel? What time?"

"Four o'clock," said Wallander. "Thank you for agreeing to meet me."

Nordlander laughed.

"Do you give me any choice?"

"Do I sound that strict?"

"Like an old schoolmaster. You're sure that nothing's happened?"

"Not as far as I know," said Wallander evasively. "I'll see you tomorrow, then."

Wallander sat down at his computer and with some effort eventually managed to buy a train ticket and book a room at the Mariners' Hotel. Since the train was due to leave early the following day, he drove home and took Jussi to his neighbors'. The husband was in the farmyard, tinkering with his tractor. He raised his eyebrows at Wallander when he saw him approaching with the dog.

"Are you sure you don't want to sell him?"

"Completely sure. But I have to go away again. To Stockholm."

"I seem to recall that only the other day you were sitting in my kitchen and telling me how much you hated big towns."

"I do. But I have to go for work reasons."

"Don't you have enough crooks to deal with down here?"

"I certainly do. But I'm afraid I do have to go to Stockholm."

Wallander stroked Jussi and handed over the leash. Jussi was used to this by now, and didn't react.

But before leaving, Wallander had a question for his neighbor. It was only polite to ask at this time of year, as fall was approaching.

"How's the harvest looking?"

"Not too bad."

Very good, in other words, Wallander thought as he made his way back home. He's usually pretty gloomy when it comes to forecasting crop yields.

Wallander called Linda when he got in. He didn't tell her the real reason for his journey; he simply said he'd been called to an important meeting in Stockholm. She didn't question that, merely asked how long he was going to be away.

"A couple of days. Maybe three."

"Where will you be staying?"

"At the Mariners' Hotel. For the first night, at least. I might stay with Sten Nordlander after that."

It was seven-thirty by the time he had packed a few clothes into a bag, locked up the house, and settled in his car to drive to Malmö. After much hesitation he had also packed his—or rather, his father's—old shotgun and a few cartridges, as well as his service revolver. He was going to travel by train and wouldn't need to pass through security checks. He didn't like the idea of taking weapons, but on the other hand, he didn't dare travel without them.

He checked into a cheap hotel on the outskirts of Malmö, had dinner at a restaurant not far from Jägersro, and then went for a long walk to tire himself out. He was up and dressed by five the next morning. When he paid his bill, he made arrangements for his car to stay in the hotel parking lot until he returned, then ordered a taxi to take him to the train station. He could feel it was going to be a hot day.

Wallander usually felt at his most alert in the mornings. That had been the case for as long as he could remember. As he stood outside the hotel, waiting for his taxi, he had no doubts. He was doing the right thing. At long last he felt he was approaching a solution to everything that had happened.

He spent the train journey to Stockholm sleeping, leafing through various newspapers, half-solving a few crossword puzzles, and simply sitting back and letting his mind wander. His thoughts returned over and over again to that evening in Djursholm. He recalled all the photos he had at home of that occasion. How Håkan von Enke seemed worried. And just one picture of Louise when she wasn't smiling. The only picture in which she was serious.

He ate a couple of sandwiches and drank coffee in the restaurant car, surprised by the prices, then sat with his head in his hands, gazing absentmindedly out the window at the countryside hurrying past.

Shortly after Nässjö, what he always dreaded nowadays happened. He suddenly had no idea where he was going. He had to check his ticket in order to remember. His shirt was soaked in sweat after this attack of forgetfulness. Yet again he had been shaken.

. . .

He checked into the Mariners' Hotel at about noon. Sten Nordlander arrived shortly after four. He was tanned, and his hair had been cut short. He also seemed to have lost weight. His face lit up when he saw Wallander.

"You look tired," Nordlander said. "Haven't you made the most of your vacation?"

"Apparently not," Wallander replied.

"It's lovely weather—shall we go out, or would you prefer to stay here?"

"Let's go out. How about Mosebacke? It's warm enough to sit out in the sun."

As they walked up the hill to the square, Wallander said nothing about why he had come to Stockholm. And Sten Nordlander didn't ask any questions. The walk winded Wallander, but Nordlander seemed to be in good shape. They sat out on the terrace, where nearly all the tables were occupied. It would soon be fall, with its chilly evenings. Stockholmers were taking advantage of the opportunity to sit outside for as long as possible.

Wallander ordered tea—he had a stomachache from drinking too much coffee. Nordlander decided on a beer and a sandwich.

Wallander braced himself.

"I wasn't really telling you the truth when I said that nothing had happened. But I didn't want to talk about it on the phone."

He was observing Nordlander carefully as he spoke. The expression of surprise on his face seemed to be completely genuine.

"Håkan?" he asked.

"Yes. I know where he is."

Nordlander's eyes never left Wallander's face. He doesn't know, Wallander thought, and felt relieved. He hasn't the slightest idea. Right now I need somebody I can rely on.

Nordlander said nothing, waited. There was a buzz of conversation on all sides.

"Tell me what happened!"

"I will. But first, let me ask you a few questions. I want to make sure my interpretation of how all these events are connected is correct. Let's discuss politics. What did Håkan stand for, during his time as an active officer? What were his political views? Regarding Olof Palme, for example? It's well known that a lot of military men hated him and didn't hesitate to spread absurd rumors about him being mentally ill and being treated in a hospital, or that he was a spy for the Soviet Union. How does Håkan fit in with that?"

"Not at all. As I've told you. Håkan was never one of the main antagonists of Olof Palme and the Social Democratic government. As you no doubt recall, he actually met Palme on one occasion. I think he thought that the criticism of Palme was unfair, and that there was an overestimation of the Soviet Union's capacity for waging war and their desire to attack Sweden.

"Have you ever had reason to believe that he wasn't being honest?"

"Why would I? Håkan is a patriot, but he is very analytical. I think he was turned off by all the extreme hatred of Russia that surrounded him."

"What were his views on the U.S.A.?"

"Critical in many ways. I remember him saying once

that the U.S.A. is in fact the only country in the world that has used a nuclear weapon to attack another country. Obviously, you can talk about the special circumstances that applied at the end of the Second World War, but the fact remains: America has used an atomic bomb on people. Nobody else has done that. Not yet."

Wallander had no more questions for the moment. Nothing of what Nordlander said was surprising or unexpected. Wallander received the answers he thought he would get. He poured himself some tea and decided that the time was now ripe.

"We spoke earlier about there being a spy in the Swedish military. Somebody who was never exposed."

"Rumors like that are always flying around. If you don't have anything else to talk about, you can speculate about moles digging their tunnels."

"If I've understood those rumors correctly they suggested there was a spy who was in many ways more dangerous than Wennerström."

"I don't know about that, but I suppose a spy you don't catch is always going to be a bigger threat than any other."

Wallander nodded.

"There was also another rumor," he continued. "Or rather, there is a rumor that still persists. That this unknown spy is in fact a woman."

"I don't think anybody believed that. Not in my circles, at any rate. There are so few women in the armed forces with access to classified documents, it's just not credible."

"Did you ever speak to Håkan about this?"

"A woman spy? No, never."

"Louise was a spy," Wallander said slowly. "She spied for the Soviet Union."

At first Sten Nordlander didn't seem to grasp what Wallander had said. Then he realized the significance of what he had just heard.

"It can't be possible."

"It not only **can be,** it **is** possible."

"Well, I don't believe it. What proof do you have?"

"The police found microfilms of classified documents, and also several photographic negatives hidden in Louise's purse. I don't know exactly what they were, but I've become convinced that they prove she was participating in high-level espionage. Against Sweden, for Russia, and before that for the Soviet Union. In other words, she was active for a very long time."

Sten Nordlander eyed him incredulously.

"Do you really expect me to believe this?"

"Yes, I do."

"Questions are welling up inside me, arguments protesting that what you say can't be true."

"But can you know beyond question that I'm wrong?"

Nordlander froze, beer glass in hand.

"Is Håkan involved in this as well? Did they operate as a pair?"

"That's hardly credible."

Nordlander slammed his glass down on the table.

"Do you know or don't you? Why don't you tell me straight?"

"There's nothing to suggest that Håkan cooperated with Louise."

"Then why is he hiding himself away?"

"Because he suspected her. He was on her trail for many years. In the end he began to fear for his own life. He thought Louise realized that he suspected her, and that meant there was a significant risk that he might be murdered."

"But Louise is the one who's dead."

"Don't forget that when her body was found, Håkan had already been missing for a long time."

Wallander watched a new Sten Nordlander emerging. He was normally energetic and straightforward, but now he seemed to be shrinking. The confusion he felt was changing him.

There was a minor commotion at a neighboring table: a drunken man fell over and knocked down several bottles and glasses. A security officer came hurrying up, and calm was soon restored. Wallander drank his tea. Sten Nordlander had stood up and walked over to the fence. He gazed down at the city stretching out before him. When he returned, Wallander said, "I need your help to persuade Håkan to return."

"What can I do?"

"You're his best friend. I want you to come with me on a trip. I'll tell you where tomorrow. Can we use your car? Can you leave your boat for twenty-four hours or so?"

"No problem."

"Pick me up at three o'clock tomorrow outside the hotel. Dress for rain. I have to go now."

He didn't let Nordlander ask any questions. He didn't look around as he walked back to the hotel. He still wasn't absolutely certain that he could rely on Sten Nordlander, but he had made his choice and there was no going back now.

That night he lay awake for hours, tossing and turning between the damp sheets. In his dream he saw Baiba hovering over the ground, her face completely transparent.

He left the hotel early the next morning and took a taxi out to Djurgården, where he lay down under a tree and slept for a while. He used his bag containing the shotgun as a pillow. When he woke up, he strolled back through town to the hotel. He was waiting there when Sten Nordlander drove up to the entrance. Wallander put his bag in the backseat.

"Where are we going?"

"South."

"Far?"

"A hundred and twenty miles or so, maybe a bit more. But there's no hurry."

They drove out of Stockholm and set out on the highway.

"What's in store for us?" Nordlander asked.

"You'll just have to listen to a conversation, that's all."

Nordlander asked no questions. Does he know where we're going? Wallander wondered. Is he only pretending to be surprised? Wallander wasn't sure. Deep down, of course, there was a reason why he had taken his guns with him. I brought them because I can't be sure that I won't have to defend myself, he thought. I just hope it won't be necessary.

They reached the harbor at about ten o'clock. Wallander had insisted on a long stop in Söderköping, where they ate dinner. They sat in silence, contemplating the river that flowed through the town and admiring all the plants and bushes coming into bloom on its banks. The boat Wallander had reserved was waiting for them in the inner dock.

By about eleven they were approaching their destination. Wallander switched off the engine and allowed the boat to drift in to land. He listened. Not a sound to be heard. Sten Nordlander's face was almost invisible in the darkness.

Then they stepped ashore.

40

They moved cautiously through the late-summer darkness. Wallander had whispered to Nordlander that he should stay close to him, without giving any explanation. The moment they arrived at the island, Wallander felt quite certain that Sten Nordlander didn't know anything about Håkan von Enke's hideaway. It would have been impossible for anybody to conceal so skillfully any knowledge about where they might find the man they were looking for.

Wallander paused when he saw the light from one of the windows in the hunting lodge. He could also hear the sound of music above the sighing of the waves. It took several seconds before he realized that a window was open. He turned to Sten Nordlander and whispered, "You find it hard to believe that Louise von Enke was a spy?"

"Do you find that odd?"

"Not at all."

"I hear what you're saying, but I refuse to believe that it's true."

"You're absolutely right," said Wallander slowly. "What I'm telling you is what they **want** us to believe."

Nordlander shook his head.

"Now you've lost me."

"There were items in Louise's purse indicating that she was a spy. But those things could have been planted there after she was dead. Whoever killed her also tried to make it look like a suicide. When I met Håkan here on the island he told me in minute detail how he had suspected for many years that Louise was a spy. It sounded very convincing. But then I began to understand what I had overlooked earlier. You might say that I held up a mirror and observed all the events in reverse."

"And what did you see?"

"Something that turned everything upside down. What is it they say? You have to stand things on their head in order to see them the right way up? That's how it was for me, in any case."

"Are you saying that Louise wasn't a spy after all, then? If not, what **are** you saying?"

Wallander didn't answer his question.

"I want you to sneak up to the house wall," he said. "Stand there, and listen in."

"To what?"

"To the conversation I'm going to have with Håkan von Enke."

"But why all this pussyfooting around in the darkness?"

"If he knows you're here, he may not tell the truth."

Nordlander shook his head. But he made no further comment and edged his way toward the house. Wallander stayed still. Thanks to his alarm system, von Enke would know that somebody was moving around on the island. The hope was that he wouldn't realize there was more than one person outside his hunting lodge.

Nordlander reached the house wall. Wallander would never have noticed him if he hadn't known he was there. But he continued to wait, not moving a muscle. He felt a strange mixture of calm and uneasiness. The end of the story is nigh, he thought. Am I right, or have I made a huge mistake?

He regretted not having explained to Nordlander that the mission might take some time.

A night bird fluttered past, then vanished. Wallander listened into the darkness for any noise that would tell him Håkan von Enke was on his way. Nordlander was standing motionless by the house wall. The music was still oozing out through the open window.

He gave a start when he felt a hand on his shoulder. He turned and found himself looking into Håkan von Enke's face.

"Are you here again?" said von Enke in a low voice. "We didn't arrange this. I could have mistaken you for an intruder. What do you want?"

"I want to speak to you."

"Did something happen?"

"All kinds of things have happened. As I'm sure you know, I went to Berlin and talked to your old friend George Talboth. I must say that he behaved exactly as I had expected a high-ranking CIA officer to act."

Wallander had prepared himself as best he could. He knew he couldn't afford to exaggerate. He had to speak loudly enough for Nordlander to hear what was being said, but not so loudly that von Enke would suspect there was somebody else in the vicinity, listening in.

"George said you seemed to be a good man."

"I've never seen an aquarium like the one he showed me."

"It's remarkable. Especially the trains traveling through their little tunnels."

A gust of wind whooshed past, then all was quiet again.

"How did you get here?" von Enke asked.

"With the same boat as last time."

"And you came on your own?"

"Why wouldn't I?"

"Questions in answer to questions always make me suspicious."

Von Enke suddenly switched on a flashlight that he'd been hiding next to his body. He aimed it at Wallander's face. Third degree, Wallander thought. As long as he doesn't shine the light at the house and discover Sten Nordlander. That would ruin everything.

The flashlight was switched off.

"We don't need to mess around out here."

Wallander followed in von Enke's footsteps. When they entered the house he switched off the radio. Nothing in the room had changed since Wallander's earlier visit.

Von Enke was on his guard. Wallander couldn't work out if that was due to his instinct, warning him of danger, or if it was just natural suspicion following Wallander's sudden appearance on the island.

"You must have a motive," said von Enke, slowly. "A sudden visit like this, in the middle of the night?"

"I just wanted to talk to you."

"About your visit to Berlin?"

"No, not about that."

"Then explain yourself."

Wallander hoped that Nordlander could hear this conversation, standing outside the window. What if von Enke suddenly decided to close it? I have no time to spare, Wallander concluded. I have to come straight to the point.

"Explain yourself," von Enke said again.

"It's about Louise," Wallander said. "The truth about her."

"Isn't that what we talked about last time we were sitting here?"

"It is. But you didn't tell me the truth."

Von Enke looked at him with the same noncommittal expression as before.

"Something didn't add up," said Wallander. "It was as if I were looking up in the air when I should have been examining the ground at my feet. That happened when I visited Berlin. It suddenly became clear to me that George Talboth wasn't just answering my questions. He was also investigating, very discreetly and skillfully, how much I knew. Once I realized that, I discovered something else as well. Something horrific, shameful, a betrayal so despicable and misanthropic that I didn't want to believe it at first. What I believed, what Ytterberg thought, what you said and George Talboth maintained, was not the truth at all. I was being used, exploited. I had stumbled obediently straight into all the traps that had been set for me. But that also opened my eyes to another person."

"Who?"

"The person we can call the real Louise. She was never a spy. She wasn't false in any way; she was the most genuine person imaginable. The first time I met her I was struck by her lovely smile. I thought about that again when we met in Djursholm. I was convinced later that she had been using that smile to conceal her big secret—until I realized that her smile was absolutely genuine."

"Have you come here to talk about my dead wife's smile?"

Wallander shook his head in resignation. The whole situation had become so repugnant that he didn't know how he was going to handle it. He should have been infuriated, but he didn't have the strength.

"I've come here because I've discovered the truth I've been searching for. Louise has never been remotely close to being a spy and betraying her country. I should have understood that much sooner. But I allowed myself to be deceived."

"Who deceived you?"

"I did. I was just as misled as everybody else into believing that the enemy always came from the east. But the one who deceived me most was you. The real spy."

Still the same expressionless face, Wallander thought. But how long can he keep it up?

"Are you suggesting that I am a spy?"

"Yes!"

"You're alleging that I spied for the Soviet Union or Russia? You're crazy!"

"I said nothing about the former Soviet Union or the new Russia. I said that you are a spy. For the U.S.A. You have been for many years, Håkan. For exactly how long and how it all started are questions only you can answer. Nor do I know what your motives are. It wasn't you who suspected Louise; she was the one who suspected you of being an American agent. That was what killed her."

"I didn't kill Louise!"

The first crack, Wallander thought. Håkan's voice is starting to sound shrill. He's beginning to defend himself.

"I don't think you did. No doubt others did that. Maybe you received assistance from George Talboth. But she died to prevent you from being exposed."

"You can't prove your absurd allegations."

"You're absolutely right," said Wallander. "I can't. But there are others who can. I know enough to make the police and the armed forces start looking at what's happened from a different perspective. The spy they've long suspected was operating in the Swedish armed forces was not a woman. It was a man. A man who didn't hesitate to hide behind his own wife as a way of providing himself with a perfect disguise. Everybody was looking for a Russian spy, a woman. When they should have been looking for a man spying for the U.S.A. Nobody thought of that possibility, everybody was preoccupied with searching for enemies in the east. That has been the case for the whole of my life: the threat comes from the east. Nobody wanted to believe that an individual might even consider the possibility of betraying his country in the other direction, to the U.S.A. Anyone who did warn of anything like that was a lone voice crying in the wilderness. You could maintain, of course, that the U.S.A. already had access to everything they wanted to know about our defense services, but that wasn't the case. NATO, and above all the U.S.A., needed help obtaining accurate information about the Swedish armed forces and also about how much we knew about various Russian military plans."

Wallander paused. Von Enke continued to look at him with the same lack of expression in his face.

"You provided yourself with a perfect shield when you made yourself unpopular in the navy," Wallander went on. "You protested about the Russian submarines trapped inside Swedish territorial waters being set free. You asked so many questions that you were regarded as an extreme, fanatical enemy of Russia. At the same time, you could also criticize the U.S.A. when it suited you. But you knew of course that in fact it was NATO submarines hiding in our territorial waters. You were playing a game, and you won. You beat everybody. With the possible exception of your wife, who began to suspect that everything wasn't what it seemed. I don't know why you came to hide here. Maybe because your employers ordered you to? Was it one of them who appeared on the other side of the fence in Djursholm, smoking, when you were celebrating your seventy-fifth birthday? Was that an agreed way of passing a message to you? This hunting lodge was designated as a place for you to withdraw to a long time ago. You knew about it from Eskil Lundberg's father, who was more than willing to help you after you made sure he was compensated for battered jetties and damaged nets. He was also the man who helped you by never saying anything about the bugging device the Americans failed to attach to the Russian underwater cable. I suspect the arrangement was probably that you would be picked up from here by some ship if it should become necessary to evacuate you. They probably said nothing about the fact that Louise would have to die. But it was your friends who killed her. And you knew the price you would have to pay for what you were doing. You couldn't do anything to prevent what happened. Isn't that right? The only thing I still wonder about is what drove you to sacrifice your wife on top of everything else."

Håkan von Enke was staring at his hand. He seemed somehow uninterested in what Wallander had said. Possibly because he had to face up to the fact that what he had done had resulted in Louise's death, Wallander thought, and now there was nothing he could do about it.

"It was never the intention that she should die," von Enke said, without taking his eyes off his hand.

"What did you think when you heard she was dead?"

Von Enke's reply was matter-of-fact, almost dry.

"I came very close to putting an end to it all. The only thing that stopped me was the thought of my grandchild. But now I don't know anymore."

They fell silent again. Wallander thought it would soon be time for Sten Nordlander to come into the room. But there was another question he wanted answered first.

"How did it happen?" he asked.

"How did what happen?"

"What was it that made you into a spy?"

"It's a long story."

"We have plenty of time. And you don't need to give me an exhaustive answer; just tell me enough to help me understand."

Von Enke leaned back in his chair and closed his eyes. Wallander suddenly realized that he was facing a very old man.

"It started a long time ago," von Enke said without opening his eyes. "I was contacted by the Americans as early as the beginning of the 1960s. I was soon convinced of how important it was for the U.S.A. and NATO to have access to information that would enable them to defend us. We would never be able to survive on our own. Without the U.S.A. we were lost from the very start."

"Who contacted you?"

"You have to keep in mind what it was like in those days. There was a group of mainly young people who spent all their time protesting against the U.S.A.'s war in Vietnam. But most of us knew that we needed America's support in order to survive when the balloon went up in Europe. I was upset by all those naïve and romantic left-wingers. I felt that I needed to do something. I went in with my eyes wide open. I suppose you could say it was ideology. It's the same today. Without the U.S.A., the world would be at the mercy of forces whose only aim is to deprive Europe of power. What do you think China's ambitions are? What will the Russians do once they've solved their internal problems?"

"But money must have come into it somehow?"

· · ·

Von Enke didn't reply. He turned away, lost in his own thoughts again. Wallander asked a few more questions, to which he received no answers. Von Enke had simply brought the conversation to a close.

He suddenly stood up and walked toward the kitchenette. He took a bottle of beer out of the refrigerator, then opened one of the drawers in the kitchen cabinet. Wallander was watching him carefully.

When von Enke turned to face him, he had a pistol in his hand. Wallander stood up quickly. The gun was pointed at him. Von Enke slowly put the bottle down on the work surface.

He raised the gun. Wallander could see that it was pointing straight at his head. He shouted, roared at von Enke. Then he saw the pistol move.

"I can't go on any longer," said von Enke. "I have absolutely no future anymore."

He placed the barrel against his chin and pulled the trigger. The sound echoed around the room. As he collapsed, his face covered in blood, Sten Nordlander came storming into the room.

"Are you hurt?" he screamed. "Did he shoot you?"

"No. He shot himself."

They stared at the man lying on the floor, his body in an unnatural position. The blood covering his face made it impossible to make out his eyes, to see if they were closed or not.

Wallander was the first to realize that von Enke was still alive. He grabbed a sweater hanging over the arm of a chair and pressed it against von Enke's chin. He shouted to Nordlander, telling him to get some towels. The bullet had exited through von Enke's cheek. He had failed to send the bullet through his brain.

"He missed," Wallander said as Nordlander handed him a sheet he had pulled off the bed.

Håkan von Enke's eyes were open; they had not glazed over.

"Press hard," said Wallander, showing Nordlander what to do.

He took out his cell phone and dialed the emergency number. But there was no signal. He ran outside and scrambled up the rocky slope behind the house. But there was no signal there either. He went back inside.

"He'll bleed to death," said Nordlander.

"You have to press hard," said Wallander. "My phone isn't working. I'll have to go get help. Telephone coverage is sometimes pretty bad here."

"I don't think he'll make it."

Sten Nordlander was kneeling beside the bleeding man. He looked up at Wallander with horror in his eyes.

"Is it true?"

"You heard what we said?"

"Every word. Is it true?"

"It's true. Everything I said and everything he said. He was a spy for the U.S.A. for about forty years. He sold our military secrets, and he must have made a good job of it if the Americans considered him so valuable that they didn't even hesitate to murder his wife."

"I find this impossible to understand."

"Then we have another reason to try to keep him alive. He's the only one who can tell us the truth. I'm going to get help. It will take time. But if you can stop the bleeding, we might be able to save him."

"So there's no doubt?"

"None at all."

"That means he has been deceiving me for years."

"He deceived everybody."

Wallander ran down to the boat. He stumbled and fell several times. When he reached the water he noticed that the wind was blowing stronger now. He untied the painter, pushed the boat out, and jumped in. The engine started on the first pull. It was so dark now that he wondered if he'd be able to see clearly enough to maneuver his way to the dock.

He had just turned the boat around and was about to accelerate away when he heard a shot. There was no doubt about it, it was a gunshot. Coming from the hunting lodge. He returned to neutral and listened carefully. Could he have been mistaken? He turned the boat around once more and headed for land. When he jumped ashore, he landed short and felt the water flowing into his shoes. The whole time, he was listening for any more sounds. The wind was getting stronger and stronger. He took the shotgun out of his bag and loaded it. Could there be people on the island he knew nothing about? He returned to the hunting lodge, his shotgun at the ready, trying to proceed as quietly as possible, and stopped when he saw the faint light through the gaps in the curtains. There wasn't a sound, apart from the sighing of the wind in the tree-tops and the swishing of the waves.

He had just began to advance toward the door of the hunting lodge when another shot rang out. He flung himself down onto the ground, his face pressed against the damp soil. He dropped the shotgun and protected his head with his hands. He expected to be shot dead at any moment.

But nothing happened. Eventually he dared to sit up and pick up his shotgun. He checked to make sure there was no soil in the two barrels. He stood up slowly, then ducked down and headed for the front door. Still nothing happened. He shouted, but Sten Nordlander didn't respond. Two shots, he thought frantically, and tried to work out what that implied.

He could still see Sten Nordlander's face when he asked his question. **So there's no doubt?**

Wallander opened the door and went in.

Håkan von Enke was dead. Sten Nordlander had shot him in the forehead. He had then turned the gun on himself, and was lying dead on the floor next to the man who had been his friend and colleague. Wallander was upset; he should have foreseen this. Sten Nordlander had been standing out there in the darkness and heard how Håkan von Enke had betrayed everyone—perhaps most of all the ones who had trusted him and seen him not so much as a fellow officer, but as a friend.

Wallander avoided treading in the blood that had

run all over the floor. He flopped down onto the chair where he had been sitting not so long ago, listening to what von Enke had to say. Weariness seemed to explode inside him. The older he became, the more difficult it seemed to be for him to cope with the truth. Nevertheless, that is what he always strove for.

How far had they come since that birthday party in Djursholm? he wondered. If I assume that his conversation with me was part of a plan to persuade me to believe that his wife was a spy, and thus divert any possible suspicions away from himself, it follows that the most important decisions had already been made. Perhaps it was Håkan von Enke himself who had the idea of exploiting me. Making the most of the fact that his son was living with a woman whose father was a stupid provincial police officer.

He felt both sorrow and anger as he sat there with the two dead men in front of him. But what upset him most was the thought that Klara would never get to know her paternal grandparents. She would have to make do with a grandmother on her mother's side who was fighting a losing battle with alcohol, and a grandfather who was becoming older and more decrepit by the day.

He sat there for half an hour, possibly longer, before forcing himself to become a police officer again. He worked out a simple idea based on leaving everything untouched. He took the car keys out of Sten Nordlander's pocket, then left the hunting lodge and headed for the boat.

But before pushing it into the water again, he paused on the beach and closed his eyes. It was as if the past had come rushing toward him. The big wide world that he had always known so little about. Now he had become a minor player on the big stage. What did he know now that he hadn't known before? Not much at all, he thought. I'm still that same bewildered character on the periphery of all the major political and military developments. I'm still the same unhappy and insecure individual on the sidelines, just as I've always been.

He pushed the boat out and despite the darkness managed to steer it in to the dock. He left the boat where he had picked it up. The harbor was deserted. It was 2:00 a.m. by the time he sat in Sten Nordlander's car and drove off. He parked it outside the railway station, having carefully wiped clean the steering wheel and stick shift and door handle. Then he waited for the first early-morning train south. He spent several hours on a park bench. He thought how odd it was, sitting on a bench in this unfamiliar town with his father's old shotgun in his bag.

It had started drizzling as dawn broke, and he found a café that was already open. He ordered coffee and leafed through some old newspapers before returning to the railway station and catching a train. He would never go to Blue Island again.

He looked out of the train window and saw Sten Nordlander's car in the station's parking lot. Sooner or later somebody would start to take an interest in it. One thing would lead to another. One question would be how he had gotten to the docks and then sailed out to Blue Island. But the man who rented the boat would not necessarily associate Wallander with the tragedy that had taken place in that isolated hunting lodge. Besides, all details would no doubt be classified.

Wallander arrived in Malmö shortly after midday, picked up his car, and headed for Ystad. As he came to the exit, he found himself at a police checkpoint. He showed his ID and blew into the Breathalyzer.

"How's it going?" he asked, in an attempt to cheer up his colleague. "Are people sober?"

"On the whole, yes. But we just started. No doubt we'll nail one or two victims. How are things in Ystad?"

"Pretty quiet at the moment. But August usually produces more work than July."

Wallander wished him good luck, then rolled up his window and drove on. Only a few hours ago I was sitting with two dead men at my feet, he thought. But that's not something that anybody else can see. Our memories don't pop up next to us in Technicolor.

He went to the store to buy a few groceries, collected Jussi, and eventually pulled into the parking area outside his house.

After putting his purchases in the fridge, he sat down at his kitchen table. Everything was quiet and calm.

He tried to figure out what he would tell Linda.

But he didn't call her that day, not even in the evening.

He simply had no idea what to say to her.

Epilogue

One night in May 2009 Wallander woke up from a dream. That was happening more and more often. All the memories of the night lived on when he opened his eyes. Until recently he rarely remembered his dreams. Jussi, who had been ill, was asleep on the floor by his bed. The clock on the bedside table said four-fifteen. Perhaps it wasn't just the dream that had woken him up. Perhaps the calling of an owl had drifted in through the open window and into his consciousness—it wouldn't be the first time.

But now there was no owl calling. He had dreamed about Linda and the conversation they should have had the day he returned from Blue Island. In his dream he had in fact called her and told her what had happened. She had listened without saying anything. And that was all. The dream had broken off abruptly, like a rotten branch.

He woke up feeling very uncomfortable. He hadn't called her at all, in fact. He hadn't had the strength to do it. His excuse was simple. He hadn't played a part in the tragedy, and calling her would only have led to an unbearable situation as far as he was concerned; if he gave her an exact version of events, he would be suspected of having been involved. Only when the tragedy became public knowledge would she and Hans discover what had happened. And with a bit of luck, he would be able to stay out of it.

Wallander thought that this case was among the worst experiences of his life. The only thing he could compare it to was the incident many years ago when he killed a man for the first time in the line of duty, and seriously wondered if he could continue as a police officer. He considered doing what Martinsson had now done: throw in the towel as a policeman and devote himself to something entirely different.

Wallander leaned carefully over the side of the bed and checked on his dog. Jussi was asleep. He was also dreaming, scratching in the air with his front paws. Wallander leaned back in bed again. The air drifting in through the window was refreshing. He kicked off the duvet. His thoughts wandered to the bundle of papers lying on the kitchen table. He had started writing a report last September, noting down everything that had happened and culminating in the tragedy in the hunting lodge on Blue Island.

It was Eskil Lundberg who found the dead bodies. Ytterberg had immediately called in the CID in Norrköping to assist. Since it was a matter for the security police and the military intelligence service, an embargo had been immediately imposed on all aspects of the investigation, and everything was shrouded in secrecy. Wallander was informed by Ytterberg of whatever he was allowed to pass on, in strict confidence. The whole time, Wallander worried about the possibility of his own presence at the scene being discovered. What concerned him most was whether Nordlander had told his wife about the trip he was going to make, but evidently he hadn't. With great reluctance Wallander read in the newspapers about Mrs. Nordlander's despair over her husband's death and her refusal to believe that he had killed his old friend and then shot himself.

Ytterberg occasionally complained to Wallander about the fact that not even he, the man in charge of the police investigation, knew what was going on behind the scenes. But there was no doubt that Sten Nordlander had killed Håkan von Enke using two shots to the head, and had then shot himself. What was mysterious and what nobody could explain was how Sten Nordlander had come to Blue Island. Ytterberg said on several occasions that he suspected a third party had been involved, but who that could have been and what role he or she played he had no idea. The real motive for the tragedy was also something that nobody could work out.

The newspapers and other media were full of speculation. They wallowed in the bloody drama played out in the hunting lodge. Linda and Hans and Klara had almost been forced to move in order to avoid all the inquisitive journalists and their intrusive questions. The wildest of the conspiracy theorists maintained that Håkan von Enke and Sten Nordlander had taken to their graves a secret linked to the death of Olof Palme.

· · ·

Occasionally during his conversations with Ytterberg, Wallander had asked cautiously, almost out of politeness, how things were going with regard to the suspicions that Louise von Enke could have been a Russian spy. Ytterberg had only extremely meager information to give him.

"I have the impression that everything is at a standstill as far as she is concerned," he said. "What facts the security police are looking for, or trying to suppress, I have no idea. We might have to wait until some investigative journalist goes to town on that."

Wallander never heard a word about the possibility of Håkan von Enke's being a spy for the U.S.A. There were no suspicions, no rumors, no speculations that this might be the cause of what had happened. Wallander once asked Ytterberg point-blank if there were any such theories. Ytterberg had been totally incredulous.

"Why in God's name should he have been a U.S. spy?"

"I'm just trying to think of any possible explanation for what happened," Wallander said. "Given there have been suspicions that Louise was spying for the Russians, why not try a different possibility?"

"I think I'd have heard if the security police or military intelligence had any suspicions of that sort."

"I was only thinking aloud," said Wallander.

"Do you know something I don't?" Ytterberg suddenly asked with an unexpected edge to his voice.

"No," said Wallander. "I don't know anything you don't."

It was after that conversation that Wallander began writing. He collected all his thoughts, all his notes, and invented a system of Post-its that he stuck up on one of the living room walls. But every time Linda came to visit him, with or without Hans and Klara, he took them down. He wanted to write his story without the involvement of anybody else, and without anyone's even suspecting what he was doing.

He began by trying to tie up the remaining loose ends. It wasn't difficult to check that "USG Enterprises," whose name he had seen in the entrance hall of the building where George Talboth lived, was the name of a consultancy firm. There was no indication that it wasn't aboveboard. But he couldn't work out who had broken into his house while he was away, nor who could have visited Niklasgården. It was obvious that they were people who had assisted Håkan von Enke in some way, but Wallander never established why they did it. Even if the most likely explanation was that they were looking for what Wallander called Signe's book. It was lying on the kitchen table as he wrote, but otherwise he continued to hide it in Jussi's kennel.

It wasn't long before it dawned on him what he was really doing. He was writing about himself and his own life just as much as about Håkan von Enke. When he returned in his thoughts to everything he had heard about the Cold War, the divided attitude of the Swedish armed forces to neutrality and not joining alliances or the necessity of being an integrated part of

NATO, he realized how little he actually knew about the world he had lived in. It was impossible to catch up on the knowledge he hadn't bothered to acquire earlier. What he could learn now about that world obviously had to be from the perspective of somebody in the present looking back in time. He wondered grimly if that might be typical of his generation. An unwillingness to care about the real world they lived in, the political circumstances that were shifting all the time. Or had his generation been split? Between those who cared, and those who didn't?

His father had often been better informed than Wallander on all kinds of events, he could see that now. It wasn't only the episode with Tage Erlander and his speech in the People's Park in Malmö. He also recalled a time in the early 1970s when his father had told him off for not bothering to vote in the election that had taken place a few days earlier. Wallander could still remember his father's fury, how he had called him "an idle idiot when it comes to politics" before throwing a paintbrush at him and telling him to get out of his sight. Which he had done, of course. At the time he just thought his father was weird. Why should Wallander care about the way Swedish politicians were always arguing with one another? The only things that were of any interest to him were lower taxes and higher wages, nothing else.

He often sat at his kitchen table and wondered if his closest friends thought the same way. Not interested in politics, only worried about their own circumstances. On the few occasions he ever talked about politics it was mainly a matter of attacking individual politicians, complaining about their idiotic shenanigans without moving on to the next stage and wondering what the alternatives were.

There had been only one short period when he thought seriously about the political situation in Sweden, Europe, and perhaps even the world. That was nearly twenty years ago, in connection with the brutal double murder of an elderly farming couple in Lenarp. Fingers were pointed at illegal immigrants or asylum-seekers, and Wallander had been forced to face up to his own opinions on the massive immigration into Sweden. He realized that behind his usual peaceful and tolerant exterior lurked dark, even racist, views. The realization had surprised and scared him. He had eliminated all such thoughts. But after that investigation, which had come to its remarkable conclusion in the market square at Kivik, where the two murderers had been arrested, he sank back into his political apathy.

He visited the Ystad library several times during the fall and borrowed books about Swedish postwar history. He read about all the discussions concerning whether or not Sweden should acquire nuclear weapons or join NATO. Despite the fact that he was reaching adulthood when some of these debates were taking place, he had no recollection of reacting to what the politicians were talking about. It was as if he had been living in a glass bubble.

On one occasion he told Linda about how he had started to examine his past. It turned out that she had much more interest in political matters than he did. He was surprised—he'd never noticed it before. She merely commented that a person's political awareness wasn't something that necessarily showed on the surface.

"When did you ever ask me a political question?" she asked. "Why would I discuss politics with you when I know you're not interested?"

"What does Hans say?"

"He knows a lot about the world. But we don't always agree."

Wallander often thought about Hans. In the late fall of 2008, in the middle of October, Linda had called him, obviously upset, and told him that the Danish police had raided Hans's office in Copenhagen. Some of the brokers, including two Icelanders, had rigged the increase in value of certain stocks and shares in order to secure their own commissions and bonuses. When the financial crisis hit, the bubble burst. For a while, all employees, including Hans, were under suspicion of having been involved in the scam. It was as recently as March that Hans had been informed that he was no longer suspected of shady dealings. It had been a heavy burden for him to bear when he was also mourning the death of another parent. He had frequently visited Wallander and asked him to explain what had actually happened. Wallander told him as much as he could, but was careful not to even imply what really lay behind it all.

Wallander was particularly concerned about how to make sure that the summary of his thoughts and the knowledge he had acquired would become public. Should he send his text anonymously to the authorities? Would anybody take it seriously? Who wanted to destroy the good relationship between Sweden and the U.S.A.? Perhaps the silence surrounding Håkan von Enke's espionage was best for everybody involved?

He had started writing at the end of September, and now he had been going for more than eight months. He didn't want what had happened to be buried in silence. That possibility made him feel indignant.

While writing he also continued his work as a police officer. Two depressing investigations into cases of aggravated assault occupied him throughout the fall. Then in April 2009 he started looking into a series of arson attacks in the Ystad area.

What worried Wallander more than anything else during this period was that his sudden losses of memory kept recurring. The worst incident was during the Christmas break. It had snowed during the night. He had dressed and gone out to shovel the driveway and the parking area. When he had finished, he didn't know where he was. He didn't even recognize Jussi. It was quite a while before it dawned on him whose house he was standing in front of. He never did what he should have done. He didn't see a doctor, because he was simply too scared.

He tried to convince himself that he was working too hard, that he was burning himself out. Sometimes he succeeded. But he was constantly afraid that his forgetfulness would get worse. He was terrified of succumbing to dementia, that he might be suffering from the early stages of Alzheimer's disease.

Wallander stayed in bed. It was Sunday morning; he wasn't on duty. Linda was due to visit him after lunch, with Klara. Hans might come too, if he felt up to it.

When he eventually got up, he let Jussi out and made breakfast. He devoted the rest of the morning to his papers. For the first time, this very morning, he believed that what he was writing was in fact a sort of "life story," a testament. This is what his life had been like. Even if he lived for another ten or fifteen years, nothing would change very much. But he did wonder, with an empty feeling deep inside himself, what he would do after retiring as a police officer.

There was only one answer, and that was Klara. Her presence always cheered him up. She would be there for him when everything else was over.

He finished his story that morning in May. He had nothing more to say. A printout was lying on the table in front of him. Laboriously, one word at a time, he had reconstructed the story of the man who had tricked him into thinking that his wife was a spy. Wallander too was a part of the story, not just the person who had written it down.

He had never found explanations for some of the loose ends. What he had perhaps spent most time thinking about was the question of Louise's shoes. Why were they standing neatly next to her body on

Värmdö? Wallander eventually came to believe that she had been killed somewhere else and didn't have her shoes on at the time. Whoever placed them by her side hadn't really thought about what he was doing. Wallander also didn't have an answer to where Louise had been during the time she was missing. She had presumably been held prisoner until somebody decided she had to die for the sake of Håkan von Enke.

The other continuing mystery as far as Wallander was concerned was the question of the stones. The stone he had seen on Håkan von Enke's desk, the stone he had been given by Atkins, and the one he had noticed on George Talboth's balcony table. He gathered they were some sort of souvenirs, taken from the Swedish archipelago by people who shouldn't have been there among the little islands and rocks. But he couldn't explain why von Enke's had eventually disappeared from his desk. There were several possibilities, but he was reluctant to choose any of them.

He had occasionally spoken to Atkins on the phone. Listened to him crying when he talked about his lost friend. Or rather, friends, as he always corrected himself. He didn't forget Louise. Atkins had said he would come to the funeral, but when it actually took place, in the middle of August, he never showed up. And he never contacted Wallander again after that. Wallander sometimes wondered what Atkins and Håkan von Enke had talked about the many times they'd met. But he would never know.

There was another question he would have liked to ask Håkan and Louise. Why had one of his desk drawers been such a mess? Did he intend to go to Cambodia if he was forced to flee? Nor did he know why Louise had withdrawn 200,000 kronor from the bank. He didn't find the money when the Stockholm apartment was cleaned out. It had simply disappeared, without a trace.

And why had Sten Nordlander decided to kill Håkan von Enke and then himself?

The dead had taken their secrets with them.

At the end of November, when Wallander was at a conference in Stockholm, he rented a car and drove out to Niklasgården. He was accompanied by Hans, who still hadn't been able to bring himself to visit his unknown sister. It was a moving moment for Wallander, watching Hans at the side of Signe's bed. He also thought about the fact that Håkan von Enke had always visited his daughter regularly. He could rely on her, Wallander thought. He had dared to trust her with his most secret documents.

He spent a long time wondering whether he should give a name to what he had written. In the end he left the title page blank. The manuscript amounted to 212 pages in all. He leafed through it one last time, stopping occasionally to check that he hadn't gotten something wrong. He decided that despite everything, he had come as close to the truth as possible.

He decided to send the material to Ytterberg. He wouldn't sign it but would mail it to his sister, Kristina, and ask her to forward it to Stockholm. Ytterberg would naturally know that it must have been Wallander who had sent it, but he would never be able to prove it.

Ytterberg is an intelligent man, Wallander thought. He will make the best possible use of what I have written. He'll also be able to work out why I chose to send it to him anonymously.

But Wallander was aware that even Ytterberg might not be able to convince a higher authority to investigate further. The U.S.A. was still the Great Redeemer as far as many Swedes were concerned. A Europe without the U.S.A. would be more or less defenseless. It could be that nobody would want to face up to the truth that Wallander was convinced he had established.

Wallander thought about the Swedish soldiers who had been sent to Afghanistan. That would never have happened if the Americans hadn't asked for them. Not openly, but behind the scenes, just as their submarines had hidden themselves in Swedish territorial waters in the early 1980s with the approval of the Swedish navy and Swedish politicians. Or as CIA operatives were allowed to capture two suspected Egyptian terrorists on Swedish territory on December 18, 2001, and have them returned in humiliating circumstances to their home country, where they were imprisoned and tortured. Wallander could imagine that if Håkan von Enke were to be unmasked, he would be hailed as a hero, not as a despicable traitor.

Nothing, he thought, is certain. Not the way in which these events are interpreted, nor what the rest of my life will be like.

. . .

The May morning was fine but chilly. Around noon he went for a long walk with Jussi, who seemed to be back in good health. When Linda arrived, without Hans but with Klara, Wallander had finished straightening up the house and checking that there weren't any papers lying around that he didn't want her to see. Klara had fallen asleep in the car. Wallander carefully carried her indoors and laid her down on the sofa. Holding her in his arms always gave him the feeling that Linda had returned in another guise.

They sat down at the kitchen table to drink coffee.

"Did you clean?" Linda asked.

"I've done nothing else all day."

She laughed and shook her head. Then she turned serious again. Wallander knew that all the problems Hans had been forced to cope with had been shattering for her as well.

"I want to start work again," she said. "I can't go on much longer just being a mom."

"But there are only four more months of your maternity leave . . ."

"Four months can be a very long time. I'm getting very impatient."

"With Klara?"

"With myself."

"That's something you inherited from me. Impatience."

"I thought you always said that patience was the most important virtue for a police officer."

"But that doesn't mean that patience is something you're born with—you have to learn it."

She took a sip of coffee and thought over what he had said.

"I feel old," Wallander said. "I wake up every day feeling that everything is going so incredibly fast. I don't know if I'm running after something or away from something. I just run. To be completely honest, I'm scared stiff of growing old."

"Think of Granddad! He just kept on going as usual and never worried about the fact that he was growing old."

"That's not true. He was scared of dying."

"Sometimes, maybe. But not all the time."

"He was a strange man. I don't think anyone can compare themselves to him."

"I do."

"You had a relationship with him that I lost when I was very young. I sometimes think about the fact that he always had a better relationship with Kristina. Maybe it's just that he found it easier to get along with women? I was born the wrong sex. He never wanted a son."

"That's ridiculous, and you know it."

"Ridiculous or not, that's what I keep thinking. I'm scared of old age."

She reached across the table and stroked his arm.

"I've noticed that you get worried. But deep down you know there's no point. You can't do anything about your age."

"I know," said Wallander. "But sometimes it feels like complaining is all you can do."

Linda stayed for several hours. They talked until Klara woke up, and with a broad smile on her face she ran over to Wallander.

Wallander suddenly felt terrified. His memory had deserted him again. He didn't know who the girl running toward him was. He knew he'd seen her before, but what her name was or what she was doing in his house he had no idea.

It was as if everything had fallen silent. As if all colors had faded away, and all he was left with was black and white.

The shadow grew more intense. And Kurt Wallander slowly descended into a darkness that some years later transported him into the empty universe known as Alzheimer's disease.

After that there is nothing more. The story of Kurt Wallander is finished, once and for all. The years—ten, perhaps more—he has left to live are his own. His and Linda's, his and Klara's; nobody else's.

Afterword

In the world of fiction it is possible to take many liberties. For instance, it is not unusual for me to change a landscape slightly so that nobody can say: "It was exactly there! That's precisely where the action took place!"

The thought behind this is of course to stress the difference between fact and fiction. What I write **could** have taken place as I narrate it. But it didn't necessarily do so.

There are many shifts of that type in this book, between what actually happened and what might conceivably have happened.

Like most other authors, I write in order to try to make the world more understandable. In that respect, fiction can be superior to factual realism.

So it doesn't matter whether or not there is a nursing home somewhere in central Sweden called Niklasgården. Nor does it matter if there is a banquet hall on Östermalm in Stockholm where naval officers congregate. Or a café just outside Stockholm that serves the same purpose, where a submarine officer by the name of Hans-Olov Fredhäll might turn up. And Madonna didn't give a concert in Copenhagen in 2008.

But the most important things in this book are built on the solid foundation of reality.

Many people have helped me in doing the necessary research. I thank them all most gratefully.

However, the responsibility for the contents right up to the final period lies with me. Completely, and with no exceptions.

Gothenburg, June 2009
Henning Mankell

A NOTE ABOUT THE AUTHOR

Internationally best-selling novelist and play-wright Henning Mankell has received the German Tolerance Prize and the U.K.'s Golden Dagger Award and has been nominated for a **Los Angeles Times** Book Prize three times. His Kurt Wallander mysteries have been published in thirty-three countries and consistently top the best-seller lists in Europe. He divides his time between Sweden and Maputo, Mozambique, where he has worked as the director of Teatro Avenida since 1985.

www.henningmankell.com